SCOTCH AND WATER

(Incomers: Book 2)

Jim Forbes

A Kinord Book

Published by Kinord Books
Edinburgh
www.kinordbooks.com

ISBN: 978-0-9928080-4-4

Scotch and Water is a work of fiction. Most contemporary and a few historical characters, organisations and events are fictitious and any resemblance they may bear to real persons, living or dead, is purely coincidental. Other characters and events are based on public domain sources and are partially fictionalised.

The cover illustration (copyright © 2014 Jim Forbes) on this edition of *Scotch and Water* shows the Forth Bridge as seen from St David's Harbour. The photograph is by the author.

To the people of Edinburgh
who have welcomed another pair of Incomers to their city

Portrait of Charlotte Nasmyth, aged 23
by William Nicholson

Original oil painting in Scottish National Portrait Gallery

1
THE UNMISTAKABLE SIGNATURE OF GOLD

THE J-WAY PURRED SOFTLY as Bob swept its coil in long arcs over the uneven ground. Occasionally it uttered a 'beep' as it encountered a large rock near the surface, but for the most part it remained placid, unexcited.

It was the third, and by far the best, metal detector he had owned since taking up the hobby five years ago. An Australian machine originally developed for gold prospecting, the J-Way could be tuned to pick up signals from a wide range of metals. For the moment, it was on a low sensitivity setting, hence the quiet purr. Later, Bob planned to sweep the same area with progressively higher sensitivity.

Up to now, he had stayed close to his Edinburgh home in pursuit of his hobby, and today was no exception. He had parked his Mercedes A-Class less than a mile away and followed a signposted right-of-way to the site, the J-Way slung from a shoulder harness. For a retired man in his sixties he was in good physical shape, and had enjoyed the walk on this fine spring day. Arriving at his chosen spot, he'd taken a moment to catch his breath and savour the fresh air before getting down to work. Now, though, his full attention had to be on the J-Way's digital display and its soft murmur.

This was not, on the face of it, a promising site for buried treasure. Not necessarily a bad thing, Bob believed, for it meant the land was probably 'virgin' – it hadn't already been scoured by weekend amateurs looking for loose change.

A steep gorse-covered slope separated his present hunting-ground from a golf course below. His search area extended from its crest up a gentler incline towards the vertical rock face of an abandoned quarry. Refusing him permission to search anywhere within the golf course, a groundskeeper had drawn his attention to this forlorn corner. A battered red twenty-foot shipping container, its white letters proclaiming 'Hamburg Süd', defiled the site; how *that* had been hauled here, and why, Bob couldn't guess. It was an eyesore in such a pretty place.

'Nothing to do with the golf club,' the groundskeeper had told him; 'in fact, that isn't part of our property. I think it's public land – you can check with the council if you like.'

Bob didn't check. He just came, surveyed the area briefly, and began sweeping with the J-Way. No one bothered him; not even the occasional duffer who came near, thrashing about among the gorse looking for a wayward golf ball.

He enjoyed the solitude. His was a pastime for men who liked their own company, and for Bob, the J-Way was company enough. It spoke to him, in a language he had come to understand very well. *There's something deep here, probably an old rusty pipe,* it would say. Or, *a few beer cans were opened here, back in the days of detachable ring-pulls.*

There had been several love affairs: with cars, with a top-of-the-range audio system, with a racing bike, though never with another human being, male or female. Now the love of his life was a metal detector. One that might make him rich.

He scanned along the brink of the steep slope, working towards the red Hamburg Süd box. As he approached its metal wall, the J-Way's purr gave way to an angry growl. Too much interference there.

Keeping a safe distance from the container, and still on the low-sensitivity setting, he had almost completed a first sweep when, at the entrance to a semicircular inturn in the rock face, the J-Way broke into a squeal. He passed the coil repeatedly across the same spot, getting the same high-pitched note each time. An abandoned quarrying tool, perhaps?

With the setting adjusted for improved discrimination, the digital readout was unambiguous: this was a non-ferrous object. Not a quarrying tool, then. A high-conductivity metal, though not quite as conductive as silver. Bob's heart skipped a beat. The J-Way was displaying the unmistakable signature of gold.

And yet, was that possible? The signal was not consistent with a small item such as a wedding ring or locket close to the surface. It had to be something deeper and much bigger. His hand-trowel would be of little use; he stuck it in the ground to mark the spot, hid the J-Way among some gorse bushes and set off towards his car.

Within forty minutes he was back, armed with a heavy-duty spade. He began to dig, totally unaware of the arrival of a heavily-built young man who lurked, cigarette in hand, behind the shipping container.

About a foot down, Bob encountered a layer of flat rock, sandstone it looked like. From the sound the spade made when striking it, there seemed to be some kind of hollow cavity beneath. Turning on the J-Way again, he confirmed that the target was under the rock, probably in the cavity. Afraid to damage the object, whatever it might be, he dug cautiously, widening the hole and sometimes scraping with his trowel to expose the surface of the sandstone.

At first, he wondered if he had stumbled on the lid of a burial chamber, dating perhaps from iron-age times. Soon he saw he had struck a portion of pavement, formed of irregularly shaped slabs. It reminded him of some crazy paving he had laid in the tiny garden of his bachelor bungalow thirty years ago. Then he had another thought. *Could it be ...?*

He was startled by a voice at his back saying, 'Found something, pal?' Twisting round, he found himself looking up into a scowling bearded face framed by a black hood.

After a pause to regain his composure, Bob replied, 'I don't know. See these slabs? They look like pictures I've seen of Roman roads. But there's no record of a Roman road here.'

'You've no permission to dig on this land,' Hoodie announced aggressively.

Bob stepped out from under the big man's shadow to set a more comfortable distance between them. 'I spoke to an official at the golf club. He said there wouldn't be any problem here, above the gorse bushes.'

'None of the golf club's fucking business. The land is private. We'll be building a house here.'

A house? Bob thought. *Isn't this a protected area?*

He decided to humour this hooligan. 'Oh, my mistake,' he said apologetically. 'I'd no idea I was on private property. Anyway, the planning people will want to know there are possible Roman remains here.'

Hoodie's tone suddenly switched to one of false amiability. Taking a long drag from his cigarette, he said, 'Yeah, yeah, we'll tell them, of course. So did your metal detector locate something under those slabs?'

Not wishing to give anything away, Bob said, 'I got a signal that probably came from the paving stones themselves. They're iron-rich. See, they have a reddish colour.'

'Stay there a minute. I just need to check something in my office.'

Office? Oh, right, the Hamburg Süd box.

As the hooligan strode off, Bob read the words in large letters on his back: *THIS HOODIE'S NOT FOR HUGGING*, an allusion to the short-lived *'hug a hoodie'* catchphrase uttered by a prime minister some years before. With a shudder, he started filling in the hole he had dug. He needed to think about how to retrieve the gold, if gold it was, from below that pavement. It wouldn't happen today. He'd come back another time and make sure Hoodie wasn't around before he did any more digging.

If this *was* Roman gold, his luck was truly in. As treasure trove, it would be the property of the crown, but he'd be entitled to a reward based on its market value. Like every metal detector hobbyist in Scotland, he knew well that the finder of the Stirling hoard in 2009 had received a reward of nearly half a million pounds. Everything the J-Way was telling him led him to believe this could be another Stirling.

Hoodie shouted, 'Hey you! Come over here!'

Hesitantly, Bob stuck his spade in the ground and made his way over to the door of the container. It was gloomy inside but as his eyes became accustomed to the dimness he saw a portable generator, a variety of tools including a chainsaw and ropes as might be used for tree-pruning, a couple of plastic chairs and several packs of canned food and soft drinks.

'Okay, pal,' Hoodie said, 'first things first. Who are you?'

'My name's Robert Bowman. Look, if I've ...'

'I'm Victor Herring. This is actually my mother's building site, but I'm managing it for her.'

'Herring, eh? Is your mother Rachel Herring, by any chance?'

Victor nodded.

'I read in the paper she's negotiating to buy the old bank headquarters near the airport. She has plans for a casino hotel. Las Vegas-style, the paper said. Is that right?'

'She's got her finger in a lot of pies, but you can't believe everything you read in the newspapers. Anyway, I just called to tell her somebody was digging around on her land. She went ballistic, said I should set my dog on you. As it happens, I don't have Gnasher with me this afternoon. So it's your lucky day.'

Just an hour earlier, when the J-Way had first signalled the possibility of gold, Bob had believed it was indeed his lucky day. Now, sitting in the semi-darkness of a dirty old shipping container with a bearded gorilla, he was not so sure.

'Doubly lucky, in fact,' Victor went on. 'You see, Mr Bowman, I've a deal for you.'

'What kind of a deal?'

'Thing is, if it turns out we're sitting on some archaeological site – a Roman fort, whatever – we'll not be allowed to build. And my Ma's dead set on making her home here. So what's it worth for you to do nothing more about those Roman slabs, eh? Forget you ever saw them? Never breathe a word to anybody?'

Bob reprised his vision of half a million pounds if there was gold out there like the Stirling hoard. Whatever Victor Herring had in mind, it wasn't going to come close. 'No, I couldn't do a deal like that,' he said. 'If this *is* a Roman site, it should be preserved. Or at least documented before any foundations are dug. But, you know, chances are those slabs aren't Roman, maybe not even very old. Let the council's archaeologist do a survey. It might hold up the project for a few weeks, but that's likely all.'

'So, no deal?'

'That's what I said.'

They were sitting on white plastic chairs, facing each other. Bob started to get to his feet. 'Don't go,' Victor said. 'You can't reject an offer without even hearing it. Like a Coke? An Irn Bru? It's cold enough in this tin box at night to keep my supplies cool.'

Bob's first instinct was to walk away, but his curiosity as to Victor's price got the better of him. 'Coke, thanks.' He settled down again in his chair.

Victor stepped behind him – for a can of Coke, he supposed. The next thing Bob knew, there was a rope around his neck. He couldn't breathe, couldn't cry out. Lashing out with his arms and legs, he sent his chair flying. Soon he was face-down on the dusty floor, with Victor on his back, twisting the rope ever tighter. In less than a minute, he blacked out.

Victor kept the rope tight around the neck of the lifeless man for another full minute. Then he got up and rolled the body over with one foot to satisfy himself that his victim was dead. Rifling through Bowman's pockets, he removed everything he found, including a wallet with seventy pounds and some cards, a couple of pounds in loose change, a set of house keys and a car key. *No mobile phone. Good.*

Outside, he completed the task Bowman had begun of filling in the hole he had dug. Carefully he replaced the turf. It was hard to see the ground had ever been disturbed. All of Bowman's belongings, including the metal detector and its harness, he gathered up and took inside his 'office'.

He opened a can of Irn Bru and drained it in a single draught.

2

AN ECONOMIC PROPOSITION

PEOPLE WOULD SOMETIMES ASK Delia Cobb how she came to be living in Edinburgh. A pretty red-haired girl in her twenties, she looked authentically Scottish, but her Chicago accent told a different story. One of a handful of U.S. graduates working at the water-infrastructure company NEPA, she had landed an international fellowship in environmental science.

It was not her first experience of Scotland. She had come the previous year to retrieve a rare and ancient artefact she had inherited. 'Taran's wheel', it was called, an object of great cultural significance*, now lodged in the National Museum of Scotland for safe-keeping.

It was there that Delia met the curator Jody Stair. In her mid-thirties, Jody had a partner, a divorcé by the name of Marcus Annandale. He owned a business on Edinburgh's Royal Mile, selling customised malt whisky blends to tourists.

Though she found her NEPA work interesting, the fellowship was for Delia primarily a reason to continue her acquaintance with what she had come to regard as her adopted country, at least for a couple of years. After that, who knew? She might find some other reason to stay in Scotland, or she might decide it was time to return to the States.

A complicating factor was her boyfriend Quin Johnson, still pursuing an academic career as a linguist in Chicago. Lately, things had cooled between them; he seemed keen to settle down

---

* See *Taran's Wheel (Incomers: Book 1)*

in the Midwest, while she had a vision of a more interesting life across the Atlantic. Not quite ready to break off their relationship – apart from anything else, he was living in her apartment and paying rent, and they talked by phone or Skype at least once a week – she was nonetheless reluctant to plan her future around him. Edinburgh, she found, was a place where she would be happy to put down roots, something she had never felt in Chicago, though she had grown up there.

North East Pipeline Aqueduct, her employer, was headquartered at South Gyle in the west of the city under chief operating officer Dennis Dickie. It was one of two similar, supposedly competitive, enterprises established three years earlier. The other, WestWater, had its offices in Glasgow.

Climate change had led to more erratic rainfall patterns in southern England, with catastrophic flooding in some years, yet severe and prolonged drought in others. Building infrastructure to transfer water on demand from northern and western Scotland to thirsty Londoners was the business that NEPA and WestWater were set up to pursue.

For decades it was believed that moving huge volumes of water from one end of Britain to the other could never be an economic proposition. The new companies were changing all that by using existing rights-of-way. NEPA, for example, was installing pipelines and open channels alongside the main railway line from Inverness through Perth, Edinburgh and Newcastle to a hub north of London, from which the water they brought would be distributed to a system of reservoirs. Even the necessary pumping stations along the way could mostly be accommodated on underutilised railway land. The rent NEPA paid to Network Rail promised to transform the economics of Britain's railways – a huge side-benefit.

All mainstream political parties in the Scottish parliament at Holyrood were supportive of the program, despite public unease about inevitable cost overruns and travel disruption.

NEPA cultivated a higher profile than WestWater, and as a result became a greater target of dissent. Yet only one political entity caught and exploited the anti-NEPA mood: a dissident faction of extreme nationalists calling themselves *Auld Stobby*, Scots for 'Old Prickly', in reference to the Scotch thistle. They campaigned vociferously against England's 'theft' of 'Scottish' water.

None of this was Delia's concern. She was glad to have a job that let her enjoy living in one of Europe's most vibrant and historic capital cities. She had found a charming flat at a rent she could just afford on Marchmont Road.

With a habit for composing anagrams, she converted the name of her street to a fictitious website: *northdrama.com*. She could not have foreseen the kind of drama Edinburgh had in store for her.

3
WATER LAIRDS

AT 81, ARCHIE KILGOUR WAS the oldest and longest-serving member of the Ancient Edinburgh Society of Water Lairds. He had been inducted as a young man by his father; his grandfather and great-grandfather had been Water Lairds in their time too.

Since his wife's death a couple of years ago, Archie had withdrawn from most of the Society's activities, but maintained a friendship with some of his fellow members. Living alone in his large Georgian terrace house in Stockbridge, he was under constant pressure from his three daughters to sell up and move to a smaller place – a pressure he had until recently resisted.

'It's not just *my* home,' he had protested to them. 'Four generations of Kilgours have owned this house. Francis Kilgour – your great-great grandfather – bought it in 1877 for 250 guineas. And I'm not done with it yet.'

Of the many historic societies and guilds surviving in 21st-century Edinburgh, the Water Lairds had the longest pedigree, and were the most secretive. While others had charters from the Lord Provost or the city council, or were registered as charities, the Water Lairds owed their existence to no authority but their own. They did not hold flashy dinners or get mentioned in the *Scotsman* for good works. Meeting once a month in a rented room above a Rose Street pub, they talked mainly about current politics and the local economy, but also recounted stories handed down through the centuries of the Society's existence.

Most members were small businessmen; there were a few professionals including a couple of doctors, a university professor, an art gallery curator and a concert violinist, but – unusually for an ancient Edinburgh institution – no lawyers. Sons followed fathers into the society, just as Archie Kilgour had, with new members quietly recruited from among friends and associates of existing Water Lairds. The roll had no more than thirty names, of whom perhaps two dozen attended regularly.

Membership records went back a little over 300 years, but unlike, say, the Merchants' Company, the Society of Writers to Her Majesty's Signet, the High Constables or the Speculative Society, the Water Lairds had no documented history or date of foundation. It was generally believed that in medieval times they had some quasi-official role as guardians of watercourses in and around the city of Edinburgh. The quality of those waters was not just of local but of national importance. After all, by act of the Scottish Parliament in 1617, wheat, peas, beans, rye and salt were to be measured in *firkins*, a volume equal to *21 pints and a mutchkin of the water of Leith*.

The Society kept a collection of old books in a locked cabinet in its meeting room. From time to time a proposal was made to donate them to the National Library of Scotland, but thus far no action had been taken. Occasionally recourse was had to one volume or another to settle a debate; this happened less and less as most of the titles, being long out of copyright, were easily accessible free on the web.

Lacking written articles of association, the Water Lairds had no explicit ban on female enrolment, but no woman had ever been admitted. It had not occurred to Archie to propose one of his daughters for membership. Instead, he had championed the recruitment five years ago of Marcus Annandale, who became his protégé and a close friend.

The day after celebrating his 81st birthday Archie fell on the stairs of his house. He would admit no connection between these events, and was lucky to have no broken bones. His confidence shaken, he finally agreed to his daughters' entreaties to move to a flat in a building with a lift. Marcus agreed to help him sort through his belongings and dispose of things he would have no room for, nor need of, in his new, much smaller, home.

For five successive Mondays (the only day of the week when his shop was closed), Marcus combed through cupboards, chests and glory-holes. Archie supervised, giving thumbs up or down as Marcus suggested disposition of articles – sell, donate, keep, bin. On the sixth Monday, Archie pronounced himself satisfied that everything had been gone through.

'Isn't there an attic?' Marcus asked.

'Haven't been up there in forty years. My stepladder got to be unsafe and I threw it out. Never got around to buying a new one.'

'We should borrow one and take a look.'

'There's no light in the attic. And as I recall, there's only some old junk of my parents' or grandparents'. Whoever buys the house can get rid of it.'

'Ancestors' junk can turn out to be worth something. There could be stuff from your great-grandparents' time.'

'Okay, you win,' Archie said at length.

Marcus bought a powerful flashlight from a little hardware store around the corner and, with the aid of a neighbour's ladder, climbed through a trapdoor in the ceiling of the top-floor landing. Decades of dust and cobwebs lay on every surface. He found some hatboxes (one containing a top hat), a melodeon from which he could coax only a wheeze, a box of children's games, a wireless from the 1930s, and a set of wartime blackout blinds.

In a corner was a large wooden trunk, its lid secured with a brass hasp. Marcus tried to move the trunk towards the trapdoor but it wouldn't budge. At first he thought it was just heavy; soon he realised it was anchored, probably nailed from the inside, to the joists. He would have to force it open where it sat. A stout screwdriver proved an effective lever.

Inside were some women's clothes, mostly Victorian underwear. Nestled among the garments was a doll with a porcelain head. And at the bottom lay a leather attaché case full of papers. Marcus brought the entire contents of the trunk down from the attic to let Archie have a look.

'Never saw this stuff before,' the old man said. 'The doll might have been my mother's when she was a little girl.' He opened the attaché case and pulled out a wad of yellowing papers. Leafing through them, he sat silent for a few minutes.

'Something interesting, Archie?'

'Looks like a manuscript. See the handwriting? Isn't it beautiful? Nobody writes like this any more.'

Marcus had to agree. The calligraphy was evenly sized and spaced without the aid of ruling; the letters sloped gently and uniformly forward and looped elegantly above and below. This was the writing of an artist, he was sure. A frugal artist – the writing ran to the very edge of the page with no margins, front and back. The slender ink-strokes suggested the pen had been held lightly, and there was evidence in places of a slight tremor, as if the writer was an old person. From perusal of a few passages in the manuscript, it appeared to be a family history of some kind.

'Where's the first page?' Marcus asked. 'That should give us a title and the name of the author.'

It eluded them until Marcus saw it stuck to the inside of the leather case. He tried gingerly to peel it off but the fragile paper threatened to tear with the slightest pull.

'Archie, I'd like Jody to take a look at this.'

The old man looked puzzled. 'Jody? Who's she?'

'I've told you about Jody a number of times. Jody Stair. She's my girlfriend. We've been seeing each other for almost a year.'

'Since your divorce from Heather?'

'Not quite. That was over two years ago. I met Jody at *Inglisleid* last spring.'

'Ingle what?'

'You know, the Scots language discussion group. Jody's a founder member. Not me – I just started going after the divorce. Anyway, the reason I'd like her to see these papers is that she works at the National Museum. She'll know somebody there with the right technique for separating the first page from the leather.'

'Is she as bonnie as Heather?'

'Yes, but in a different way.' He took a photo out of his wallet and showed it to Archie: a woman slightly younger than Marcus, with regular features, dark hair and eyes, slim athletic build, and a radiant smile.

'You can pick them. A bit on the thin side, isn't she?'

'No excess fat, for sure. She runs a lot. Finished the Edinburgh marathon this year.'

'Mm. Divorced like you, I suppose?'

'Too many questions, Archie. But as a matter of fact, no. She never married.'

Archie took a moment to digest this information. Then he said, 'Marcus, you've been so kind and helpful these last few weeks. I want you to have the manuscript, if you'd like it. To keep, I mean. By all means share it with your girlfriend. Maybe you could ... what is it they do nowadays? ... scan it so that it's preserved, and give me a copy.'

'Thank you,' Marcus said. 'I'll do that, and treasure it.'

Little did he realise what a treasure it would turn out to be.

A roll of builder's heavy-gauge polythene and some duct tape in Victor Herring's shipping container proved ideal for wrapping the corpse. Leaving the still-warm body well sealed in its plastic cocoon on the floor, he locked up and walked down a path through woods – skirting around the golf course – to where his green Land Rover was parked. Soon he was home at his spacious flat in Merchiston, an upmarket area in the south-west of Edinburgh. That evening he checked the weather forecast and tide tables.

The following day was wet and unseasonably cold. Early in the morning he headed for his mother's building site. Putting the Land Rover in all-wheel drive, he followed the track through the deserted golf course. It was like negotiating a muddy river, but the LR was well up to the job.

It was no day for golf or dog-walking. But he kept an eye open for passers-by, just in case. Entering his 'office', he saw everything was exactly as he had left it the day before.

He hauled the polythene-shrouded body outside. Though it was much heavier than he expected, he was able by stages to lift and shove it into the back of the LR, accompanied by his chainsaw, a can of fuel, some bin-bags, a plastic bucket, and Bowman's metal detector and harness. Not fully trusting the privacy afforded by the LR's tinted rear windows, he threw a black cover over his cargo.

Back in the Hamburg Süd container, he thoroughly swept the floor to remove any visible traces of the previous day's struggle. It was thirsty work, and he gulped down a can of Irn Bru before setting off. Halfway to the public road, he met a hardy soul in a parka and waterproof trousers who was taking a walk in the rain. Victor slowed down so as not to splash him, then gave him a cheerful wave as he drove by.

At 11:20 am, just ten minutes before high tide, Victor stopped at a lonely spot he knew well near Carriden on the south shoreline of the Firth of Forth. He'd been along this almost deserted road on many a Sunday ride on his motorbike – a five-year-old Harley 1200cc Nightster that spent far too much time in the back of his garage – but never before in the Land Rover. Certainly never on business like today's.

The rain continued unabated, and a cold fog lay over the firth. Though the north shore was less than two miles away across the water, it was invisible, as were the towers of the Forth Road Bridge and the new Queensferry Crossing about five miles downstream. The ghostly shape of a container ship could just be discerned making its way upriver to Grangemouth. Victor lit a cigarette and planned his next move.

4
BOX-CUTTER BALLET

JODY LEAFED THROUGH THE PAPERS. 'Yep, you're right,' she said to Marcus. 'It's a family history.' Turning to the last page, she noted the initials *C.N.* and a date, 1883. 'I wonder who *C.N.* was. It's a shame we can't see page one. That might give us her full name.'

He gave her a sceptical look. '*Her* full name? What makes you so sure this was written by a woman?'

'There's a feminine quality about the handwriting, don't you think? I'll take the attaché case to work tomorrow, get the first page separated from the leather.'

Next morning, she called Shilpa Chandrasekharan in the conservation department of the National Library of Scotland. Putting the case in a plastic pouch to protect it from the rain, she hurried over to the NLS.

Entering the library at street level, most visitors are unaware that most of the building lies below them, and that they are actually on the eleventh floor. Far below, she found the conservator at her desk in a tiny room.

'This is a common problem,' Shilpa said in her Indian-inflected Edinburgh accent. 'A little mildew on leather acts as a kind of adhesive for any paper that gets pressed against it for a prolonged period. But I have a way of freeing it. Just in case the paper gets damaged – which it shouldn't – I'll scan the visible side before I begin. You don't care about the case, do you?'

'No, it's the document that matters.'

Almost before Jody had finished saying those words, Shilpa brought a box-cutter out of a drawer in her desk and began attacking the inside of the case. She worked rapidly and rhythmically – a box-cutter ballet, Jody thought admiringly. Soon Shilpa had a rectangle of leather, just slightly bigger than the paper adhering to it, that could be laid flat on the platen of a scanner.

'I'll have the first sheet in good condition for you by five o'clock tomorrow.'

'Thanks, Shilpa, you're a gem. I'll take the rest of the manuscript out of your way.'

'Actually, a manuscript of this age is going to be quite fragile and prone to fading. Why don't you leave it with me? I can have the original archived here and send you a scan of the whole thing tomorrow afternoon. Just email me details of the provenance of the document, for proper cataloguing.'

Jody was initially reluctant – she wanted to start reading the document that evening. But Shilpa had made a good point. And if *C.N.*'s writing had lain undisturbed since 1883, it could wait one more day.

'Okay, that makes sense,' she said. 'But I'll take what's left of the case.' Replacing the bits of ancient leather in the plastic pouch, she stepped back out into the rain.

Marcus's shop was close by. She headed up there to tell him they'd have a scan of the manuscript by the following evening. Since he was busy with a customer, she put the plastic pouch on his desk at the back of the shop, then signalled to him, putting her thumb and little finger to her right ear and mouthing 'call me.' On the way back to her office, she stopped in a sheltered doorway and rang Delia's mobile.

A box-cutter ballet of a different kind was about to take place on the dismal, deserted shore of the Firth of Forth. From inside the Land Rover, Victor Herring shoved with his feet against the large polythene-and-duct-tape package until it fell out the back door, landing with a heavy thump on the ground. Taking a box-cutter from his pocket, he slit the bands of duct-tape holding the package together. Soon he was able to unroll the heavy-duty polythene to reveal Robert Bowman's corpse, lying face down on the plastic sheet.

Working quickly and methodically, he removed every stitch of clothing from the body and stuffed it all in a bin-bag. He then inspected the naked corpse for tattoos or other distinguishing marks, and saw nothing of significance. It was at this stage that he almost missed Bowman's gold wristwatch, but caught it in time. Severing the leather strap with his cutter, he noted the initials *R.J.B.* engraved on the back of the watch. *Probably a retirement gift,* he thought as he pocketed it.

Next, with his chainsaw he made short work of decapitating the body. He sealed the head in a bin-bag, then double-bagged it just to be sure there would be no fluid escape. *Better take the hands off as well.* He tried to restart the chainsaw. No joy: the rain had got to it. *Ah well, if the police have Bowman's fingerprints on file, they'll also have his DNA. And there's nothing I can do about that.*

So on to the main event, dumping the headless corpse in the firth. Grabbing it by the feet, he hauled it down over the shingle beach, leaving a trail of blood and tissue fragments. Soon the water was lapping around his ankles, but he kept going. By the time the water was up to his knees, the corpse was floating. It was time to let the outgoing tide do its work. The body would be carried away from this spot, to wash up anywhere on the downstream shoreline. It might even find its way out into the open sea, then who knew where it would end up? Denmark possibly. An interesting subject for one of those Scandinavian crime dramas.

Having gathered up and bagged the polythene sheet and duct tape, he filled the bucket several times from the firth and splashed the water over the shingle to wash away the bloody trail the body had left above high-water mark. The rain helped with the clean-up.

He removed his shoes, socks and outer clothes and put them all in a bin-bag. Returning to the lapping shore, he shivered in the drenching rain but took time to thoroughly wash his hands and face in the brackish water. Back inside the LR he towelled himself and slipped on dry jeans, hoodie, trainers and gloves. He turned up the heat as he drove back into Edinburgh.

What remained of his task was more fun. First he disposed of the J-Way metal detector and its harness in the doorway of a charity shop on St Johns Road. Then, driving randomly around the city, he dropped off the bin-bags, one at a time, in communal rubbish bins belonging to different blocks of flats. Nobody paid the slightest attention. He took time to move the existing rubbish around in each bin, so that his deposit wouldn't be sitting on top. The last bag, the one with the severed head, was left at an address in the Grange. Mission accomplished.

Rachel Herring took his call in the study of her five-bedroom house in the Isle of Man countryside. 'I don't need details, son. Just pleased you've averted what could have been a sticky situation. As it is, Planning's asking for too many changes, and I don't want the question of an archaeological survey coming up again. It cost me ten thousand to get it waived last time.'

'You know, Ma, I could get a digger up to the site and work the whole place over before any archaeologist comes near.'

'Yes, I thought of that, but it would attract too much attention. Plus, it would be obvious we've been excavating before the planning approval comes through. I've another idea. I'll discuss it with you tomorrow when I'm in Edinburgh.'

'You're coming over? I'd better clean the house.'

'I'll stay at the Balmoral. But you should clean your house anyway. Or get a wife to do that for you.'

'Love you, Ma.'

The customer Marcus had been preoccupied with when Jody dropped in was an elderly well-to-do lady named Kirsty Morton. Unlike most of his clientele, Kirsty was no tourist. Home for her was a large house in Murrayfield surrounded by an acre of gardens, all enclosed behind high walls, on the lower slopes of Corstorphine Hill. With no children of her own, she had a favourite grandnephew, Hugh Leggat, whom she indulged on special occasions. A flyer for *A Malt O' My Ain* among her junk mail one day gave her the idea of having a unique Scotch whisky created for Hugh's 28th birthday.

A Malt O' My Ain was Marcus Annandale's brainchild. Five years ago, he had been an up-and-coming marketing executive with one of Scotland's biggest distillers, headquartered in Edinburgh. Following a hostile takeover by a French-Irish conglomerate he and over a hundred other employees suddenly found themselves surplus to requirements. The severance payment was generous beyond his wildest expectations. With it he purchased a retail whisky shop on the High Street, part of the Royal Mile in the Old Town, that had been in decline for years.

A business concept he had tried unsuccessfully to push through the bureaucracy of his former employer could now be given the breath of life. The notion was a custom blending operation, in which high-quality single malts could be mixed to an individual's precise specification to provide a unique 'signature' blend with its own label.

In principle it was no different from the colour mixing found in any paint store, except that the sensory properties of malt whiskies – smoothness, peatiness, smokiness, fullness, aromaticity and so on – were highly subjective. Punters would taste a variety of 'standards' and rank them on a number of criteria, providing data for the design of a specific blend of up to six single malts tailored to their preferences.

Depending on the rarity of each single malt used in the blend, a customised bottle of whisky from *A Malt O' My Ain* could retail for anything from £50 to £500. Buying a case of a dozen bottles brought the unit price down significantly: £29.99 upwards a bottle, with free shipping. It was at the low end that Marcus did most of his business, which still left a healthy profit margin.

Kirsty was not a low-end customer. Nothing younger than twelve years was to go in the blend. Marcus suggested her grandnephew come into the shop to take the 'taste test'; meanwhile Kirsty could select a label design.

'Have you a name in mind for this malt?' Marcus asked.

'*Poacher's Poison*. Private joke – Hugh will understand.'

'No problem. I just have to run a wee check to make sure it's not somebody else's trademark – but I doubt it.'

'Hi, Delia.' Jody's voice on the phone sounded excited. 'I've come across a manuscript – well, it's Marcus's, really – that might be quite interesting. It's from 1883, by the looks of it a family history left to posterity. You're good at reading between the lines. Would you go through it with me?'

'Sure, Jody. I'd love to.'

'How about tomorrow, after work? We can meet at La Toscana – say at 6:30.'

No sooner had Jody ended her phone conversation with Delia than she received a call from Marcus.

'What's up, sweetheart?' His usual phone conversation starter. 'Sorry I was busy when you came in.'

'Shilpa at the National Library did quite a number on the attaché case, as you've probably noticed.'

'I saw you left a plastic pouch on my desk, but haven't had a chance to see what was in it.'

'Don't bother. It's not salvageable. The important thing is, Shilpa will send me a scan of the whole manuscript tomorrow. Including the sheet that was stuck to the leather. Soon as I get it, I'll shoot you a copy. You coming over after you close up?'

'Can't tonight. Promised Archie I'd meet him for a beer at the Stockbridge Tap. He wants to celebrate getting his place cleared out. Tomorrow?'

'If you're finished by 6:30, come to La Toscana. Delia will be there.'

5
PERSUASIVE

THREE ITEMS OF BUSINESS brought Rachel Herring to Edinburgh. First, a mid-afternoon meeting with Councillor James Swift. Second, an unlikely rendezvous with a couple of members of the ultra-nationalist group *Auld Stobby*. And third, dinner with her son Victor, to discuss what to do about those damnable Roman remains – if that's what they really were.

Rachel was a slim, good-looking woman of 55 with neat dyed-blonde hair, who favoured expensive clothes and jewellery. Her son had inherited none of her fine features, spare physique or cultured tastes; for these deficiencies she blamed his father, her first husband. Dead these last 26 years, it was Cyril Herring who had built up the business interests she now owned and managed.

Not that she complained about her marriage to a man thirty years her senior. It had made her a wealthy woman, and had been mercifully short – just over three years from wedding to cremation, during which she had borne her only child, Victor, now 27. Although recently wed to the fourth of her husbands (a pretty boy about the same age as her son), she had kept her first married name. To none of them had she been the kind of wife she wanted for Victor: someone who would clean him up a bit, do his laundry and provide a bunch of grandchildren.

Swift hated his meetings with Rachel. Invariably she made demands requiring all his political skill and deviousness to satisfy. Already he had used his powers of persuasion to swing the council's acting director of planning behind giving consent in principle to plans for a luxury home on possibly the best undeveloped site in Lothian – maybe all of Scotland. A local conservation group had protested vehemently, but Rachel's promise to make a huge business investment in the area had been his trump card.

The councillor stood to be well rewarded. A 'fee' of £25,000, plus £10,000 for securing a waiver of the normally mandatory archaeological survey. All payable in a few weeks, assuming the committee signed off on detailed planning approval.

Still, it was with some trepidation that he came to the one-on-one meeting in the Balmoral Hotel. Rachel Herring had leverage. Having once accepted her money, he couldn't back out of his business relationship with her; better to keep it going than risk her outing him for corruption. Anyway, he told himself, it was for the public good. Her commercial development plan would create hundreds of local jobs. She had made it clear that her proposed casino resort near Edinburgh airport was contingent on a building permit for her new home. Swift was doing the right thing for the Lothian economy.

He arrived at the Balmoral early, giving himself time for two stiff drinks before Rachel appeared. Alcohol and apprehension turned his ordinarily florid complexion a deeper puce. But the meeting in an otherwise deserted lounge turned out to be relatively benign. Rachel was all sweetness and light; she ordered coffee, a large cognac for him and a Tio Pepe for herself. All she apparently wanted was an update on the progress of the full planning application. And it was going fairly well: a few changes would be demanded, but it appeared there were no serious snags.

Privately, Swift found the proposed seven-bedroom, eight-bathroom house hideously vulgar in appearance; a tasteless excrescence on such a prominent site. But none of that mattered. So long as the house was built, Swift's secret, and his augmented bank account, would be safe.

The meeting over, Rachel ordered another large cognac for him, then made her apologies. She was running late for another appointment. He stood to bid her good day, then sat down to nurse the soothing, warming brandy.

Ten minutes later, Rachel was shown into a small cheerless room below street level in a narrow close off the High Street. It reeked of mould, rancid chip fat and stale beer. A tiny window high on one wall admitted a cold draught but little in the way of light; illumination came from an ancient fitment containing two buzzing, flickering fluorescent tubes. In the centre of the floor stood a cheap laminate-topped table surrounded by four chairs.

Left alone for a few minutes, she began to wonder if she'd been wise in coming here. After all, *Auld Stobby* wasn't exactly a mainstream political organization. It had failed to distance itself from the vague threats of violence against English-owned businesses in Scotland uttered by some of its adherents.

Though born in Lancashire, Rachel didn't consider herself English; when asked her nationality she always replied 'Manx', the Isle of Man having been her home since her first marriage 29 years ago. Now she was contemplating giving up her 'non-dom' tax status and taking up permanent residence in Scotland, though this would hardly make her Scottish.

A couple entered. The woman was small with a boyish figure, her black hair in an asymmetric post-punk crop, a naturally pale complexion emphasised by deep purple lipstick, set off by a single large black earring in the shape of a raven's feather. A Goth, presumably. Heavy black eyeliner and mascara contrasted with her hazel eyes, which looked unusually green in the fluorescent light. She wore knee-high boots, tights and a tiny flared skirt, all black, and a white Primark top cut to show cleavage, though she didn't have much.

Her slightly older companion was tall, muscular but pasty-faced, with cold eyes. Lank fair hair fell over the collar of his Italian leather jacket, which was teamed with designer jeans.

The pair introduced themselves as Isla Younie and Hendrik Vandenbrouck.

'You're not Scottish, I take it?' Rachel said by way of greeting to the tall man, on hearing his name. Evidently a man of few words, he let Isla do the explaining.

'He's Belgian, from Ghent. Was active for many years in – what was it, Hendrik, the Free Flanders Army? – but left when they started getting too soft. Now he's joined our movement for a free Scotland.'

'I suppose your movement has links to the Scottish National Party?'

'The SNP?' Isla sneered. 'They're politicians like all the rest. They'll sell Scotland down the river. We, on the other hand, won't rest until Scottish assets are safely in the hands of the Scottish people.'

'And by "we" you mean *Auld Stobby*?'

'That's right.' Isla smiled to reveal even white teeth. 'We're well named, *stobby* – prickly, just like the Scotch thistle. *Wha daur meddle wi me.*'

Isla's recitation of the Latin motto *'Nemo me impune lacessit'* from Scotland's royal coat of arms, in its usual Scots translation, was lost on Rachel. 'So I'm surprised you wanted to meet with *me*,' she said. 'I'm an incomer, not one of the "Scottish people" you want owning Scottish assets.'

'We've heard you're negotiating to open a big gambling resort out west, by the airport,' Isla said, coming to the point of the meeting.

'And you're against it?'

'Not at all. It'll bring in foreign money. Aye, *English* money. And that's okay by *Auld Stobby*. Your English punters – Americans, too, and Chinese – will fly in, lose their shirts and fly out again. We won't be too troubled by them on the streets of Edinburgh. Perfect. But see your Scottish Parliament? And your Edinburgh Council? They'll be holier than the Pope.

"Gambling?" they'll say. "Las Vegas on our doorstep? No, we don't want *that*."' For this last remark, Isla adopted a mock 'Edinburgh genteel' accent.

Rachel saw the pitch coming. 'So I suppose you're after some funding from me, as the price of your support?'

Hendrik Vandenbrouck, who hadn't said a word up to this point, pushed his chin forward and said, in his Flemish accent, 'We can be *very* persuasive.'

Rachel was taken aback by his sudden aggression. Isla immediately clarified. 'When Hendrik says "persuasive", he means we can persuade people to favour your scheme. He wasn't talking about putting pressure on you, in case that's what you thought.'

Vandenbrouck nodded, saying nothing more.

'But you *are* after money, aren't you? Isn't that what this meeting is about?'

'We always need money to continue our work.'

'And what exactly can you do for me? *Who* can you persuade? You're not exactly a legitimate lobbying organisation, are you?'

'It's a few years ago now, but when Donald Trump wanted to destroy a prime Aberdeenshire coastal habitat to open a golf resort for tourists with bags of money and zero taste, the local council turned him down. That seemed to be the end of the matter, until their decision was overturned by the SNP-led government at Holyrood, and the bulldozers were soon at work. Who do you think made that happen?'

'*Auld Stobby* did that? If it's true, I'm impressed.'

'You better believe it,' Vandenbrouck said.

Isla studied Rachel's inscrutable expression. 'We're not expecting anything right now, Mrs Herring. All we ask is you give it some thought. We can meet again in a few weeks.'

'Leave it with me. I'll get in touch if and when I think there's something to discuss.'

With that, the meeting broke up. Rachel returned to the Balmoral to freshen up before having dinner with Victor. Her clothes and hair stank of the basement room where she'd just had her first encounter with *Auld Stobby*.

⬠

When Kirsty Morton arrived home from her gift-shopping, she was pleasantly surprised to find her grandnephew waiting for her on the driveway.

'Hugh!' she cried. 'Why are you waiting out here? You could have let yourself in.'

'I just arrived. There's something I want to talk to you about.'

'Me too!'

Over freshly brewed coffee and a scone at the kitchen table, Hugh Leggat said, 'Okay, Aunt Kirsty, you go first.'

'Your birthday's coming up in less than a month, and I've just been arranging your present. Unfortunately it can't be a surprise this year, because you need to go for a fitting, as it were.'

'A fitting? What for? Not a kilt, for sure. You gave me one just two years ago.'

The gift would be a case of custom-blended Scotch whisky from *A Malt O' My Ain*. One that would be blended to his precise preference. Hugh made his usual protestations that the gift was too much, but promised to go for a tasting session within the next few days. Then it was his turn to share some news.

'You know I've been speaking out against NEPA,' he began.

'Speaking out? No, I didn't know.'

'I had a letter printed in the *Scotsman* last week, saying what a boondoggle it is for all those executives. They're drawing huge salaries, and are in line for massive bonuses that aren't tied properly to project timelines. And in the end, what's it for? Just to keep London in cheap water.'

'I don't take the *Scotsman*, dear.'

'I know. You get some English paper. The *Independent*, isn't it? You don't learn about what's really important to Scotland.'

'Hugh, darling, I've never heard you take such a parochial attitude! You used to rail against the nationalists for exactly that kind of thinking. Now it sounds like you've joined the SNP. Is that what you're going to tell me?'

'Not the SNP. They're in bed with the NEPA board. I'm a member of *Auld Stobby*.'

Kirsty was stunned. Her grandnephew was a forensic accountant. He hobnobbed with prosecutors, solicitors, judges even. It could only hurt him professionally to be associated with those tattooed, multi-pierced skinheads. She begged him to reconsider.

'It's too late, I'm in. And I expect to be very active. But I wanted to tell you myself before you hear it from another source.'

'Well, I can't pretend I'm not shocked and disappointed. But you know your own mind. I just hope you're not putting your career in jeopardy over this.'

'If something's worth fighting for, a career sometimes has to take second place. It's not as if I'm married with kids. I'm not putting anyone else's wellbeing on the line. Only my own. I can understand how you're having a hard time taking this in, but it'll all seem perfectly normal to you in a few weeks.'

Kirsty thought otherwise but decided to leave it at that for now.

⬠

Rachel's preference would have been a hushed, expensive restaurant with starched tablecloths and an à-la-carte menu in French. But she couldn't take Victor to a place like that. So she settled for a slightly seedy bistro on Rose Street with 'today's specials' scrawled in chalk on a blackboard. Victor liked that 'today's specials' never changed – he came here often and knew exactly what would be on offer.

'Okay, Victor,' Rachel said after they'd ordered their food and had a bottle of wine on the table, 'we need to do something about those damned remains.'

'I know. I still think a few hours with a digger is the answer.'

'No. Here's what we're going to do. What was the name of that little man we got to fix the fire doors at Learmonth?'

'Cameron Lewis. Calls himself Cammy.'

One of Rachel's existing business interests in Edinburgh was the Learmonth Club, a small casino operation. A year or two earlier, the premises were found to be in violation of fire code; to avoid losing its licence, the club was required to install new doors meeting very stringent – and expensive – specifications. The manager, Ciaran Mortimer, had mentioned this to one of his regular punters who happened to be a building contractor.

Actually, 'building contractor' was a slightly grandiose term for Cammy Lewis's operation. He did odd jobs for the cash he needed to fund his gambling habit. At that time, however, his habit was costing more than he earned, and he'd maxed out his credit card with no obvious means of paying off the debt. He proposed installing the fire doors for a combination of cash and gambling chips; he just *knew* that those chips would get him on a winning streak and he'd be back in the black.

Victor, who kept close tabs on the Learmonth Club, instructed Mortimer to accept Lewis's offer. Furthermore, at his mother's suggestion, he made it clear that the chips Lewis received had to be 'lucky' ones. Not *too* lucky, mind. Just enough to keep their contractor in credit, at least until the job was finished and approved by the licensing authority.

'Does Lewis still play at Learmonth?' Rachel asked.

'He does. And still loses. From time to time he goes off in despair to the Genting, but I assume he does no better there – he always comes back.'

'Give him a bigger line of credit as he's such a faithful customer. I want him in our debt. Then we'll have him dig up whatever it is we have at the building site. By hand, under cover of darkness. Does he have a wife? Kids?'

'I think so.'

'Good. If he shows any sign of backsliding, or threatens to tell anyone what he's doing, remind him how unfortunate it would be if anything happened to them. Now pour me another glass of that merlot.'

6

A TRUE MEMOIR

THOUGH HE OWNED A SMALL FLAT in Newington (Heather had held on to the matrimonial home after their divorce), Marcus spent most nights at Jody's place off Morningside Road. It was there that his most treasured possessions – his Kindle, his best scotch, his guitar – had taken up residence.

There was an unseasonable chill in the air when the three of them left La Toscana. At her flat, Jody turned up the heat and opened a bottle of Argentine shiraz. On the kitchen table lay three hard copies of the Stockbridge attic manuscript, printed from the scan she had received that afternoon.

All she said to Marcus and Delia was, 'Let's read.'

MY FAMILY: A TRUE MEMOIR

To an old woman of 79, it comes as a shock to find her illustrious brother publishing an Autobiography she never knew he had written. It is even more shocking to find so much deliberate misrepresentation in the chapters dealing with his – and her – family.

James (I used to call him Jamie but cannot now bring myself to do so) has engaged the famous Dr Samuel Smiles to edit this Autobiography of his. I have nothing to say against Dr Smiles; indeed in my opinion his notable works Self-Help *and* Thrift *point the way to a better Britain. Many years ago he put his name to an estimable biography of George Stephenson. No doubt my brother, considering himself at least as great an engineer as Stephenson, calculates that with Dr Smiles's endorsement he will be as favourably regarded by generations to come.*

However, Dr Smiles could know only those things that James chose to divulge. The facts that James suppressed, altered or (if I must be charitable) misremembered, were not open to his editor's scrutiny. I therefore put the blame squarely and exclusively on my brother's shoulders for the false record he has sought to create as to the Nasmyth family.

'Nasmyth!' Marcus exclaimed. 'The writer was a sister of James Nasmyth, inventor of the steam hammer.'

'Yes,' Jody chimed in, 'and a daughter of the painter Alexander Nasmyth.' Turning to Delia, she added, 'Nasmyth, father and son, are among Edinburgh's most celebrated figures of the 18th and 19th centuries. This *Memoir* is by Charlotte Nasmyth.'

A quick Google search revealed that Charlotte died at the age of 80 in 1884. The manuscript was dated 1883, near the end of her life. Google confirmed that James's autobiography was indeed published in 1883, under the editorship of Samuel Smiles.

As I do not wish, at my advanced age, to become embroiled in public controversy, this Memoir will remain private until after my death. Mr Duncan Murison of Edinburgh, in his youth a good friend of my dear brother George (departed this life 16 years ago), has agreed to hold my writings and keep them secret for as long as I shall live. My health is failing and I suspect he will not have to hold them for very long.

How could a document entrusted to Duncan Murison have ended up in Archie Kilgour's attic? Maybe, Jody surmised, he and a Kilgour ancestor had been Water Lairds together. Marcus said he could check that out.

Mention of George Nasmyth's name prompts me to note that it is the total omission of any reference to him in his brother's Autobiography that has most deeply offended me. James has sought to create a fictitious Nasmyth family in which no George ever existed; yet in fact until 1843 the two brothers were equal partners in their highly successful engineering business. By means of this Memoir I intend to correct the record with regard to George and other matters.

I shall begin with my parents, for any Memoir of the Nasmyths must be anchored in their story.

Alexander Nasmyth, born 1758, was the fourth generation of his family to operate a business in Edinburgh as architect and builder. His father, Michael, had made a great success of it, cashing in on the development of the New Town which had recently been laid out in a classical rectangular pattern. The street plan drawn up by James Craig had been inspired in part by the 'divine proportions' of Luca Pacioli, a late 15th-century mathematician who was a formative influence on the great Leonardo da Vinci. The same 'divine proportions' are evident in many of the buildings in the New Town, including those designed by my grandfather. Among Michael Nasmyth's commissions was a house on St David Street, the gateway from Princes Street to St Andrew Square, for the world-renowned writer and thinker David Hume.

To digress, Hume was a controversial figure in his day – he still is, in some quarters – because of his questioning of religious faith. Some called him an atheist; how remarkable it is that a man with such views should now be revered as one of the fathers of the

Scottish Enlightenment! My grandfather was initially confounded by Hume's request to fashion a belvedere for the rooftop of his new home. It was not the demand for a belvedere that my grandfather found odd, for these glass-enclosed lookouts were becoming fashionable accessories to grand townhouses. It was the shape of it that puzzled him. Hume specified that it take the form of one half of a Platonic dodecahedron, requiring six windows each in the shape of a regular pentagon. It seemed to smack of paganism, even of some satanic influence, but according to Hume the dodecahedron was believed by ancient philosophers to be the shape of the cosmos. What better place from which to view the stars?

Normally my grandfather's elder son, also called Michael, should have succeeded to his enterprise, but Uncle Michael turned out to be a gadabout, too flighty to take on the responsibilities of business. He ran off to sea, and by default his younger brother Alexander, my father, became the natural heir to the Nasmyth architectural legacy.

In 1786 Alexander wed Barbara Foulis, daughter of a Lothian baronet (the Foulis family were lairds of Woodhall and Colinton, and formerly of Ravelston – of which more anon). Over two decades she became mother to myself and no fewer than ten other children, of whom all but two survived into adulthood. She was well educated and refined, and possessed of an artistic talent to which my father was apparently blind and for which my brother James has given her no credit. The words of his Autobiography damn with faint praise the remarkable woman who gave him life:

'My mother did not bring with her any fortune, so to speak, in the way of gold or acres; but she brought

something far better into my father's home – a sweetness of disposition, and a large measure of common sense, which made her, in all respects, the devoted helpmate of her husband. Her happy cheerful temperament, and her constant industry and attention, shed an influence upon all around her. By her example she inbred in her children the love of truth, excellence, and goodness. That was indeed the best fortune she could bring into a good man's home.'

To set the record straight, Barbara Foulis was much more than a 'devoted helpmate' with a sweet disposition and, for that matter, not a mere brood-mare, however industrious and attentive. She, more than her husband, ensured that her daughters (of whom I am one of six who survived infancy) developed their individual talents to become at least as competent as her sons.

It was Mama, I truly believe, who inspired me as an artist to strive for the 'quinta essentia' *in my work – the fifth element or 'quintessence' that, when added to the four classical elements of earth, air, fire and water, can add life to a landscape. Her domestic grind left her hardly any time to hone her own skill as an artist, but she used to draw humorous little sketches – cartoons, really – of city life. To my great regret, none of these seem to have survived.*

I do not intend by any of this to deny the accomplishments of Papa as a landscape painter. That he has been called the 'Father of the Landscape School of Scottish Art' is no small tribute, even if coming from a close personal friend, since that friend was Sir David Wilkie, himself one of the finest painters Scotland has so far produced. Yet Alexander Nasmyth came first to prominence in the field of portraiture; even now his most famous work is a portrait of Robert Burns he executed in 1786, the year of his marriage to Mama.

James implies that our father's re-emphasis on landscape art was driven economically by dwindling commissions for portrait work, resulting from his political views. It is true he had what would nowadays be called a liberal bias in his opinions, and it is also true that most of the potential clientele for portraiture was of a Tory bent. But I think he had a different motivation. In a way it was his misfortune to be a contemporary of Mr (later Sir) Henry Raeburn, whose great talent as a portraitist was legendary, even in his own time. Sir Henry commanded a very high fee, and all who could afford it beat a path to his door. That left only second-class commissions for everyone else.

The Raeburn home was just across the street from ours in York Place, a broad and elegant thoroughfare in Edinburgh's New Town. Sir Henry and Papa were not only neighbours but friends, the more so when Papa turned away from portraiture and emerged from the Raeburn shadow. Both artists enjoyed the company of like-minded men in informal gatherings such as the Poker Club and the Dilettanti Club.

I cannot mention Sir Henry Raeburn without saying something about The Skating Minister, *his oil painting of the Reverend Robert Walker at Duddingston Loch. Some have found it charming or whimsical but not of great artistic merit. Papa, on the other hand, thought it a work of genius. I don't believe he said this just as Sir Henry's friend, and I have to agree with his assessment. Although I have never myself aspired to portraiture, I appreciate the* <u>*life*</u> *in that painting, the* 'quinta essentia' *as I have described it. Perhaps in pursuit of the 'fifth element' in my own work, I was inspired by Sir Henry's masterpiece to attempt several landscapes at Duddingston Loch.*

Another of Papa's eminent friends was James Hutton, the Edinburgh polymath now revered as the founder of modern geology. It was Dr Hutton more than any other scientist who convinced a sceptical world that our planet must be incomparably older than the few thousand years implied by a literal reading of the book of Genesis. He demonstrated, by his studies at the Salisbury Crags in his native city, that many rock formations owe their origin not to deposition in a primordial flood but to the long-ago solidification of molten rock, like lava from modern-day volcanoes.

I recall Papa taking George, James and me to the very spot on the Crags where his friend had experienced the flash of inspiration that formed the basis of his theories. It was, however, not Papa but Sir Henry Raeburn who was commissioned to paint Dr Hutton's portrait.

I must mention one more of Papa's acquaintances – I dare not call him his 'friend'. William Brodie was a respected cabinet-maker and locksmith, and rose in Edinburgh guild society to become president, or Deacon, of the Society of Wrights. By day he installed fine furniture in the homes of the rich in the New Town; by night he returned with copies of their keys to burgle them. It is said that he constructed a new improved gallows for the city, and in 1788 became one of the first on whom it was successfully used.

An organization to which both Papa and, for a time, Deacon Brodie belonged was the Ancient Edinburgh Society of Water Lairds. Although this was a rather secretive group, I cannot put James's omission of it down to ignorance of Papa's membership. I believe he would have found it difficult to mention without bringing up the subject of his brother George. It was habitual in the Society for fathers to enrol a son, generally the eldest. Patrick, the firstborn of Alexander and Barbara Nasmyth, left Edinburgh at the age of 21; the next son George was therefore Papa's choice to join him as a Water Laird.

'Your guess was good, I think,' Marcus said to Jody. 'George Nasmyth was a Water Laird, so his good friend Duncan Murison might well have been one, as you surmised. And I know Archie Kilgour's great grandfather was one. He probably got Charlotte's *Memoir* from Murison, but didn't get the message he was supposed to make it public after Charlotte's death. Instead it languished unread for over 130 years in Kilgour's attic.'

'You never told me the illustrious membership of the Lairds included Deacon Brodie,' Jody said, with a laugh.

'Until he was "suspended", you mean? To be honest, I didn't know until now. But I can tell you his infamous exploits are fodder for many a discussion over a glass of whisky. A couple of months ago our topic was Stevenson's *Strange Case of Dr Jekyll and Mr Hyde*. Brodie was his main inspiration – indeed Stevenson co-wrote a play, *Deacon Brodie, or the Double Life*, several years before the more famous novella. We discussed how *Jekyll and Hyde* in turn became the prototype for 20th-century superhero comics, TV shows and movies. *The Incredible Hulk* is the most obvious example.'

One of the three had said hardly a word since they sat down to read. 'You're very quiet, Delia,' Jody said.

Delia took a sip from her wine glass. 'Your instinct was right, Jody. This is a fascinating manuscript. Cryptic, actually.

7
FAMILY TREE

THE NASMYTH FAMILY OF 47 York Place consisted in 1808 of Papa, Mama and nine of their sons and daughters.

Patrick, the eldest, was born in 1787. By the age of 21 he had already embarked on a career as an artist, and in 1808 he abruptly left the parental home, soon afterwards setting himself up in a studio in London. He had been a sickly child and continued to suffer poor health all his life. Sadly he died aged just 34.

After Patrick came a succession of daughters, beginning with Jane in 1788. She was blessed with great common-sense and practicality and, by the time she was in her teens, was already immensely supportive to Mama. It is perhaps uncharitable of me to describe Jane as domineering, but as I have set myself the task of writing a true Memoir I cannot pretend otherwise.

After Jane came Barbara in 1790, Margaret in 1791, Elizabeth in 1793 and Anne in 1798. A gap of six years separated Anne's birth from the arrival of the next Nasmyth daughter, Charlotte (myself), in 1804. That made me the eldest of a 'second' family including George, born in 1807, and James, 1808. Two more, Mary and Alexander, died as infants; sad to say I barely remember them.

Artistic talent was a gift bestowed to a greater or lesser degree on all the Nasmyth children. In giving my assessment of the talent each one of us has displayed in our time on this Earth, I freely admit that my 'true' Memoir will become a little subjective. But first I must record and acknowledge the contributions of both Papa and Mama to the heritage of our family as landscape artists.

Despite Papa's accolade as a landscape painter, portraiture was his greater strength. Indeed, his landscapes have been criticised by some as 'lifeless'. This is not a charge that can be laid against the foremost of his English contemporaries, in particular Mr John Constable, for whose work I have the highest admiration (though the Royal Academy was inexcusably slow to appreciate the depth of his talent).

Papa's training as an architect and builder may have overburdened his art with an obsession for anatomical correctness. He would tell how the great Leonardo's sculpture and painting were informed by a study of human anatomy, internal as well as external, and he felt the same principle should apply to the artistic representation of a flower or tree. For this reason he made us all study botany.

Our home was a short walk from the Edinburgh Botanic Garden on the Leith road; when it moved to a grand new site on the Hill of Inverleith in 1824 it was scarcely further, and remained a frequent destination. From our rooftop belvedere (yes, we had one, though not like the one my grandfather designed for David Hume with its pentagonal panes) we enjoyed watching its colours change with the seasons. Behind it lay the firth with its scattering of islands and, still farther beyond, the hills of Fife, the distinctive rounded summit of East Lomond being our marker for due north.

James's Autobiography tells of Papa engaging us in fashioning a sculpture of a tree from strands of wire.

He neglects to say, however, that the strands running from the finest twigs through the branches and limbs to the trunk, were conceived by Papa to represent the true anatomy of a living tree. It was because of this that the sculpture looked so realistic.

Delia was tapping on her computer. 'Have you reached the bit about Alexander Nasmyth's wire model of a tree?' she asked. 'I've found James's *Autobiography* online. On page 38 there's a drawing of what he called the "Family Tree". Look.'

'It does look amazingly lifelike,' Marcus said.

'Yes,' Delia agreed. 'And as Charlotte suggests, that's because it's constructed along anatomical lines. In my master's program I took an advanced course in plant form and function, and still remember something called the Pipe Model Theory.' She tapped again on her computer. 'Yes, here it is. Shinozaki, 1964. In his theory a tree stem can be thought of as a bundle of "pipes" – a kind of plumbing system – connecting roots to leaves. As the stem branches, the bundles get smaller and smaller, until the finest twigs have only one "pipe" each. Every one of those "pipes" is continuous down though the branches and main stem to the roots. It was the same insight Alexander Nasmyth had a century and a half earlier.'

Papa's ability to reproduce on a flat surface the intricate architecture of a tree or a building stood him in good stead early in his career, when he made his living as a stage decorator for theatre productions. In later life, he didn't talk much of those days, and I never actually saw any of the backcloths he created, but I can imagine they were as lifelike as a critical theatre audience demanded. The trees of his later landscapes were no less perfect in form. Yet where Mr Constable's elms come alive on the canvas – you can almost hear the breeze whisper among their leaves – Papa's oaks, pines and sycamores seem to my eyes as dead as the wire model we constructed under his tutelage in our York Place drawing-room.

Well aware of the missing spark in Papa's work, Mama confided as much to my sisters and me some time after his passing in 1840, though she would never have given voice to such criticism while he was alive.

Papa's landscapes attracted their share of negative appraisal during his lifetime. Much of the adverse commentary came from members of the English art establishment, who tended to regard their Scottish contemporaries as rude and unsophisticated. As a prime example of this attitude, I have only to quote from the diary of the late Mr Joseph Farington, a pillar of the Royal Academy. This extract was recently given to me by one of his descendants, not, I fear, with the kindest of motives:

'On seeing Alexander Nasmyth's landscapes, I thought them much inferior to what I expected, being deficient in style and colouring and executed in a puerile and feeble manner. In short, they do not look like the works of a master learned in the art, but are likely enough to please people not conversant with superior art and to be esteemed by such as pleasing furniture.'

Whatever I may have said about Papa's talent as a landscape artist, I would happily ask anyone, whether or not 'conversant with superior art', to compare Alexander Nasmyth's *Edinburgh from Corstorphine Hill* with Mr Farington's *Scotch Landscape* and say which is the more 'puerile and feeble'! I am proud to say that my father would never have stooped so low as to criticise his rivals' work in such snide language.

Papa continued throughout his life to apply his talent to architecture as well as painting. James, however, has done our father's memory no favours by exaggerating his accomplishments in that arena. Most egregiously, he insists that Alexander Nasmyth 'was the architect of the Dean Bridge, which spans the deep valley of the Water of Leith, north-west of the New Town.' In a footnote, he (or perhaps his editor Dr Smiles) remarks that 'Mr Telford was afterwards called upon to widen the bridge. He threw out parapets on each side, but it did not improve the original design.'

It is true that Papa submitted a design for a bridge to connect the New Town of Edinburgh to the land on *the north side of the Water of Leith. But it was, from the start, Thomas Telford's design that was adopted. The challenges of bridging the ravine at Dean Village could have been met only by a master of viaduct design. Telford was, indeed, such a master, and the Dean Bridge is his triumph.*

For my brother to attempt to appropriate this dramatic and beautiful engineering masterpiece to our father's legacy is shameful, but ever since James was a child, arrogance and boastfulness have unfortunately accompanied his undoubted brilliance of mind. I shall have more to say about this when I return to the subject of his unforgivable attempt to delete George Nasmyth from the record of our family.

A quick internet search confirmed that the Dean Bridge, opened in 1832, was indeed the work of Scotland's greatest civil engineer Thomas Telford, as acknowledged by the plaque on its east parapet. He had perhaps overlooked the attraction of the 106-foot-high viaduct to those wishing to commit suicide; in 1888 the parapets were heightened and overlaid with iron spikes, which are still there.

Among Papa's genuine architectural works may be mentioned the pump-room for St Bernard's Mineral Well by the Water of Leith near Stockbridge, which he designed in 1789. Though unquestionably elegant, it owes more to ancient Rome than to fresh inspiration, being copied from a temple of Vesta, complete with a statue of the goddess Hygieia. Soon after its completion, the estate on which it stood was acquired by none other than Henry Raeburn, already a very wealthy man.

I have mentioned my brother Patrick's artistic career, sadly curtailed by his early death. During his lifetime his work was regarded as inferior to his father's, but more recently his landscapes have become better appreciated. Perhaps the romantic view of Scotland fostered by our Queen and her late Consort has contributed to this reappraisal. Patrick adhered to a tried and tested formula, never experimenting or deviating from the principles he learned as a young man. He had no 'early' or 'middle' period, and perforce no 'late' period. A landscape painted in his thirties was no different in style from one executed at the age of twenty. If you buy a Patrick Nasmyth, you know exactly what to expect.

With the work of his sisters, and I like to include my own efforts in this generalisation, you can be less sure of what you will get. Instead you will see what the celebrated Mr Darwin might call an 'evolution' in our style. Jane's early work is indistinguishable from our father's; indeed, he was often able to pass her work off as his own. Later, she experimented with colour, creating more vivid scenes than Papa ever envisaged. I have tried to emulate Jane's inventiveness in this regard, with some modest success.

Barbara has been less prolific, perhaps because she is excessively critical of her own endeavours. I have some of her landscapes displayed in my home, and consider them at least as accomplished as any of my own.

Of all of the Nasmyth 'girls', Margaret (Meg, as we called her in the family) is the one who has most studiously broken free of Papa's influence. I like to think that her deliberate sacrifice of detail for freer, more spirited brushwork was an early harbinger of the style known as 'impressionism' that has recently become the rage in the salons of Paris, under the influence especially of M Claude Monet.

Meg left the family home in 1836 to become James's housekeeper near Manchester; it was perhaps good for her to escape the homogenising pressure of remaining closeted with her sisters. Her delightful defiance is exhibited in the bold signature at the bottom left of each of her paintings, which seems to shout, 'I am an artist in my own right, not just one of the Nasmyth clan!'

The next two Nasmyth daughters, Elizabeth and Anne, also left the family home, in their case for husbands. (The rest of us remained spinsters all our days.)

Lizzie married the famous actor Daniel Terry, a close confidant of Sir Walter Scott; after Daniel's death her artistic talents were put to use by Sir Walter in designing the interior of his grand home at Abbotsford. Later she became the wife of an eminent lexicographer, Charles Richardson.

Anne continued to paint after her marriage. Her work, submitted always under her married name of Anne (or Mistress) Bennett, strove to conform to public taste and thereby lost its individuality, becoming more typical of what we are beginning to call the 'Victorian' period after our long-reigning Queen.

8
THE SIXTH DAUGHTER

NOW WE COME TO THE sixth daughter, Charlotte. How can I characterise my own style of painting? I must begin by returning to the family home at 47 York Place, Edinburgh where my art was inspired by my famous father and tempered by my beloved mother.

Like Jane, I learned my craft in part by adding small details or fine brushwork to Papa's landscapes, always under his critical eye. Jane's contribution to his work expanded as she matured, until in the later years of his life it was Papa who was making minor additions to her work! This did not happen with me.

'Charlotte,' he would say, 'unless you precisely reproduce my habits with the paintbrush, I cannot give you a bigger part to play in creation of a Nasmyth landscape. You hold the brush too loosely, allowing it a life of its own! If you wish to travel down the path your sister Meg has chosen, your technique is fine; but that is not the path that will earn us good commissions.'

I sometimes regret that I did not give even freer rein to the brush as Meg did. But in deference to Papa's instruction, I learned to control its strokes more firmly, though not exactly in the way he liked. It was a tiny rebellion on my part, but one that ensured a Charlotte Nasmyth landscape would never be signed by Alexander Nasmyth. My independence as an artist was secure, enabling me to try out ways of injecting a sense of movement, of life, into my paintings as Mama constantly encouraged me to do. And those paintings sold – not, of course, at the kind of price an Alexander Nasmyth landscape could command, but enough to give me confidence in my work.

Mama influenced me in another way too. Of a Sunday afternoon in the summer, while Papa was in the company of friends, she and I (sometimes with my younger brothers George and Jamie in tow) would take a cab ride out of the city. The driver was often none too pleased at such a journey, but it seemed his horse rejoiced to leave the smoke of the town and breathe the fresh air of the countryside. We would pack a picnic and head for high ground to the south and west: the Blackford, Craiglockhart and Corstorphine Hills.

A favourite destination was the ancient estate of Ravelston on the city-facing slope of Corstorphine Hill. Mama had an emotional attachment to the place, once owned by the Foulis family. Sir Archibald Primrose, the last family member to dwell there, was executed at Carlisle for having supported the 'wrong' – that is, losing – side in the Jacobite uprising of 1745–46.

She loved telling stories of her ancestral home. One tale was of a former laird who, it was said, buried a treasure chest in a secret spot on the property to avoid his riches going to an heir of whom he disapproved. A hundred years later, his descendant as laird was deeply in debt and was deceived into paying a fee he could ill afford to a 'seer' who claimed he could divine where the treasure was hidden. As digging began, the 'seer' ran off with his fee, and the laird, realising he had been tricked, gave up the excavation and prepared to sell his lands to clear his debt. At the last minute, he was persuaded by a local beggar to continue to dig; a chest containing enough gold to clear his entire debt was found under a stone, precisely where the 'seer' had indicated.

Once, Papa embarrassed Mama when his friend Walter Scott was taking tea at our house. 'Tell Mr Scott about the hidden gold of Ravelston, my dear,' he said.

'Hush, Alexander,' Mama replied. 'It's just a foolish tale I made up for the children.'

'Nevertheless,' Mr Scott insisted, 'I would love to hear it.'

Shyly she told the story to the attentive poet and novelist. When she had finished, he complimented her on having preserved for future generations, and on so eloquently recounting, such a charming fable.

'If I may confide in you, Mistress Nasmyth,' he then said, 'I have been working, as time and inspiration permit, on a poem in celebration of that great Jacobite warrior James Graham, a truly handsome man known to his followers by the well-earned soubriquet "Bonnie Dundee".' (Mr Scott had a tendency in speech to be almost as wordy as he was with his pen.) 'There is much still to be written, but I settled some time ago on the final couplet, which refers to the lands of your ancestors. May I recite it?'

Papa, whose Whiggish politics did not hold with glorifying Jacobite heroes, gave a clucking sound of disapproval, but there was no stopping Mr Scott in full flow:

... On Ravelston's cliffs and in Clermiston's lee
Died out the proud war-notes of Bonnie Dundee.

Shortly afterwards – it must have been in 1816, when I was 12 – we were all amused to read in his latest novel, The Antiquary, *of treasure hidden under a stone. Mama's story had been much embellished by Mr Scott, but was still recognisable.*

Yet it took him many years to complete his now-famous poem, with 11 stanzas. Before its publication he shared it with my sister Lizzie, for whom he had an almost fatherly affection. She visited us in 1828, together with her 12-year-old son Walter Scott Terry (her husband Daniel was sick and unable to accompany her; he died a few months later), and gave a rendition of the poem. Papa hated its pro-Jacobite partiality and, though never one to take the Lord's name in vain, was moved to call out, 'Last verse, for God's sake!' during the seemingly interminable recitation.

Set to music, Bonnie Dundee *has become one of the most popular of Scottish songs, though mercifully only a few of its verses, together with a rousing chorus, are usually sung.*

Marcus left the room briefly and returned with his guitar. He began strumming then broke into song: the chorus of *Bonnie Dundee*, which was all he could remember of the song.

Come fill up my cup, come fill up my can,
Come saddle my horses and call out my men,
Unhook the West Port and let us gang free,
For it's up wi' the bonnets o' Bonnie Dundee!

'More!' Jody and Delia shouted in unison.

'After I've had another glass of wine,' was the response.

It was in 1820 that the writer was elevated to a baronetcy, becoming Sir Walter Scott. Curiously enough, this was not in recognition of his writing but for his part in recovering a real-life buried treasure:

neither the legendary gold of Ravelston nor the fictitious silver hoard of The Antiquary, *but Scotland's crown jewels, hidden within the walls of Edinburgh Castle since the time of Cromwell.*

He and Papa remained close friends, in spite of their political differences. Papa was immensely proud of Sir Walter's achievement in 1822 in organising the visit to our city of King George IV. My recollection, on the other hand, is one primarily of disappointment at seeing what a fat ugly man the king was.

Mama confided in me that if his physical appearance was repulsive, his conduct was even more so. It was a shock to hear her speak so ill of our monarch. She told me well-founded stories of his cruelty to his wife, Caroline of Brunswick, who had died the previous year aged 53. For years he accused her of adultery, despite his own infidelities (most notably with Mrs Maria Fitzherbert, who bore him several children). Though queen for little over a year, she has been immortalised by schoolchildren, who can still be heard chanting to the rhythm of a skipping rope:

Queenie, Queenie Caroline
Washed her hair in turpentine
Turpentine to make it shine
Queenie, Queenie Caroline

By the time I was in my early twenties, I was already giving painting lessons, mostly to well-to-do young women. Not all of my students had great artistic talent, but I gained a reputation as a supportive and effective teacher.

In 1827 Mr William Nicholson, who had earlier executed a fine portrait of my brother-in-law Daniel Terry, invited me to sit for him. I think Lizzie may have put Mr Nicholson up to this in an attempt, fruitless as it was to turn out, to improve my eligibility in the marriage stakes.

Returning to those excursions with Mama to the hills around Edinburgh, it was at that time that I first conceived the notion of painting a suite of landscapes, each providing a distant view of the city from one of five surrounding hills. It was not until 1832 that I began the task and 1835 that I completed it. In addition to views from the hills of Blackford, Craiglockhart and Corstorphine, I set up my easel on Arthur's Seat, by far the highest of the five eminences, and on the Hill of Inverleith, which is but a low rise within the confines of the Botanic Garden, of which I have already written.

It was my ambition that this suite of five paintings would find a single home. But securing a purchaser for even one Charlotte Nasmyth was no easy task, let alone a patron willing to dip into his coffers for five! Had my name been Charles rather than Charlotte, I suspect the task would have been easier; the simple truth was (and still is, alas) that the work of a woman was worth less than half that of a man. In the end, the suite went to five different buyers with homes from Perthshire to Massachusetts.

9
INSEPARABLE

AULD STOBBY HAD ORIGINATED as an under-the-radar activist cell of the Scottish National Party, but soon proved too radical. Within months of its formation the SNP had disowned it. Rather than disband, it turned itself into an independent political pressure group.

Unashamedly xenophobic, *Stobby*'s platform was defined mainly by what it was against: immigration, the European Union, above all England and the English. Ironically, its hysterical hate-mongering may have tipped the balance of the vote *against* Scottish independence on 18th September 2014. In June of that year it had helped orchestrate the torrent of personal abuse on social media that followed J.K. Rowling's measured contribution to the referendum debate and her donation of a million pounds to the 'Better Together' campaign. Vilifying one of the country's best-loved authors was not politically smart: at that moment the steady opinion-poll rise of the pro-independence movement went into reverse for a time. And, despite a late surge in support for a 'yes' vote, *Stobby*'s rent-a-mob tactics, designed to disrupt and intimidate, instead alienated voters still undecided in the closing days of the campaign.

The convincing victory for 'no' was not the chastening experience for *Auld Stobby* that its critics expected. Indeed it became even more strident, blaming everyone for the 'wrong' result – including the SNP for favouring the 'English' pound and EU membership. But by then most Scots were ready to put the divisions of the referendum behind them, and *Stobby* found itself marginalised and irrelevant.

The setting up of North East Pipeline Aqueduct as a quasi-commercial operation with the financial backing of the British (or, as *Stobby* saw it, English) government gave the group a new target, an opportunity to reboot. Locating the company's headquarters in Edinburgh didn't soften *Stobby*'s hostility; they pointed out, with some measure of truth, that hardly any Scottish jobs had been created. The South Gyle offices of NEPA, *Stobby* maintained, were full of 'foreigners' who remitted their earnings to Australia, America, France, you name it – and England. Even its internships, which could have been restricted to graduates of Scotland's universities, were 'international'.

In short, NEPA was a gift. That it existed solely for England to 'steal' Scotland's water was a pitch that played well among certain sectors of the voting public. *Auld Stobby* began to look less like a nutty fringe group, more a semi-respectable political movement.

At the same time its 'underground' origins were not forgotten. It still had a core of militant activists intent on using any means, foul or fair, to advance the separatist agenda. The problem was, they were rank amateurs. There was no deep well of experience in guerrilla tactics to draw on as in Ireland, for example, or the Basque country. The movement's leaders recognised this deficiency and set about correcting it, by looking outside Scotland for a 'professional' commander to take charge of *Stobby*'s covert activities. They found him in Belgium.

Hendrik Vandenbrouck had founded the Free Flanders Army, a cell of 'freedom fighters' based in Mechelen, with funds siphoned from *Vlaams Blok*, a right-wing Flemish nationalist party. As *VB* sought to break into mainstream Belgian politics, its finances came under closer media scrutiny. Vandenbrouck found his 'army' starved of cash. He considered alternative sources of funding, including bank robbery, forgery and the drug trade, but these were all too carefully controlled by organised gangs. Furthermore, success in raising money through crime required a lot of effort, a serious distraction from the central objective of his cell. So when he was headhunted by *Auld Stobby* he decided to take them up on their offer.

From the start, Vandenbrouck instructed his new Scottish cohorts that, although he would be calling the shots, to all outward appearances he would be just a regular operative. The meeting with Rachel Herring was a case in point: it was at his initiative and Isla Younie was just following orders, but it was Isla who did virtually all the talking and appeared in charge.

Within the privacy of the group there was no doubt who was boss. In his accented but fluent English, embellished with a few choice profanities, the Belgian could always be assured of having the last word.

Monthly meetings were held in a rented light-industrial unit in Granton with a sign above the door proclaiming 'Firth TV & Audio' followed in smaller letters by 'Rental & Reconditioning'. Eleven attended the April session, at which Vandenbrouck introduced a new recruit.

'Mr Hugh Leggat joins us tonight. He's a forensic accountant. No, nothing to do with the fucking police. He has access to all kinds of financial records and he'll keep an eye on NEPA for us. Where their money comes from, how they're spending it. Their top executives will be under his microscope. He'll sniff all their arses, he'll find out who they're screwing and what they're buying for their wives to make up for it. But listen: he's new, and I don't trust him for a damned shit. Nor should any of you. Mr Leggat understands he needs to *earn* our trust.' Vandenbrouck locked eyes with Hugh and held his gaze until the other looked away.

The meeting then got down to operational matters. There was the usual debate about small harassment activities – setting fire to English-owned holiday cottages in the Highlands, vandalising cars of foreign-born footballers playing for Scottish clubs, and so on.

But Vandenbrouck was adamant. 'I put it in the middle,' he said in literal translation from idiomatic Dutch. 'Crap like that just turns the media against us. We keep our powder dry for now. Soon there will be something big we can do, something that will really hurt NEPA.'

⬠

George was the only one of us to show little interest in art. From childhood he was fascinated by mechanical things; a toy held little attraction for him unless it could be taken apart and reassembled. In this regard he was like his younger brother James, except that where George liked to construct things exactly to a plan, his brother would always look for ways to improve on the original design. James pleased Papa by learning to paint, though surprisingly his inventiveness did not show in his art. Like Jane in her early work, he adopted Papa's style and would not deviate from it.

It is hard to credit from a reading of James's Autobiography that he and the unmentioned George were close. Yet in their childhood and formative years they were inseparable. Both had an intense interest in astronomy, which I shared despite discouragement from Papa, who saw the sciences as an unsuitable calling for girls. (He did allow that women could excel as authors of novels, an opinion shared with, perhaps influenced by, his friend Sir Walter Scott. In 1816 Papa presented me with what he called an exemplar of feminine authorship, the newly published novel Emma *by an anonymous 'Lady' now known to have been Miss Jane Austen. I still have that book.)*

From our belvedere we acquainted ourselves with the heavens. Unfortunately by that time Edinburgh was well deserving of the name 'Auld Reekie'*: its skies* *were often obscured by smoke from the hundreds of coal fires that moderated the chill of a winter's night. To the south of us, the huddled tenements of the Old Town generated a particularly constant blanket of smoke. For this reason, we got to know the northern sky much better than the southern. The circumpolar constellations – those that wheeled around the North Star without ever dipping below the horizon – became as familiar to us as the streets of our city.*

One of my most vivid childhood memories is of Mama getting me up at midnight, wrapping me in a blanket and hustling me up the steep staircase to the belvedere. Once there, she snuffed out the candle she was carrying, but not before I saw George already there with Papa. James was not there – I think he had earlier been given a draught of laudanum to allay a persistent cough and could not be roused.

It was an eerie experience. The whole northern sky seemed aflame. Sheets of light, now green, now red, swept upwards from the horizon. I instinctively drew closer to Mama. Noticing my anxiety, George told me, in the most authoritative tone his childish voice could muster, 'It's the Northern Lights.' I had read of the phenomenon but had never before seen an auroral display with my own eyes.

Next day, when George recounted what he had seen, James threw a tantrum at having been left to sleep and remained in a sulk for a week or more. His anger arose not so much from disappointment at missing the Northern Lights as from envy that George had seen them. Less than ten years later James, still in his teens, built himself a telescope; now he could see all manner of heavenly phenomena to which he could introduce his brother. As he has written in his Autobiography, on directing his telescope to the Milky Way: 'it revealed such countless multitudes of stars that I had only to sit before the eyepiece, and behold the endless procession of these glorious objects pass before me.'

In other words, a pox on your pathetic Northern Lights!

That first sight of the aurora initially terrified me – I thought for a moment our beloved city was on fire. Some years later, in November of 1824, our belvedere afforded a 'grandstand' view of a real conflagration: what has become known as the Great Fire of Edinburgh. The devastation of a substantial section of the Old Town between the Tron and St Giles, the loss of life more tragic than the destruction of property, is forever seared on my memory. James's boast that as a 16-year-old he ascended the tower of St Giles in dangerous proximity to the blaze so as to 'look down into it' seems far-fetched – even for him.

Through their teens James and George collaborated on a variety of projects. A model of a condensing steam engine, accurate in all details, was constructed by the two brothers for the Edinburgh School of Arts when both were not yet twenty. The finished model bore a brass plaque engraved with the names 'G. & J. Nasmyth', yet according to the Autobiography it was solely James's accomplishment.

When he decamped for London to perfect his talents as an engineer under Mr Henry Maudslay (whose name is unfortunately misspelled in the Autobiography), George inevitably went with him. In 1829, during their tenure as assistants to Mr Maudslay, they were jointly awarded a silver medal (and a prize worth, I seem to recall, 5 guineas) for an invention relating to pulleys. And in 1831 the two inseparable brothers returned to

Edinburgh. How happy I was to welcome them back to their native city! I admit it was an especial joy to see George again. He and I had always been close, whereas James distanced himself from me by his arrogant braggadocio. How George put up with his constant boasting I cannot imagine.

George now being 24 years of age, Papa decided it was time to introduce him to one of his clubs, the Society of Water Lairds. Though James was envious that his older brother had been chosen for this honour, Mama was very supportive of the decision. She felt George was too much in James's intellectual shadow and the Society might enable him to gain some prestige.

It probably breached the rules of membership, but George used to share his recollections of Water Lairds meetings with me. I especially loved the tales he told of the ancient history of our city, tales that had been passed down by word of mouth from the earliest days. How true they were I cannot judge, but they spoke to me from a time before Edinburgh was the capital of Scotland, before there even <u>*was*</u> *a Scotland!*

Marcus remarked that historical lore was still a feature of Water Lairds meetings. And it *was*, he said, a breach of the rules for George to tell his sister what went on in these meetings. Not, he hastened to add, because she was a woman, simply because she wasn't a member.

That happy period ended in 1836, when George left again for England, to join James in setting up a business partnership at the Bridgewater foundry in Patricroft, five miles from Manchester. I prayed the venture would be successful, not only financially but in terms of sibling relationship. Though James provided the technical brains of the operation and George assumed more of a marketing role, I was pleased to note that theirs was an equal partnership.

It saddened me at first that my dear brother George was no longer in Edinburgh. But I resolved to capture, as it were, our time together by writing down all I could remember of the tales of the Water Lairds he had shared with me. It was 47 years ago that I committed his tales to paper, under the title A New Story of Edinburgh's Earliest Beginnings. *Since then nobody has read them but me.*

'Now I'm getting *really* interested,' Jody announced. 'Charlotte collected tales of the history of Edinburgh. I'd love to read *that* document.'

'Me too,' Delia said. 'Wonder what happened to it?'

'I bet she destroyed it,' Marcus said. 'She realised George shouldn't have told her the Water Lairds' stories.'

'Yeah, pity,' Delia said. 'Even this *Memoir* has subtle clues in it. To what, I've no idea. But she's trying to leave a message of some kind, a message that might have been clearer if we had the *New Story* as well.'

'Clues?' Marcus drew her back. 'What do you mean?'

'Well, for example, in the hunt for Taran's wheel, I kept coming up against the number six.'

Jody nodded; Marcus looked blank.

'It was a kind of magic number,' Delia explained. 'Now for Charlotte, the magic number is five.' She elaborated: the suite of five paintings, the five hills around Edinburgh, the five-sided windows of David Hume's belvedere, the *'quinta essentia'* Charlotte strove for in her art.

'Her five sisters, all artists,' Jody said, getting into the spirit. 'The five-guinea prize George and James received for their pulley contraption.'

'Okay, my turn,' Marcus said. 'George Nasmyth was a Water Laird for five years, from 1831 to 1836.'

Delia laughed. 'We're getting carried away here. To figure out what *might* be important, let's look for bits of information that aren't really relevant to the whole story she's put together. Then ask ourselves, why is she telling us this? Why, for example, does she go into all that detail about David Hume's belvedere? It was designed by her grandfather, who otherwise scarcely features in the story at all.'

'Okay,' Marcus said, 'I can play that game. What about the buried treasure, the supposed basis of Scott's novel *The Antiquary*? That's a bit of a digression, isn't it? And, Jody, what are you grinning at?'

'I *knew* you'd pick up on the buried treasure. Another *Secret Seven* mystery for the Water Lairds.'

'Huh?' With her American upbringing Delia had not been exposed to Enid Blyton's prolific output.

'Just a joke at my expense,' Marcus explained, 'and it's getting a wee bit tiresome. The *Secret Seven* are a bunch of kids who have adventures and solve mysteries. A bit like your *Nancy Drew*. According to Jody, the Edinburgh Water Lairds are a kind of *Secret Seven*, forever having pointless meetings, just with Scotch whisky in place of milk and biscuits. Right, sweetheart?'

'You're the one saying it.'

'But you're thinking it. It's true that buried treasure would have been right up the *Secret Seven* alley. But buried treasure has a great literary pedigree in Edinburgh. As Charlotte reminds us, Scott planted it firmly in *The Antiquary*. And Stevenson later wrote a whole book about it: *Treasure Island*.

Turning to Jody, Delia said, 'Marcus makes a good point. I'm not saying we should be looking for a stash of gold, but that passage of the *Memoir* reads to me like a coded reference of some kind. Maybe Charlotte wants us to read *The Antiquary*.'

'Life's too short,' Jody said, a little miffed that Delia seemed to be taking Marcus's side. 'There's a reason Scott's been out of fashion for years.'

10
FRAUDULENT ACCOUNTING

LIFE AT 47 YORK PLACE resumed its regular pace after George's departure. Papa's health was declining, and, though he continued to paint, most of the works he signed were really Jane's. Mama, on the other hand, seemed to have a new lease of life now her child-rearing days were far behind her. Remarkably, I do not recall her ever smiling and laughing so much as she did after she turned 70.

Jane and Barbara were now well beyond marriageable age, but in spite of their own spinsterhood they continually questioned my unmarried state – I was 28 by that time. 'You must find yourself a husband, like Lizzie and Anne,' they would say. But I had seen how Mama had devoted her life to the needs of a husband and children, and I did not wish to forgo laughter until I reached seventy. By the time I was 30, the subject no longer came up.

In 1840, Papa died and we were forced to take stock of our situation. We no longer needed a big house, nor did we have the income to continue supporting two servants. It was Jane's suggestion that we move close to George and James, now living and working at Patricroft.

Though I was keen to live in a place that would furnish opportunities nearby for landscape painting, Jane ignored my wishes and settled us in Pendleton, between Manchester and Patricroft. Our new home was in a grimy industrial town bristling with cotton mills and collieries. I took every chance I could find to get out into the countryside to paint; I particularly loved the ancient Forest of Pendle, whose rustic charm will forever be tempered by the awful memory of its infamous 17th-century witch-hunts.

James, at the age of 32, had recently married 21-year-old Miss Anne Hartop, and Meg was no longer his housekeeper. The Bridgewater foundry business that he and George had established was doing well, though George confided in me his dismay at James's handling of a labour dispute. Rather than concede what George saw as legitimate demands by his local workforce, James had simply fired them and recruited a whole new gang of labourers from Glasgow in their place. (James tells the story rather differently.) It was perhaps a critical point in the evolving relationship between my younger brothers, one at which George may have begun to think about pursuing a solo career.

In the early 1840s, the business suffered a downturn – those were difficult times – and the brothers were obliged to lay off a substantial number of men. George wanted at least to pay their train fares back to Glasgow, but James would not agree. 'We are not a charity,' he said laconically. For George it was the last straw, and he decided to leave for London to set up as an independent engineering consultant. James bought out his brother's share of the partnership.

The timing could hardly have been worse for George. Not long afterwards, James's invention of the steam hammer transformed the company's fortunes, making him very wealthy. So wealthy, in fact, that a few years later he was able to retire from business and pursue the leisurely life of a gentleman.

As an equal partner, George could have shared in this good fortune. Instead, he faced a constant struggle to secure contracts for his services. He did achieve some success during this period, including obtaining several patents for his engineering inventions. One of which he was especially proud was for fireproof steel beams, which were installed in the Bank of England among other buildings. But the financial rewards were small.

Meanwhile, our life at Pendleton took a turn for the worse. Mama was now in her eighties and becoming frail. Jane, Barbara and I took turns nursing her as best we could, and reading to her from her favourite books and newspapers. She was happy to hear of James's business success but, like me, regretful that George was no longer sharing in it. In 1846 Mama died.

A few years later, we made the decision to move to London, and found a house we loved at 13 Charlwood Road in Putney. We named it Woodhall, after Mama's parental home near Edinburgh. Our neighbours probably thought us an odd bunch; I have heard they referred to the three of us as the 'Scotch Sisters'.

George used to visit from time to time and give us news of his business dealings, though I always suspected things were a little less rosy than he painted them. In 1849 he married Miss Isabella Sanford, who was almost twenty years his junior; following that his fortunes seemed to pick up somewhat. Perhaps the pinnacle of his career came in 1851, when he showed some of his work at Prince Albert's Great Exhibition in the Crystal Palace in Hyde Park. Among distinguished men who saw his display were Mr Charles Darwin and Mr Charles Dickens, both of whom he admired greatly.

By 1857, George was finding it ever harder to keep his business afloat. A lifeline was thrown to him when he was invited to become the first curator of a museum being set up by the Patent Office. He paid us a visit around that time, without Isabella. It was obvious, without his telling us, that the marriage had foundered. And as for his new position, he was not excited at the prospect; he told us he found the salary of £300 a year demeaning.

What followed was a sad downward spiral. Just two years into the job he was suspended, and shortly thereafter dismissed. It emerged that he had indulged in fraudulent accounting. Accused of misappropriating public funds in excess of £300, he had no means of repaying the debt. He boarded a ship for America, and we never heard from him again. Isabella returned to her parents' home. In the spring of 1867 she sent us a telegraph telling us George had died in America. She had no other information.

It could be assumed that James's comprehensive deletion of his brother from the narrative of his life and work arose from shame. Somehow, he may have felt, George's fall from grace would reflect negatively on him, tainting him by association.

It would not surprise me, however, if the real motivation was to claim for himself all credit for the success of the Bridgewater Foundry partnership, and expunge any memory of 'the Nasmyth brothers' from the record. I do not deny that James was the more brilliant engineer or that the steam hammer that made his fortune was truly his sole invention. But how much more secure his reputation among future generations could have been had he been generous enough to give George his rightful place in the Nasmyth story!

In the same year that news arrived of George's death in exile, the three 'Scotch Sisters' became two, with the death of Jane at the age of 79. Three years later, she was followed by Barbara, aged 80. Now 79 myself, I will no doubt join them soon.

I continued painting until quite recently, but my eyesight is too weak now to afford me any pleasure in it. In my long life I have exhibited or sold well over 200 paintings, mostly landscapes, and I can see all of them still in my mind's eye.

The ones I return to most often are the series of five views of my native city from the hills of Inverleith, Corstorphine, Craiglockhart, Blackford and Arthur's Seat. Each one of these I sold under the title A Prospect of Edinburgh*; I would love to think that one day they will be united under one roof as I earnestly hoped when I painted them.*

C.N., 1883

'Charlotte concludes her *Memoir* by coming back to the number five,' Delia observed. 'Of the many ways she could have chosen to wrap up her story, she elected to return to the five hills where she painted her five landscapes.'

⬠

Victor stood a few paces behind Cammy Lewis's seat at a poker table in the Learmonth Club, watching the run of play. Lewis had a dwindling stack of chips by his right hand; even Victor found himself willing this loser to play more intelligently.

Down to his last £50, Lewis wasn't ready to give up but he needed a break. Looking round to attract the attention of someone who could bring him a drink, he found himself making eye contact instead with Victor.

'Let me buy you one, Cammy,' Victor said in a friendly tone. 'How about a single malt?' He signalled to a pretty blonde cocktail waitress. 'Irina, bring Mr Lewis a Balvenie twelve, double, no ice. And I'll have an Irn Bru, virgin, rocks.'

At an almost imperceptible gesture from Victor, the croupier announced the table was closing. As the punters gathered up their chips Victor sat down at Cammy Lewis's shoulder.

'Not doing too well tonight, pal?' he remarked, eyeing the gambler's meagre pile of chips.

'I've done better. This isn't a good spot. If he hadn't closed I'd be moving to another table anyway.'

The drinks came. 'No hurry, pal. Enjoy.'

'I will, Victor, thanks. Gimme some water in that. I take it there's something you want to talk to me about?'

Victor grabbed a bottle of mineral water from Irina's tray and handed it to Lewis. He swirled the ice in his Irn Bru and seemed to concentrate for a moment on the fizzy orange liquid. Then looking straight into Lewis's eyes, he said, 'I've another job for you. Not here in the club this time. At my mother's place.' He took a sip of his drink, spat it on the floor and yelled at Irina, 'What's this, you stupid cow? Did I *ask* for sugar-free?'

Lewis looked away in embarrassment. As Irina ran off to fetch a replacement drink, he turned back to Victor. 'Did you say your mother's place? Doesn't she live on the Isle of Man?'

'She does, but she's building a house not too far from here. Or at least she will be as soon as the detailed planning approval comes through. Which it will.'

'And the job's at her new place?'

Victor ignored the question. 'How's Mrs Lewis? Karen, isn't it? The kids? They must miss you – working all day, playing the tables all evening?'

'Never mind about them. They're doing okay.'

'Yeah, yeah. 'Course they are. But wouldn't you like to go home and say, "Hey, Mrs Lewis, how about a nice holiday in the sun? Cyprus, Egypt, Dubai? Somewhere exotic – Mauritius, maybe?" Or, "Karen, *darling*, close your eyes while I put this diamond pendant round your pretty neck." Well, zircon probably, but you get the idea.'

'I'm overdue for a big win. I can take care of Mrs Lewis.'

'Your next win, won't that just go to pay off the credit card? Look, Cammy, I know you're in a bit of shit with the bank. But it doesn't have to be like that. Here's the deal. An enhanced line of credit from the club. Twenty-five thousand. Enough to pay off the card, take the wife and kids to Sharm-el-Sheikh, trade in that old van of yours. Or, if you like, parlay it into fifty thousand here at the club. Your choice. If you do the job, you owe nothing. If you don't do it, or quit half-way through, we'll work out a repayment plan.'

'So, what's the job, for Christ's sake?' Lewis was hooked.

Victor explained what physically had to be done: dig over his mother's building site and remove any archaeological remains 'for safe-keeping'. Now for the tricky part. It had to be done by hand, at night, to avoid prying eyes. Turf to be replaced exactly as found. And not a word to be breathed to a living soul.

'Sounds like a lot of hard work. How big is the site? Maybe 25 grand's not enough.'

'Okay, 30. Deal, pal?'

Lewis poured some water into his Balvenie, knocked the whole drink back in a gulp and slammed the glass down on the table. The contract was sealed with a handshake.

11
SCOTCH AND WATER

A CRISIS MEETING HAD BEEN CALLED at headquarters. The Perth-to-Edinburgh segment of the planned aqueduct was in disarray, threatening a major delay in project completion. For NEPA's senior directors, that would be a career-killer.

A large map of Britain displayed prominently in the atrium lobby at South Gyle showed the line of the aqueduct running south-west from Perth to Stirling, then south-east from there to the outskirts of Edinburgh. For almost the whole way it ran alongside, sometimes under, rail lines. As recently as two weeks ago, the project manager responsible for that segment had assured the NEPA board that everything was on track. It then emerged that he was hiding significant problems and, worse, that he had received kickbacks from certain contractors bidding for engineering and construction work. He was summarily relieved of his post.

Pending a permanent replacement, his responsibilities were to be shared between Stan Dalton, Inverness-to-Perth manager, and Helen Brewer, who had responsibility for the difficult cross-city segment from west to east of Edinburgh. Their first action was to call the crisis meeting. Senior engineers, accountants, business analysts, PR specialists and environmental scientists among others were required to drop everything and attend.

From eight until noon, the problems besetting the line from Perth to Edinburgh were scrutinised. If there had been a single issue, a solution would have been quickly found. But it turned out there were several, some of them so complex and intertwined that the only way to resolve them would involve massive overruns of both budget and timeline. Dalton and Brewer made it clear that such overruns were politically impossible. The meeting broke for a sandwich lunch with no obvious way forward.

NEPA folklore has it that the solution was suggested by a security man who brought in the sandwiches at noon.

'See yer big map in the front loaby?' he reputedly said. 'I look at it every workin day, an' I've never understood why ye want tae cairry that water aw the wye roond by Stirling. Shairly it wid be mair direct tae tak it through Fife. The wye the train comes fae Perth.'

It was tactfully pointed out to him that the Fife route was impossible; you'd have to find some way of crossing the Firth of Forth. There was no question of the 130-year-old Forth Bridge carrying a high-capacity water pipeline as well as a railway.

At which point Helen Brewer reportedly asked, 'Why not?'

By the time the meeting broke up at half past five, a feasibility study of the security man's 'direct' route, focusing primarily on the Forth Bridge, was under way.

⬠

A week or so after disposing of Bob Bowman's remains, Victor Herring was preparing a bag of laundry when he found some unfamiliar keys in a jeans pocket. It took a few seconds to register. *Of course! Bowman's car and house keys!*

On his way to the full-service launderette along the street from his Merchiston flat he dropped the house keys down a drain, but decided to hold on to the car key. He figured Bowman's car must be parked not far from his mother's building site; it might be a good idea to move it before it attracted attention.

Soon he was driving along a number of streets, pointing and pressing the remote 'unlock' button on the key at every parked car. In a residential avenue, he saw a small Mercedes being hauled on to a flat-bed recovery vehicle. A quick point-and-click caused the lights to flash on the Mercedes. *Shit! Should have taken care of this sooner.*

He drove on. Once on a quiet country road just outside Edinburgh, he pulled over briefly and tossed the key into a hedge.

The police had identified Mr Robert Bowman of an address in Greenbank as owner of the Mercedes. They notified the Transport and Streets department, who had the vehicle removed to a pound in Leith, and sent a letter advising the owner how he could retrieve it. No response was received.

⬠

Hugh Leggat was in the tasting room at *A Malt O' My Ain*, selecting single malt whiskies to be blended to make the unique *Poacher's Poison* that his great-aunt Kirsty was giving him as a birthday present. His scotch would include five malts – three from Speyside, one from Islay and one from Aberdeenshire – which Marcus Annandale was now mixing in small quantities to provide a first sample.

While he waited, Hugh admired some prints of old Edinburgh street scenes that decorated the walls of the tasting room. Soon Marcus returned with a small jug of golden-brown liquid and two long-stemmed tulip-shaped glasses. Not brandy snifters, as Hugh had expected.

'Your *Poison*'s ready to taste, Mr Leggat,' Marcus said. 'Watch me to see how best to appreciate this fine Scotch whisky.'

He first poured a tiny amount into a glass and, holding it by the base, swirled it around so that the whole inner surface was coated. Then, to Hugh's surprise, he discarded the liquid into a bowl. 'Let the glass have its share,' he said, 'then it won't hold back what is yours.'

Next, he poured a larger amount, what his customer recognised as a typical 'nip' or 'dram', into the glass. 'In our fathers' or grandfathers' time, a nip of whisky in a pub was usually a fifth of a gill – that's one fluid ounce – sometimes a wee bit more or less. Today it's metric, 37 mils, but it's still the same amount. That's about what I've got in this glass.'

Hugh nodded, wondering when he was going to get to taste his own whisky.

Marcus swirled the 'nip' in the glass, then examined the 'tears' or 'legs' running down the inside. 'See, the tears are well separated, the sign of a well-matured scotch. All the single malts you selected are at least 12 years old. They've blended well. Okay, Mr Leggat, here's a clean glass. Your turn.'

Though he felt the preamble was unnecessary, Hugh went through the motions of wetting the glass and discarding the first small volume of liquid. Then he poured himself a 'nip' and swirled, as he had been shown.

'Hold the glass nearer the base,' Marcus insisted. 'This isn't cognac. People who think a brandy snifter is appropriate for scotch are mistaken. We don't want the warmth of your hand to transfer to the whisky. That's why we use these more slender, long-stemmed glasses.'

Now it was time to inhale the aroma. Marcus demonstrated and Hugh self-consciously imitated the art of filling the nostrils with volatiles emanating from the glass. It was apparently important to let the nose accustom itself to the vapours before breathing in deeply.

'Tell me, Mr Leggat, why the name *Poacher's Poison*?'

'I'm a forensic accountant. A couple of years ago, I gave evidence in the trial of an estate manager accused of illegal poisoning of protected bird species in the north-west Highlands. He blamed local poachers for the poisoned kites and golden eagles. One newspaper believed him and ran a story under the headline 'Poacher's Poison'. The case hinged on the guy's records of purchase and use of a particular pesticide, which I showed he had falsified. He went to jail. Lawyers still refer to it as the

Poacher's Poison case. Aunt Kirsty seems to think it was my finest hour.'

'Well done! So are you ready to taste your poison?'

Hugh was surprised to see Marcus pour water from a stone jug into his whisky. 'Don't you taste it neat?' he asked.

'I suggest you try it first with water. Not too much, about half and half. All the flavours will be revealed. Sipping it neat will partially anaesthetise your taste buds and you'll lose some of the complexity. Go on, try it.' As Hugh diluted his dram, Marcus continued, 'Scotch and water, a great combination. Afterwards you can try your *Poacher's Poison* neat, if you like.'

The whisky was very much to Hugh's liking and he pronounced himself satisfied. As he sipped what was left in his glass he said to Marcus, 'I was admiring the prints on your wall. Aunt Kirsty would be interested in them. Did she see them when she was here?'

'No, I don't think I showed her the tasting room. Is she an art collector?'

'Big-time, yes. Anything Scottish, especially from the 19th century. She has no room on her walls for any more, but she keeps going to auctions and buying.'

'Nineteenth century, eh? Does she have any Nasmyths?'

'Alexander Nasmyth? I don't think so, unfortunately. His work fetches a pretty price these days. She has a few, though, attributed to some of his daughters. You know, Nasmyth had three daughters, as well as a son, who exhibited their own work.'

'Not three, six. Jane, Barbara, let's see ... Margaret, Elizabeth, Anne and Charlotte.'

Leggat gave a little gasp of amazement. 'Wow, you know your stuff. Have you made a study of the Nasmyth family?'

'Erm ... you could say that. But I don't have any of their work.'

'I'm sure Aunt Kirsty would love to show you her collection.'

'I'd like that.'

Hugh was still inspecting Marcus's prints of street scenes. 'Where did you buy these?' he asked.

'Actually, I didn't buy them. They're copies of illustrations from an old book I borrowed from the Water Lairds library.'

'*Which* library?'

'The Ancient Edinburgh Society of Water Lairds. Have you heard of it?'

'No, can't say I have.'

'It's existed since medieval times, some think even longer. At one time it was responsible for policing the city's water supplies, lochs and streams, but nowadays it's just a discussion group for people interested in local politics, history and culture. We have a couple of accountants who attend regularly ... but not a *forensic* accountant, as far as I know.'

'I'm curious,' Hugh said. 'Anyone I might know?'

Marcus paused before replying, disinclined to reveal members' names to this customer, whom he hadn't known until he walked into the shop. So he answered vaguely. 'One's with a big chartered accountancy firm in the West End. Rutland Square, I think. The other's with NEPA at South Gyle.'

Hugh's ears pricked up. 'Hmm, sounds like something I might be interested in, if you think the society could tolerate another accountant.'

'Well, Mr Leggat, you have to be nominated by an existing member, then there's a vetting procedure. I'd be glad to nominate you, once I know you a bit better.'

'For a start, call me Hugh. Could you come over to my office sometime, see my modest little operation? It's in the Pleasance, not ten minutes away. Here's my card.'

'Sure, Hugh, that'd be fine. Maybe one lunchtime? I usually close for an hour or so around one o'clock unless I'm busy.'

They settled on the following Tuesday.

It was nearly the end of the business day when Councillor James Swift caught up with Donald Lindsay in his office. Strictly, it wasn't *his* office; it was the Planning Director's office, but, as his deputy, Lindsay was 'acting director' during his boss's leave of absence. Enjoying the more spacious accommodation and nicer furniture than he had in his cubby-hole down the hall, he was hopeful that he would be confirmed as the new Director when, as expected, the present incumbent was finally obliged to resign 'to pursue other career interests'.

'I just wanted to find out where we stand on the Rachel Herring application,' Swift said. 'She's on a bit of a knife-edge with regard to her resort development, maybe thinking twice about making such a large investment. Getting the house she wants could be key. You've already given consent in principle, but a final decision could seal the deal. A *favourable* decision, of course.'

'It's an ugly bugger of a house,' Lindsay remarked.

'You know, Donald, I agree with you, but it's off the beaten track. Nobody will see it. If you can recommend approval, I'll be able to hold my nose and support it in the committee, in view of the economic benefit to the whole region if her resort development goes ahead.'

Lindsay pulled up the Herring file on his computer. 'Let's see what we're still waiting for,' he said as he tapped on his keyboard. 'Okay, here's Edinburgh airport, usual remark about bird roosting patterns; traffic, no concerns; Scottish water, likewise; archaeology, signed off subject to visits during excavation of foundations. Nothing yet from schools, shouldn't be an issue. As far as regular consultees are concerned, it's a go. But there's a lot of hostility among local residents. The committee will need to take that on board.'

'I'm well aware of the residents' comments. Concerned about amenity, tree cover, quality of architecture, stuff like that. I think we can safely ignore those.'

The acting director of planning raised an eyebrow at Swift's cavalier attitude to local feeling, but said nothing. After all, Swift was the elected official, not Lindsay; any public anger would be directed at Swift when he came up for re-election. There seemed to be no reason to delay approval – it would be good to get the matter off his docket. And he could be a hero if, by fast-tracking the application, he made Rachel Herring's casino resort happen. The kind of hero that would be a shoo-in as Director of Planning.

'Yes, Councillor,' he said, 'I'll send a "minded-to-grant" letter up to the committee first thing tomorrow.'

James Swift was happy. 'Good work, Donald,' he said.

12
A BRIDGE TOO FAR

SURVEYING THE PROPOSED alternative route for the aqueduct threw Delia into ten-hour days and seven-day weeks for the latter part of June and most of July. Under orders to keep quiet about the new route, she said nothing to Jody or Marcus. NEPA's PR department would announce it to the press, with the right spin, when and if the project was a 'go' *and* it was clear a deal could be done with Network Rail, owner of the Forth Bridge. When she wasn't in the field she was processing samples in the lab at South Gyle. Charlotte Nasmyth's memoir slipped to the back of her mind.

Jody, meanwhile, took a couple of days' leave. The cool but dry weather was ideal for a run along the entire 12 miles of the Water of Leith walkway. Approaching the Dean Bridge from the downstream side, she was disappointed not to have a view of its soaring arches from river level; last time she had come this way had been in winter, when Telford's magnificent creation was not totally obscured by foliage.

That afternoon she began a hunt at NLS and on the web for any publication of Charlotte's retelling of the Water Lairds tales, her *New Story of Edinburgh's Earliest Beginnings*. She also did a search for an unpublished manuscript among NLS's 40,000 such items. No luck.

Thinking the tales might have been entrusted to a Nasmyth relative, she ran a genealogy search. Although Alexander and Barbara Nasmyth had raised nine children to adulthood, Lizzie was the only one to have borne them grandchildren. Out of her marriage to Daniel Terry came three offspring. The eldest,

Walter Scott Terry, joined the Bombay Artillery and was killed in battle at the Khyber Pass at the tender age of 26. There were also two younger daughters, Jane and Elizabeth, but Jody was unable to find evidence of any continuing line of descent.

In any case, she observed, the *Memoir* had been rather brief on the subject of Lizzie. Nothing suggested the sisters had remained close enough for Lizzie's children to have been likely recipients of the *New Story* manuscript.

'We have to accept,' she told Marcus, 'that Charlotte's *New Story* is probably lost forever.'

He agreed. 'She really only wrote it for herself, as a means of adjusting to her brother George's departure from Edinburgh. That much is clear from her *Memoir*. Incidentally, I have a customer who owns some paintings by one or more of the Nasmyth daughters. Don't know if any of them are Charlotte's. I may be invited to go and see them.'

'That'd be interesting. Though what would be better is if your customer had a copy of the *New Story*.'

Marcus laughed. 'In your dreams. To be honest, it would be kind of embarrassing for me to have a hand in exposing the tales of the Water Lairds to a wider audience.'

'Are you saying you'd put your little secret society before the chance to publish such a rare insight into Edinburgh's history?'

'I'm not saying any such thing. Just that there would be some members who would think it improper. It's moot, anyway.'

'Unfortunately.'

Of the several islets in the Firth of Forth, Cramond Island is the only one accessible on foot at low tide. For a few hours each day, it is possible to walk the narrow, kilometre-long causeway from Cramond village to reach it. A young couple, having gone there one day in late June, were exploring the north end of the island when they made a gruesome discovery on the rocky shore.

They called the police to report that a headless human body had washed up on the island. Within the hour the 19-acre island had been designated a crime scene and was off-limits to the public. Soon the causeway was flooded by an incoming tide, and crime scene investigation continued from a police dinghy. After removal of the corpse to the pathology lab, a small group of officers remained on the island, under orders to search for the missing head.

From time to time police had to identify bodies found on the rocks, beaches and mudflats of both shores of the firth, mostly suicides who had ignored the Samaritans' notices on the Forth Road Bridge walkway. Following a tally with some missing person, formal ID was usually straightforward based on facial features or, where the corpse was in an advanced stage of decomposition, dental records.

With a headless torso, identification was a more difficult matter. Gender and, within limits, age were easily ascertained – this body was male, aged fifty to seventy – but beyond that nothing could be said with certainty. There were no tattoos or distinguishing marks, and no fingerprint or DNA match in the system. Cause of death could not be immediately established, but for sure it was no suicide; he could hardly have cut off his own head then thrown himself from the Forth Road Bridge.

The pathologist's report noted that, despite decomposition and post-mortem damage resulting from the action of waves on the rocky shore, signs of tissue shredding on the neck had survived. It appeared the head had been severed by some kind of rough sawing action. Minute traces of oil on the wound suggested a power-driven saw might have been used: a circular or table saw, for example, or more likely a chainsaw. The victim had probably been dead for several hours before the head was removed.

Evidence of bruising near the wound was consistent with death by hanging or strangulation. The degree of decomposition of internal organs, taking into account water temperature in the firth at that time of year, put the time since death at 4 to 6 weeks.

The *Evening News* carried a short report including an interview with the couple who found the body. Victor Herring had been scanning the paper daily and read it with interest. *Bowman didn't get far,* he mused. *From where he was launched to where he went aground was little more than ten miles.* Victor wasn't worried in the slightest.

⬠

Hendrik Vandenbrouck had received a call from one of his operatives in Dundee, and was driving through Fife to a rendezvous in Auchtermuchty. Lex Durno, about thirty years of age with athletic build and a curly mop of fair hair, flagged him down at a filling station on the outskirts of the village.

'Okay, Durno, tell me again what the fuck's going on.'

'There's a couple of NEPA vans at the Loch of Lindores. That's way off the route the pipeline's supposed to take – unless they're looking at another option.'

'And this matters why?'

'Well, because the railway line that runs by Lindores eventually crosses the Forth Bridge into Edinburgh. There's enough anger about England stealing our water. Using Scotland's most iconic example of 19th-century engineering to transport it would be the last straw. A bridge too far, you might say.'

Vandenbrouck gave no indication he caught the movie reference. 'Jesus Christ. The Forth Bridge. We could stir some shit up about this, if you're right.'

'That's what I was thinking. Why don't we leave your car here and take my pickup over to the loch? It's about five miles away.'

With a shrug Vandenbrouck got into the passenger seat of the pickup. 'I hope I'm not wasting my fucking time,' he said. 'There could be another explanation for the NEPA vans.'

The road to Lindores was narrow and winding. To Vandenbrouck it seemed longer than five miles. As Durno drove, he filled in some more background. 'Just south of Perth, the railway divides into two branches. The west branch heads towards Stirling – the line NEPA's maps show for the pipeline. The other goes east before turning south past the Loch of Lindores towards the Firth of Forth. Now, why would NEPA be doing environmental studies on the *east* branch, unless they're thinking about relocating the pipeline?'

'Beats the shit out of me. How do you know it's environmental studies they're doing?'

'There's a lassie – red hair, nice figure in jeans, 25-ish – been setting up equipment, taking soil and water samples. Drives one of the vans with the NEPA logo that's been parked near the loch this last few days. I followed her one evening after she'd gathered up her stuff. She's in a B&B in Strathmiglo.'

'So?'

'I spoke to her landlady yesterday. You know, friendly chat, price of bacon, that kind of thing. Turns out the redhead's American, an intern.'

'NEPA's full of English and American interns. Fucking foreigners,' the Belgian remarked, without a trace of irony.

The Loch of Lindores nestled in a narrow gap in the low ridge that formed the easternmost extremity of the Ochil Hills. A gap that accommodated the railway from Perth to the Forth Bridge, and might in the near future be delivering Scotland's water to thirsty English mouths. Durno parked by an anglers' hut on the east shore.

A brisk breeze raised wavelets on the surface of the loch. As a result the resident drift of swans congregated on the more sheltered water near the opposite shoreline, above which four high-vis jackets could be seen. 'Those are NEPA people,' Durno said. 'See where they're walking? That's the railway. I've a pair of binocs in the glove-box. Take a look.'

Vandenbrouck trained the binoculars on the four figures. ‘Three men and a girl,’ he said. ‘That the redhead you liked the look of?’ He handed the binoculars to Durno.

‘Aye, that’s her all right.’

‘Okay, get to know her. Use that charm I keep hearing about. Get between the sheets, between her legs, you know the drill. Find out what NEPA’s screwing around at here. Learn if they’re planning to use the Forth Bridge.’

Lex Durno had a woman and 3-year-old twins in Dundee but was no stranger to this kind of assignment. Just over a year earlier, he’d seduced Chloe, an assistant to a Conservative candidate for the Scottish parliament; the campaign information she provided during their liaison helped Lowell Blackett, an SNP hardliner and *Auld Stobby* sympathiser, win the election. Funny thing was, Chloe thought all along *she* had seduced *him*, so was less upset than she might have been when he disappeared from the scene immediately after the election. Durno was good at this.

But something told him the American beauty from NEPA would be more of a challenge. For one thing, girls this good-looking were usually attached and always picky. For another, she mightn’t be attuned to his line of Scottish patter. But he was ready to give it a go; in any case, an assignment from Hendrik Vandenbrouck couldn’t easily be refused. And he had his reputation within *Auld Stobby* to consider.

13
USEFUL LITTLE OPERATION

CAMMY LEWIS'S FIRST TASK at the building site was to erect a security fence. The materials had already been delivered – 2x3 metre wire panels, stabilisers, concrete feet, heavy-duty nylon privacy backing and all necessary fixings. The uneven, sloping ground presented some complications but, with improvisation here and there, he had the job done in a day.

The following afternoon he played blackjack at the Learmonth Club. The table was kind to him and by 5:30 he was up £380. When he saw Victor enter, he collected his chips, tipped the croupier and headed for the cashier's cage.

'Had a better day, I see,' Victor said. 'Now I'll buy you dinner so you're set up for the dig tonight.'

Dinner was no gourmet experience for Lewis – fish and chips with garden peas washed down with a good Edinburgh-brewed ale – but it would fortify him for the work ahead. Victor had as hearty a meal as his contractor, though he planned to take no physical part in the upcoming 'archaeological' excavation. As usual, his beverage of choice was Irn Bru.

Scotland's most popular carbonated drink, Irn Bru perennially relegated Coke and Pepsi to second and third place. It once claimed with self-evident hyperbole to be *made in Scotland from girders*, though a single one-ton girder would supply enough iron to fill 100 Olympic-size swimming pools with Irn Bru. Put another way, if you extracted all the iron from 750 cans of the stuff you could just about make one paperclip.

After their meal, the two men drove in Victor's green Land Rover up the rough track to the future site of Rachel's home. It was after 9:30 but there remained a good hour of daylight. The last golfers of the day were on the 17th and 18th holes, a long way from the newly fenced area where the job was to be done. Lewis opened the gate he'd made in the fence to let Victor drive in. From the Hamburg Süd container he selected tools for the job.

'Let me show you where I want you to start.' Victor guided Lewis to the spot where Bob Bowman's metal detector had come alive.

'Why here?'

'No reason. It's as good a place as any.'

'Okay, you're the boss.'

'As you say. Now, remember, the ground has to be left looking undisturbed. So, first off, remove the turf and stack it before digging any deeper. When you've finished, replace it exactly as you found it.'

Though a little annoyed at Victor's micromanagement Lewis said nothing, and began digging out squares of turf. After a few minutes, he stopped. 'It's been turned over here before,' he said. 'Not too long ago. The turf hasn't knitted where it was broken.'

It was Victor's turn to be irritated. 'What the hell does it matter?' he said. Then, after a moment's thought: 'The drainage survey, the subsoil survey, who knows? Everybody's been making holes here.'

'The archaeology survey too, I suppose?'

'Yeah, that too. Look, pal, I'll leave you to get on with it. I'll be in my office until midnight. If you find anything, don't shout. Just come and tell me.'

Lewis resumed his spadework. In minutes, he hit the same hard horizontal surface that Bowman had struck a few weeks earlier. He needed to clear a larger area of turf around the hole he had dug to explore the extent and nature of the hard layer. A number of bushes including a particularly thorny wild rose had to be uprooted, scratching his face and tearing his trousers.

The sun had gone down but the long summer twilight, together with the reflected glow of city lights off the cloud base over his head, gave enough illumination for his work. He had a flashlight but, at Victor's orders, used it sparingly to avoid attracting attention.

By 11:30 he had excavated about twelve square metres. He could now tell that the hard horizontal surface was made up of paving stones. Three metres from his starting point, the paving came up against what had once been the base of an upright wall. It was time to go knock on the door of Victor's 'office'.

Wrapped in a blanket, Victor was lounging on a plastic chair to watch a police drama on his iPad. He signalled Lewis to be quiet as a pair of NYPD detectives carried on a good-cop-bad-cop interrogation of a suspect. In a couple of minutes, the show was interrupted by a commercial break.

Turning to face his labourer, Victor asked, 'Found anything?'

'You'll have to see this for yourself.'

Outside, Lewis shone his flashlight on the paving and then on the remains of the wall that marked its boundary. 'I don't know what this is,' he said, 'but it's manmade. Your mother's not the first to want to build something here.'

'Shit. Well, you're going to have to dig it all up and get rid of it.'

'That could take weeks.'

'You think so? Okay, cover it up again and replace the turf until I figure out what we're going to do.'

'What about the bushes?'

'Dump them in a corner somewhere. We're allowed to clear brush, not supposed to be excavating yet.'

A scuffling sound caught their attention. Lewis shone his torch in its direction, and saw a distinctive pattern of three white stripes converging at a point, and a pair of eyes reflecting the torchlight. 'Just a badger,' he said.

It was eight o'clock on a drizzly morning in the north of Fife. Delia had eaten a generous 'full Scottish' breakfast at her digs in Strathmiglo and was ready to get on the road again. Several times she tried without success to start the engine of the little white NEPA van.

At that moment, a young man in full cycling gear rode by, then stopped and turned back. Taking off his helmet and shaking free his curly hair, he shouted to Delia, 'Having trouble?'

She lowered her driver's side window.

'Mind if I have a go?' the young man asked. 'I'm in the army reserve. I know a couple of things about engines.'

'Well ... it's a company van but I'd appreciate if you could try to get it moving.' She got out to let him into the driver's seat.

'I'm Lex,' he said.

'Delia.'

'Hi, Delia. What brings NEPA to this neck of the woods? I didn't think your pipeline was going to come anywhere near Strathmiglo.' He turned the key a couple of times, with the same lack of success as Delia had experienced.

'We're doing a study at the Loch of Lindores. But you're right, the aqueduct doesn't come through this way.'

Lex Durno released the bonnet of the van. Reaching down into the engine compartment he fiddled with something. 'Give it another go now,' he said.

The engine fired and, after a little cough, began to run smoothly. He lowered the bonnet and said, 'Should be fine now. Just a bit of grit. You've probably been off-road somewhere.'

'Yes, as a matter of fact,' Delia said. Her eyes briefly met his, then dropped. She couldn't help noticing his muscular arms, shoulders and thighs and his flat belly under the spandex. Shame about the girlish blond locks – but then who was she to pass judgment on anyone's hair, after the grief she'd taken all her life about her red tresses? 'I'm very grateful, Lex, thank you.'

'My pleasure. Will you be around for a day or two?'

She nodded towards the guest-house. ‘I’m staying here until the middle of next week.’

‘Your landlady giving you dinner as well as B&B?’

‘No, I’ve been eating in the pub. It’s fine, but I’d kill for a crisp green salad.’

Lex laughed, showing nice white, straight teeth. ‘This isn’t America. Salad’s a rare commodity round here. We’ve a lot to learn.’

‘It’s a two-way street.’

‘Listen, there are some places to eat in Falkland, just three miles from here. Would you like to have dinner with me tonight?’

‘That sounds nice, but I’ll be working quite late. Won’t get back here until after seven. I’d need to clean up a bit.’

‘See you here at eight, then. I’ll book a table for 8:30.’

Delia gave the offer some thought, then replied, ‘Okay, deal. But we go Dutch, right? My expense allowance covers dinner for one.’ She waved to him as she drove off.

Durno grinned as he put his helmet back on and got astride his bicycle. He’d always known it would come in handy, that engine immobilisation trick. It had been a cinch to open the NEPA van’s bonnet late last night to perform that useful little operation. Delia might not be such a challenge after all.

A little later that same morning, at home in the Isle of Man, Rachel Herring took a call from her architect in Edinburgh. ‘Good news,’ he announced. ‘Yesterday afternoon the council issued a “minded-to-grant” decision on your new house.’

‘Minded to grant? What does that mean?’

‘Subject to certain conditions and due consideration by the Planning Committee, your application has been approved. I wouldn’t worry about them. They usually just do a rubber-stamping job.’

‘You mentioned conditions?’

'Nothing too onerous. Tree preservation, ensure access road can take construction traffic and any damage is put right afterwards, seven-to-seven rule, ...'

'What's that?'

'Construction work can't start before 7 am and must stop by 7 pm, no Sunday working.'

'Shouldn't be a problem.'

'Oh, and one more site report before any excavation begins.'

'Jesus, I thought we had a waiver from archaeology.'

'Not archaeology. Badgers.'

'Badgers?'

'Yes, it's a local ordinance. No development on any site containing one or more badger setts.'

'Surely it wouldn't scupper the project, if we found a sett?'

'Sorry, but it might. We haven't seen any evidence of such a thing up there, have we?'

'No.'

'Then it's just a formality. We can hire an environmental or wildlife consultant to survey the site and prepare a report.'

Rachel immediately called her son. Before she could give him the news, Victor told her Lewis had begun the excavation. 'Could be a bigger job than we were thinking, Ma. Remember the paving slabs the metal detector guy found? They cover a big area. They're bordered by a ruined wall – could be some kind of terrace or courtyard, or an interior floor. We'll need weeks to dig them all up and get rid of them.'

'Whatever it takes. Even if he needs more money, the little shit. But tell him to hold off for a few days. There's to be one more damned inspection. For badgers, would you believe. I'm assuming there aren't any badgers up there?'

In response, Victor said, 'I hope you're sitting down, Ma.'

14
GOLDEN

THE CONVERSATION WITH HUGH LEGGAT at his office in the Pleasance and immediately afterwards in a nearby café had satisfied Marcus that he would be a worthy recruit to the Water Lairds. The Lairds met on the first Thursday evening of every month; now, at their 1st July meeting, Marcus was introducing the young forensic accountant to the assembled members. If they accepted him, formal induction would take place three months hence, on 7th October.

The principal subject of debate this evening was the rise and fall of 'tartan nationalism'. The keynote speaker, a member of forty years' standing, began by blaming the origin of tartan tat – the tacky souvenirs sold in gift shops on Princes Street and the Royal Mile – on Sir Walter Scott's invention of a romantic past that Scotland never had.

Scott was an affirmed Tory and as such had sympathy for the long-lost Jacobite cause; this did not, however, prevent him from organising the welcome for a Hanoverian king, George IV, to Edinburgh in 1822. It was the first time since 1650 that a British monarch had deigned to set foot in Scotland, and Scott choreographed a feast of 'traditional' pageantry made up out of whole cloth for the occasion. The hideously obese king was decked out like a pantomime dame in a kilt of lurid red, set off by pink tights.

Later, George's niece Queen Victoria committed a slightly lesser offence against good taste by festooning her new Scottish castle at Balmoral with tartan floor-coverings and draperies and decorating the walls with generic romanticised Highland scenes.

Mention of the queen's taste, or lack of it, in art rang a bell in Marcus's mind. Hadn't Charlotte Nasmyth referred in her *Memoir* to her sister Anne Bennett's work as losing its edge by conforming to 'Victorian' values?

The speaker noted that the new respectability of what was supposedly true Highland tradition led to an explosion in demand for all things pseudo-Scottish, a demand that had not altogether subsided. Among the more grotesque manifestations in the first half of the 20th century was the popularity in England of Scottish music-hall stereotypes, probably the worst offender being Sir Harry Lauder, whom Churchill (one hopes tongue firmly in cheek) called 'Scotland's greatest ever ambassador'. By the 1970s, when Edinburgh's Bay City Rollers once again used tartan as a stage prop, they did so in a way that was less pernicious for its obvious self-mockery.

However, there was no self-mockery in 'tartan nationalism', a narrow chauvinistic tendency within the independence movement. Its most dangerous excesses, the speaker said, were exemplified by the group calling itself *Auld Stobby*. At this Hugh Leggat neither blushed nor protested.

During the discussion that followed, Marcus expressed the view that the worst aspect of 'tartan nationalism' was its belief, sometimes stated and always implied, that the Scots are somehow a race apart from the English. First he invoked Robert Burns to argue that if it were true

That man to man the world o'er
Shall brothers be, for a' that,

how could our neighbours on this small island not be our brothers?

He then turned to the language spoken by almost all Scots, *Auld Stobby* included. The Scots tongue, Marcus reminded his listeners, is derived from the Germanic language of the Angles, 5th- and 6th-century settlers who founded the kingdom of

Northumbria, a realm that extended from the Humber to the Forth. The same Anglo-Saxon language is also the foundation of modern English. Indeed what we now think of as the Scots tongue was originally called *Inglis*.

A thousand years ago the *Inglis* speakers of Lothian, the northernmost province of Northumbria, joined the Gaelic and Cumbric speakers to their north and west to form the new nation of Scotland. Our nation, Marcus said, has roots at least as firmly planted in the Anglo-Saxon culture of Lothian as in any Highland tradition, and certainly not in the faux-Highland myth concocted by Sir Walter Scott. He concluded with a plug for *Inglisleid*, the Scots language group of which he was a member.

As the meeting was breaking up, Hugh took the opportunity to introduce himself to Craig Wetherby, a small bespectacled man of about fifty who was chief accountant of NEPA. He had encountered him a couple of times at professional gatherings, and had heard him deliver an after-dinner speech at some award ceremony or another. One useful fact he remembered: Wetherby was a malt whisky drinker like himself, but one who didn't know when he'd had enough.

'If you're not in a hurry to get home, Craig, how about a nightcap in the bar downstairs? I noticed they have an 18-year-old Talisker I've been meaning to try. Have you tasted it?'

'I believe I have, but I've no objection to sampling it again.'

The younger accountant drank his whisky diluted with water while the older knocked back doubles, neat. Thus did Hugh Leggat, *Auld Stobby* operative, ease his way into the confidence of Craig Wetherby, the man who had every detail of NEPA's budget and spending at his fingertips.

⬠

Rachel Herring absorbed the news about badgers on her building site and texted Isla Younie asking her to call. Her phone rang within ten minutes.

'You said you have influence,' Rachel reminded her *Auld Stobby* contact. 'Very persuasive, your Flemish colleague said you could be. I might need some of that persuasiveness.'

'Sure,' Isla said. 'What's your problem?'

'I've got badgers on my building site.'

'Badgers? On your casino resort site by the airport?'

'No, the site of my new house.'

'I'm not sure I understand.'

Rachel explained: if the upcoming survey found badger setts, there would be no house on that site. And no house, no casino, period. She would invest her money in Ireland instead.

'So you're looking for us to influence the survey?'

'Right. Or better still, get it dropped.'

'Mm.'

After a few seconds' silence on the other end of the line, Rachel said, 'You can't do it? Glad I didn't commit to a donation.'

'No, no! It's not that, Mrs Herring. I was just thinking. Listen, we probably can't stop the badger survey, but what we might be able to do is make sure you get a friendly surveyor. Of course, an expert like that costs money.'

'How much money?'

'I'd have to make inquiries. But how about this? You make us a gift of £25,000 for our action fund, and we'll find a surveyor for you.'

'Twenty-five K? That's a lot for a few fucking badgers.'

'Fucking badgers are the worst kind,' Isla retorted with a laugh. 'Before you know it you've a whole army of badgers.'

'Very witty. I can do fifteen thousand. But not just for the stupid badgers. I can still use your help on my casino.'

They settled on twenty. 'Leave it to me,' Isla said, a reassuring note of confidence in her voice. 'I'll send you instructions for getting the funds to us.'

It was just that morning that Vandenbrouck had informed Isla and a few other front-line operatives of NEPA's possible interest in using the Forth Bridge to carry its aqueduct across the firth, and had charged them with assembling a war-chest. Isla was pleased with herself. She'd raised the first £20,000, almost without lifting a finger. She was golden. All she had to do now was figure out how to deliver on the badger surveyor.

⬠

Falkland. The location of a royal palace. King James V, at the age of 30, retired there in a state of depression after a heavy defeat in battle. And there he died, leaving a six-day-old infant daughter to succeed him to the throne of Scotland. That daughter was Mary, Queen of Scots. Another fact: Falkland Palace boasted the oldest functioning real tennis court in the world, opened by King James in 1539. (Real tennis is the forerunner of modern tennis and other racquet sports.)

Delia had agreed to have dinner that evening with a man she knew nothing about. What had she been thinking of? Then again, what was wrong with it? It wasn't like it was a *date*. Or was it? Standard test: would she tell Quin about it? Probably not. Okay, it was a date. But it was dinner, nothing more. And Lex Durno *had* been kind in getting her van to start.

She tried to focus on her work. But wading out into the loch to sample water weeds, counting branches and feeding the data to CCD was a tedious business, not enough to keep her mind from wandering. Around the middle of the day, another line of thought began forming in her brain, one that did manage, for a while, to drive Lex into the background.

It was CCD that sparked it. Computerised comparative dendrometry was a fairly new technique that had been developed for studying tree growth in forests and subsequently adapted for growth analysis of perennial plants of any kind, including the water weeds that Delia was collecting in the loch. It yielded a measure of ecological health of a habitat, through analysis of year-to-year branching ratio. A relatively stable ratio over several years was indicative of a robust habitat, one that could tolerate a considerable degree of human interference without serious damage. A ratio that fluctuated wildly from one year to another suggested a habitat that was more fragile.

What made branching pattern such a useful environmental indicator was that, like tree rings, it recorded *history*, opening a portal not just to current growth but to how things had been over the past five, ten, twenty years. In many species, the average ratio over several years was found to come close to the so-called golden ratio of 1·6180339887... – one of those irrational numbers, like pi, that can't be expressed as a precise fraction. It was usually rounded to 1·618, close enough for most purposes.

Delia wondered idly what CCD would make of the Nasmyth 'family tree', the model constructed by Charlotte and her siblings from bundles of wire, under their father's supervision. That thought led to another: how near would branching in the Nasmyth 'tree' approach to 1·618?

Charlotte herself had mentioned the golden ratio, though not by that name and not in connection with trees. She had claimed that Pacioli's *divine proportions* underlay the street plan in Edinburgh's New Town and the design of the buildings lining those streets. It was the same concept; perhaps the term 'golden ratio' wasn't yet in use at the time Charlotte was writing.

Many beautiful things, Delia knew, obeyed the golden ratio in one way or another. Architecture since the building of the Parthenon had been influenced by it. Everyday objects having dimensions close to the golden ratio include mobile phones, business cards and flat-screen TVs. In the natural world, the spirals of a sunflower head, a pineapple and a nautilus shell all testify in their beauty to the aesthetic power of 1·618.

Once again, Delia pondered the significance of the number five that cropped up so often in Charlotte's *Memoir*. Could the recurring five be a coded reference to the golden ratio? After all, 1·618 was constructed from fives:

·5 times the square root of 5, plus ·5.

Likewise its reciprocal, 0·618:

·5 times the square root of 5, minus ·5.

In addition, the golden ratio could be derived from the series of numbers beginning 1, 1, 2, 3, 5, 8, 13, ... where each number is the sum of the preceding two numbers. It's the famous Fibonacci series much loved of mystery writers from Philip K. Dick to Dan Brown. The ratio between any number and the one immediately before it in the series gets closer and closer to the golden ratio, the bigger the numbers become. And the Fibonacci series also has five embedded in it: every fifth number is exactly divisible by five. For example, fifth in the sequence is 5, tenth is 55 and fifteenth is 610, which is 555 + 55. Fifty-five is especially interesting: not only the tenth Fibonacci number but also the sum of whole numbers from 1 to 10 and the sum of squared numbers from 1 to 5.

The regular five-sided figures from which Charlotte's grandfather constructed David Hume's belvedere also embody the golden ratio. The total height of a regular pentagon is 1·618 times the height from its base to its 'shoulders'.

Delia planned to call Jody and tell her that if Charlotte's *Memoir* contained a hidden message, it might be something to do with the golden ratio, 1·618. A few minutes later, she found herself thinking about Lex again.

15
IDLE CURIOSITY

'HEADLESS CORPSE IDENTIFIED' was the *Scotsman* headline. Victor read the story while eating a pie-and-beans lunch in a Queensferry Street pub he frequented. On noticing the headline, he had asked the bartender to fortify his Irn Bru with a double shot of vodka.

It was reported that the search for a head to go with the body found on Cramond Island had so far proved unsuccessful. However, the pathologist had noticed tiny, almost invisible, well-healed scars on the left leg – scars consistent with varicose vein surgery at some time in the past year.

Hospitals throughout central and south-east Scotland were contacted. As it happened, one vascular surgeon had been trialling a new procedure and had kept meticulous records. In his file was a photograph of a left leg with a distribution of incisions exactly matching the victim's scars. The owner of that left leg, it turned out, was a missing person, a 63-year-old male whose identity the police were withholding from the press until next-of-kin could be found and informed.

'*I* could tell you the name,' Victor said silently to the newspaper. 'Robert Fucking Bowman.' A name the police had no doubt already linked to the Mercedes towed from a street not half a mile from Ma's building site. It was only a matter of time until they would come snooping around. Not that they'd find any evidence of Bowman ever being there. But it could be embarrassing if they arrived to find Lewis digging the place over.

Should he tell his mother about this latest development? No, not for now, he decided. Better to act dumb, like he would when the cops eventually showed up. *Bowman? Never clapped eyes on him, never heard of him.*

That afternoon, back at the casino, Victor had an acute bout of indigestion. The pie, probably. Or maybe the double vodka.

⬠

At precisely eight o'clock, dressed casually in blue jeans, a white tee shirt and smart leather jacket, Lex rang the bell at the front door of Delia's B&B in Strathmiglo. In his hand he held a bunch of flowers, nothing too presumptuous like red roses, just a mixed floral bouquet. Hell, if Delia didn't want them her landlady would. In fact, he owed her, for telling him what she knew of her American boarder.

When they met they burst out laughing to find they were dressed almost identically. Graciously accepting the flowers, Delia asked the landlady to put them in a vase in the breakfast room.

They took Lex's car. Approaching the village of Falkland, she read the sign by the roadside and said aloud, '*Dank fall.*'

'Eh?'

'Sorry, just a crazy thing I do. When I see a place name for the first time, I often make an anagram of it in my head. I do it with movie titles, product names, notices, anything. I've done it since I was a child.'

'It's clever,' he said, admiringly. Did you do the same for Strathmiglo?'

'Yup. *Tight morals.*' Again they laughed together.

'Nice place,' she said at the restaurant, picking up a leaflet explaining the history of the area. After a cursory look at the menu, she asked Lex what he did for a living.

He volunteered some details of his background. That none of them had even a grain of truth wouldn't matter, at least to him. This was to be the briefest of relationships. After he'd learned what NEPA had in mind for the new pipeline route, in particular what they intended to do about a Forth crossing, he'd disappear. And Delia would never track Lex Durno down, for there was no such person, at least not in *this* skin.

'So you manage a cycle shop?' she said. 'Here in Fife?'

'Yes, in St Andrews. We do sales, rentals and repairs.'

'Is it your own business?'

'No, it's a chain, with stores in Glasgow and Aberdeen as well. There's a local manager in each place.'

'Mm. What's it called?'

'Two-Wheeler Dealer. Naff name, but it brings in the punters. Scottish students, mainly. See, they don't have fees to pay, so they're not as hard-up as students from England, Wales or Northern Ireland.'

'Not exactly fair, is it? I mean, that if you happen to be Scottish, you get thousands of pounds' worth of free university tuition, but if you're from across the border you've to rack up all that debt to get a degree.'

'Fairness is a matter of opinion, Delia. If *you* were studying at a Scottish university, you'd have to pay your full whack, being American. So why shouldn't other foreigners pay the same?'

'You consider English people foreigners?'

'Like I said, matter of opinion.'

This line of conversation was going nowhere. Fortunately, the waitress was keen to take their order. A bottle of wine came, a fruity Italian red, and Delia complimented her companion on his choice.

'So, how long have you been with NEPA, Delia?'

'Just a few months. It's a temporary internship for a couple of years, max.'

'And after that you'll go back to the US?'

'Possibly, we'll see. I'm enjoying being here for the time being. I might look somewhere else in Europe next.'

Despite her signal that she was a free agent with no strings and no connections, he didn't seem to pick up on it. Instead, he came back to her job. 'What are they like to work for? NEPA, I mean?'

'Okay, I guess. They treat me well – pay and conditions okay, gym membership, all that good stuff. The job's a bit repetitive, but it's kinda what I expected. It's work that has to be done, might as well be me.'

'They let you in on strategic thinking? Or are you a corporate mushroom?'

'Kept in the dark and fed a load of shit?' She'd heard that old joke many times. 'No, there's open discussion within the company. When you're sent out to the field to work ten-hour days, seven-day weeks, it's good to understand how your little operation fits into the grand scheme.'

'So with this project of yours at the Loch of Lindores, you're helping scout out a new route for the pipeline? The *aqueduct*, I should say?'

'Exactly.' *Damn!* That was confidential information, but Lex had guessed and she'd just confirmed. She tried to recover from her slip: 'I mean, *exactly*, you should call it the aqueduct, not the pipeline.'

She wasn't fooling him. He grinned. 'It's obvious you're checking a new route, alternative route, whatever. I had a customer the other day, told me as much.'

The food arrived. 'This looks good,' she said. 'Let's eat.'

When he judged the moment was right Lex steered the conversation back to the only subject he cared about. 'If NEPA *was* thinking about coming through Fife instead of Stirling, they'd have to take the aqueduct across the Firth of Forth, wouldn't they?'

'If. I suppose so, yes. Look, Lex, I ...'

'I'm sorry. Just idle curiosity on my part. Here, have some more wine. I'd better switch to water since I'm driving.'

The expression on his face was that of a good little boy who'd been denied a new toy or another piece of cake, but in spite of wanting to appear stoic was letting the hurt show. And Delia could see the hurt wasn't about forgoing another glass of wine, but about her clamming up on the stupid aqueduct route. She sipped her drink, saying nothing. Then, what the hell: 'Yes, we've all been briefed. It's supposed to be a secret but pretty soon it'll be all over the papers. The plan is to take the aqueduct over the Forth Bridge.'

Bingo! 'The *rail* bridge?'

'Why not?'

'It was built in 1890. It was never designed to carry anything other than the railway line. And it's world-famous. Putting an aqueduct on it would change its appearance altogether, even supposing it could structurally support such a thing.'

'You may be right, but we're in negotiation with Network Rail to secure access. I'm sure all the necessary engineering analysis will be done, design studies too. It'll be important not to compromise the aesthetics of the bridge.'

'Wow, I'm impressed!'

'Please don't spread this around. The negotiations with Network Rail are quite sensitive. NEPA will want to keep the lid on this until they have a deal. Promise me it'll go no further.'

'The secret's safe with me.'

Back at Strathmiglo she said, 'Sorry I can't invite you in for coffee or anything,' she said. 'You know how it is in a place like this.'

'There'll be another time, I hope,' he said. 'Can I have your mobile number?' He tapped it into his phone list.

She planted a friendly kiss on his cheek and stepped out of the car.

⬠

It had been a busy day, a day of constant interruptions. Marcus closed up for the evening, but before going home he had a few back-of-store jobs to do. Three separate customers had selected labels for their malts and he still had to set them up for printing. He had recorded their individual selections, but was damned if he could find his notes. Trouble was, his desk was cluttered with paperwork. He'd already had to rifle through various piles looking for a repeat order he'd received by mail.

I should get help, he thought, not for the first time. But not every day was like today. An assistant's wages and benefits would have to be paid through all the quiet spells, the weeks on end when scarcely a soul might darken the door of *A Malt O'My Ain*.

As he searched for the elusive information, he accidentally knocked a stack of papers off the edge of his desk on to the floor. The pile had been balanced precariously on the plastic wallet containing the old leather attaché case. 'My God!' he said to himself. 'Am I still holding on to that?'

Butchered though it was, he decided he'd better offer it back to Archie Kilgour. Looking inside, he noticed that two leather dividers had been sewn together. A slight bulge suggested there might be something in the sealed compartment between them. He attacked the stitching with scissors. The thread had long since rotted but the leather panels were firmly stuck together along the seam. His scissors were not up to the task but a stout knife did the trick.

Pulling apart the dividers, he found a silk envelope. Inside was a wad of paper covered with elegant but dense handwriting, similar to that of Charlotte's *Memoir* but bolder and less shaky. It was difficult to read, as the sheets were thin and translucent, letting the writing on the reverse side shine through.

But it was easy to make out the heading in capital letters on the top sheet:

A NEW STORY OF EDINBURGH'S EARLIEST BEGINNINGS.

16
INVASION AND CONQUEST

'WHAT'S UP, SWEETHEART?'

'You tell me, Marcus. I just answered *your* call.' Jody was totally unprepared for what he had to say next.

'The story of Edinburgh begins on the south shore of an eastern firth.'

'Eh? I know that. What are you talking about?'

'Just reading something to you. A document I became aware of just five minutes ago. It's titled *A New Story of Edinburgh's Earliest Beginnings*.'

There was silence on the phone line for a moment. Then: 'Marcus! Are you serious?'

'Absolutely. It's in Charlotte's beautiful hand.'

'Get over here this minute!' Whatever Jody had planned for the rest of the evening was forgotten. She wanted to get her hands on the *New Story*, having tried in vain for days to find any record of it.

'Just closing up. Haven't eaten yet.'

'I'll microwave something for you. Don't keep me in suspense any longer!'

In fifteen minutes he was at her door. While she rustled up a ready-meal for him, he opened a bottle of wine and told her how he'd found the manuscript. As he ate, she began reading.

> *The story of Edinburgh begins on the south shore of an eastern firth: not, as we might expect, the Firth of Forth but the Firth of Flensburg. That firth is locally*

known as a fjord, for it is situated in Denmark, on the east side of the Jutland peninsula. On its south shore is a low-lying region known since antiquity as Angeln, the ancestral home of a people calling themselves Angles. They were a Teutonic race, like their neighbours the Jutes to the north and the Saxons to the south; all three spoke a similar language, which can be called Anglo-Saxon.

Though the calligraphy was bold and clear, its legibility was compromised by the writing on the back of each thin sheet. Jody wondered if her friend Shilpa at the National Library might have a system for copying or scanning this document that would heighten the contrast between front and back, improving its readability. It would make sense, in any case, to archive this delicate original and work from a digital or paper copy. But for now she continued to read the very ink Charlotte Nasmyth had committed to paper 180 years before.

Around the year 100, the Roman historian Tacitus wrote an account of the Angles' worship of a goddess he called 'Nerthus', though according to tales of the Water Lairds her name in Anglo-Saxon was Neadreth. She was believed to have power over both land and water. At her pleasure the Angles could enjoy rich harvests from their fields and bountiful fishing from the sea. Her home, according to Tacitus, was in a sacred grove on an island in the ocean.

From there the goddess would ride in a chariot drawn by female oxen, to visit her people. Although invisible, she could communicate with them, and they with her, through the medium of a priest who travelled alongside her chariot. During her sojourn among them, the Angles would put away all weapons and refrain from battle, instead feasting and rejoicing in a time of peace. Eventually, she would grow tired of her travels and return to her island home, where she, her chariot and her oxen would be purified of all human taint by washing in a sacred watercourse – sometimes described as a spring, a stream or a lake.

In Tacitus's account, the invisible goddess is washed by slaves, and immediately after their ritual is performed they are drowned in the sacred water. I believe this detail was pure invention designed to appeal to a Roman audience.

Uh, oh, Jody thought. Our old friend Tacitus up to his usual mischief. What he doesn't know he makes up, the first-century equivalent of a tabloid journalist who focuses on and often invents salacious details to help sell his stories.

'What has this Neadreth to do with Edinburgh?' she asked Marcus.

'Read on', he said.

Despite Neadreth's pacifying effect, the Angles, like their cousins the Jutes and Saxons, were at heart a warlike race whose reputation for fighting became known throughout Europe. By the 5th century Anglian warriors were in demand as mercenaries to win battles for foreign kings. In Britain at this time, the collapse of Roman rule had left a patchwork of small kingdoms vying for supremacy, and at least one of the warring British kings invited Angles, Jutes and Saxons to help defend or expand his realm.

The mercenaries brought word back to Angeln that Britain was ripe for invasion and conquest, and by the year 500, substantial Anglian settlements had been established on the east coast, from the Thames estuary in the south to the Firth of Forth in the north, and in inland Mercia (now the English midlands). Around the same time, Saxons colonised large swathes of what is now central and southern England, and Jutes found homes in Kent, Hampshire and the Isle of Wight.

Initially, the Angles kept very much to themselves, interacting little with the indigenous Brythonic (British) people, who spoke a language akin to Welsh. As time went on, trade and intermarriage began to blur the boundaries of Brythonic and Anglian culture.

At the northernmost extremity of Anglian settlement was the region now known as Lothian, a corruption of the old Welsh name Gododdin *pertaining to the tribe already inhabiting that region, whom the Romans had called* Votadini. *The story of Neadreth and the Angles must be interrupted here while we say something about the* Gododdin.

The principal inheritor of Roman rule in what is now northern England and southern Scotland was a Brythonic chieftain by the name of Coel or Colud. He remains better known than many later rulers, at least to children, through the traditional song Old King Cole. *His name survives in places such as Coldingham and Coldstream in the Borders and Coylton in Ayrshire, where he was reputedly buried.*

On his death his realm splintered, forming numerous smaller kingdoms of which Gododdin *was one, occupying not only Lothian but a tract of land to the south and a small province known as* Manaw *(present-day Clackmannan) taken from the Pictish kingdom north of the Forth.*

Another Brythonic warlord who may have held sway over Gododdin *in the early 6th century was the legendary King Arthur. The Water Lairds hold that the battle of Camlann, in which both Arthur and the usurper Mordred lost their lives, was fought at the place now called Camelon, in the eastern borderlands of the* Gododdin *kingdom.*

The principal seat of power in the kingdom was initially a fortified hill, Traprain Law near present-day Haddington. Sometime in the 6th century, King Clydno moved his capital to an even better defensive position 20 miles to the west, in a part of Lothian then known as Eiddyn.

Some scholars have connected Eiddyn *with the biblical Eden, but the similarity of names is probably accidental. The river and vale of Eden in Cumbria, and the rivers Eden in Fife and Ythan north of Aberdeen, suggest an ancient, pre-Christian, origin for the name.*

Long before Clydno's time, the Romans had built several forts in Eiddyn, *including one the* Gododdin *called* Caer Eiddyn *(Carriden) at the eastern end of the Antonine wall and one near the mouth of the River Almond –* Caer Amond *(Cramond). But these were now in ruins and Clydno chose a more spectacular location. His castle on a rock came to be called* Din Eiddyn.

Though a site of human settlement for over a thousand years, only now did the rock assume strategic and political importance. It became a fortified stronghold with principal defences to the west, the line of approach of marauding Picts.

Gododdin*'s relationship with the Picts was uneasy. As the one British realm that had never yielded to Rome, the Pictish kingdom (whose southernmost lands were clearly visible across the Firth of Forth from* Din Eiddyn*) was regarded with wary respect.*

However, there was one curious aspect of the Pictish nation they were able to exploit: the matrilineal descent of kings. The king of the Picts was always chosen from the maternal line, making princesses, as potential bearers of future kings, both prized and vulnerable. A deal was struck whereby Pictish royal daughters, while still virgins, would be safeguarded by the Gododdin *on their castle rock, where potential suitors could have controlled access. These unfortunate girls were essentially prisoners in the fortress, which came to be called the 'Castle of Maidens'.*

The Water Lairds tell of one resident of the Castle of Maidens by the name of Hermutrude. She was a 6th-century Pictish princess, though Danish folk-tales refer to her as a 'Scottish queen'. (There was no such thing as 'Scottish' at that time.) Hermutrude had received many suitors, but accepted none. It was not so much that she didn't like any of them, rather she realised that matrimony would take away such power as she had. Once she had borne a son or two, her usefulness would be at an end. The story goes that she killed each of her suitors in the midst of their wooing.

A young man by the name of Amlode changed all that. Better known to us as Shakespeare's Hamlet, he was a prince of Jutland in Denmark who, having just killed the usurper of his father's throne (his uncle Feng – Shakespeare's Claudius), arrived in Britain to be reunited with his wife, a daughter of a Brythonic king.

The king loved his son-in-law well, but had sworn an oath with Feng that if either should die through villainy, the other would avenge his death. Not having the heart to see Amlode die at his court, yet unwilling to break his solemn oath, the king, a widower, conceived the idea of sending him on a mission to Din Eiddyn *to woo the beautiful but cruel Hermutrude on his behalf. Amlode would surely not return alive.*

However, the plan failed when Hermutrude fell in love with the prince. After a brief courtship, the pair were wed, notwithstanding that Amlode was already married to the British king's daughter. The king was enraged at this turn of events and tried to kill Amlode, but the prince escaped to Jutland with his two wives. There he found a new king had installed himself on the throne, which he believed was rightfully his. Battle ensued in which Amlode was slain, whereupon Hermutrude transferred her devotion to the victor, and married him. Thus did Din Eiddyn's *Castle of Maidens provide a queen for Denmark.*

During much of the period of Gododdin *rule, Anglian incomers settled in Lothian, clearing forests to grow their crops while giving little provocation to the indigenous population. From Angeln they brought their spiritual beliefs, in particular their veneration of Neadreth, but made no attempt to convert their new neighbours, whose attachment to Celtic gods was already being challenged by Irish missionaries of yet another religion, Christianity.*

To the south, the Anglian immigrants were less peaceable. They took up arms in Bryneich, *a Brythonic kingdom with its capital at Bamburgh, and by 550 had installed an Anglian king by the name of Ida. His realm, now known as Bernicia, stretched from the River Tees to the borders of Lothian. Still farther south, from the Tees to the Humber estuary, another Anglian kingdom, Deira, arose around the same time.*

In 598 the Gododdin *king Mynyddog (his name means 'mountainous') perceived a threat and, rather than wait for Bernician or Deiran forces to invade Lothian, assembled an army at* Din Eiddyn *to march into Anglian territory. Remarkably, they crossed the whole of Bernicia into Deira before meeting significant resistance. Their path was easy: the Romans had built a great road called Dere Street from their stronghold of* Eboracum *(York) all the way to the Firth of Forth.*

Jody was familiar with the history of Dere Street, constructed as a Roman supply route to the Antonine Wall. She had travelled it many times, for the modern route from Edinburgh to York via Jedburgh, Corbridge and Catterick follows the Roman road closely much of the way.

It was at Catraeth *(Catterick) that the* Gododdin *force encountered an army raised by the allied kings of Bernicia and Deira. Disastrously, before launching an assault on the Angles, Mynyddog's men spent the night drinking. When dawn broke they were massacred mercilessly in their drunken state, Mynyddog among them; few if any returned to* Din Eiddyn.

In the aftermath of that fateful battle, the Lothian Angles swore allegiance to the Bernician king Aethelfrith, a grandson of Ida. Shortly afterwards, the alliance of Anglian kingdoms foundered and, in 604, Aethelfrith conquered Deira, driving out its king, Eadwine. Not for nothing was he known as Aethelfrith the Twister.

The Anglian realm now covered all the land north of the Humber as far as the Forth and became known eventually as Northumbria. In 616 Eadwine returned with an army, killed the Twister and established himself as ruler. The vanquished king's three sons, Eanfrith, Oswald and Oswy, went into exile, waiting their chance to retake the throne.

Eanfrith's exile was among the Picts. While there, he was permitted to travel south to Din Eiddyn *to woo a Pictish princess in the still* Gododdin*-held Castle of Maidens. That princess's name does not appear in any historical record, but the Water Lairds call her Eithne.*

More amenable to courtship than the earlier Hermutrude, she agreed to marry Eanfrith the Angle, in due course bearing him several daughters and a son, Talorcan, who became king of the Picts. The mixed Pictish and Anglian blood of Eithne's daughters has flowed in the veins of Pictish, Scottish and ultimately British monarchs right down to the present day.

Jody was beginning to have a new respect for the Water Lairds. Where medieval scribes felt it unnecessary to record the names of historical figures if they happened to be female, the Lairds obviously recognised, even in the mid-19th century, that someone as significant as Eanfrith's Pictish queen deserved to have a name. Slightly odd, Jody thought, that they would give her an *Irish* name; then she remembered that by 616 the Picts had largely been converted to Christianity by Irish missionaries, who probably insisted on 'proper' – that is, Gaelic – Christian names for their flock. And 'Eithne' had a nice ring to it, suggesting a link to *Eiddyn*.

Eadwine's reign ended in 632 with the break-up of Northumbria once again into its two constituent parts. Eanfrith returned from Pictland with Eithne his queen to rule the northern portion, Bernicia. A year later Oswald took control and reunited Northumbria under a single throne. Dissatisfied to find that pockets of Gododdin *control remained in the north, including* Din Eiddyn *with its Castle of Maidens, he took the fortress on the rock in 638 and established Anglian hegemony over all of Lothian for the first time.* Din Eiddyn *was translated into the Anglo-Saxon language as* Eidin Burg, *eventually becoming Edinburgh.*

17
SWITCH

SOONER OR LATER, VICTOR WAS SURE, the police would come snooping around his mother's building site. Last night, he had wakened in a cold sweat with Bob Bowman's words echoing in his brain: 'I spoke to an official at the golf club.' At least one other person had met Bowman on the day he disappeared; that 'official' had even directed the treasure hunter to the Herring site.

Victor had done a very thorough cleaning job in his red Hamburg Süd box, the scene of Bowman's demise, but a microscopic trace of the victim's blood, skin or hair could give the game away. He was less worried about evidence outside. It had rained so heavily the day he hauled the body down to the firth, he was confident they would find nothing incriminating.

Then he thought, the chainsaw. He'd cleaned it well, but had he removed every strand of Bowman's DNA from the blades? No, it would have to go. The Land Rover? Probably okay – the body had been well wrapped in builder's polythene.

The priority was the shipping container. He got on the phone to a contractor friend. A fresh one would be delivered that afternoon, and his present Hamburg Süd 'office' with all its contents would be taken away. By day's end his furniture, tools and equipment would have been dumped in landfill at Polmont and the battered red box would be steam-cleaned inside and out, stacked with dozens of similar twenty-footers at Grangemouth docks. Soon it would be reloaded with scrap metal, bound for Gdansk or Valencia or Mumbai. A substantial bonus payment would ensure its records would somehow be lost or muddled.

The main hazard was the on-site switch. People might get curious. Well, the story would be that the old box was damaged and letting in rainwater, so he ordered a replacement.

In the event, the operation went like clockwork. Now there stood a pale grey twenty-footer emblazoned with the red logo of OOCL, looking no less out of place than its predecessor.

⬠

Delia's mobile phone pinged twice in the space of five minutes. The first text message read:

> Great news – Magnus found Charlotte's 'New Story'. Am reading it now. After scanning will email it for your enjoyment. Hope you're having a good time in Fife ☺. Jody.

The second:

> Hi, Delia! Enjoyed our evening together, hope you did too. I'll be in Dundee for company meeting Friday to Sunday. Can you join me for dinner Saturday? My treat. Lex X.

It was all happening. In her reply to Jody she said she was looking forward to reading the *New Story*; and, yes, she was liking Fife more than she expected.

Lex's invitation needed more reflection. She had enjoyed his company but, when she replayed some of their conversation, something bothered her. He had been very attentive, quite open in answering her questions. The problem was, he had been more interested in her work than in her. He had pressed her for NEPA information, and stupidly she had shared company secrets with him, including the plan to use the Forth Bridge. Yet he had never asked her where her home was in America, where she had studied, what her interests were outside work, any of that.

Still, in spite of herself, she wanted to see him again. She called the Premier Inn in Dundee to ensure the Two-Wheeler

Dealer meeting wasn't to be there, before making a booking online. Only then did she reply to Lex's message:

> Yes, that would be great. Working Saturday but should get to Dundee by about 6. Let me know where you want to meet and when. Delia X.

⬠

NEPA's chief accountant had a lot on his plate. The switch to a new aqueduct route had to be costed down to the last penny, while preserving intact the overall construction budget. Savings elsewhere had to balance the added expense, a trick that was well-nigh impossible given uncertainties around the Forth Bridge. But, hey, he was paid to make the numbers balance, and that's what he'd do. Or what he'd have his two assistants do. Craig Wetherby didn't keep two dogs and bark himself.

His secretary buzzed him. 'Call for you on line one, sir. A Mr Leggat. Says you'll know what it's about.'

Leggat? Oh yes, the chap he'd got drunk with after the Water Lairds meeting. Wetherby picked up the phone.

'Sorry to trouble you at work, Craig. I just wondered if you'd be free to have dinner with me sometime soon. I'd appreciate your angle on the Water Lairds, to see if it's something I really want to commit to. Marcus Annandale has done a great selling job, but I'd like to hear another member's view before I sign up.'

Visions of a whisky-soaked dinner with Hugh Leggat played in Wetherby's brain. 'Sure, Hugh, I'd be glad to. As it happens, I'm free tonight. Would that work for you?'

⬠

Jody kept on reading.

> *During the early part of the 6th century, a feeling grew among the Angles of Lothian that Neadreth dwelt among them, indeed that Britain was the very 'island in the ocean' where the goddess had her home.*

Furthermore, they came to believe that her sacred grove and watercourse were right here in Eiddyn. *By around 530 they had consecrated a place of pilgrimage and worship, and given it her name. It was a peaceful, sheltered spot where, in the sun-dappled shade of hazel trees, there flowed a limpid water.*

The Angles were not the first to recognise the charms of this secluded place. Almost 400 years earlier, the Roman emperor Antonine had appointed an aggressive new governor of Britain by the name of Lollius Urbicus and charged him with pushing the frontier of the empire north from Hadrian's wall, hitherto the limit of effective Roman control.

To Urbicus's advantage, an earlier governor, Agricola, had made a partial and temporary conquest of northern Britain and had extended the road known as Dere Street as far as the Firth of Forth. Marching three legions north along Dere Street in 141, Urbicus led a blistering campaign, defeating at least four British tribal kingdoms including Gododdin, *to secure control of all the territory south of the Forth valley. It was soon clear, however, that the people the Romans called* Caledonii, *whose territory was the vast wild land north of the Forth, would be less easy to subdue.*

Antonine may have been disappointed at this setback, but by 143 he accepted the inevitable and ordered the building of a wall marking the new frontier. That wall would cross the island of Britain at its narrowest point, from the Firth of Clyde at Old Kilpatrick to the Firth of Forth at Carriden.

The building of what became known as the Antonine wall, with its chain of 19 forts, took about twelve years. For such a massive undertaking, it had a very short useful life. By around 160 it had been abandoned in favour of the relative safety of Hadrian's wall a hundred miles to the south. A later occupation of the land between the walls was attempted by the emperor Septimius Severus in 208 but was similarly short-lived, due to continual harrying by the Caledonii *(who were later to acquire the pejorative name of* Picti *– painted people).*

During the period from 141 until 160 and the even briefer period of Severus's occupation, large numbers of legionnaires and support workers were deployed along the Antonine wall and around the ancient centres of native power, ready to quell any insurrection. Garrisons in Lothian included Carriden at the east end of the wall, as well as Cramond and Inveresk.

During this time the Romans used certain locations as bathing places, dedicated to their gods. One such location was the shady hazel grove later rediscovered by the Angles and consecrated in the name of their goddess Neadreth, believing the remains of Roman construction at the site to be the work of her mystical priesthood.

Though there were other deities in their pantheon, they revered Neadreth as the fountainhead, the wellspring of all their fortune – <u>mis</u>fortune too, for if she was angered, she could cause famine and pestilence. A legend grew that the stonework concealed a store of wealth amassed during her travels among her people; but that anyone unwise enough to steal from that store would be accursed.

18
THE OLD RELIGION

A STORE OF WEALTH HIDDEN in Roman stonework in a *shady grove* where the 6th-century Angles worshipped their water-goddess? Jody gave an involuntary start, then read the paragraph again. Was Marcus aware of the legend from storytelling sessions at the Water Lairds? Is that why he focused on the mention of buried treasure in Charlotte's *Memoir*?

She read on.

The incomers felt they were on familiar territory. Lothian was a fertile land bordered on the north by a firth, just like Angeln. To the east was open sea, not the Baltic of their homeland but a stormy yet bounteous water nonetheless. And by night, the heavens looked <u>*exactly*</u> *as they did in Angeln.*

The 6th-century Angles may have lacked the modern concept of a spherical, rotating earth on which Angeln and Lothian lay at a very similar latitude. But being a widely-travelled people, they knew the heavens did not look the same everywhere. In Rome, some bright stars appeared near the southern horizon that were unknown at home; in the cold lands away to the north the familiar celestial beacon we know as the 'dog star' failed to put in its winter appearance. But here in Lothian, all was just as it had been in Angeln.

According to Anglian legend, Neadreth toured the northern sky by night. The goddess in her chariot was identified with the star pattern classical astronomers named Cassiopeia. The chariot was drawn by a pair of oxen (the constellation Cepheus). Pursuing Neadreth around the sky, but never catching up, was a great bear (the Plough).

Although the Gododdin *had been largely converted to Christianity, the Angles who lived peaceably among them held fast to their own beliefs, and for a time the worship of Neadreth – and some other Anglo-Saxon deities including a wind-god, a thunder-god, a dawn-goddess and a war-god – was the dominant religion of Lothian. This continued even after King Eadwine of Northumbria took up the Christian faith, for his rule over Lothian remained tenuous. In 633, Eadwine was killed in battle against Cadwallon of Wales, and with Welsh support Eanfrith became king.*

This was a high point for the old religion, as Eanfrith would have nothing to do with the strange cult his predecessor had embraced. That cult, of a single omnipotent god whose son lived among the people until he was betrayed, crucified and rose from the dead, was something the backward Gododdin *had been talked into, and was not for the more sophisticated Lothian Angles under Eanfrith.*

Eanfrith's years of exile with the Picts had fostered in him a resistance to the march of Christianity, for he had witnessed how their society and culture, even their language, was being assailed by evangelists of the new religion. Now as king, with his Pictish queen Eithne by his side, he resolved to restore Neadreth to her rightful place as the supreme goddess of the Anglian people.

But his brother Oswald had other ideas. His period of exile had been not in Pictland but in Dalriada to the west, an enclave of Christians who were to adopt a name Latin writers used for their Irish tribe – Scoti *or*

'Scots'. There, on the island of Iona, Oswald was brought up to deny his Anglian heritage and accept the Christian faith unquestioningly.

In an effort to halt the spread of the new religion, Eanfrith allied himself with the powerful Cadwallon. One year into his reign, he was treacherously killed during a visit to the Welsh king. Oswald seized the opportunity to take power over all of Northumbria, banishing Eithne to her Pictish homeland.

Such was Oswald's piety that he set about wiping the native Anglian religion off the pages of history. He began by establishing a bishopric on the island of Lindisfarne from which missionaries travelled all over his kingdom. Although the Gododdin *who still held pockets of land in Lothian were Christian, like him, he could see that they would never convert the local Angles. When in 638 he finally destroyed what was left of* Gododdin *culture by making Edinburgh's Castle Rock a Northumbrian fortress, the new religion supplanted the old in short order.*

Yet the long-forgotten creed of the followers of Neadreth has a link, albeit tenuous, to present-day Edinburgh. The water-goddess's priesthood, who tended her sacred grove and ensured the purity and clarity of the water that flowed there, took on a new, even more demanding charge: to look after the fresh waters all around the Castle Rock. As the population of the rock expanded, a reliable water supply became an ever more precious resource. So came into existence the Edinburgh Water Lairds.

⬠

It was a quiet morning at *A Malt O' My Ain*. Marcus was catching up on some overdue VAT paperwork when Jody walked in, carrying two cups of Costa coffee. 'Thought you might be ready for a java jolt,' she said.

They kissed, then Marcus eased off the lid of the cup she handed him and sniffed the warm dark liquid. 'This is a pleasant surprise,' he said. 'And not just the coffee.'

'I've given the *New Story* to Shilpa. She can prepare a more readable copy with some fancy scanning software at the National Library, and she'll email it to me this afternoon. Last night I read the original, well, just the first dozen pages or so. I started to get the feeling that ... how can I put this? ... either Charlotte or George Nasmyth had added details of their own. Parts of it are well-accepted historical fact, but other parts ... well, I suppose she does call it a "story".'

'I'm looking forward to reading it myself. I'll be interested to see if any of the tales the Lairds tell nowadays were being told back in the 1830s.'

'Do the Water Lairds talk about a *store of wealth* at Neadreth's sacred grove? And disaster awaiting anyone who finds it?'

'Well, since Charlotte's time, some of the details will have obviously have shifted in the telling. But it's still said that Neadreth promised good fortune.'

'And the *mis*fortune part?'

'That too. Most myths about becoming rich include some serious side-effect.'

'The Midas touch, yeah.'

'And every "three wishes" joke you ever heard.'

At that moment a customer walked through the door of *A Malt O' My Ain*. 'See you later,' Jody said, pecking Marcus on the cheek. 'Enjoy the coffee.'

19
PROJECT MEETING

THE PREMISES BEARING THE SIGN 'Firth TV & Audio' usually hosted gatherings no more than once a month, but a special meeting had been called for a small working group, who sat down around a collapsible white table. At the head of the table was Hendrik Vandenbrouck; to his right sat Isla Younie and the man who called himself Lex Durno, to his left Hugh Leggat and a woman Vandenbrouck introduced as Mariane, whom none of the others had met before. Sitting silently in a corner of the room was a bearded man of about thirty with a resemblance to a young Billy Connolly and the unfriendly mien of a nightclub bouncer. He spoke not a word during the entire session.

Mariane turned out to be Belgian, a former fellow soldier of Vandenbrouck's in the Free Flanders Army. With her ratty brown hair, bad teeth and battle fatigues, Durno hoped this was one woman he would never be instructed to seduce. Probably a lesbian anyway, he concluded on the flimsiest of evidence.

'We will review where we stand on the matter of the Forth Bridge,' Vandenbrouck announced with little preamble. 'Mariane, what are our options?'

She shrugged and pouted. 'Depends how much money you wanna spend.'

'God dammit, Mariane,' Vandenbrouck said, slamming a fist on the table. 'We'll raise as much money as we need.' Switching into Flemish, he spoke to her at some length, and Mariane responded in kind. When she finished what she had to say, he announced he was satisfied, then told her she could leave.

The three Scots around the table looked expectantly at Vandenbrouck. He saw the questioning expressions on their faces, but said, 'If you didn't understand, you'll learn in good time. Now, Younie, tell us how much money we have so far.'

Isla brought a notebook out of her shoulder-bag and flicked over a few pages. 'From our friends in Glasgow, £2600 from the whisky job, with another thousand or so still to come ...'

'Whisky job?' Durno queried.

'Yeah,' Isla explained, 'the Glasgow group, er, *acquired* a lorry-load of whisky, unbranded supermarket stuff for Lidl or Aldi or somewhere. They've had lads selling it around the estates. We get a fiver a bottle, the sales team get whatever they can charge over that.'

Hugh Leggat's accounting antennae were twitching. 'You say *we* get £5 a bottle. I take it you mean *Auld Stobby*? How much of the £5 goes into our war-chest?'

'Four,' Isla replied. 'One pound goes into the Glasgow group's kitty.'

'So the £3600 we'll end up with represents 900 bottles – 75 cases, is that right?'

Isla got a little flustered. 'I dunno. The police report said over two hundred cases went missing.'

Vandenbrouck cut in. 'Who's made off with the rest of it?'

'I'll look into it,' Isla said. 'Could be an insurance scam.'

'Bastards,' Vandenbrouck said. 'The distiller or the delivery company on the fucking make. Can't trust anybody. But see you check it out, Younie. If our Glasgow boys are screwing us, it'll be a job for the enforcers.'

Hugh refrained from asking who *they* were, and how they did their 'enforcing'. He had a hunch it would be unpleasant.

Isla continued her income report: £220 collected at a pro-independence rally in Paisley, £250 received so far in response to requests from regular donors. A couple of bigger items. A thousand from a couple in Lanark who'd won a lottery prize,

£8,000 in 'silence money' from a senior bank executive who'd been playing away from home – he'd hardly notice it out of his bonus – and, the highlight, £20,000 from Rachel Herring.

'Twenty thousand, that's good,' Vandenbrouck commented. 'Delivered, or just promised?'

'It's firm,' Isla replied, 'so long as we can arrange a favourable badger survey. Anybody know a crooked wildlife expert?'

It was Durno who spoke. 'As a matter of fact, yes. My Conservative friend Chloe let me into a secret about her candidate – the son of a landowner in the Perthshire glens. He needed a friendly ecological report to overcome local resistance to a wind farm. Chloe found him a consultant who would turn a blind eye to a bird migration path for not a lot of money.'

'You have contact information for him?' Isla asked.

'Believe so,' Durno replied.

'Or if not, can you get the information from Chloe?'

'Er ... no, I don't think I can do that. We're not exactly on speaking terms any more. But I'm sure I kept the guy's name and phone number. I'll let you know.'

'While we're on the subject of your sex life,' Vandenbrouck said to Durno, 'what news of the American?'

Lex had a smug expression on his face. 'Got her in the sack the night before last. Premier Inn, Dundee. Her tab, not mine. She wasn't a pushover, this one. Cost me dinner. But after some wine, couple of after-dinner drinks, she ...'

'Yeah, yeah, we don't need the sweaty details. Just the info. What did you learn about the pipeline?'

'NEPA's determined to take it over the Forth Bridge. They're negotiating with Network Rail.'

'You told me that. You got as much from your first date. What did you get out of her at the Premier Inn?'

'Well, erm ... there's no backup plan. It's the Forth Bridge or nothing.'

'They can always go back to the original route, can't they?'

‘Apparently not. Some major cock-up. That route’s no longer an option. Tried to find out why not, but she couldn’t tell me.’

‘Maybe you should try harder.’

Durno guffawed at what he took to be Vandenbrouck’s *double entendre*, then realised it was unintended. ‘She’s told me all she knows, I’m sure of it. Anyway, it’s a sticky negotiation, this Forth Bridge access. Network Rail sees the pipeline as a way to pay off debt from its restoration work. But for NEPA to settle even a portion of that debt would blow its budget to pieces. And there’s another complication – UNESCO.’

‘*UNESCO*? You’re shitting me. What the hell has UNESCO to do with it?’

‘They want to declare the bridge a World Heritage Site. If they do, it creates a huge additional liability. Network Rail’s been fighting tooth and nail to prevent that from happening. But it probably can’t be stopped now. So the hope will be for NEPA to take on some of the liability.’

‘What about a structural study? Do they know the bridge can take the extra weight of all this water?’

‘Apparently it was colossally over-designed. Everybody was shit scared after the Tay Bridge collapsed in 1879. They didn’t want *this* one falling down too. NEPA’s got engineers doing a study, but they’re pretty confident there’s no structural problem. *Two* pipes will cross the bridge, three metres diameter each, with a heavy-duty pumping station, probably at Dalmeny at the south end. The plan is for the pipes to deliver up to a hundred cubic metres of water per second.’

‘So everything hinges on the deal NEPA’s able to do with Network Rail?’

‘So it seems.’

Hugh had been paying close attention to Durno’s report. ‘Hey, Lex, I’m impressed that you know the year of the Tay Bridge disaster off the top of your head, like that.’

‘Not just the year, the actual date.

On the last sabbath day of 1879
Which will be remembered for a very long time.

I'm from Dundee. I know my McGonagall.'

Visibly annoyed at this diversion from the business in hand, Vandenbrouck turned to Hugh. 'What have *you* found out, Leggat? Anything that calls in question what Durno learned?'

'I've been cultivating Craig Wetherby, chief accountant of NEPA. Fortunately he's a lover of Scotch whisky – or thinks he is and doesn't put water in it. So he loosens up nicely. But on the new route, he's so far stayed tight-lipped. When I told him I'd heard a rumour they were looking to put the aqueduct over the Forth Bridge, he looked at me as if I was stupid. However, I did glean from him that budget sensitivity at NEPA is all about construction cost, not operating cost.'

'And that matters because ...?'

'Because it means if NEPA can do a deal with Network Rail that shoves a big part of the cost into future operation, they might be able to do a Forth Bridge crossing without blowing the construction budget.'

'What kind of deal?'

'Well, for example, NEPA might agree to pay a variable rent. So if UNESCO World Heritage status adds liability in future years, the rent could be increased to reflect that.'

Vandenbrouck began to speak in wrap-up mode. 'Okay, here's where we're at. Younie, good start but we need at least another fifty.'

'Fifty thousand? Jeez, Hendrik ...'

'Never mind the "Jeez, Hendrik". Just do it. You have three weeks. Now Durno, get that consultant's name to Younie, even if you've to put your leg over Chloe again. And if you've got all there is to get out of the redhead, dump her. Can't risk her tracking you down.'

Vandenbrouck turned his attention to Hugh. 'Leggat, I'm expecting much more from your accountant friend. You're not getting him drunk enough. See you get us some specifics on the Forth Bridge by this time next week.'

Hugh saw little point in remonstrating. He had no idea how he would get Craig Wetherby to open up further, but nodded in response to Vandenbrouck's demand. He stood and left the meeting.

A moment or two later, heading for the door, Isla Younie took the opportunity to have a word in Vandenbrouck's ear. 'You're right not to trust Leggat,' she said. 'You never know what he's really thinking. I say we ditch him now.'

'Not yet. But you'll understand why I didn't translate any of what Mariane said while he was in the room.'

'Yeah, I get it. Hopefully Leggat doesn't understand Belgian.'

'Flemish.'

'That's what I meant. So what exactly did Mariane have to say?'

Vandenbrouck motioned her to sit down, then answered her question at some length.

20
THE REAL LEX DURNO

THE EVENING FOLLOWING the rendezvous in Dundee, Delia waited for a call from Lex but it never came. She thought she knew why.

Dinner had been very good; they'd gone on to spend the rest of the night dancing at a club, which was fun, then he'd shared her taxi back to the Premier Inn, some distance from the city centre. He had clearly expected to spend what was left of the night with her, but she wasn't ready to take that step. Setting him back in the cab for a return to his own lodgings, she had noticed that petulant little-boy sulk once again on his face. Her decision was the right one.

He'd pumped her for information about NEPA's Forth Bridge plans – why he should be so concerned about that she couldn't fathom – but, as before, had shown little interest in her personal background. Still, she enjoyed being with him, and would have been open to a follow-up date if he'd called.

Ah well, she had something else to occupy her. Jody had emailed her *A New Story of Edinburgh's Earliest Beginnings*. She read as far as the origin of the Water Lairds before putting down her tablet and turning off the light. Her last conscious thought before sleep overcame her was not of Neadreth or her priesthood, not of Hermutrude or Eithne, but of Lex Durno.

Next morning, a text message came in from one of her work colleagues that a piece of equipment had developed a fatal malfunction. It would be early afternoon before a replacement could arrive from Edinburgh. There was no reason to be at the Loch of Lindores until one o'clock at the earliest.

After breakfast, she drove to St Andrews ('*Want dress,*' she said aloud as she passed the sign at the entry to the town) to walk in its ancient streets and along the beach in front of the famous championship golf course. Suitably exhilarated by the salty wind off the North Sea, she made straight for a shop she'd passed earlier on Market Street. Not a dress shop. 'Two-Wheeler Dealer' was the sign above the door.

Inside, a young woman was arranging a display of biking accessories. 'Can I help you?' she said, looking up from her task.

'I'm thinking of buying a bike, and somebody recommended I speak to Lex Durno. Is he here today?'

'Yes, he's in the back. Let me get him for you.'

The man who emerged and introduced himself as Lex Durno was not an athletic young man with good teeth and curly fair hair, but a fifty-something bald man with heavy-rimmed glasses and decidedly irregular dentition. 'Somebody gave you my name?' he said.

Somebody gave himself your name. 'Mm ... yes. I'm looking for a bicycle that I can use for getting around town. But I'm not quite ready to buy.'

'No problem,' the real Lex Durno assured her.

Delia took her mobile out of her pocket and looked at the screen, pretending she'd just received a text message. 'Sorry, I have to fly. I'll be back later.'

Outside, she called the other Lex's number, ready to vent, but the display on her screen said 'number not in use'. She'd been well and truly had. On the drive to Lindores she began to connect up his misappropriation of another man's identity with his consuming interest in NEPA's plans. It felt like industrial espionage, but on whose behalf?

Network Rail, to give it some kind of hidden advantage in the upcoming negotiation?

WestWater, NEPA's Glasgow-based twin and notional competitor?

Some other corporate entity developing an alternative option for solving south-east England's water deficit?

Whoever it was, the plan to carry twin pipelines across the Forth Bridge would pretty soon become public knowledge anyway. If the shit hit the fan it would be time enough then to come clean. She allowed herself a wry chuckle at the mixed metaphor as she approached the Loch of Lindores.

⬠

The *Auld Stobby* operative who went by the name of Lex Durno was nervous. Vandenbrouck and Isla Younie were talking quietly together after the meeting broke up; he was excluded from the conversation. He hadn't been given any significant task, other than to get the crooked wildlife consultant's contact information to Isla.

If he could have admitted it to himself, he was disgusted at his failure to get Delia into bed and his need to lie about it at the meeting. Should it ever come out that he hadn't made the conquest he'd boasted about, it would do his reputation no end of harm. He removed and destroyed the sim card from the pay-as-you-go phone he had used to contact Delia, then, on his regular mobile (the one registered in his real name, Paul Bissett) called the mother of his children in Dundee to let her know to expect him for supper.

21
AEBBE

BRITONS WERE STILL numerically dominant in the northern reaches of Oswald's Northumbria, and his imposition of the new faith, which they already embraced, helped integrate them into the cultural life of the kingdom. However, adoption of Christianity by the Angles of Lothian was not completed without some resistance.

A tale of that time illuminates the hesitant progress of conversion of the 'pagan' Angles. It concerns a sister of Oswald who, like him, grew up in exile among the Scots of Dalriada and adopted their uncompromising Christian faith. Her name was Aebbe or Ebba.

The Water Lairds' version of her story is generally consistent with her life as chronicled by the 8th-century historian Bede, but adds a significant new dimension. I have been 'protected' from some of its more bawdy details, but I understand that, as told within the confines of the Lairds' meeting-place, the story has salacious elements that could not be divined from Bede's writings.

Jody and Marcus were reading the *New Story* together on opposite sides of her kitchen table, she on a printed copy and he on his laptop. Shilpa's scanning technique had greatly improved the manuscript's readability.

'Is this true?' Jody asked. 'Do the Water Lairds still tell the story of this Aebbe, and does it still have naughty bits?'

'Yes, and yes,' he replied.

'Okay, Marcus, you're under orders to fill in the "bawdy details" that Charlotte either didn't know or couldn't bring herself to write down.' She ran a bare foot up the inside of his trouser-leg.

'I certainly will, but don't be disappointed if what passed for "bawdy" in the 1830s seems quite tame today.'

In 633 Aebbe and her brothers returned from exile. Despite her upbringing, she was content to revert to the ancient Anglian religion promoted by Eanfrith, and may have especially liked its emphasis on the goddess Neadreth. But its renaissance was brief. The following year, when Oswald established himself as king of Northumbria, she was obliged to follow his lead and once again commit totally to the Christian faith.

Her first major act to prove her sincerity was to found a monastery on Dere Street south of Hadrian's wall. The location she chose was a long-abandoned Roman fort called Vindomora, within the confines of which her monastic buildings were erected. The place was later renamed Ebchester in her honour; the village of that name still has a church dedicated to 'St Ebba'.

Later, Aebbe convinced the king that his people (by which she meant specifically the Angles) in the more northern parts of his realm had greater need of Christian example. She proposed establishing, beyond the Tweed, a place of contemplative piety and forbearance from worldly pleasures.

King Oswald granted his sister a charter to do just that. This time she selected not a location on Dere Street with Roman connections, but a hilltop site off the beaten track, on the bluff North Sea coast. It was a place formerly associated with the patriarch Coel of the Britons: Coldingham.

The abbey she founded there was a double monastery – one housing men and women of religion in separate buildings. Oswald expressed concern that such an arrangement would not be conducive to the celibacy required of those dwelling there. However, Aebbe convinced him that testing the chastity of monks and nuns living in close proximity would illuminate their path to true Christian piety.

So it was that, around 640, a princess of the ruling Northumbrian dynasty became abbess of Coldingham. At first she governed her double monastery strictly by the book: monks and nuns could be out in the grounds only at separate, prescribed times to avoid any risk of them meeting or even seeing one another. To enhance her authority she spun a tale of her own rejection of earthly romance, a tale that survives to this day as 'evidence' of a miracle qualifying her for sainthood.

(The tale went that she was courted by Aidan, a prince of Dalriada. She refused him, professing her love of God alone, but he persisted until, by the power of prayer, she made the tide around the abbey hill remain high for three days, protecting her from his attentions.)

Having, with Aebbe's aid, christianised the Lothian Angles, the increasingly arrogant Oswald turned his attention to a bigger challenge: the still 'pagan' Angles of Mercia, whom he regarded as a tributary people. In 642 he led an army into the Mercian heartland. On this occasion the God he trusted to bring victory failed him; he was killed and his body cut into pieces for display at the site of his death. His brother Oswy was waiting in the wings to become king of Northumbria.

Aebbe seems to have regarded the succession of Oswy as an opportunity to relax the firmness with which she ruled her abbey. Her charges, both men and women, were clearly missing the gaiety, feasting and drinking that had accompanied the now forbidden worship of Neadreth. Their hair-shirt existence in the clammy cells of Coldingham needed at least an occasional respite – a time when they could dress up in stylish clothes and enjoy the company of their neighbours – that is to say, the opposite sex.

That Aebbe allowed this to happen is put down, in the 'official' record, to ignorance that it was going on or an inability to enforce discipline despite her own piety; but as the Water Lairds tell her story, she deliberately turned a blind eye and may even have participated in the fun. Whatever her role, such festivities became more and more frequent; life in her Coldingham monastery was now far from monastic.

'One of our oldest members, a retired school inspector, tells stories of the "far from monastic" life of the abbey,' Marcus said.

Jody raised her eyes from Charlotte's manuscript and gave him a look that said, *I'm listening*.

'Supposedly the monastery took the form of individual beehive-like cells scattered in two walled enclosures, one for the monks and one for the nuns. There may also have been a refectory and a chapel that served both sexes, though not at the same time. Once a week, a particular hour was set aside for self-flagellation as an act of atonement, to take place in the privacy of each cell. When, with Aebbe's active encouragement and participation, it became habitual for men to invite women into their cells, or vice versa, what could be more natural than to time such visits to coincide with "whipping time"? And how better to disguise the sounds of lovemaking than as yowls and moans from the laying on of birch or hazel rods?'

'A 7th-century *Fifty Shades of Grey*,' Jody observed.

'Yes, but without 21st-century birth control, in a place where pregnancy or babies would be a dead give-away. Well, Aebbe had a solution for that, too. As a charitable act, the monastery began taking in orphans, especially the infants of mothers who died in childbirth. Any wailing newborn was easily explained away; even a nun's obvious pregnancy could be justified as self-sacrifice: *somebody* had to wet-nurse those orphan babies. And on more than one occasion Aebbe herself was that somebody.'

By and by, a young Anglian monk by the name of Cuthbert came to stay at Coldingham. (In later life he was bishop of Lindisfarne and is now revered as the patron saint of Northumbria and founder of St Cuthbert's church and parish in Edinburgh).

Ascetic and hermitical, he could not adapt to the laxity of Aebbe's monastery. To quell any rising passion, he made a habit of going down to the sea at night where he would stand in the cold chest-deep surf, all the while singing and praying aloud. For this he was deemed eligible for sainthood.

In 670 Oswy died and his son Ecgfrith came to the throne with Aethelthryth or Audrey, a princess of East Anglia, as his queen. Throughout their marriage she had resolutely resisted consummation, while Ecgfrith took his pleasure elsewhere. Upon becoming king, he insisted that she become a proper wife to him and give him a child and heir, a demand she continued to reject.

At some personal risk, Aebbe intervened and welcomed Audrey into her monastery as a nun. It is not recorded how the queen reacted to Aebbe's flexible view of the nun's vow of chastity, but she was no doubt grateful for her place of refuge.

The king sent men to Coldingham to try to extract his reluctant queen by force, but they were unsuccessful – according to myth because Aebbe performed her trick with the tide again. Ecgfrith gave up the chase, had his union with Audrey annulled, and married another. Eventually it was safe for Audrey to leave the monastery and return to land she owned at Ely in East Anglia, where she is credited with founding the cathedral.

Sooner or later, Aebbe's chickens were bound to come home to roost. Ecgfrith heard rumours that not all was as it should be at her monastery. His half-brother Aldfrith had a close friendship with Eunan, abbot of Iona, and a plan was laid for him to visit Coldingham.

There Eunan uncovered the depravity that had been going on for years, yet was convinced that Aebbe herself was blameless, merely an incompetent administrator. He took no action against her, but, according to legend, prophesied destruction for the monastery after Aebbe's death.

In 683, having been abbess of Coldingham for over forty years, Aebbe died; within months of her death the entire monastery was consumed by fire and was never rebuilt. The promontory on which it stood is still known as St Abb's Head. A fishing village established nearby in the 18th century has been named St Abbs – the name of Aebbe lived much longer than the monastery she founded.

'Hi, it's Delia,' the voice said on Jody's mobile. 'I've been reading about the abbess of Coldingham.'

'Amazing! So have Marcus and I, just in the last few minutes! And Marcus added a few juicy details that Charlotte left out from the Water Lairds' story.'

'Really? What struck me was the reference to destruction of the monastery or abbey.'

'As prophesied by the abbot of Iona. What about it?'

'In her *Memoir* Charlotte makes a point of mentioning Scott's novel *The Antiquary*. Scott borrowed a tale of buried treasure he heard from Barbara Nasmyth, Charlotte's mother, and used it as a plot device.'

'I'm not getting the connection.'

'I read a summary of *The Antiquary* on the web. Haven't had time to read the full novel yet, but the buried treasure is under a tombstone in a ruined abbey.'

'So you think Charlotte wants us to look in the ruins at Coldingham?'

'I dunno. I just think it's odd that she would write at such length about Aebbe, who wasn't from Edinburgh, in a place that's not particularly near Edinburgh, in her *New Story of Edinburgh's Earliest Beginnings*. Unless she had a good reason for it.'

'Maybe she just liked a good yarn,' Jody suggested.

'I suppose. By the way, did you notice another reference to the number five?'

'What, in the Aebbe story?'

'No, earlier. The Angles believed the northern constellation Cassiopeia was a heavenly manifestation of Neadreth.'

'So?'

'There are five bright stars in Cassiopeia. They form a W-shape.'

22
GROUND DISTURBANCE

THE WILDLIFE CONSULTANT WAS a thin, dishevelled man with a straggly goatee, dressed in an anorak and corduroy trousers worn smooth at the knees. He carried a tape measure, a notebook and a pointed stick.

'Have you ever seen badgers on this property?' he asked.

'No, never,' Victor lied.

'In that case, this will be a formality. I'll poke around with my stick and tell you if I find anything. Doesn't look like badger territory to me.'

Victor retired to his recently replaced 'office' while the caller went about his business. After ten minutes, there was a knock on the door of the grey OOCL container. 'There's a sett over there by the base of the cliff,' the consultant announced. 'But it's been abandoned. And there's evidence of ground disturbance, which might have scared the critters off. In any case you're all clear – I won't be mentioning these observations in my report. Have you an email address for the report and my invoice?'

'Invoice?' Victor queried. 'I thought this had all been arranged by my mother. Isn't the job fully paid up?'

'Without getting into details, Mr Herring, your mother paid a finder's fee. To ensure everything's above board, it's best if we create a proper record of you paying the normal industry rate for this survey. I'm sure you understand.'

'I understand you're trying to con us into paying twice, you weaselly fucker.'

'So I assume you don't need my report? Fine. If you change your mind, call me.' He handed Victor his card. 'I'll be off, then.'

'Send the report and your goddamned invoice. I'll discuss it with my mother.' Victor realised as his temper cooled that in fact it wouldn't do to lack a proper paper trail showing billing of the survey to the applicant for planning approval. And, though it still galled him that the £20,000 'finder's fee' his mother had paid wouldn't cover the cost of the stupid report, that fee would also buy *Auld Stobby*'s help in pushing the casino resort through planning. So, back to business. Time to get Cammy Lewis back here to get on with the job of eradicating those Roman remains, or whatever the hell they were.

Victor stepped outside to light a cigarette. Looking down the track leading to the site, he saw two figures in high-vis jackets approaching. They stopped to talk briefly with the consultant, then continued walking up the slope.

Shit – police! He stubbed out his cigarette, returned to his desk inside the container and waited for the inevitable knock.

The two officers introduced themselves, presenting their badges. PCs Peter Crawford and Shona Kilmartin.

'I'm Victor Herring. How can I help you today?'

PC Kilmartin did most of the speaking while Crawford nosed around the inside of the container. 'Just routine, Mr Herring,' she said. 'We've a missing person on our books and we're checking the area in case anyone might have seen him.' She showed Victor a photo that looked like it had come from a driver's licence.

'Doesn't look familiar.'

'Take another look. A groundskeeper at the golf club down there said he recognised him. He'd come with a metal detector, to do some prospecting – you know, treasure hunting, like. It would have been about six weeks ago. Sure you don't remember this man?'

'Yeah, I'm sure.'

'He'd asked the groundskeeper about this piece of land – what is it, a building site? – and was told it wasn't part of golf club property. Could our missing man have been up here with his metal detector, say between the 5th and 25th of May?'

'It's possible, I suppose. But I wasn't up here all that often in May. I would certainly remember if I'd seen him.'

PC Crawford was rooting about at the back of the container. 'I noticed you'd been cutting some brush and tree branches out there, Mr Herring,' he said. 'Used a chainsaw for that, did you?'

'Er ... yes.'

'The chainsaw here, is it?' PC Kilmartin asked.

Victor was thinking quickly. 'No, it's in my garage at home. A leylandii hedge is getting out of hand and I've been intending to cut it back.'

'I see. And home would be where?' She wrote down Victor's address as he gave it. 'Now back to our missing person. If he'd come while you weren't here, how would he have got in through your security fence?'

'He wouldn't. The fence has only been up a couple of weeks.'

'So before that, he would have easily gained access?'

'I suppose.'

PC Crawford spoke up. 'D'you think he found anything?'

'How would *I* know?'

'I saw some ground disturbance over by the gorse bushes, where there's that kind of inturn in the cliff face. Might he have been digging there?'

Victor was uneasy about police interest in the excavations that had been going on at the site. But if he stonewalled, they might think he was hiding something – like Bowman's head, for example. 'So many holes have been made – you know, for soil cores, drainage tests, all the crap planning needs to give you approval to build – it would be hard to tell if anyone else had done a spot of digging.'

The two officers looked at one another, then PC Kilmartin said, 'Thank you for your help, Mr Herring. If we need to see the chainsaw in your garage, what's the best number to call?'

Victor gave her his mobile number, then asked, 'Why are you so interested in my chainsaw?'

The policewoman shrugged. 'No reason. Chances are we won't be bothering you again.'

Victor walked the two officers to the gate in the security fence. As he watched them head off down the track he rang Cammy Lewis. 'I need you here tonight,' he told him.

⬠

The Acting Director of Planning was on the phone to James Swift's office. 'Just a courtesy call, Councillor. The Herring application, you know, the big ugly house? We've received and reviewed the badger report. Looks clean. So your committee can finalise approval at today's meeting.'

'Great stuff, Donald, thank you. With her house approved, Mrs Herring will be ready to commit fully to her business scheme by the airport. Scotland's biggest casino development is primed for take-off.'

23
LEGACY OF GREATNESS

King Ecgfrith gathered his nobles in his Edinburgh stronghold. It was 671, just one year into his reign, with Northumbria at the height of her power. Putting behind him the humiliation of having a wife who would not submit to his marital demands, he was determined to build for himself a legacy as the greatest ruler the island of Britain had ever seen. Greater even than the famous King Coel, or the already legendary Arthur.

The assembled men had eaten heartily of the finest salmon from the Tweed, wild boar from Jed Forest and venison from the nearby Pentland Hills, yet the table still groaned under the weight of uneaten food. Ale brewed from Lothian barley by monks at Tyninghame was brought in by the barrel and every man's tankard was kept filled. 'My faithful knights,' the king announced, 'I have brought you together in my castle on the rock to seek your wise counsel. How should I enlarge my kingdom?'

The nobles had not reached or maintained their position of influence at the Northumbrian court without learning to read their ruler's mind. There was a reason he had gathered them in his northern outpost, they supposed. He must be thinking of taking on the Britons of Strathclyde or the Scots of Dalriada, to rebuild the Old North of the powerful Coel. Only this time it would be an <u>Anglian</u> empire.

'Well,' the king said, 'I'm waiting. You've eaten my meat, drunk my ale, now I want to hear your boldest thoughts.'

Nobody was keen to be the first to speak, but eventually one noble broke the silence. 'The Scots, my lord. They are Christian, like us – indeed, they made us Christian – and they gave refuge to your brave father Oswy. Your brother Aldfrith still enjoys their trust and affection.'

'Your point, sir?' the king interjected.

'Only, my lord, that a union with the Scots would create dominion from one side of our island to the other. From the sea crossed by our ancestors to the western ocean. That would be something to behold.'

'A union? You want me to sit down with the king of Dalriada and agree to some kind of shared power? You have drunk too much of my fine ale. Who has a better idea?'

Another noble spoke up. 'My lord, your father of blessed memory acquired, and bequeathed to you, the Cumbric kingdom of Rheged through his marriage to the princess Rhiannon ...'

'Rhianmel,' Ecgfrith corrected him.

'Rhianmel, yes, of course. And her homeland is now firmly within your realm. North of Rheged, to the west of Lothian, lies another Cumbric kingdom: Strathclyde, ruled from Dun Britan, a castle on a rock just like Edinburgh.

'And you would have me send an army to take this castle and its petty kingdom?'

'Petty it is indeed, my lord, but the Scots of Dalriada covet Dun Britan; if they won it they would control the rich lands of Kyle and would threaten us on our western flank.'

Ecgfrith pondered a moment. This idea made more sense, but still did not ensure a legacy of greatness. Strathclyde, including Dun Britan *(Dumbarton) and Kyle, would indeed be a worthy addition to the Northumbrian kingdom, but failed to stir the blood. If none of his idiot nobles could come up with the right answer, he would just have to voice it himself.*

'I will not seek first to absorb the Scots of Dalriada into my realm, nor yet the Britons of Strathclyde. I raise my eyes rather to the north.'

They looked around at each other in disbelief. The Picts? Surely not. Christ be praised, even the armies of Rome failed to conquer the Picts. They are a savage race, their land is vast and mostly worthless, yet our king would march an army against them. How to talk him out of this foolish notion?

'To the north, my lord?' one said. 'In truth, the name of Ecgfrith would forever be remembered if some part of the Pictish kingdom of Alba were ceded to Northumbria. Perhaps the territory of Manaw, which once Gododdin *ruled but is now part of Alba again.'*

'Come, look out from our battlements,' the king said. 'That land across the shimmering firth is the Pictish province of Fib.' (It is now known as Fife.) 'Beyond it is another great firth, then begins the land of mountains the Romans called Mons Graupius. *We will take Fib first, then proceed to the Pictish heartland.'*

In vain they tried to divert Ecgfrith from his grandiose plan. He thundered that the Romans had inflicted a massive defeat on the Picts in the battle of Mons Graupius, *therefore so could he. They reminded him that the victors in that battle lost the war. The Picts were never subdued; Roman attempts to hold the line at the Antonine wall were doomed.*

But Ecgfrith would listen to no such defeatist talk. Where Rome failed, he declared, the Angles of Northumbria would triumph.

Later that same year, Ecgfrith led his troops north-west from Edinburgh, expecting to engage the forces of Alba near its ancient southern capital, Scone. To the Angles' dismay, before they had even crossed the Forth they were ambushed by a much larger Pictish army lying in wait for them. The Picts must have had foreknowledge of Ecgfrith's plan, perhaps from a traitor among his coterie.

Despite the element of surprise and the superiority of numbers in favour of Alba, the Angles fearlessly hacked down their attackers, by day's end, it is said, filling two rivers with their bodies. Victory was Ecgfrith's; no longer did his knights doubt him. Official histories do not identify the location of the battle of Two Rivers, but in the Water Lairds' tale it was fought between the Rivers Avon and Carron, on the flat plain near Abbot's Grange.

Emboldened by this success, Ecgfrith sent armies north, pushing the boundary of Anglian power almost to Aberdeen. One of his farthest fortresses was on a windswept headland high above the North Sea at Dunnottar. It was only a matter of time, he told his courtiers, before the whole of Alba would be subsumed into the great Anglian kingdom of Northumbria.

Two Rivers proved a political as well as military disaster for the Picts. In its aftermath, the provinces of Alba began fighting against one another; the situation was stabilised only when the weak King Drest was deposed by Bridei III.

Meanwhile, Ecgfrith had to divert his attention to attacks on his southern borders. Taking advantage,

Bridei's forces laid siege to Dunnottar in 680 and wrested it out of Anglian hands.

By 685, Ecgfrith was ready to reassert Anglian dominance over Alba. Cuthbert, bishop of Lindisfarne counselled him against further aggression, but the king believed the time was right. He marched his army to Scone, meeting little resistance. Continuing north, he eventually encountered the enemy, and was delighted to see the Picts flee before him.

Unfortunately for Ecgfrith the Pictish retreat was a ruse; he allowed his army to be lured into an ambush at Nechtansmere, where he and most of his troops were slain. All the lands the Angles had gained following the battle of Two Rivers were recovered by the Picts. Ecgfrith's ambition to go down in history as the most famous king in all of Britain was not realised; today few remember his name.

Expecting to remain on the throne for many years (he was 40 when he died at Nechtansmere), Ecgfrith had not planned for his succession. His half-brother Aldfrith, bookish and monastic, was thought unsuitable for the rough-and-tumble life of a Northumbrian king. However, through Cuthbert's persuasiveness, he was elevated to the throne and oversaw a more peaceful chapter in his kingdom's history.

Aldfrith devoted most of his attention to the southern portion of his realm, leaving Lothian in the hands of his lieutenant Beornhith, a capable governor. For the first time since the Gododdin *era, Lothian was effectively ruled from within, a situation enabling it to play an important part in the eventual formation of Scotland as a nation.*

24
TEN-EIGHTEEN

STILL SMARTING FROM HER MISADVENTURE with 'Lex Durno', Delia drove back to Edinburgh. It had rained much of the day but now the evening sun shone between layers of cloud on the western horizon, casting long shadows across the road. Passing the signs for Rosyth (anagram '*Shorty*') she was soon on the southbound carriageway of the Forth Road Bridge. To her left, the massive steel towers, girders and trusses of the original Forth Bridge glowed red in the setting sun.

Strange, she mused, that those majestic old cantilevers were soon to support not just a railway but, alongside or below the tracks, the North East Pipeline Aqueduct carrying up to half a billion cubic metres of water a year. NEPA was highly unpopular among Scots; perhaps, however, the project would gain in prestige through association with that bridge, a much-loved triumph of Scottish engineering.

Had Delia read the true history of the bridge instead of believing local folk-wisdom, she would have known that the Forth Bridge is, in fact, one of the greatest triumphs of 19th-century *English* engineering.

Originally, the firth was to be crossed by a bridge built to the design of the Edinburgh engineer Thomas Bouch, whose one-year-old Tay Bridge had so impressed Queen Victoria in June 1879 that she knighted him.

On 28th December of that same year, Bouch's Tay Bridge collapsed with the loss of 75 lives; inferior design and shoddy construction were blamed for the disaster. His Forth Bridge plans were quickly abandoned and a new contract was given to

Benjamin Baker and John Fowler, two of England's most highly regarded railway engineers. The bridge that has spanned the Firth of Forth from Dalmeny to North Queensferry since 1890 is their masterpiece.

By the time Delia had returned the NEPA van to South Gyle and caught a bus home it was almost nine o'clock. Having called from the bus to order Chinese, she ate it quickly. By 10:30 she was in bed. On her tablet she opened *A New Story* and resumed reading.

> *From the time Aldfrith came to power, the Angles had just a hundred years to enjoy their Northumbrian kingdom before the seeds of its destruction were sown, paradoxically in Denmark, the very land that had nurtured their ancestors.*
>
> *Throughout much of the 8th century, Christian missionaries worked patiently among the peoples of Scandinavia to convert them from their worship of deities such as Tyr, Odin, Thor and Freyja. (By this time, devotion to Neadreth in Denmark seems to have been transferred to a male counterpart, the minor god Nerthur.) Adherents of the old religion resented the new and fought to retain their ancient culture, often destroying the Christians' places of worship in an effort to stem the relentless tide. By the late 700s, their resistance was becoming futile.*
>
> *A magnificent invention, the longship, was their salvation. 'Pagan' Danes, Swedes and Norsemen took to the sea to find new lands where they could worship the old gods in peace. Most places they reached were already inhabited by Christian communities and had to be taken by force. The first step was to destroy their most venerable sites of religious devotion; this disheartened the natives to such an extent that they fled the coastal areas, leaving the land free for*

colonisation by the invaders, Vikings as they were called.

In 793 a fleet of longships arrived at Lindisfarne bearing Viking warriors who killed the monks and captured the abbey's most sacred valuables, including the relics of St Cuthbert. One year later Norsemen launched a similarly destructive raid on Iona, the most holy site of the Scots of Dalriada.

By the middle of the 9th century, the northern and western isles were firmly in Norse hands. Not long afterwards, in 867, most of Northumbria fell to Scandinavian invaders, who established a major military and commercial centre on the site of the ancient Roman city of Eboracum, renaming it Jorvik (York).

The Danelaw, as the Scandinavian-ruled part of England became known, was for over a century more or less constantly at war with the Anglo-Saxon rump. Lothian in the north suffered Viking raids but never came fully under the rule of the Danelaw. Meanwhile, Alba and Dalriada, both weakened by Norse incursions, had formed a united kingdom under Kenneth MacAlpin.

The kings of the now-enlarged Alba took advantage of Viking harassment of Lothian to gradually extend their domain south of the Forth, and around 960 King Indulf seized Edinburgh Castle from the Angles, their stronghold since 638. For the first time the Anglo-Saxon language spoken in Edinburgh came under threat from the Gaelic language of Alba.

In 1005, Malcolm II became king of Alba, his domain extending from the northern Highlands to the Forth valley. Having designs on Lothian and the more southerly lands of Northumbria, he launched an attack in 1006, culminating in the siege of Durham. Eventually his army was repulsed and he withdrew to his Highland fastness to plot a new approach.

His first task was to secure his northern flank. This he did by marrying his daughter to Sigurd the Stout, Earl of Orkney, a Norseman having effective dominion over the northern and western isles and a large part of the northern mainland. Next he forged a strong anti-Viking alliance with Owen the Bald, king of Strathclyde. In 1018 he was ready to launch a renewed attack on the coveted territory of Northumbria.

By this time Anglo-Saxon control of southern Britain had been replaced by Danish rule, following a stunning defeat by the invading forces of Knut the Great. However, Knut had not fully secured dominion over Northumbria and left defence of its northern border to the local Angles under their leader, Uhtred.

In August 1018 a comet appeared in the northern sky, with a tail that spanned one third of the heavens. To the Northumbrians this was an omen of disaster. One month later (according to the Water Lairds, on 18th September), a massive combined army of the kingdoms of Alba and Strathclyde met Uhtred's men at Carham on the river Tweed. Both sides suffered heavy losses – Owen the Bald lost his life in the battle – but the day was won by Malcolm's coalition. In the peace conference that followed, Uhtred surrendered to Malcolm all lands north of the Tweed, including Lothian that for over 200 years had already been semi-independent of its nominal Northumbrian overlords. For what King Knut considered this treasonous act, Uhtred paid with his life.

Upon Owen's death at Carham, Malcolm became overlord of the Strathclyde Britons as well as the

Lothian Angles. For some reason the enlarged kingdom of Alba began to be known as Scotland*, although the Scots of Dalriada were in truth a very minor component.*

It can therefore be said that the battle of Carham on 18th September 1018 marked the day the Scottish nation was born.

Soon, all peoples of the kingdom, whether Pict, Scot, Briton or Angle, began calling themselves Scots*; perhaps in an effort to integrate his diverse subjects, Malcolm took the formal title King of Scots rather than of Scotland, a style that was maintained by his successors until 1707.*

The Picts' own language having been ruthlessly extinguished as part of the process of conversion to Christianity, all of Scotland north of the Forth spoke the Gaelic language of Dalriada. Strathclyde had already been heavily exposed to Gaelic through the efforts of Dalriadan missionaries and its Cumbric language gradually died out after 1018.

But the language of Lothian – Inglis *as it was called, the speech of the Angles, persisted even in Edinburgh where the ruling classes were now Gaelic-speaking. That* Inglis *survived, and eventually became the first language not just of Edinburgh and Lothian but of almost all Scots, is an accident of history; had an 11th-century struggle with a Norwegian earl turned out differently, our native tongue might have been a variant of Old Norse, like modern Icelandic or Faroese.*

Odd, Delia thought, that Scotland, for all its pride in nationhood, was set to ignore its millennium in 2018. Could it be that identifying ten-eighteen as the year of foundation was a fiction of the Water Lairds as relayed by George Nasmyth to his sister Charlotte? Or had the significance of its putative date,

18th September, been tarnished by the defeated independence referendum on that very date in 2014? Was it just that Delia brought an American way of thinking to the question? Her native country had a birthday, 4th July 1776, that was celebrated every year; but there was, she supposed, no particular reason that other countries should have a similar occasion.

If the Scottish nation *was* born in September 1018, how fitting, she thought, that its birth should be presaged by the appearance in the north of a great comet *'with a tail that spanned one third of the heavens'*. An internet search quickly took her to Kronk's *Cometography*, which confirmed that a comet or 'hairy star' was widely observed across Europe and Asia, traversing the northern constellations for about a month from August to early September of that year.

Charlotte's discourse on the languages of early Scotland was in Delia's mind as she settled down to sleep, making her think of Quin back in Chicago. Her romance with the Ph.D. linguist that had blossomed during her previous adventure in Scotland had hit the skids, yet somehow she missed him. It might have been a reaction to the 'Lex Durno' affair. For whatever reason, she dreamed of Quin Johnson that night.

⬠

'Okay, Cammy,' Victor said, 'we need to work as fast as we can. I'll give you a hand. We'll clear the turf, then dig down to those paving stones again. We should be able to lift them – if they're too big we'll smash them, okay? I'm thinking they'll make a nice patio, so we'll stack them over in the corner there, and cover them with the gorse and brambles you cleared.'

Cammy Lewis gave a 'you're the boss' shrug and got down to work. In half an hour the turf was removed from the previously excavated area and both men began shovelling away the loose soil that covered the paving. With pickaxe and shovel they levered up the stones one by one, revealing a bed of clay beneath.

At ten-eighteen by Lewis's watch they were working on a particularly large slab. It was in precisely the spot where Bob Bowman had dug in response to a signal from his metal detector. 'This'll be a bugger to lift,' Victor remarked. 'I'm gonna try to smash it through the middle with the pick.' Ignoring Lewis's protest, he wielded the pickaxe above his head and brought it down as hard as he could on the big slab, which responded with a dull reverberation but remained intact. A few chips flew off the surface where the point of the pickaxe had struck.

'Did you hear that?' Lewis said. 'There's a cavity of some kind. Let's lever up the slab and see what's underneath.' He shone his torch. 'If we get the end of the pick under that edge, we should be able to raise it enough to take a look.'

'First I need a drink,' Victor said, making for his 'office'. 'You want one?'

'Irn Bru, is it? No, I'll pass, thanks.'

While Victor sought refreshment, Cammy Lewis stuck the point of the pickaxe into a space between the big slab and its neighbour, and used all his weight to press down on the handle. The stone moved, enough to wedge the pickaxe below it. In a deft move, Lewis applied just the right leverage to upend it. Illuminating the spot that the slab had been covering, he wasn't quite sure what he was seeing. He got down on his hands and knees for a better look.

What seemed to be the almost rusted-away remains of an iron box were embedded in the clay. As he put his hand on the lid it gave way, revealing its hollow interior. Covered with a layer of rust fragments was an object between thirty and forty centimetres long. He looked up – no sign of Victor. Sitting down taking a breather with a can of his favourite fizzy drink, no doubt. Reaching into the cavity with both hands, Lewis lifted the artefact, finding it surprisingly heavy.

He set it down on a horizontal paving stone and began picking off the rusty deposit with his fingers. Having cleaned off a few square centimetres he shone his torch again. The newly exposed surface was shiny and metallic. The colour was difficult to determine by torchlight, though it was too pale to be bronze. From the absence of oxidation, Lewis had a strong feeling he was looking at solid gold.

That was when he became aware of Victor Herring standing at his shoulder.

25
THORFINN THE MIGHTY

DELIA HAD THE DAY OFF WORK. Jody called in the morning to invite her for a light lunch at her flat, after which they would begin a thorough review of Charlotte Nasmyth's writings.

'Fine,' Delia agreed, 'but I still have a few pages of the *New Story* to read. I'm up to the age of the Vikings and the creation of Scotland by King Malcolm. And I need to do some laundry. I'll be over there by about 12:30.'

'Great. I'm going for a run first. See you then.'

> *Far from Edinburgh, trouble was brewing among the sons of Sigurd, Earl of Orkney. The Norse sagas recount events of the time, but the Water Lairds have a tale, not found in the sagas, of an incursion as far south as Lothian by one of those sons, Thorfinn Sigurdsson.*
>
> *Sigurd's earldom, along with the rest of Norway, became Christian in the reign of King Olav I. How that happened gives a chilling flavour of the times.*
>
> *As a younger man still adhering to the old Nordic religion, Olav had become known for wanton cruelty during his raids throughout the Baltic and all around the British Isles. In 994 he accepted Christian baptism at Canterbury and a year later came to the Norwegian throne. His subjects proving resistant to giving up their ancient gods, Olav embarked on a reign of terror to 'persuade' them to adopt Christian piety like his. All of the skills and inventiveness in the arts of torture and*

killing he had deployed as a pagan plunderer were applied with the newfound zeal of the convert; he took personal pleasure in overseeing the protracted and excruciating death of anyone suspected of adhering to the old religion.

Orkney was remote enough from Olav's centre of power at Trondheim to permit Sigurd and his four older sons to pay little more than lip-service to the new faith. But when his second wife, a daughter of King Malcolm II of Alba, gave him a fifth son, Thorfinn, she raised the boy as a true believer.

In 1014 Sigurd led an army against the king of Ireland, in support of the Norwegian enclave of Dublin. At the battle of Clontarf he was killed, leaving his earldom to be fought over among his sons. Thorfinn was only about five years old, but Malcolm set him up as nominal ruler of Norway's possessions on the mainland, to the north of his own kingdom. Through 'advisers' from his own court, Malcolm thereby gained effective control of the Norse lands of Caithness, Sutherland and Ross. Meanwhile, three of Thorfinn's older half-brothers took joint charge of the northern and western isles, which little interested Malcolm.

In 1028 the Danish king Knut the Great, whose kingdom already embraced England as well as Denmark, conquered Norway and thus became overlord of the earldom of Orkney. By then Thorfinn had grown into a strong young warrior. Knut took a liking to him and supported him in gaining effective control of the entire earldom.

A much bigger opportunity arose for Thorfinn in 1034 when the death of his grandfather Malcolm II resulted in the ascent of Duncan I as King of Scots. Duncan was weak and unpopular among his subjects, and the ambitious Thorfinn believed he could defeat him in battle. If his undoubted military prowess held up, he could secure the whole of Scotland in the name of Knut the Great. Knut would add Scotland to his kingdom, uniting the whole of Britain as one nation for the first time. For a brief period in 1034–35 the destiny of our entire island appeared to be in Scandinavian hands.

As any warrior Norseman would have done, Thorfinn led his army by sea. Sailing south along the east coast, he defeated Scottish forces in several battles. The sagas recount that he reached as far as Fife and won nine Scottish earldoms. According to the Water Lairds, while in Fife in 1035 he sailed into the Firth of Forth, made a landing at Cramond and marched a small army over the hill to a place affording a view of Edinburgh's famous Castle Rock. The sight of it brought a brilliant idea into his head.

It was Yule and the weather was mild and wet. Camp was pitched on a south-facing hillside overlooking an expanse of flat marshy land, watch was posted and Thorfinn and his men settled down for the night. Next morning he called one of his most trusted young lieutenants to his tent.

'Einar,' he announced, 'a great day beckons for the earldom of Orkney. We will lay siege to yon fortress on the rock and, with God on our side, we will make it ours. From there we will rule the whole of Scotland!'

The young man stood open-mouthed, at a loss for words. His master's ambition knew no bounds – and this time he truly had his head in the clouds. 'Are you struck dumb, Einar?' Thorfinn prompted.

'It is in truth a bold plan, my lord,' Einar said. 'But ...'

'But what? You think it can't be done? That Thorfinn the Mighty cannot take and hold that little rock? Have we not captured nine earldoms on our way here from Orkney?'

'My lord, we are less than two hundred men here in Lothian. How are we to lay siege to such a fortress? How are we to resist the two <u>*thousand*</u> *armed men the King of Scots will send to support his garrison?'*

'Behold the reason why I am commander of our army and you my lieutenant. This is no wild adventure I have come up with in a dream. My stratagem for success is to be a secret between us for the moment. The enemy must not suspect what we have in mind, but I need <u>*you*</u> *to know, for a reason that will soon be clear. Are you ready to hear it?'*

Einar still looked incredulous but nodded. 'Yes, my lord.'

'It is little over seventeen years since Malcolm my grandfather brought the Angles of Lothian into his kingdom. He was a brave and just ruler, but his successor Duncan, my cousin, acts like a petty tyrant, taxing the hard-working Angles to pay for his extravagances. There's a good reason we Norsemen call him Hundason *– Son-of-a-Bitch. No doubt the Angles here in Lothian call him something similar, or worse. They would rather have Norsemen in that castle on the rock than Duncan's Gaelic-speaking minions. After all, the Angles are in a way our kinsmen; long ago they came here from Denmark.'*

'So your plan is to enlist local support? To raise an army from among the people of Lothian to help overthrow the Scottish king?'

'Not exactly, though it will be helpful to our cause if we give the Angles reason to like us, not to fear us.

No, our support will come from our glorious monarch Knut. You will sail to Southampton and from there reach his royal palace at Winchester, where you will crave an audience with the king. I will write a letter and put my seal upon it, as your introduction. The letter will not reveal any part of our plan, in case it should fall into the wrong hands. But once at King Knut's court, you will lay out the plan for him. He cannot fail to agree to join with us in the taking of Edinburgh.'

'But, my lord, what exactly is the plan? Why should King Knut commit an army to support us? If he wished to add Lothian to his kingdom, wouldn't he have sent his forces here already?'

Thorfinn drew a long breath, giving himself a moment to finally decide whether he could trust Einar with his strategy. Then he spoke. 'We offer him not just the tiny land of Lothian, but the whole of Scotland. His rule will then extend from the English Channel to the northernmost skerries of Shetland. Together with his dominions in Denmark and Norway, this will give him undisputed command of the entire North Sea.'

'And you, my lord?' Einar put in.

'As grandson of King Malcolm, I will be the rightful King of Scots as well as Earl of Orkney, but in both realms I will be subject to Knut as high king. He will know that I have already conquered most of Scotland – so all that remains is for his army and mine to take Edinburgh. That will secure Lothian; soon afterwards Hundason *will give up what territory he has not already lost, and die like the dog he is.'*

'A brilliant plan, my lord. It will, of course, take a little time. Southampton is far from here and will take weeks to reach, then, if at Winchester the king agrees ...'

'When, not if.'

'When the king agrees, it will be a month or two before an English army is in position to join us in besieging the Castle Rock.'

'I have thought of all that, Einar. You will make first for Jorvik, where you can be assured of a friendly reception. I will give you another letter, this one for Earl Sigurd (his name is the same as my late father's, and his reputation no less distinguished). He governs the north of England for the king, and I will beseech him to grant you safe and speedy passage to the royal court at Winchester. And while you are gone, our time here will not be wasted. We will offer gifts to the Angles, gain their trust and thereby establish reliable supplies of food and other provisions to sustain us during our siege of Edinburgh.'

Without delay, Einar set sail from Cramond with a small crew. A week or so later he entered the Humber estuary, where his boat was intercepted on the first day of 1036 and escorted upstream to Sigurd's palace at Jorvik. Presenting himself humbly to the earl, he handed over his master's letter.

'As an emissary of our kinsman Thorfinn the Mighty,' Sigurd announced, 'you are welcome here in Jorvik. But I cannot offer you safe passage to the royal court. You clearly have not heard: Knut the Great is no more. He died six weeks ago, and only his bones now lie in Winchester.'

Einar was shocked by the news. 'A tragedy for all of England,' he said reverentially. 'My lord the Earl of Orkney will be sad to learn of the king's passing. Who now wears his crown?'

'No one,' was Sigurd's surprising reply. 'Prince Harold, who may not have the blood of Knut in his

veins, has declared himself king but has not been crowned. He has forsaken Christ and prefers hunting to attending church on the sabbath. The true heir is in Denmark, at war with a usurper king of Norway – a bastard child by the name of Magnus. Has the Earl of Orkney sworn allegiance to him?'

'My lord Thorfinn has been campaigning in Scotland these ten months and may know nothing of events in Norway. Certainly this is all news to me.'

'You may partake of our hospitality in Jorvik in the coming days, but you would be well advised to return forthwith to your master, forgetting any idea of travelling to Winchester.'

Einar saw Thorfinn's grand plan unravelling before his eyes. The only hope was that Sigurd, now beholden to no one in Winchester, might be persuaded to send a Northumbrian army north to join Thorfinn's men in laying siege to Edinburgh. But could he, Einar, take the risk of disclosing Thorfinn's strategy for uniting Scotland and England under the English crown? After a moment's thought, he realised he could not. Apart from anything else, there was no English crown at present. England might fragment in the absence of the powerful king that Knut had been. And Thorfinn would not wish to subordinate himself to Sigurd, a mere regional governor.

'I will follow your sage advice,' Einar told Sigurd. The next day he began the voyage back to the Firth of Forth, not looking forward to the reception he would get from Thorfinn on his early return.

Meanwhile, Thorfinn himself received unwelcome intelligence. A rival to King Duncan had emerged in Scotland, a man of greater military prowess who commanded more respect among the Scottish people.

That rival – whose name is nowadays remembered as Macbeth – was already beginning to regain territory that Thorfinn had wrested from Duncan, particularly on the coastal plain by the Moray Firth. If word did not come back soon that English forces would join him in the siege of Edinburgh, Thorfinn would be forced back north to defend his recently conquered earldoms.

So, when Einar returned with the news that Knut was dead, that England was in disarray and would provide no support for the planned siege, Thorfinn the Mighty quietly struck camp and departed Lothian with all his men.

A wooden cross outside a hut that had served as the camp's chapel was the only physical evidence that remained of their sojourn; known as the cross of Thorfinn, it gave its name to the place where it stood – Corstorphine. Edinburgh remained Scottish, and the nation of Scotland, which might have come under the English crown just 18 years after its birth at the battle of Carham, survived to develop its distinctive identity over the centuries that followed.

26
A BEAUTIFUL THING

Cammy Lewis's strange find now stood on Victor Herring's kitchen table. Victor had brought it home at three in the morning, wrapped in a black bin-bag. Though eager to remove the clay adhering to almost every surface, he decided to leave it until next day.

Lewis remained at the site with instructions to replace the soil and turf over the whole excavated area. It would take him at least until sunrise. His noises about declaring the find to the authorities – he was presumably after a cut of its value – had been met with 'Yeah, yeah, we'll talk about it tomorrow.'

It was 11 am when Victor got down to work. He immersed the artefact in lukewarm water in the kitchen sink, which was only just big enough when he set it in diagonally.

Conscious that damage could seriously impact the price a collector might give for whatever kind of thing it would turn out to be, he worked carefully with a variety of small tools. In some places the clay was so impacted that it was impossible to remove; in others it fell away cleanly to reveal the deep yellow colour of antique gold. By noon he could finally see the proper contours of the object.

It was a statuette of a two-wheeled chariot drawn by two animals and driven by a solitary charioteer. Surprisingly the animals were not horses but long-horned oxen; even more curiously the charioteer was a bare-breasted woman.

As he continued the delicate cleaning operation, he saw she had long, flowing hair. Beside her in the chariot were two barrel-shaped objects, each about half her height. And sufficient fine detail of the draught animals had emerged to reveal that they were heifers.

The female symbolism meant nothing to Victor. What did mean something was the weight of the piece (over five kilos on his bathroom scale), and therefore its value as scrap gold. At current prices he estimated it would fetch £160,000. Of course, it might not be *pure* gold. But even if it was one-third base metal, he still had over £100,000 worth in his possession at that moment. Not bad for a night's work! Actually, Lewis had done most of the work, but he was being paid well. He wouldn't be getting a cut of the value of the statuette over and above, oh no. Hell, if he did, he would just gamble it away!

As Victor continued to soak, pick and scrape to remove the last deposits of clay from the gold, he accidentally broke off one of the heifers' horns. Not to worry, if the thing was going to be melted down anyway, what did it matter if it was in pieces? On the other hand, he realised the object's value as an antique might be much greater than its worth as scrap. To avoid any further damage, he decided to stop working on it. He would consult his mother on maximising its value. He placed the statuette back on the kitchen table to dry off on a newspaper.

The video entry system whistled. On the tiny screen Victor saw Cammy Lewis at the lobby door. *Shit! How does he even know where I live?* Picking up, he said, 'What the hell are you doing here?'

'We need to talk. Now. About the gold thing.'

'What's to talk about?'

'I think we need to declare it as – what's it called? – treasure trove. It could be an important find. We'd still be entitled to its value.'

We? The guy's delusional. 'Look, Cammy, it's probably of no historical interest. It's certainly not worth opening up the building site to a bunch of fucking archaeologists. You agreed to keep this whole operation quiet.'

‘Do we continue having this conversation through your entryphone, or do I leave now and go to the police?’

Victor buzzed in the visitor.

Seeing the now gleaming gold statuette on the kitchen table, Lewis picked it up and examined it closely. ‘It’s beautiful,’ he said. ‘Wonder if it’s Roman?’

‘I don’t give a shit what it is,’ Victor said. ‘It’s our secret, as we agreed. And it belongs to my mother, since it was found on her land. She’ll be the one to decide what to do with it.’

‘Well, I hope she’ll do the right thing.’

‘She doesn’t even know about it yet. And frankly, Cammy, it’s none of your goddamned business what she might do or not do.’

‘Actually, it *is* my business. *I* found the thing, and I’m not prepared to be silent. I’m not going to implicate myself in an illegal act.’

‘God, Cammy, just listen to yourself, will you? I gave you this job to get you out of a financial hole of your own making. If you want to go back under a mountain of debt, go ahead and be a “good citizen”. What will your wife and kids think of you then, eh?’

‘I can sort out my own affairs,’ Lewis retorted, knowing full well he absolutely depended on the promised £30,000.

‘Look, let’s not rush into something here. There could be more stuff waiting to be found up there. Why don’t we finish digging up those pavers, check for any more hidey-holes, then decide what’s best? By that time I’ll have talked to my Ma and we’ll know what *she* wants to do.’

Lewis nodded cautiously. ‘Okay,’ he said, ‘I’ll be there at nine tonight to get on with the job.’

As soon as he’d escorted Lewis out of his flat, Victor called his mother.

⬠

Marcus had almost forgotten Hugh Leggat's offer to have his great-aunt show her collection of Scottish paintings. When the call came, it took him a moment to register who 'Kirsty Morton' was. It was arranged that he would visit on Monday at eleven.

Kirsty showed him into her elegant sitting room, which was tastefully if not too comfortably furnished with antique chairs and occasional tables. She left him there for a few minutes while she prepared a cafetière and a plate of assorted biscuits.

'Hugh told me you had an interest in the Nasmyth family,' she said, beckoning him to sit down and pouring him coffee.

'Just a passing interest, really. I read recently somewhere about the Nasmyth daughters, how some of them stuck close to their father's style while others tried to do their own thing.'

'Indeed. If you ask me, some of their work is actually *better* than their father's. But it's still Alexander Nasmyth who commands the high prices at auction. I'm hoping that will change, because I've bought quite a number of the daughters' paintings – and didn't pay too much for them. That one to the left of the fireplace is by Margaret Nasmyth. The one above the davenport is – I believe – by her sister Anne Bennett, though it isn't signed.'

Marcus got up to take a closer look at both paintings. It was exactly as Charlotte had said in her *Memoir*: Margaret's work was bold and unrestrained, impressionistic almost, whereas Anne's stuck close to Victorian convention. 'I don't suppose you have any of Charlotte Nasmyth's landscapes?' he asked.

'I do. Follow me,' Kirsty said, getting to her feet.

In the dining room, all four walls were laden with art. Kirsty first drew Marcus's attention to two landscapes bearing Charlotte's neat signature. One was a scene in Pendle Forest, Lancashire, the other a woodland scene in Essex. 'I especially like this Essex one,' she said. 'The way she renders these old dead trees is inspired, I think. Are you especially attracted to Charlotte's work, Mr Annandale?'

'Er ... not really,' Marcus replied untruthfully. 'It's just that you hear so little about her.'

'Her only problem was her gender. Even now, she's not taken as seriously as if she had been a man. Yet a portrait of Charlotte by William Nicholson is on display in the National Portrait Gallery, in Queen Street. Have you seen it?'

'No, I knew of the portrait but didn't realise it was there. I must go in and look at it. Strange to think she grew up in a house just a few doors away.'

Kirsty was impressed. 'You *do* know your Nasmyth history!'

Marcus's eye alighted on a row of three landscapes above the sideboard. 'Views of Edinburgh, I see. Are those Nasmyths?'

'Attributed. In the opinion of some expert or other they are Nasmyths, but there's no clear provenance. They're unsigned, which is not unusual. I bought them because I like them, and because I love Edinburgh.'

'Which Nasmyth, do you think?'

'Definitely not Alexander. The brush strokes aren't quite disciplined enough. They could be Jane, but my guess is Charlotte. Funny thing is, two of them have the same title. *A Prospect of Edinburgh*. The third, that one in the middle, has no title, but I'm sure it belongs to the same set. As you see, I've hung them as a triptych.'

'Where did you get them?' Marcus asked.

'These two at auction sales and this one at a gallery in Selkirk. Or Peebles.'

'So they weren't a set when you bought them?'

'No. I can't help thinking the artist intended them as a set, but they seem to have gone in different directions. I'm happy to have brought them back together.'

Marcus inspected the three paintings in an effort to identify the viewpoint for each. The middle one was easy – a view looking west, presumably from Arthur's Seat. Centre-stage was the castle and, in a direct line behind it, the south end of

Corstorphine Hill. Of the other two, one seemed to be from the south-west, and he deduced it had been painted on Craiglockhart. The third was from the north. It had to be the view from Inverleith.

The view looking west was painted on a bigger canvas than the other two. Wider but not taller, like a wide-angle photo. With Kirsty's permission he took each painting down to examine the back. The larger one had received a new backing paper at some stage and lacked the dog-eared label confirming *'A Prospect of Edinburgh'* for the other two. Replacing all three on the wall, he took a few photographs of each with his smartphone.

Kirsty showed off her extensive collection of other artists before they returned to the sitting room to finish their now tepid coffee. It was best meantime, he decided, not to tell his hostess that he knew Charlotte Nasmyth had painted *five* landscapes titled *A Prospect of Edinburgh*, nor that he was in possession of some writings by the artist.

Taking his leave, he felt guilty at holding back so much when Kirsty had been so welcoming. 'You know, Mrs Morton,' he said enigmatically, 'though I'm no expert, I think you're absolutely right in thinking your three paintings are by Charlotte rather than Jane Nasmyth. And that they formed a set she intended to be displayed together. I wonder if your set is complete?'

'I don't know,' Kirsty replied, 'but I keep checking the auction catalogues in case there might be more.'

⬠

Isla Younie was in a spot of trouble, still waiting for the £20,000 Rachel Herring had promised. Somehow she had to raise another £50,000 to fund *Auld Stobby*'s Forth Bridge operation. With just three weeks to find the additional money demanded by Hendrik Vandenbrouck, she had no idea where it was going to come from. Little did she imagine when she took out her phone to call Rachel that the problem was about to solve itself.

'I know what you're calling about, Isla,' the voice said on the phone. 'I have to tell you, I'm delighted at the outcome of the badger survey. All so quickly and efficiently organised, thank you.'

Isla was taken aback by Rachel's grateful tone. This was not what she was expecting. 'So you're ready to give us the agreed sum?'

'I have an even better proposition for you.'

The *Auld Stobby* operative was on her guard. 'I'm listening,' she said, cautiously.

'A certain – what should I call it? – *objet d'art* has come into my possession. Well, it's my son who's holding it but it's mine to dispose of as I please. The slight difficulty I have is that I've no papers documenting how I came by it, which rules out selling it through conventional channels. Now if your organisation can take advantage of any *less* conventional channels (if you follow me), maybe you could convert my *objet d'art* to cash for, say, half the proceeds.'

'What kind of thing is this ... this *budgie da*?'

'I'll give you my son's number. Call him and he'll let you see it. It'll be worth your while, I promise you – it should fetch more than £100,000. With luck, *a lot* more. So if we went fifty-fifty, wouldn't that be better than me giving you just £20,000 in cash?'

Yes it would, Isla thought, *if* this isn't some kind of scam. Problem was, she couldn't tell a *budgie da* from a ham sandwich. Even if she saw it, how would she know what it was really worth? Someone else who knew more about such things should go along with her. Someone like Hugh Leggat, the forensic accountant, though she trusted him no further than she could spit. 'Okay,' she said at length. 'I'll give your son a call, take a look at the *budgie da* and get back to you. No promises.'

'Fair enough,' Rachel said. 'When you see it, you'll know it's a good deal. It's a beautiful thing.'

27
FROM MYTH TO HISTORY

THORFINN NEVER BECAME King of Scots. It was Macbeth who toppled Duncan from the throne in 1040. He then wasted little time in regaining the territories lost to Thorfinn during his predecessor's ineffectual reign. Before long the Norseman had been beaten back to Orkney.

The country began to enjoy relative peace, but trouble was brewing in the shape of one of Duncan's sons, in exile in England. The English king, Edward the Confessor, was grooming him to take Macbeth's place. After several years of fighting, Edward's puppet ascended the Scottish throne in 1058 as Malcolm III.

Known as Canmore ('Big-head'), the new king was crowned at Scone like his predecessors. For a time, everything he did was at the English king's bidding. However, this changed when Edward reneged on an agreement that his grandniece Margaret would become Canmore's wife. Incensed at such duplicity, Canmore began paying more attention to his fractious nobles who sought a return to the greater independence from England they had enjoyed in Macbeth's time.

But the popularity he craved from his subjects was slow to materialise. So he did what many national leaders before and since have done in an effort to rally his people: he went to war.

In 1061 he launched a raid across the English border to plunder Lindisfarne Abbey. It was the first of many such incursions, which continued even after the Norman-French invasion under William the Conqueror in 1066 swept away England's last Anglo-Saxon dynasty.

Canmore's constant, often pointless provocation of his English neighbour began a relentless cycle of hostility, of attack and counter-attack, that went on for centuries, denying Scots the peace and prosperity they might otherwise have enjoyed. But for a happy circumstance, this would have been the sum total of the sorry legacy that Malcolm Canmore's 35-year reign bequeathed to his nation.

The happy circumstance that was a boon to Scotland, and most especially to Edinburgh, was a matrimonial one. On the rebound from Edward's breach of promise of the Saxon princess Margaret's hand in marriage, Canmore first married Ingibiorg, the recently bereaved widow of Thorfinn the Mighty. In 1066, following the Norman conquest of England, Margaret and others of her family took refuge in Scotland; and upon Queen Ingibiorg's death in 1070, Canmore was finally able to take Margaret as his second wife.

Queen Margaret had a huge influence on the development of Edinburgh as a focus of cultural and religious activities, leading ultimately to its status as Scotland's capital city.

First, she refused to speak Canmore's Gaelic language, preferring the speech of the ordinary people of Lothian, which was still Inglis, *the forerunner of modern Scots. Though starting to diverge from her own Anglo-Saxon tongue, it was at least intelligible to her.*

Second, her fondness for Edinburgh over Scone and the Highland fortresses enjoyed by the king led to establishment of an Inglis-*speaking royal court on the castle rock.*

Third, in her piety, intellect and cultured demeanour she offered an attractive contrast to her profane and illiterate husband, and it is to Margaret that the first stirrings of Edinburgh as a centre of learning can be traced. The oldest building now standing on the castle rock is a chapel she began building before her death in 1093; it was completed by her son King David I and dedicated to her memory. In 1250 she was canonised as a saint.

Scottish institutions – political, legal, cultural and commercial – began gravitating to Queen Margaret's favourite town from the 12th century forward, though Edinburgh's status as Scotland's capital was not truly cemented until 25th March 1437, more than three centuries after her death. It was on that date that her descendant King James II was crowned, not at Scone, but in Holyrood Abbey at the east end of the Royal Mile leading down from Edinburgh Castle.

Such was the influence of Edinburgh by then that all of Scotland, except its remotest Highland glens and western isles, had adopted the tongue of the Angles as its first language, which began to be called Scottis *or Scots – as it is to this day. Gaelic, never the speech of the people of Edinburgh, retreated to the margins whence it came.*

This 'New Story' of Edinburgh's earliest beginnings is therefore not a tale of Celtic romance, nor is it solely a catalogue of kings and their military triumphs and defeats. As recounted by the Water Lairds, it is a story principally of the Anglian incomers, and of their culture, religion and language, a story in which women play as big a part as men. The influence of those women – from myth to history, from Neadreth the goddess to Margaret the queen and saint – can still be felt in the streets of Edinburgh today.

'Today' in Charlotte Nasmyth's *New Story* was 1836. Was it still true in the 21st century, Delia wondered, that Edinburgh wore its Anglian heritage, in particular the part played by women in its earliest beginnings, on its sleeve? Was it even true then, or had it been a fiction propagated by the Water Lairds or possibly invented by Charlotte herself?

That, however, was a side-issue. Now that Delia had reached the end of the *New Story*, she was ready to join Jody in dissecting the artist's 19th-century writings. What had Charlotte's real motivation been for writing the *New Story*? Should it be taken at face value, as a slightly idiosyncratic history of Edinburgh up to the 11th century? Or did it have some hidden meaning – clues, perhaps, to the location of Neadreth's sacred grove and its legendary *store of wealth*?

Similarly, was her *Memoir* just a way of setting straight the omissions, deceptions and lies of her brother's autobiography, or was it another document to be mined for clues? By the time Delia arrived at Jody's door her mind was still racing.

After lunch the two of them began their analysis. Delia placed great emphasis on the number 5, a recurring feature of Charlotte's writings, starting with David Hume's belvedere – the half-dodecahedron with its five-sided windows. 'Y'know, Charlotte wasn't the last artist to take an interest in the dodecahedron.'

'Who else?' Jody felt obliged to ask.

'Salvador Dali. In his rendering of the Last Supper, he framed the scene in pentagons, forming part of a regular dodecahedron, just like Hume's belvedere. I saw the painting once in Philadelphia.'

Returning to Charlotte's apparent fixation on the number 5, Delia began rattling off some more examples. The *quinta essentia*, that 'fifth element' Charlotte strove for in her art. The five stars of the constellation Cassiopeia. Jane Austen's *Emma*, presented to Charlotte by her father.

'What has *Emma* to do with 5?' Jody asked. 'Just that it begins with the fifth letter of the alphabet?'

'Well, that too, I suppose. But I checked it out: it's a book with 55 chapters. Then there's the golden ratio in Edinburgh's New Town architecture and street layout, with the number 5 embedded in it.'

Delia wrote down the formula and showed it to Jody:

$$1{\cdot}618 = {\cdot}5 \times \sqrt{5} + {\cdot}5$$

'I can see,' Jody said, 'you're saving the best for last. The five hills around Edinburgh where Charlotte painted her suite of five landscapes.'

'Exactly. Any one of those could be the location of Neadreth's grove.'

'But there are other locations, too, aren't there? Duddingston Loch, for example, that figures in Raeburn's painting of *The Skating Minister*. The Roman forts at Carriden, Cramond and Inveresk – the grove was supposedly on the site of a Roman bathing place. Coldingham, where Aebbe had her monastery.'

'Or pleasure-palace,' Delia put in. 'And Corstorphine, which gets several mentions. One of Charlotte's five hills, also the only one of her father's landscapes she specifically refers to, and the site of the camp set up by Thorfinn the Mighty, who gave the place its name.'

At this point Marcus entered, fresh from his visit to Kirsty Morton's. Jody outlined what she and Delia had discussed; on the subject of the suite of five *Prospect of Edinburgh* paintings, he stunned them by saying he had just viewed three of these at Kirsty's. He showed them the photos he had taken on his mobile phone.

'Does she know who has the other two?' Delia asked him.

'No, she doesn't even know that there *are* more, though she keeps looking. She said she'd let me know if she tracks down any others.'

'Those paintings are our best lead,' Delia said confidently.

'Actually,' Marcus said, 'I think there's an even better lead.' He leafed through a copy of the *New Story* until he found the paragraph he was looking for, then read from it.

> *During this time the Romans used certain locations as bathing places, dedicated to their gods. One such location was the shady hazel grove later rediscovered by the Angles and consecrated in the name of their goddess Neadreth, believing the remains of Roman construction at the site to be the work of her mystical priesthood.*

'The grove was given Neadreth's name,' he said. 'I think it still bears her name.'

'You mean you know a place called Neadreth?' Jody asked.

'Well, of course it's changed a bit over the centuries. Now it's Niddry with a "y" or Niddrie with an "i-e". It's an obvious modification of Neadreth.'

'Where is this Niddry?' Delia wanted to know.

'There are at least three places with that name,' Marcus said, 'that is, not counting Niddry Street in the Old Town. One's in Midlothian, now within Edinburgh's city boundary, on the east side towards Musselburgh. It's sometimes called Niddrie Marischal to avoid confusion with the other Niddries. In East Lothian there's the town of Longniddry. And in West Lothian you'll find Niddry Castle.'

28
THE GOLDSMITH

THE CONVERSATION ON THE WAY to Victor Herring's flat was strained; Hugh had developed a mild antipathy to Isla, who in turn made it obvious she mistrusted him. Attempting to open discussion of the recent meeting at Firth TV & Audio, he asked, 'Who was the guy with the beard who sat in the corner and never opened his mouth?'

'His name's Rory. He's an enforcer.'

'Sounds ominous.'

'Long as we all follow instructions, we've nothing to fear.'

'Instructions? Like, you've to raise more money, and I've to get more NEPA secrets out of Craig Wetherby?'

'Those are just the preliminaries. When we get down to business, when we're *using* the money I raise and whatever you learn from Wetherby, that's when Rory's job kicks in.'

'What kind of business are we talking about here? I saw you stayed behind to talk to Hendrik after the meeting.'

'Look, Hugh, you'll be told everything you need to know once it's decided what your role will be. *If* you have a role.'

'But I still don't understand why we need an enforcer. You're committed, I'm committed, to *Auld Stobby*'s agenda. That should be enough, shouldn't it?'

Isla gave a dry laugh. 'You've a lot to learn, haven't you? First rule, don't trust *nobody*. You shouldn't trust me, I sure as hell don't trust you. Step an inch out of line, Mister Hugh Leggat, and Rory will have a suitable punishment for you, maybe involving a baseball bat. So, y'see, we don't need *trust* between us. Just the knowledge that Rory's very good at what he does.'

Victor was guarded when he admitted them to his flat. To Isla the statuette on the kitchen table resembled objects she'd seen in antique dealers' windows on Causewayside or Dundas Street. If that was what a *budgie da* looked like, she wasn't particularly impressed.

Hugh, on the other hand, saw right away that it was no run-of-the-mill antique. 'Where did you come by this?' he asked.

'Shit, Hugh,' Isla butted in before their host could speak, 'we're not here to question where it came from, okay?'

'Of course. Just couldn't believe my eyes.' He lifted the statuette with both hands, noticing how much heavier it was than it looked. As heavy as lead, in fact. 'Feels like solid gold to me.'

'Weighed it on my bathroom scale last night,' Victor said. 'It's between five and six kilos. Say 5·5. Melted down, it's worth well over £100,000.'

'Mr Herring's right,' Hugh said to Isla. 'But this is an extremely rare piece, I think. Its value to a museum or collector could be much greater. Millions, maybe.'

Victor's eyes seemed to light up at the word *millions*. 'Okay, put a value on it.'

'I can't,' Hugh replied, 'but I know who can. There's a goldsmith over on ...'

'It's going to no fucking goldsmith,' Victor interrupted. 'He'll start asking questions. No, no, the deal is, we agree a value, you pay us half of that and take it away. And you *never* mention my name or my mother's when you dispose of it.'

'The guy I work with is very discreet,' Hugh said. 'See, my day job is forensic accountancy. I often have jewellery retrieved from criminal suspects and need a valuation. He knows I can't disclose how I came by it; he just tells me what it's worth on the bullion, estate jewellery or art market, no questions asked.'

Giving Victor a little time to reconsider, Hugh began examining the statuette closely. The female charioteer was beautifully rendered, as were the two heifers, apart from one broken horn. The chariot was exquisitely detailed, with five stars engraved on each side in a W-pattern. 'Pity about the missing horn,' he said. 'Otherwise it's in almost perfect condition.'

'I have the horn,' Victor said. 'It broke off when I was cleaning it.'

'Tell you what,' Hugh suggested, 'let me take just the horn to my goldsmith. From it, he'll be able to determine the purity of the gold, then we can agree a value based on the weight of the statuette. We should be able to get back to you in a week or so.'

'Will you have the money then?'

It was Isla's turn to speak. 'We can't give you your fifty percent until we've raised the cash on it ourselves. I made that clear to your mother on the phone. But we'll be disposing of it pretty damn quick. You won't have long to wait.'

Victor seemed comfortable with the arrangement and handed over the broken horn, a piece about the length of a thumbnail.

⬠

A few days later, Hugh was in the familiar cramped premises of Norris Trimble in the Old Town. Trimble had operated a goldsmith's business from this tiny shop for almost forty years, making most of his money from jewellery repairs and alterations and from insurance appraisals.

'Well, this is an interesting sample, and no mistake,' Trimble began. 'You know I never ask where you get your stuff, but I must admit I'm curious.'

'Can't tell you, Mr Trimble, sorry.'

'Worth a try. What you have is the purest gold I've seen in a long time. It's 23·7 carats – about 98·5 percent. Last time I saw gold this pure was in an *aureus* – a Roman coin from the reign of Septimius Severus, circa 200 AD. Those coins turn up from time to time – Severus was quite active in Scotland. He tried to re-garrison the Antonine Wall, years after it had been abandoned.'

'So you think the artefact is 3rd century Roman?'

'I didn't say that. More likely it's later, made from melted-down Severus *aurei*. How big is the whole piece?'

'About five and a half kilos.'

Trimble whistled. 'At $1,600 an ounce, that's nearly $300,000 worth of bullion.'

'That's what I figured, Mr Trimble. Send me your invoice as usual.'

⬠

For their next visit to Victor Herring's flat, Hugh and Isla equipped themselves with a postal scale. Before setting the gold statuette on the scale, Hugh asked Victor if he'd any unopened food packages in his pantry.

Victor's response was 'What the fuck are you talking about? Food packages?'

'Just want you to see that the scale's accurate.'

'Oh.' Victor rummaged in one of his kitchen cabinets and produced an unopened bag of sugar. On the scale it was a smidgen over one kilo, including the packaging.

Carefully, Hugh placed the statuette on the scale, together with the small fragment he'd had tested by the goldsmith. 'You weren't far out,' he told Victor. 'Exactly 5,460 grams.' He produced a calculator. 'Purity of this gold is 98·5 percent, so you have ...' (tap, tap, tap) '... 5,378 grams of pure gold. Divide by 31·1, that's ...' (tap, tap) '... 173 troy ounces. Today's gold price is 1,618 dollars an ounce, so as bullion your statuette is worth ...' (tap, tap, tap) '... call it 280,000 dollars. In pounds, 175,000, give or take.'

'Wait a minute,' Isla said. 'We won't get the official gold price, you know that. Whoever we sell it to will have to get a cut. So take, say, fifteen percent off that figure.'

‘Okay,’ Hugh said, ‘that leaves just under £150,000.’

Victor was following Hugh’s calculations as carefully as he checked the books at the gambling club. ‘Give me 80K and it’s yours,’ he said.

‘The deal’s fifty-fifty,’ Isla demanded. ‘Seventy-five K each.’

‘Who’s doing who a favour here? Tell her, Forensic. Eighty thousand to me, or the deal’s off.’

‘Fair enough,’ Isla said, ‘we’re all friends here. As soon as we raise the cash, £80,000.’

‘Friends or not, don’t try to screw me, okay? I’ve got your address, Mister Forensic, and me and some of my buddies will pay you a call if I don’t see the money by the end of the month.’

Hugh Leggat paled slightly. Though he hadn’t mentioned his name, he had been stupid to tell Victor Herring he was a forensic accountant – there weren’t too many of those in Edinburgh. It was easy to track him down.

⬠

‘All right, *Mister Forensic*,’ Isla said with a grin as they drove off with the statuette under a coat on the back seat, ‘will your goldsmith buy this thing for cash?’

‘I can ask him, but I doubt it,’ Hugh replied. ‘Don’t you have some underworld connections you can flog it to?’

‘Yes, there’s a wee man in Glasgow we’ve used before, but we’ve never had anything worth more than about 10K. This is in a different league. Not sure he can deal with gold by the kilo.’

‘In any case, we could be missing out on a really big payoff if we just sold the thing as bullion. My goldsmith friend won’t buy it, but I could ask him to appraise it as an antique. We’d see what it’s really worth.’

‘Won’t he be suspicious?’

‘Probably, but I often bring him articles of dubious provenance.’ Noticing Isla’s puzzled expression, he searched for simpler language: ‘Things we can’t say where they came from.’

'Okay, if you're sure,' she said. But from the roll of her green eyes he knew she was sceptical.

⬠

When Hugh set the heavy object on the counter, Trimble's eyes bulged out of their sockets. 'Trove, is it?' he asked.

'Don't know,' Hugh said. 'What makes you think it's trove?'

'One, it's very old. Two, it's very unusual. And three, it's still got traces of clay on it.' Using a jeweller's loupe, he peered at the surface of the object. 'It's been cleaned up, quite recently, by somebody who doesn't know what he's doing. There are tool-marks all over it. Damned shame. Because it's an absolutely beautiful piece.'

'Is it Roman?'

'No.'

'That sounded quite definite.'

'Aye, it's definite. What are those things in the chariot, one on either side of the pretty lady?'

Hugh took a close look. 'They look like barrels of some sort.'

'Exactly. The Romans didn't use barrels like these, made of wooden staves bound together with iron rings. At least, not until the 4th or 5th century. Up to the time they left Britain, they stored liquids such as wine and oil in earthenware vessels. So this dates from post-Roman times.'

'But you said it was very old.'

Trimble turned the statuette around and around on his counter, as if trying to make sense of something. 'This isn't a war chariot and the lady isn't dressed for battle like Boudicca. You wouldn't go into battle flashing your breasts, and you'd have horses, not oxen, pulling you. Plus, you'd likely have some kind of weaponry. Not beer barrels.'

'So who is she?'

'My guess is the Anglo-Saxon goddess Nerthus. Supposedly she rode in a chariot drawn by heifers. Did this object come from Denmark or northern Germany, perhaps? The cult of Nerthus was common there in pre-Christian times, but isn't known among the early Anglo-Saxon settlers in Britain, as far as I'm aware.'

Hugh pointed out the markings on each side of the chariot. 'These stars look like the constellation Cassiopeia to me.'

'They certainly do,' Trimble agreed. 'I've no idea what the significance of that might be, but I'll do some research – it's possible the stars will help date the object.'

'So, for the moment, you couldn't guess at its value? Not even a notional amount that I could enter in a spreadsheet for the case I'm working on?'

'If it's Anglo-Saxon, pre-Christian as it seems to be, it could be worth twenty times its bullion value or more. But only if its provenance is known. If it's treasure trove, as I suspect (and I know you can't confirm that), its full value will be realised only if it's declared.'

29
CANTY

MARCUS'S SUGGESTION THAT the place bearing Neadreth's name had to be one of the Niddries was too good to be ignored. Support came from another source: the opinion of a linguist whose specialism was the quasi-Darwinian evolution of words. An email dated 9th July from Quin Johnson of the University of Chicago, otherwise Delia's live-in partner before she moved to Edinburgh and still resident in her apartment in a Chicago suburb, popped up in her inbox.

> Hi Delia:
>
> Your latest hunt sounded v. interesting when we talked!
>
> Neadreth/Niddrie: yes, v. likely the same word. Did a quick web search, found Dixon's 'Place-Names of Midlothian'. He traces Niddrie back to 12th c. as Nodref, suggests it's Cumbric or Old Welsh for 'new farmstead'. Neadreth is just as plausible, I think, consistent with well-documented evolutionary trends in place-names. So go for it!
>
> Corstorphine: little doubt it means 'Cross of Thorfinn'. Found on internet a convoluted theory that it's derived from Gaelic – 'torr fionn', meaning 'white hill'. Unlikely, in an area where Gaelic was never the language of the common people.

> I miss you more than I can say. Could I come and join you in Edinburgh for a couple of weeks? You haven't told me what exactly it is you're hunting for, but I might be of some help. We worked so well together on Taran's wheel last year! I'll give you a call on Sunday evening, your time, okay?
>
> Love, Quin.

Pleased though she was that Quin wanted to visit, something held her back from replying *Yes, I miss you too, please come as soon as you can.* Instead, her response was a businesslike *Sunday evening after 7 would be fine.*

The first of the three Niddries didn't hold out much hope. Jody and Delia drove to Niddrie Marischal on a sunny but cool Sunday morning, leaving Marcus to mind the store at *A Malt O' My Ain.* The Wauchope family, many of whom held the title of Marischal of Scotland, had been given a charter to lands by the royal castle of Craigmillar to the east of Edinburgh as long ago as the reign of Robert III, king from 1390 to 1406. By the 16th century a tower house occupied the site, and in 1636 a grand mansion, Niddrie Marischal House, was built around it. Wauchopes lived there until 1944.

The primary reason for pessimism was the more recent history of the estate. Having been purchased by the City of Edinburgh for just £8000, the house and grounds were allowed to fall into a grievous state of disrepair, until in 1959 the house was totally destroyed by fire – many suspect not accidentally. In 1968 the ruins were finally demolished, leaving not a trace of the elegant mansion that had once graced the Wauchope lands. In their place now stands one of Edinburgh's bleaker tracts of social housing.

Whatever might have served as a marker for Neadreth's sacred grove – if such a marker ever existed here – would have been erased by 20th-century 'development'. *A peaceful, sheltered spot where, in the sun-dappled shade of hazel trees, there flowed a limpid water:* that was Charlotte Nasmyth's description. Old maps showed a tiny stream, the Niddrie Burn, running through the estate; at one time this might have qualified as a *limpid water*. But no trace of it was visible, nor was there any other point of interest to keep the two women here.

Next stop: Longniddry in East Lothian. Many places with 'Long' or 'Lang' in their name were once a single row of cottages along a road or lane; Longniddry had no doubt been such a place but, being close to Edinburgh, had grown into a commuter town. Delia was most interested in the wooded dell named Longniddry Dean on the Ordnance Survey map, forming the western boundary of the town. Leaving the car nearby, they followed a footpath into the Dean.

They found it to be *a peaceful, sheltered spot*. Though the trees were not hazels, they did provide a *sun-dappled shade*. It was something of a stretch to describe as *a limpid water* the tiny stream that ran through the Dean to trickle across Seton Sands to the waiting firth, but once upon a time it might have been just that. 'For all its size, this stream has a name,' Delia remarked, consulting the map. 'It's the Canty Burn.'

'D'you know what *canty* means in Scots?' Jody asked.

'Sure don't.'

'Pleasant, cheerful, happy.'

'Mm. I wonder, could Neadreth's followers have given the stream that name because it flowed through their sacred grove? I mean, it was a place they came to in search of happiness, joy and peace.'

'Just what I was thinking,' Jody said.

They sensed they were on to something. This could be the place where, 1500 years ago, the incomers from Angeln set up a shrine to their water-goddess. Together Jody and Delia walked the full length of Longniddry Dean several times, looking for any durable marker – a waterfall, perhaps, or a large rock – as a starting point for a search, but nothing presented itself.

Thinking aloud, Delia said, 'Didn't Charlotte claim that Neadreth's grove had been used earlier by the Romans as a bathing place?'

'If she was right about that, there's no record of Roman activity here. The nearest Roman site is probably the fortress of Inveresk at the north terminus of Dere Street. That's in Musselburgh, five or six miles away.'

So Longniddry Dean checked some but not all the boxes. Jody gave Marcus a call to report what they had seen. On the ride back into Edinburgh, Delia felt unaccountably happy. *Canty*, in fact. It might have had something to do with a call she was expecting from Chicago that evening.

⬠

Hugh had arranged to meet Isla at a particular park bench in Princes Street Gardens on Sunday at two o'clock. He was surprised, but not displeased, to see Hendrik Vandenbrouck waiting for him as well.

'Got a valuation?' Isla asked peremptorily.

'Yes and no,' he replied cautiously.

'Don't fuck with us, Leggat,' the Belgian said.

'What I mean is, I've an estimate of what it would fetch if it was all above board. For example, if it was declared as treasure trove. Three to four million, maybe more. It's a very rare piece. Absolutely unique, probably.'

'And if not declared?'

'Bullion value, £150,000.'

'Less £80,000 to Herring,' Isla put in.

'Damned shame to miss out on a million plus,' Vandenbrouck said. 'Think what we could do with that!'

Hugh took a deep breath. 'You know, in the course of my work I've made a lot of contacts, on both sides of the law.

There's a collector I've dealt with, in London, who would love the statuette. He might pay up to a million in cash for it, no questions asked. He could buy it from a bullion dealer, making *him* rich instead of *Auld Stobby*. Or he could buy it from us.'

'A million, you say?' Vandenbrouck asked.

'If you like I'll sound him out.'

'Shit, do it,' Vandenbrouck said without a second's hesitation.

30
THE SALISBURY CRAGS

DELIA'S PHONE RANG AT EXACTLY one minute past seven. International, the caller display indicated. Though the phone was at her elbow, she let it ring four times before picking up.

Quin first reported that all was well in the apartment. He'd attended a condominium association meeting on her behalf, where an argument had got up about satellite dishes on balconies. Delia inquired if his Grampa was still happy enough in his retirement home; he gave the usual 'good days and bad' response. He asked how the search was going at the Niddries. 'We've so far checked out two of them,' she told him; 'one of them seems a possibility. I've a full schedule at work this week, but I hope to visit the third Niddry next weekend.'

'I could be there by Friday,' Quin announced. 'If you don't mind, that is.' There was an uncomfortable pause as he waited for Delia to speak. After a few seconds of dead air, he said, 'Of course, I completely understand this is your project, nothing to do with me. I just thought, since we have a good track record together ...'

'We do, Quin, we do. Yes, I'd love you to come over. It's time we were together again.' Her words seemed to pierce a barrier that had arisen between them.

'Like I said, I can be there by Friday. I have two weeks' vacation due.'

'Quin, I'm really swamped at work for the next couple of weeks at least. Can you come at the end of the month instead?'

'Sure. Let me check airfares for late July.'

⬠

The Pleasance is an ancient Edinburgh street that runs along the foot of the Salisbury Crags, once the principal highway out of the city towards Dalkeith, the Borders and Carlisle. In Hugh's modest office there, it was a quiet Monday morning. Having dealt with a few routine requests from police headquarters nearby, he settled down to the main business of the day: raising a million pounds or more on a piece of antique gold with a bullion value of a fraction of that sum. By lunchtime, 15 phone calls later, he had a deal to present to his *Auld Stobby* comrades.

At 2 pm, an unexpected visitor arrived wearing a black hoodie. Without a word, Victor Herring sat down opposite him at his desk.

'Mr Herring,' Hugh said, making to stand up. His visitor remained resolutely seated and motioned him to sit down again.

'Where's my golden chariot, Forensic?' Victor demanded, looking Hugh in the eye.

Hugh cleared his throat. 'As we agreed, Mr Herring, it's with a goldsmith awaiting valuation. Then we have to find a buyer – we're making progress on that front, and with luck we'll have cash in a couple of weeks. As soon as that happens, you'll get your eighty thousand.'

'Why should I trust you?'

'Because, if I were to act dishonestly, all you'd have to do is go to the police along the street and tell them the whole story. My career would be over. I'm not going to risk my professional livelihood over this.'

'Fuck the police. You have more to lose than your "professional livelihood" if you screw me, Forensic.'

Hugh found the need to clear his throat again. 'Would it help if I wrote you a receipt?'

Victor threw his head back and laughed derisively. He got up from his chair and leaned over the desk, close enough that Hugh could identify from his breath what he'd had for lunch.

'Look, I know you've got my property, *you* know you've got my property, that's all we need to know. Except this: I'll be here again with one or two friends if I haven't got the money in a fortnight. Receipt? Hah!' He laughed again, kicked the chair out of his way and walked out.

⬠

Monday being his day of leisure, Marcus decided on a drive out to Longniddry to see for himself what Jody and Delia had found ... or not found. But first he uploaded the photos he'd taken of Kirsty Morton's Nasmyths – the three landscapes from Charlotte's *Prospect of Edinburgh* suite. As he viewed them on the larger computer screen, something didn't seem quite right, though it was hard to identify exactly what. The largest of the three, the view to the west supposedly from Arthur's Seat, particularly puzzled him.

Getting out a map, he soon figured it out. From the summit of Arthur's Seat, Corstorphine Hill should lie well to the left of Edinburgh Castle, yet in the painting the castle was directly in front of the southernmost part of the hill. The view the artist had captured was from a lower vantage point, closer to the city; Marcus reckoned she must have set up her easel at the north end of the Salisbury Crags, near Holyrood – indeed, right above where the Scottish Parliament building now stands.

On his way to Longniddry, he parked at Holyrood Palace to take a walk. The Radical Road – a path built by unemployed weavers from the west of Scotland in the aftermath of the 1820 'radical war' – invited him along the base of the cliffs. Instead, he followed a less-travelled track that winds around the back of the Crags, eventually leading up to the crest. At a spot from which the castle appeared to lie directly in front of the south end of Corstorphine Hill, he took a photograph. It would be interesting, he thought, to compare the view now with that painted in 1835 by Charlotte Nasmyth.

That evening, having visited Longniddry Dean and reached the same conclusion as Jody and Delia, that it *could* be Neadreth's hazel grove, he found himself humming a familiar tune, about another hazel dean. He knew the words well; they were by Sir Walter Scott and told of a maiden betrothed to a nobleman's son but in love with another. He tuned his guitar and sang:

'Why weep ye by the tide, lady?
Why weep ye by the tide?
I'll wed ye tae my younger son,
And ye shall be his bride.
And ye shall be his bride, lady,
Sae comely tae be seen.'
But aye she let the tears doon fa
For Jock o' Hazeldean.

The kirk is decked at morningtide,
The tapers glimmer fair,
The priest and bridegroom wait the bride
And dame and knight are there.
They seek her baith by bower and ha
But never is she seen –
She's ow'r the border and awa
Wi' Jock o' Hazeldean.

31
COUP

IT HAD BEEN ANOTHER LONG WEEK. Three full days at the Loch of Lindores and a day and a half in the lab back at South Gyle. But the hard part was finished, thank goodness. Next it would be a case of report-writing, which she could do as well at home – or anywhere – as in her cubicle at NEPA.

Not that Delia's report was going to make a whit of difference to the planned rerouting of the aqueduct through Fife and over the Forth Bridge. Scuttlebutt around headquarters was that a deal of some kind had been struck with Network Rail giving NEPA right-of-way across the bridge. And at 3 pm on Friday 16th July, scuttlebutt was replaced by a formal announcement to the assembled staff in a crowded conference room.

No one was surprised to hear chief operating officer Dennis Dickie confirm that the North East Pipeline Aqueduct would cross the Firth of Forth on the iconic 1890 railway bridge. What caused a loud collective gasp, however, was the nature of the deal that had been negotiated. A press release, put out simultaneously with the meeting, expressed it succinctly.

> In a joint statement issued today by NEPA and Network Rail, it is announced that an outright purchase of the Forth Bridge, including its associated lands, buildings, works and other assets, has been agreed. NEPA will acquire full ownership of the bridge, together with all rights, obligations and liabilities, at 12:01 am on 6th August of this year. A purchase price of one pound (£1) has been negotiated. Network Rail will pay NEPA a

> monthly rent, the amount of which is not presently disclosed, for continued use of the bridge as a rail crossing. Maintenance of the railway track and bed will remain a responsibility of Network Rail; costs of all other maintenance and repairs to the bridge will be borne by NEPA.

An excited chatter erupted in the room as NEPA employees grasped the implications of the deal. The hubbub was allowed to continue for about five minutes before Dickie brought the meeting back to order.

'This is a coup for NEPA,' he announced. Laughter broke out as he took a pound coin from his pocket and flipped it in the air, saying, 'The price, as you see, is quite a bargain.' Pointedly, he placed the coin in the centre of the table in front of him.

As the laughter subsided, chief accountant Craig Wetherby rose to speak. So short was he, not everyone noticed he'd got to his feet; to gain attention he had to pick up the coin and rap loudly on the table with it.

'Buying the Forth Bridge for £1 will make tomorrow's headlines,' he said. 'But be in no doubt, this purchase comes with heavy liability, which is why it's a good deal for Network Rail as well as for us. From our perspective, that liability represents future cost, which will be factored into the price of the water we supply. The good news is that it puts no pressure on our construction budget, which remains healthy. For that reason, I echo Mr Dickie's words: this is a *coup* for NEPA. We have cause for celebration tonight.'

Wetherby knew how *he* at least would be celebrating. At home he had a bottle of The Glenlivet, a fifteen year-old reserve, that he'd received in a gift from his forensic accountant friend at the Water Lairds – what was his name again? – and planned to uncork it that evening.

Isla Younie's phone buzzed close to her ear, waking her abruptly at eight o'clock on Saturday morning. It took her a moment to tune into the Belgian-accented voice.

'Vandenbrouck on the line. Have you seen the news today?'

'Oh, it's you, Hendrik. No I haven't. What's up?'

'NEPA's bought the bridge. It's to be turned over to them on 6th August.'

'*Bought?* You mean they will *own* the Forth Bridge?' Isla was now wide awake.

'That's what I said, dammit. Now wouldn't it be a fucking *coup* if we were to implement our plan on that very day?'

'Well ... yes it would. But the money's not through for the gold chariot. Last I spoke to Leggat, he was still haggling with his contact in London.'

'You need to get up earlier in the morning, Younie. Leggat texted you and me both, an hour ago, saying he'd sold it. Didn't get a million, though. Eight fifty.'

'Eight hundred and fifty thousand? Still a lot better than bullion value. And we have only 80K to pay Victor Herring.'

'Yeah, yeah, but make sure he thinks we just sold it for scrap, or he'll come after us wanting more. Anyway, the money will be in our hands on Monday. All in used twenties, coming in two Sony TV boxes. Each of them will weigh about twenty kilos.'

'Did Leggat tell you that?'

'Didn't have to. I've handled that amount in Belgium, more than once. Believe me, I know the weight of money. I'm more familiar with euros, of course, but this'll be similar.'

'Shouldn't the cash be in something more secure? Like a suitcase with a combination lock?'

'This isn't a fucking James Bond movie. We don't want attention. Nobody looks twice at a Sony TV box.' Vandenbrouck waited a moment for Isla to speak, but she had no more silly questions. 'Okay, Younie,' he said, 'be at Granton on Tuesday at ten o'clock, for the first team meeting of Operation Nightjar.'

'What ...?'

'*Nachtzwaluw*. I think you call it nightjar. It's a bird.'

Isla thought better of asking any more questions. All would become clear soon enough.

⬠

The job was finished. The last turf had been replaced over the excavated area and all the ancient paving stones were stacked neatly in an inconspicuous corner of the building site. It was five in the morning and the sun was up.

Victor had gone home to bed around 1 am leaving a clear instruction to his henchman to call him once the work was completed. It was a gruff, drowsy voice that answered when Cammy Lewis called.

'I'll be over to inspect the site in a few hours. You get off home. Make sure the gate is properly locked before you go. Did you find anything else?'

'No, it seems there was only the one piece.'

'Or there's more, but you're thinking you can make off with it, eh?'

'Christ, no, Victor.'

'I hope not.' The tone was coldly threatening.

'You promised we'd talk about reporting the find. You want to do that now?'

Victor uttered a string of expletives into the phone. Then: 'Not now, not later, not ever. God dammit, don't you get the picture? We report it, we kiss goodbye to building on that site. And you're in serious trouble for destroying historic remains.'

'Not only me.'

'Whatever, it's too late. I've sold the chariot thing for scrap gold. It's probably already been melted down.'

'Jesus, Victor, we could have got a lot more for it as trove.'

'*We?* None of it's yours, pal. You're getting your £30,000 out of it, remember.'

'Make it fifty and I won't say a word, to the police or anyone.'

'The deal's thirty. Not a penny more. We shook on it. And I don't think you'll want to talk to the police. You're complicit in this whole thing, remember. But tell you what, pal. Come over to Learmonth next Monday evening. You'll get your 30K, then we'll see what we can do to find you a table that'll make your money grow. Meanwhile, not a cheep, okay?'

'I'll be there,' Lewis said.

Later that morning, Jody and Delia were setting off to visit the third Niddry, the one in West Lothian, when Marcus called to say he would join them. He'd put a notice on the door at *A Malt O' My Ain* saying he'd open at 1 pm.

He had a hunch, he said, that the Niddry Burn, which rises near the famous neolithic site of Cairnpapple Hill and runs east to join the River Almond at Kirkliston, would turn out to be the *limpid water* that flowed in Neadreth's *sun-dappled grove*.

'You think it's more promising than the Canty Burn at Longniddry?' Jody asked.

'Well,' he said, 'based on your description, I thought Longniddry was a strong possibility, and when I saw it last Monday I had to agree. But now, having done a little reading, I think I like the West Lothian Niddry better.'

'Why's that?'

'You're the *Inglisleid* expert. Have you noticed there's a place called Faucheldean by the Niddry Burn, near Winchburgh?'

'Faucheldean,' Jody repeated. 'A *dean* is certainly a wooded valley, like Longniddry Dean, or, for that matter, the *dean* that gave Dean Village its name. So, okay, a grove with a burn flowing through.'

'And *fauchel*, like *faw*, meaning dappled or speckled. As in Falkirk. *Fauchel dean* could be a sun-dappled grove, couldn't it?'

'More likely it's from *fauchle*, a lazy person ... maybe referring to a slow-running stream.'

'A *limpid flow*, you could say. Let's go.'

⬠

In 1870, West Lothian – or as it then was, Linlithgowshire – was in the grip of an oil boom. Deposits of an oil-bearing shale had been discovered deep underground; mines were being bored and oil works were springing up all over the hitherto green agricultural landscape between Linlithgow and Edinburgh. It was the legacy of the Scottish industrial chemist James 'Paraffin' Young, who developed and patented processes for extracting oil from coal and other oleiferous deposits. Among the shale mines coming into production at this time was one on the south bank of the Niddry Burn, operated by the Uphall Mineral Oil Company.

Half a mile downstream stood Niddry Castle, three centuries earlier a stronghold of the Setons, who were stalwart supporters of Mary, Queen of Scots throughout her troubled reign and after her forced abdication. In 1568 the 7th Lord Seton assisted her in a famous escape from imprisonment in Loch Leven Castle, reputedly by dressing in her clothes and standing in a lighted window. The following night, after paying a loyal ferryman to carry her secretly over the firth, he sheltered Mary in Niddry Castle. His sister, Mary Seton, was immortalised in a much-loved folk-song:

Yestre'en the Queen had four Marys,
The nicht she'll hae but three,
There's Mary Seton and Mary Beaton
And Mary Carmichael and me.

From that time forward, only passing traffic on the Union Canal, inaugurated in 1822, and the North British railway from Edinburgh to Glasgow, opened twenty years later, disturbed the area's tranquillity until the sinking of the first shale mine by the Niddry Burn.

So promising was this mine that the Uphall Company built a new plant adjacent to it, to extract crude oil from the shale by a process called retorting. If mining the shale was unhealthy, dangerous work, the retortman's job was no better; yet the company did not see fit to pay him more than a subsistence wage. Its largesse did extend to the building of cheap houses for its workers and their families, in a series of blocks to the east of the works, which became known as Niddry Rows. About 100 tiny homes here relied for water on just four communal standpipes.

Profits from the exploitation of shale – and of the miners and retortmen – enriched the company's already wealthy shareholders, many of whom enjoyed a luxurious lifestyle in their large, well-appointed homes in Edinburgh's New Town. In 1883, they made themselves even wealthier by selling out to Young's Paraffin Light Company.

Soon the nearby reserves were unable to satisfy the retort capacity of the Hopetoun works, but Young's company had sunk new pits at Glendevon to the north-west, and a railway was constructed to bring the shale from these pits. Another railway carried the crude oil produced by the Hopetoun retortmen to the company's refinery at Uphall. There the black gunk would yield heavy oil, an excellent lubricant for steam engines and industrial machinery; paraffin or kerosene, perfect for lighting and heating; and a dangerous volatile by-product (later known as petrol) which, until the advent of the automobile, was of little use and was burned off or dumped in the nearest watercourse.

Now there was a bit of a problem. For every hundred tons of rock brought to the retort works, 75 tons of waste – spent shale – had to be disposed of. Rendered brick-red by the heat of the retorting process, it accumulated in vast heaps known locally as *shale bings*.

The first of these bings, on the north side of the works, gradually encroached on, and soon half-filled, a shady dell called the Fauchel Dean through which ran the cool clear water of the

Niddry Burn. Except the water didn't stay clear; stained red by runoff from the Faucheldean Bing (as the waste tip became known) and poisoned by heavy metal residues in the spent shale, the burn became a toxic industrial ditch. Every time it rained, raw sewage effluent from the communal cesspit at Niddry Rows also found its way to the burn.

By now, the Rows were dominated by this manmade hill to their immediate north and west. Whenever the wind blew, red dust accumulated in every corner around and even inside the tiny hovels. At least, their residents might have consoled themselves, they could still feel the warmth of the sun shining over the open fields lying between their Rows and the canalside village of Broxburn a mile away to the south.

That warmth would not last long. By 1900, Faucheldean Bing had outgrown its limited footprint and a new tip was started on the south side of the Rows. Less constrained in area, it became a veritable mountain. The outbreak of war in 1914 further increased the demand for oil and the new Greendykes Bing, as this mountain was named, grew at an accelerating rate, soon approaching 200 feet in height, to put Niddry Rows in permanent shadow. By the time the bing was abandoned in 1925, it had accumulated fifteen million tons of spent shale, the waste from production of forty million barrels of oil.

The oil works of West Lothian had all ceased operation by 1960, but Greendykes Bing (now a scheduled historical monument) and its smaller neighbour Faucheldean Bing survive as reminders of a time when extraction of wealth from the ground was not beset by modern concerns for the natural environment or the welfare of workers and their families.

⬠

So Jody, Marcus and Delia found no *limpid flow*, no *sun-dappled grove* at Faucheldean. What they saw was an industrial wasteland. If the early Angles had built a shrine to their goddess

Neadreth here, it was now buried under tons of brick-coloured spent shale. It was impossible to gain any sense of how this place might have looked at the time of Anglian settlement; it was a landscape ravaged.

The three gazed silently at the red hills. It was Marcus who gave voice to what they were all thinking. 'This was the place. Named for Neadreth, the Niddry Burn once trickled through a hazel grove on this very site.'

The others nodded in agreement: the search was over. In a sense, this place had indeed been a *store of wealth* as the Water Lairds' legend, and Charlotte Nasmyth's writings, promised, though the people who lived in the depressing shadow of the bings and who generated the wealth got no share of it. That, and the destruction of a pastoral landscape, was perhaps the curse the legend foretold.

Marcus, Jody and Delia took a short walk from a roadside building that was all that remained of Hopetoun Works, along the line of the dismantled railway that had brought shale from the Glendevon mines. Having crossed the Niddry Burn into the tiny hamlet of Faucheldean, they continued their walk downstream, heading north-eastward in the direction of Winchburgh. Before long they returned to their car, having toured the entire periphery of the bing.

'Could there really have been a Roman bathing-place here?' Delia wondered aloud. 'An already established site of pilgrimage that became, for the Angles, a shrine to *their* goddess?'

'It's quite possible,' Jody said, unfolding a map. 'There's lots of evidence of Roman activity around here. See, they had a settlement just a couple of miles away on the other side of Broxburn, and we're not too far from the fort at Carriden, on the Antonine Wall.'

'Yes, this is the place all right,' Marcus said, a tone of resignation in his voice. 'Ah well, let's go. Time I was opening up the shop.'

Driving back into Edinburgh along Corstorphine Road, they passed a newsbill outside a convenience store at Western Corner displaying the principal headline of the day:

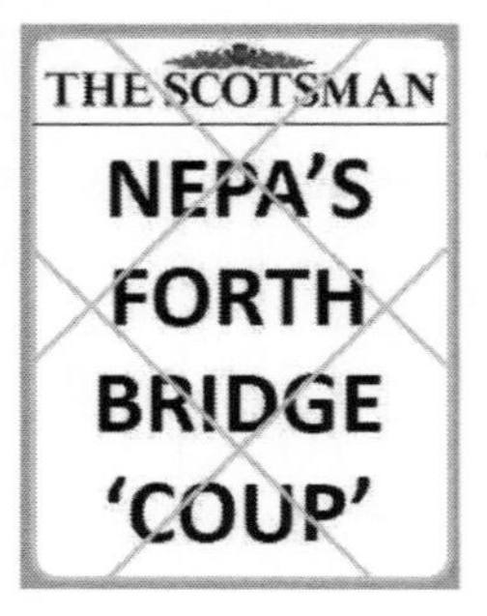

'Your company's certainly made today's news, Delia,' Marcus said. 'Buying the Forth Bridge for a quid? If that's not a coup, I don't know what is.'

But Delia made no reply. She seemed to be deep in thought.

32
OPERATION NIGHTJAR

FOR THE REMAINDER OF THE WEEKEND, by day and during waking moments at night, Delia's brain nursed an image of the *NEPA'S FORTH BRIDGE 'COUP'* billboard. Why had it made such an impression?

Was it just that she'd had a personal role, albeit a minor one, in making the now-famous 'coup' come about? No, that wasn't it – the eye-popping deal with Network Rail had nothing to do with her. So why did it stick in her head?

At 5:15 on Monday morning she knew why. Subconsciously, she had been working on an anagram of the four-word headline. And now she had the solution, one that seemed to have meaning in the search for Neadreth's sacred grove. Nothing to do with any of the three Niddries, no matter how suggestive that place-name was.

Excitedly she picked up her phone, then realised it was a little early to call. Jody and Marcus would not appreciate being wakened at this time in the morning. Instead she texted them both:

> NEPA'S FORTH BRIDGE 'COUP': the letters spell A PROSPECT OF EDINBURGH! We've been looking in the wrong place.

It was Marcus who called her at six. 'Clever,' he said, 'but why should this mean the grove isn't at Faucheldean? Are you suggesting someone at *The Scotsman* is giving us a subtle hint?'

Delia laughed. 'No, of course not. It's just that when I worked out the anagram, I realised we had to refocus. Charlotte had so much to say about her landscapes painted on the five hills around Edinburgh – and made all these other references to the number 5. We got hooked on one little phrase, where she says the location was named for Neadreth. It was probably an insignificant detail.'

'So you think we should be looking on those five hills?'

'Yes, or somewhere that's visible from all five hills and appears in each of her paintings. Edinburgh Castle, for instance. It gets mentioned a lot in the *New Story*.'

'Y'know, as I look at Kirsty Morton's three landscapes, the castle is bang in the centre of each one. I suppose it's worth thinking about.'

'Glad you agree,' Delia said. 'Think I'll take a day off work, do some research. Your shop's closed today, isn't it? Want to meet later for coffee or lunch?'

'Sure. Jody's got an important meeting, so it'll be just the two of us.'

'Can you email me your photos from Kirsty's? I'd like to take another look at them. Also the one you took on the Salisbury Crags above Holyrood.'

By the time they met at Sambuca on Causewayside, Delia had discovered that an oil painting said to be 'after Nasmyth' and titled *A Prospect of Edinburgh* was to be auctioned in Leith on 31st July. No photograph of the item was yet posted on the Ramsay Cornish website, but she had made up her mind to view the painting prior to the sale, in hope that it would be one of the two missing Charlotte Nasmyth landscapes from the suite of five.

She chewed a mouthful of pepperoni pizza and washed it down with mineral water. Dabbing her lips with a paper napkin, she pulled up Marcus's photographs on her tablet. 'Okay,' she said, 'here are the three landscapes. Remind me which is which.'

'Inverleith, Craiglockhart, Salisbury Crags,' he said, pointing to each one in turn.

'So we're still missing Blackford and Corstorphine Hills.'

‘Right. One of those might be sitting in Leith right now.’

‘You should alert Kirsty to the auction,’ Delia said. ‘She might be interested in acquiring another *Prospect of Edinburgh*. In fact, why don’t you give her a call right now? And ask her if you can bring Jody and me along to see the three she has already.’

Within five minutes it was set up. They would all pay a visit to Kirsty Morton the following evening at 7:30.

⬠

Tuesday at 10 am saw the inaugural Operation Nightjar meeting in Granton. Hendrik Vandenbrouck took his accustomed seat at the head of the table. To his left were his Flemish compatriot Mariane, Hugh Leggat and a gaunt, stubble-chinned man of about fifty called Willie Thomson. Facing them across the table were Isla Younie and Fraser Cadenhead, a young man with curly red hair and the build of a junior league footballer. Rory the enforcer sat silently in the corner.

Without a word of introduction, Vandenbrouck stated the objective of the operation. ‘Early in the morning of 6th August, just under three weeks from now, we will detonate a large explosive device on one of the main towers of the Forth Bridge. Willie, tell the team how we’re going to do this.’

Thomson handed each of the others a photograph showing the familiar profile of the bridge as seen from Queensferry, about half a mile upstream on the south shore. An Edinburgh man, he spoke in short sentences with staccato delivery.

‘Okay, see the bridge here. It’s cantilevered. Ye dinnae need tae ken whit that means. Point is, its weight’s cairried at three places. See them: one, two, three. Number one’s on the shore at North Queensferry. Number three’s in deep water – a hundred feet, near as dammit – a quarter mile oot fae Dalmeny. Now it’s number two in the middle I want yiz tae focus on, eh?’

He paused to check his audience was following him before continuing.

'Ye cannae really see fae this photo, but the middle section stands at the end o' a wee island. Inchgarvie. There's four steel towers there, each on a granite plinth. Awthing else is attached tae thae towers. Bolted, welded, riveted, it disnae matter how.'

'So we're going to blow up those four towers?' Isla asked.

'Well, that wid bring doon the bridge, for sure. But aw we need tae dae is tak oot one o' them. That'll jist gie her a bit o' a scare.'

'A scare?' Mariane cut in.

'Aye, that's right. She'll wobble a bit, but that's aw.'

'How do you know this?' Leggat asked. 'Are you a structural engineer?'

'Aye,' Thomson replied laconically. 'Worked on the bridge for 30 years. Got early retirement because o' ma health. Okay, now. Whit's important is this. They'll hae tae stop aw the trains till they're sure it's safe, maybe till they pit in a replacement tower. That could tak years. An' the pipeline boys'll no risk pittin mair weight on the bridge. It's them that'll own it, them that'll hae tae find the money tae fix it, eh? It'll no be cheap.'

While he let this information sink in, he handed out copies of a hand-drawn map, then continued his discourse.

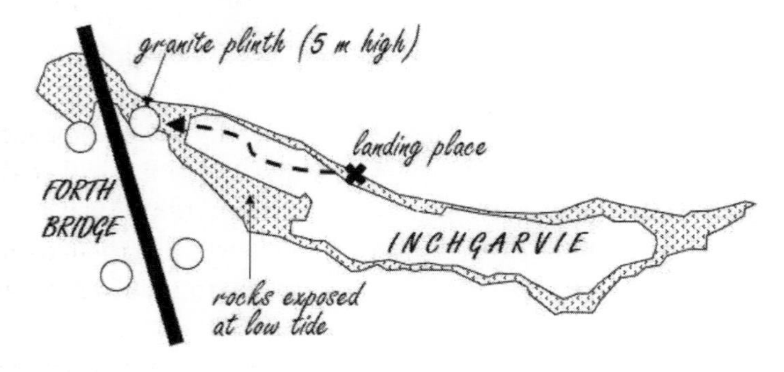

'This is Inchgarvie. It taks jist a few minutes to get there in a boat fae the east side o' North Queensferry. The best place tae land is on the north side o' the island – see the X on the wee map. Fae there it's a short distance tae the nearest tower.'

'But the plinth is five metres high according to your map,' Isla put in. 'Won't it be hard to get up there to place the explosive?'

'There'll be a ladder on the boat.'

Hugh was keen to know how the charges were to be set and detonated.

'That's for Mariane tae tell yiz.'

The Flemish woman took her cue to speak. 'I will supply the device. It will attach by magnets to the steel, like a limpet mine. Its explosion will generate enough heat, not exactly to melt the steel, but to make it lose all its strength. The base of the tower will turn to butter. Detonation will be by mobile phone. But I have a question. Why attack only one of those towers? We've plenty of explosive.'

Vandenbrouck was adamant. 'One will be enough. The Scots love that fucking bridge, even though it's an English design. Right now it's NEPA they hate, so it's NEPA we want to hurt. This plan does just the right amount of damage.'

Isla was taken aback by something Vandenbrouck had said. 'English? I don't think so.'

'Check it out, Younie.'

'I will. Anyway, I take it Fraser will be the boatman.'

Fraser Cadenhead nodded.

'And who's gonna set the explosive?'

Ignoring her question for the moment, Vandenbrouck addressed Hugh Leggat. 'This device of Mariane's has to be paid for, up front. You promised the money today. Where is it?'

'It's in two Sony TV boxes, as arranged, in a white van on its way up from London. An hour ago it was on the M6 at Bamber Bridge. Should be here by mid afternoon.'

This news brought forth an uncharacteristic compliment from Vandenbrouck. 'Good work, Leggat. Without you we'd have a lot less money. But thanks to you, on 6th August the whole of Scotland will sit up and notice. This will destroy NEPA.'

Hugh demurred, saying that raising the money had been a team effort between Isla and himself.

'Agreed,' Vandenbrouck said generously, 'and as a reward, the two of you will be entrusted with blowing the bridge.'

Hugh and Isla looked at each other, each with an audible intake of breath. Cadenhead said he would give them a precise time to meet him at North Queensferry. 'We'll make the crossing at about midnight, unless there's some unexpected shipping in the firth. There'll be no moon, so even if the sky is clear it'll be nice and dark. Only the lights on the bridge to guide us.'

'You keep an eye on the moon, do you?' Hugh asked him.

'I do a lot of night fishing from my boat, so yes, I do.'

Isla seemed pumped up at being given such a key role in Operation Nightjar. Hugh's expression gave little away, but Vandenbrouck's stare seemed to say: *What's the matter, boy, nervous?*

⬠

Two large Sony boxes were delivered to Firth TV & Audio in Granton just after 4 pm on Tuesday. Vandenbrouck, Isla and Hugh were on hand to open them and verify their contents. Exactly as arranged: 85 bundles of 250 used £20 notes in each box – £850,000 in total.

At Vandenbrouck's prompting, Isla counted out 16 bundles for Victor Herring, and threw them into a blue gym bag. 'I'll take them to his house in Merchiston tonight,' she said. 'You wanna come along, Hugh? I don't fancy meeting that guy on my own.'

Hugh found it amusing that this woman had no problem consorting with the terrorists and criminals of *Auld Stobby*, yet seemed afraid of Victor Herring. On the other hand, he himself had been physically threatened by the hooligan just a few days earlier; Isla's nervousness was probably well justified.

'Yes, I'll go with you,' he said unenthusiastically. About the only thing he relished *less* than escorting Isla to Victor's place was making up a double-act with her at the Forth Bridge on 6th August.

They helped Vandenbrouck seal up the boxes again with packaging tape and carry them out to his car – a black Renault. A passing policeman paused on the pavement to avoid getting in their way, glanced at the boxes and the 'Firth TV & Audio' sign, and walked on. Vandenbrouck locked up the premises and sat in the driver's seat. Once the constable was out of sight, Mariane emerged from a nearby car and got into the Renault. Watching the Belgians drive off together, Hugh and Isla might have been excused for thinking they would never see the money again.

Isla's worry about a one-on-one meeting with Victor was unfounded. When she and Hugh pressed his entryphone button at 6:50 that evening, it was a female voice that said, 'Come in.'

The owner of the voice met them at the door of the flat; she and Isla immediately recognised one another. She introduced herself to Hugh: 'I'm Rachel Herring, Victor's mother. We've been expecting you, but I'm afraid Victor has had to take care of business.' Her eyes lighted on the blue gym bag. 'Let's see what you've got there.'

Isla dumped the bag on a kitchen chair and unzipped. Apparently no stranger to this kind of transaction, Rachel lifted each bundle of money, one at a time, and flicked the wad of notes with her thumb. 'I take it you made enough profit on the sale not to need any further contribution from me to your funds.'

'It was a good deal for you and for us,' Isla responded.

'Don't forget your side of the bargain,' Rachel said. 'You're going to pull strings to ensure my casino resort goes ahead. You're going to do for me what you did for Donald Trump.'

33
SECRETS

COUNCILLOR JAMES SWIFT FELT SICK. After all his hard work, all his lobbying, it had become evident there was no clear majority on the Planning Committee to nod through the casino resort development by the airport. Best he could determine, the committee was split seven-seven, across party lines, and he could not rely on the convener's casting vote.

He had managed to get Rachel Herring's dwelling-house approved over loud opposition from an environmentalist group. That was now a done deal, with £35,000 in his offshore account to show for it. She had promised him another fifty grand if he secured approval of the casino development. But unless he pulled that off, he stood to lose much, much more.

He worried that she would take her revenge on him personally, by exposing his acceptance of her bribes, which would put an end to his career and possibly land him in jail. And he couldn't point a finger at her in retaliation; he'd met her son Victor, who would ensure jail was the least of his sorrows.

For perhaps the twentieth time, Swift checked off the names of the seven 'antis' on the committee. Two SNP councillors, two Labour, a LibDem, a Conservative and a Green. All of them implacably opposed to allowing a massive new gambling mecca in their city, regardless of the jobs and revenue it would bring.

The Conservative was usually business-friendly in his voting habits, but Swift had pulled an underhand trick on him earlier in the year and this was his payback. How childish some of his colleagues could be, with so much at stake! Might a grovelling apology appeal to his better nature? No, that was a non-starter.

What about the fresh-faced SNP lad, Steven Lawrie? A new recruit to the committee, he ought to be malleable – but his ward bordered on the development site and he seemed afraid of upsetting the voters who had elected him with a very slim majority. Ah well, no harm in giving him another call on the subject. There might just be *some* point on which he could be nudged out of the 'antis' into the 'pros'.

'Steven? James Swift here. Look, I know you're new to the Planning Committee, and I thought you might appreciate a few tips from an old hand. Dynamics of the committee, who's got hot-button issues, that kind of thing. It's always difficult for a new member to get traction. What about a cup of coffee downstairs? Just an informal chat.'

'Is this about the casino resort again? If it is, James, I've told you, my mind's made up. Over my dead body will that go ahead.'

'I know how strongly you feel, Steven, really I do. It does you credit that you're prepared to take a stand against something that's going to be hugely popular all across the city. Matter of principle and all that. But I don't think you're seeing the full picture.'

'With respect, James, it's you who's ignoring the downside. The gambling addiction, the influx of criminal elements, the drawing of tourist spending away from the city centre ...'

'And what about the upside? The jobs, the increased takings on the trams, ...'

'Don't lecture me on the trams. You're one of the "old hands" – your words – whose mismanagement brought so much pain and debt to our city. Made us a laughing-stock. No, James, you can count me out. My vote *against* planning approval is one hundred percent solid. Now, if you'll excuse me, I have a meeting with a constituent in five minutes. Goodbye.'

Swift had written 'Lawrie?' on a pad. Now he drew three heavy lines through the name. 'Little shit,' he muttered.

⬠

The gate leading into Kirsty Morton's driveway had been left open for their arrival. As Marcus parked on the gravel in front of the rambling Victorian house, Delia remarked on the large, colourful, well-stocked but slightly unkempt garden. She loved the herbaceous borders, the shrubbery, the tall cedars.

'A bit wild, though, don't you think?' Jody said.

'All the better for not being manicured' was Delia's opinion.

Kirsty was at the door even before they got out of the car. Marcus introduced Jody and Delia as she ushered them in.

'First things first,' their hostess announced. 'Let's have a glass of something in the sitting room.'

Having sat her guests down and poured four pale sherries from a crystal decanter, Kirsty said, 'So, ladies, you want to see my Charlotte Nasmyths. Of course, Marcus, you've seen them already but I dare say they'll stand another look. I gather, Jody dear, you're a curator at the National Museum. Is your interest in Charlotte Nasmyth related to your work?'

'Not really,' Jody replied. 'It's a little project we've all embarked on ... we came across some documents that got us thinking how under-rated she has been as an artist.'

'Never escaped her father's shadow, d'you mean?'

'Well, yes, that's true, but she may have been the *better* landscape artist. It seems she made a determined effort to differentiate her work from his.'

'Couldn't agree more,' Kirsty nodded. 'The freer brush-strokes, the more inventive palette, yet always the influence of Alexander Nasmyth coming through in the composition.'

Delia began, 'As Marcus told you, Mrs Morton, ...'

'Call me Kirsty, dear.'

'... *Kirsty*, there's a painting coming up at Ramsay Cornish this Saturday that might be a Charlotte Nasmyth. Do you plan to bid for it? It's titled *A Prospect of Edinburgh*. Could be one of her suite of five.'

'Five? How do you know there are five?'

Marcus stepped in to answer. 'Jody mentioned we'd found some documents. There's a suggestion there that Charlotte might have painted views of Edinburgh from five hills around the city. That wasn't yet clear when I came here last time,' he finished, not entirely truthfully.

'How exciting!' Kirsty exclaimed. 'I always thought there might be more than three, but it's fun to think there are only two that aren't already in my collection. Which makes it all the more disappointing that I'll not be able to go to the sale on Saturday. I'm going into hospital for a small procedure.' The last word was said in a lowered voice and was specifically directed at the two women.

'We're going to be at the auction,' Delia said. 'Well, Jody and I will, for sure. Perhaps we could bid on your behalf, if it seems the painting is a genuine Charlotte Nasmyth. You'd just have to tell us your ceiling.'

Kirsty looked doubtful. 'That depends on condition, authenticity, and so on. I'll have to think about it. Meantime, let me fill up your glasses and we'll take them through to where my Charlotte Nasmyths are.'

In the dining-room, Marcus stood back to let Jody and Delia have a closer look at the three paintings. Already familiar with their subject matter from Marcus's photographs, Delia asked Kirsty if she thought the frames were original.

'The two smaller ones could be. They're mid-19th-century in style. The bigger one in the middle, probably not. It's certainly had a new backing applied at some stage. Take it down from the wall if you like. Marcus already did, last time he was here.'

With Jody's help, Delia lifted the middle painting – the view from the Salisbury Crags – off its hook and carefully set it on the floor, leaning against a dining chair. Then she rummaged in her purse and brought out a small retractable measuring tape. 'Exactly 21 inches by 34. That fits.'

The others looked puzzled.

'The 8th and 9th Fibonacci numbers. The proportions of the frame conform to the golden ratio. The *divine proportions*.'

Kirsty said, 'I've no idea what you're talking about.'

'I'm a scientist, Kirsty. I never really know if I like something until I've measured or quantified it in some way. The golden ratio, 1·618, is something I handle in my work, but it's also a feature of all sorts of beautiful things. That cabinet over there, for example. This buffet.'

'Sideboard,' Jody translated.

'Tomayto, tomahto,' Delia said with a smile. She turned the painting over to examine the back. 'I'd like to take a peek at the stretcher bars. Would it be okay if I made a little cut in the corner of the backing paper? I'll tape it up again.'

Kirsty nodded assent as Delia dived into her purse again, this time bringing out a small pocket-knife. She slit the backing paper at one corner, then pulled it back to look underneath. 'The stretcher bars look original to me,' she said. 'What do you think, Kirsty?'

The older woman peered through the slit Delia had made. 'You'll have to open it up a bit more.'

'Sure it's okay?'

'Yes, go ahead. In fact, you can remove the whole backing sheet. I can easily have it redone.'

Kirsty was as surprised as her three guests to see what had been concealed under the backing for as long as she'd owned the painting. On yellowed paper stuck to the top stretcher bar they read:

Come Yesterday, at ten upon the hour
And cast thine eyes from high atop my Tower.

And, on the bottom bar:

A Message from the one thou callest Queen
Hand over Heart, will lead thee to her Dene.

The handwriting was small and compact, but unmistakably the work of the artist herself, Charlotte Nasmyth. Delia copied down the words in a notebook.

'Another "5" for your collection, Delia,' Jody said.

'Huh?'

'It's iambic pentameter, isn't it? Five feet in each line, di-da, di-da, di-da, di-da, di-da. Like most of Shakespeare.'

Kirsty Morton was curious. 'This means something to you?'

'Not much,' Delia said. 'Not yet, at any rate.'

'We'll let you know what we come up with, Kirsty,' Marcus said. 'Please send the bill for the rebacking to me at *A Malt O' My Ain*. By the way, how is your grandnephew enjoying his whisky? His *Poacher's Poison*?'

'Don't talk to me about Hugh,' Kirsty said in a despondent voice. 'He's been a bit of a disappointment to me lately.'

'Oh? How?'

'Can you believe he's joined those ultra-nationalist goons, *Auld Stobby*?'

Marcus was taken aback. Nothing in any conversation he'd had with Hugh Leggat indicated such extreme political views. It was a good thing he hadn't yet been confirmed as a Water Laird. There was still time for Marcus to withdraw the nomination, something he planned to take care of immediately.

He was doubly concerned, familiar as he was with *Auld Stobby*'s anti-NEPA rants. Now he realised he had been used as an inroad to Craig Wetherby. Might Hugh have been recruited by *Auld Stobby* specifically to 'spy' on NEPA's business? This could be dangerous – Wetherby was notoriously loose-tongued after a few drams.

'No, Kirsty, that's hard to believe, even harder to understand.'

'He wasn't even an SNP supporter, as far as I knew,' Kirsty said, shaking her head.

34
THE DEAN BRIDGE

RACHEL HERRING HAD INDICATED her son was 'taking care of business'; that business was at her casino in a handsome sandstone building in Learmonth Terrace. The Learmonth Club had been Rachel's first foray into the Edinburgh market, still a small-scale operation relative to her Blackpool, Brighton and Dublin enterprises. From it she had learned there was an opportunity for a really first-class casino resort, a Vegas-style facility, in the Scottish capital.

The 'no' result of the 2014 independence referendum had dented her enthusiasm for the project to some extent (she was more confident of being able to manipulate the amateurs of Holyrood than the seasoned pros at Westminster), but all was now looking rosy. As she sifted through the wads of used twenties the *Auld Stobby* fools had just brought her – notes that would be a piece of cake to launder through her various businesses – she hoped Victor was following through in the task she had set him tonight.

At Learmonth, only one table was still open at 3 am. Mondays and Tuesdays, the quietest sessions of the week, were Ciaran Mortimer's nights off; Victor was looking after the club, as normal. Sid the croupier had made several moves to close, but each time Victor had signalled him to keep going, for the single punter doggedly playing down through his ever dwindling stack of chips.

Cammy Lewis *knew* that his luck had to turn; it would be madness to cash in now. He'd gone to the trouble of putting on his best suit and a crisp white shirt; he always had the best luck when smartly dressed. He was even wearing the brand new Italian loafers he'd paid £300 for during his last winning streak.

What's more, he could see Sid was getting tired. A lapse of concentration by the dealer would be the turning-point. Meanwhile, his favourite cocktail waitress, Irina, had just served him another drink. And Victor had hinted this table would 'work' for him.

It *had* to work.

Karen and the kids had finally walked out on him a week ago, when he had refused once again to seek help with what she called his gambling addiction. He didn't know where they'd gone – his mother-in-law in Dumfries swore they hadn't shown up there. If you could believe anything *she* said.

But once he'd recovered the 20K he was down and parlayed that into 50 or 60K, he'd stop. For that kind of money, Karen would be glad to come home.

It was only when he got up from the table to go to the toilet that he realised how drunk he was. Still, his legs were one thing, his mind another. Back at the table, he was confident of his ability to keep focusing on those cards. 'Irina!' he called. 'Another scotch, with soda this time!'

'I've just sent her home,' Victor said. 'It's late. Let me get your drink.'

In another twenty minutes Lewis was almost cleaned out, and Victor instructed Sid to close the table. Placing an arm around Lewis's shoulder, he announced quietly in his ear: 'Time to call it a night, pal. Here's fifty quid for the chips you have left.'

With an incoherent sound Lewis rose from his seat to stagger back to the toilet, where he emptied his bowel and bladder, then vomited on the floor. When he emerged, he demanded another drink. 'No more scotch, pal,' Victor said. 'I'll see you home.'

'No need, I'll call a taxi,' Lewis slurred.

'Look at you, you've barfed down your shirt front. No cabby will take you. Come on, pal, grab your jacket and let's go.'

Leaving Sid to lock up, Victor threw on his hoodie and led Lewis out the back door to the garage. Unwilling to pollute his car with the reek of fresh vomit, he walked him out to the dark lane beyond, then pointed him in the direction of town. 'This way, Cammy, you drunken sod. I'll go at least part of the way with you.'

Unusually for late July a fog seemed to rise up from the Water of Leith and envelop them as they walked. On the Dean Bridge, Lewis tried to shake off his companion, at one point breaking free and crossing to the pavement on the upstream side of the bridge. There he stumbled and fell on his face.

The moist night air was heavy with malt, Edinburgh's signature scent. Victor was momentarily relieved to have that aroma in his nostrils in place of the stench from his charge's puke-sodden clothing. But duty called: crossing the road, he helped the drunken loser to his unsteady feet.

Lewis leaned back on the parapet and started to berate Victor for running a crooked casino. Voluble if not exactly coherent, he announced he was heading for the Torphichen Street police station right now to tell them everything, and to lay claim to the treasure trove he had uncovered.

Patiently Victor listened to the rant, then said, 'You've had shitty luck tonight, pal.' With that, he grabbed Lewis round both legs and hoisted him on to the parapet, making him howl with pain as the sharp iron spikes dug into his rear end. Before he knew what was happening, Victor had grabbed the heels of Lewis's Gucci loafers to swing his legs up, sending him tumbling backwards off the Dean Bridge into the foggy ravine beneath.

No more than two seconds of screaming were followed by a crunching sound. No splash, Victor noted.

Oops, must've missed the river.

He listened for a few moments, but heard only the rushing water a hundred feet below. Lighting a cigarette, Victor walked back to the Learmonth Club to collect his Land Rover.

A voice in the darkness: 'Hey, Victor, I thought you were going to give Cammy a lift home.'

Damn! He'd forgotten Sid might still be around.

'I thought so too,' he said, quickly composing himself, 'but he stank so bad I couldn't let him in my car. So we started walking, until he took an ill will at me for some reason. I left him this side of the bridge. He's plastered, but I think he'll make it home okay. Last I saw, he was staggering all over the road. Good thing there's no traffic. On a foggy night like this he could easily have been hit. I'd hate it if he got hurt.'

At 6:10 on Wednesday morning, the sun was beginning to shift the fog that had settled over Dean Village, not yet penetrating to the lowest level, 100 feet below the parapet of Thomas Telford's viaduct. Beth, a large golden retriever being walked by the Water of Leith, suddenly placed her front paws on the low wall between the path and the river to bark at something. A momentary break in the mist revealed the source of the dog's excitement: a human body, spread-eagled face down on a rock in the middle of the fast-flowing water. Beth's owner immediately called 999 on his mobile. Obviously another suicide, he told the dispatcher, though normally they landed in the flow, to be borne down to Stockbridge or Leith.

35
BREAKFAST

OVER BREAKFAST IN HER Marchmont Road flat, the kitchen radio tuned at low volume to Forth One, Delia read and reread the strange quatrain. Soon she knew it by heart.

Come yesterday, at ten upon the hour,
And cast thine eyes from high atop my tower.
A message from the one thou callest queen,
Hand over heart, will lead thee to her dene.

Though a long way from deciphering the verse (how can you ask someone to *'come yesterday'*, where is this *tower*, and who is this *queen*?), she was convinced Charlotte had intended it as a key to the location of the Neadreth grove; yet how she could have come into possession of that knowledge was not at all clear. Perhaps the combination of an intelligent woman's intuition and an artist's power of observation had led her to the spot.

Or was it just a figment of her imagination?

A *dene* was the English rendering of the word the Scots spelled *dean* (or *den* north of the Forth): a wooded valley with a stream – a *limpid water* – in the bottom, like the Canny Burn in Longniddry Dean or the Niddry Burn in Faucheldean. If a *dene* was the place to look, as the verse suggested, they had already visited those two.

She began thinking about Edinburgh's most famous dene, the one spanned by Telford's tall arches – the Dean Bridge, which featured in Charlotte's *Memoir*. Might the grove be there? Might the four-line verse, once decoded, point to *that* dene? Might ...

An item on the radio interrupted her thoughts, one that spooked her by coincidentally referring to the very place that was in her mind at that moment.

> *In breaking news, police are this morning at the scene of an apparent suicide at the Dean Bridge in Edinburgh's West End. A body was found just after 6 am on a rock in the middle of the Water of Leith, directly below the upstream parapet of the bridge. The man's name is being withheld until his family have been contacted. A spokeswoman for Police Scotland said that although suicide seems likely, foul play has not been ruled out. The northbound lane of the Dean Bridge is meantime closed to traffic, and motorists are advised to seek an alternative route.*

Delia recalled the history of the bridge, with the metal spikes added to its parapets to discourage suicide leaps. If those were still there, they were clearly not a hundred percent effective. That poor man must have been desperate to end his life.

In the shower before heading off to work, she had a happier thought. Quin would be arriving tomorrow. Unless Jody or Marcus solved the riddle of Charlotte's verse before then, there would be a fourth head to work on it.

⬠

Victor slept late. Rubbing his eyes, he stumbled through to the kitchen to put on the kettle and toaster, and was surprised to find his mother sitting at the table.

'Ma! I thought you were at the Balmoral. What're you doing here at this time?'

'*This* time? It's nearly half past ten. Anyway, I made up the spare bed, cleaned the guest bathroom – which was disgusting, by the way – and stayed here last night. Don't you have muesli?'

'If I'd known you were going to stay, I'd have laid some in for you. You know that, Ma. There's granola, I think.'

'Too much sugar. Anyway, did you do the needful last night?'

'Yes, all taken care of, just not quite as planned.'

'Not as planned? Christ, Victor, can't you ever do a simple thing the way I ask you? Did you put the Mogadon in his drink?'

'Yes, and he drank it all down. Only a few minutes later he spewed it all back up.'

'Then you gave him more?'

'No, I'd used all you gave me.'

'You're a bloody idiot, you know that? I *told* you, give him half. Too much, the body reacts by vomiting. Jeez, I should have come over to the club and done it myself.'

'It's okay, Ma. I moved to Plan B.'

'What did you do?'

'Tipped him off the Dean Bridge. It'll be in the local headlines this morning. Check it out.'

Rachel Herring quickly scanned the news on her smartphone and saw the report of a suspected suicide, the deceased not yet named by police. 'How many people saw him at the club last night?' she demanded.

'A dozen. So what? He lost all his money, decided on the way home to end it all. When the police come round, I'll tell them the whole story.'

'The *whole* story?'

'He played blackjack until three in the morning. Drank too much, so I offered to walk him home, but after a short way he insisted on going on without me. I went back to the club, met Sid who had just locked up, got in my Land Rover and came home. End of.'

'I don't like it. We had it worked out, remember? You were to get him zonked on alcohol and Mogadon, haul him out the back door into your Land Rover, drive away and strangle him like you did the treasure hunter ...'

'Yeah, yeah, I know that's what we talked about. After that I still have to get rid of the body.'

'You get rid of the body *where it won't immediately be found*. The last one you dumped in the firth, and that worked. You could have done that again. But oh, no – you have to throw Lewis off a bridge in the middle of Edinburgh.'

'Look, Ma, I know it's not *exactly* how it was supposed to go down, but it'll be fine. Nobody saw us in the fog at three in the morning.'

'You hope. Did you deal with the glass?'

'Glass?'

'The one he drank from, the one with Mogadon residue. What the hell glass do you think? Did you get rid of it, like we discussed?'

'It's in the washer. Irina always turns it on when she comes in.'

Rachel shook her head in despair and disbelief. 'You could have washed it yourself. You know, Victor, it won't take the police long to place Lewis at the club last night – they'll be there before you know it. They might even show up before Irina gets there today. You need to get over there right now.'

'Soon as I've had breakfast.' Victor opened the fridge and took out a can of Irn Bru.

Rachel wasn't done. 'Did you disable the CCTV in the gaming room?'

'It goes off automatically at two-thirty. I didn't override.'

'Okay, good. What about the cameras outside on Learmonth Terrace?'

'We went out the back door, as planned. No cameras there.'

'Could Sid have seen you prepare Lewis's drink?'

'No, I was in the back room. Sid was out front dealing cards.'

'How about the vomit? Has that been cleaned up?'

'Not yet, no. The cleaners come in at twelve. They'll take care of it.'

‘The hell they will. Get your clothes on, we’ve got some scrubbing to do. If there’s any trace of Lewis’s vomit, the cops will find Mogadon residues.’

Victor turned uncharacteristically pale.

‘What’s the matter? What have you just remembered?’

‘He spewed down the front of his suit.’

‘God dammit. So they’re going to find the drug anyway. Well, we still don’t want them to find any at Learmonth. Come on, there’s not a second to lose.’

A few minutes later, mother and son were on their way. ‘I don’t know how you can bear such a filthy car,’ Rachel said, a look of disgust on her face as she looked round the interior of the Land Rover. ‘If you can’t be bothered cleaning it up yourself, why don’t you take it to one of those full-service places?’

‘I gave it a good clean in the spring,’ Victor protested, ‘after I gave Bob Bowman a lift down to the firth, remember?’

‘I should damned well hope so. But look at the mess it’s in again.’

In no humour for such nagging, he merely grunted. To change the subject, he said, ‘Better go round by Murrayfield and the Dykes, I suppose. If the police are working at the Dean Bridge the traffic could be backed up there.’

Rachel consulted her smartphone. ‘They are, and it is.’

36
MOGADON MAN

With Operation Nightjar less than two weeks away, Isla remained deeply distrustful of the man with whom she would share the key role of setting the explosive. She had given no straight answer to Hugh's question: 'What exactly is *Auld Stobby* going to do for Rachel Herring that they did for Donald Trump?'

Now to see to that little piece of business, without Hugh looking over her shoulder. She had an appointment with Lowell J. Blackett MSP in his Scottish Parliament office at Holyrood.

Although English by birth, Blackett sat towards the 'ultra' end of the Scottish Nationalist spectrum – avowedly republican and europhobic in contrast to his party's official policies. He was tolerated by the SNP leadership, because he was well liked and responsive to his constituents on a wide range of local issues, though if his willingness to accept money in return for favours ever became known, he would be quickly disowned by the party. There had been hints in the press that he was close to, even (some said) beholden to, the extremists of *Auld Stobby*, but nothing stuck. He was, he liked to say, a maverick who put his constituents' needs above party politics; his leader tended to dismiss his errant ways as the behaviour of a mischievous but lovable schoolboy – an *awfy laddie* was the term she used.

Blackett eyed the Goth in his office with evident disdain. 'Ms Younie, I've made it clear that I'd prefer not to receive known *Auld Stobby* activists here in Holyrood. There are other places, with fewer inquisitive eyes, that we could meet. But since you're here, how can I help you?'

'It's the casino resort development by Edinburgh Airport. It promises a huge boost to the Scottish economy, but it seems to have got stalled in planning.'

'And what would you like me to do about it? Bring it up at First Minister's question time?'

'I was thinking more of having you use your influence behind the scenes, if you know what I mean.'

'I believe I know what you mean, Ms Younie. It's not really a matter for Parliament, more for Edinburgh Council ...'

'Where you must have SNP contacts. Including members of the Planning Committee.'

'Let me check on the status of the application and get back to you. Leave me your phone number.'

'I was hoping ...'

'I'll be in touch, Ms Younie. You'll have to excuse me now.'

She'd heard this 'check on the status' line many times from politicians and officials. Always a fob-off. She bloody well *knew* the status. What was needed was a *change* in the status. A positive one. Still, at least she'd be able to tell Rachel Herring that she'd set the wheels in motion.

⬠

After an overnight flight from Chicago to Heathrow, Quin Johnson arrived at Edinburgh Airport on Thursday 29th July at midday. As Delia had advised, he took the tram to Princes Street. The smooth, quiet, comfortable ride impressed him: a whole different experience from the 'El' in Chicago. At the Mound, he picked up a 41 bus to the top of Marchmont Road.

The elderly lady across the hall had been primed to let him into the building and give him the keys to Delia's flat. He freshened up, drank some fruit juice from the fridge and went out for a short walk. Buying some flowers on the way back, he put them in water and sat down to wait for Delia to arrive home. Just after five she walked in to find him fast asleep on the sofa.

Later, after they'd eaten, Quin asked, 'Any progress on Neadreth's grove?'

'Nothing yet. Hope you can give us some help with that.'

'Us? The three amigos, I suppose?'

'Yes. Jody, Marcus and myself.'

'Mm. Is there room for a fourth amigo?'

'Always room for you,' Delia said, as their eyes met for a full ten seconds across the kitchen table. 'But you've got some catch-up reading to do. Two 19th-century manuscripts by Charlotte Nasmyth got us into this whole search. You can start tomorrow.'

'Just like old times.'

'I know. Meanwhile, what do you make of this? It was written by Charlotte sometime around the 1830s.' She passed him a piece of paper on which she'd written the verse.

'*Come yesterday, at ten upon the hour*,' she recited. 'What's that supposed to mean? You can ask someone to come today, or tomorrow, but not *yesterday* for goodness' sake.'

'Could be we're meant to read *"come"* as "having come". Then it makes more sense.'

'I suppose so, yes.'

'*At ten upon the hour*. Ten o'clock. Pretty precise, isn't it? *And cast thine eyes from high atop my tower*. Again, I suppose we have to read that as "having cast". What tower is this? Does Nasmyth mention a tower in any of her other writings?'

'I don't think so. And it's odd she refers to it as *my tower*.'

'Maybe it's figurative, as in a towering achievement. A tower of strength. The Tower of Babel. Or a tower of her creation. Her artistic portfolio.' Quin was enjoying the conversation but fighting drowsiness.

'You're ready to sleep,' Delia said. 'Why don't we call it a night? I'm taking vacation starting tomorrow. Let's look at this again in the morning, when we're both fresh.'

'Sure thing. You haven't told me how you came by this little piece of iambic pentameter.'

'Pentameter, yes. The number 5 is all over Charlotte's writings. I'll tell you more over breakfast.'

When Delia came to bed an hour or two later, she put an arm over her sleeping partner. He awoke and turned over to kiss her; soon they found he was less jetlagged than they both had thought.

⬠

By that evening, the police had tracked down Karen Lewis and her children to a guest-house in Kilmarnock. In time for the late-night Scottish news bulletin, they announced that the man found dead below the Dean Bridge was Cameron Lewis, a 40-year-old building contractor and father of two. More significantly, they were treating his death as suspicious and appealed to the public for any sightings of Mr Lewis between 1 and 3 am on Wednesday.

A number of factors had already led the police to suspect this might not be a simple suicide. There was a high level of alcohol in the blood, accompanied by non-lethal amounts of the benzodiazepine drug nitrazepam, better known as Mogadon. Analysis of the victim's clothing showed evidence of the drug, indicating he had thrown up shortly after swallowing what would otherwise have been a fatal dose.

Experienced investigators considered that if 'Mogadon Man' had attempted suicide but failed, it was unlikely he would immediately throw himself off a high bridge. More typically he would make a second attempt on a later date by the same method. Furthermore, overdosing with a drug as a means of ending one's life most commonly occurs in the home.

Another curious thing: Mogadon Man was dressed in what had been a smart, though not expensive, suit and Italian designer shoes, one of which he was still wearing when his body was recovered; the other was lodged in a tree overhanging the river. According to his widow, he almost never got himself dressed up, except for weddings and funerals. Unusual to go to that trouble if he was contemplating killing himself – unless, as one wag put it, he'd decided he should be well dressed for his *own* funeral.

But the evidence that most clearly pointed away from suicide was found, curiously enough, on Mogadon Man's buttocks.

A straight line of small bruises, some with puncturing of the skin and corresponding tears in the seat of his trousers, was consistent with him having sat on the spiked iron rail that runs the length of the bridge parapet – a painful experience, even for a very drunk man. The precise geometry of the wounds showed he had been seated facing the roadway, with his back to the 100-foot drop, and had then fallen, or been pushed, backwards to his death, which would have been instantaneous. He had tumbled in such a way that he hit the midstream rock face down. The buttock wounds were therefore not obscured by more catastrophic injury on impact with the rock. Traces of the victim's blood, skin and trouser fabric were found on parapet spikes directly above where his body was recovered.

Among the calls to police headquarters shortly after the Thursday evening news was one from a man who had been gambling at Learmonth from late on Tuesday until about 1:30 am on Wednesday. He reported that Cameron Lewis, a regular like himself, had been playing blackjack at a neighbouring table and appeared to be losing heavily.

So it was that, on Thursday at 11:45 pm, a pair of police officers entered the Learmonth Club; simultaneously, the entryphone at Victor Herring's Merchiston flat whistled insistently, though no one was there to answer.

⬠

It wasn't the easiest of telephone calls to make, but he had no alternative.

'Hugh?'

'Speaking.'

'It's Marcus Annandale here.'

'Hello, Marcus. I heard you saw some of my great aunt's art collection.'

'I did. And she told me something that I found troubling.'

There was silence on Hugh Leggat's end of the line. Marcus went on, 'She told me you're a member of *Auld Stobby*. Is that true?'

'Er ... yes, though I can't imagine why she decided to tell you.'

'Thing is, Hugh, I can't continue to support your joining the Water Lairds in view of your membership of an extremist organisation. I wish you'd told me up front. It's embarrassing to have to withdraw my endorsement.'

'I thought the Lairds welcomed men of all political persuasions. You have some rank Tories, and one or two socialists. Even a Green, if I'm not mistaken. Is it just nationalists you're against?'

'Nationalists, no. I can think of at least three of our members who are pretty outspoken SNP supporters. But *Auld Stobby*? That's something else. To be honest, I'm shocked to learn you're a member.'

'Can I ask one favour, Marcus? As it happens, I'm not going to be able to come to the next Water Lairds meeting. The 5th of August, isn't it? There's a big case I'm working on that's going to come to a head on the 6th. Could you hold off on saying anything until after then?'

'I don't think so, Hugh. The longer this drags on, the more embarrassing it's going to get. I feel I have at least to warn Craig Wetherby. You guys have made some threatening noises against NEPA.'

'It's just rhetoric. Look, I give you my word I'll have no contact with Wetherby until after the August meeting. And I'd really appreciate if you could keep this whole thing under your hat, just for the next two weeks, until this case is off my docket.'

'What kind of case is it?'

'Under a gagging order, I'm afraid, so I can't talk about it yet. But you'll know all about it on the 6th, I promise.'

'Whistleblower, eh?'

'Not exactly, you'll see.'

'You're asking a lot, Hugh.'

Later that night, Jody ribbed him again about his *'Secret Seven'* club, and he began to think he might be over-reacting. True enough, it wasn't like the Water Lairds were a serious professional association. Just a bunch of men who enjoyed a crack and a glass of scotch.

Had he been given the tiniest inkling of what *Auld Stobby* was planning for 6th August, he would have been less sanguine.

37
THE TOWER

UNIFORMED POLICE OFFICERS hanging around the gaming floor are bad for business. As soon as Ciaran Mortimer spotted them on a CCTV screen, he invited them to his office.

'Were you in charge here,' one of the two inquired, 'in the early hours of Wednesday 28th July?'

'No, that would have been Victor. Victor Herring. He covers for me on my day off. He's not here tonight. Went to Brighton.'

'Brighton?'

'Yeah. Business trip. His mother owns a couple of clubs there as well. What's it about?'

'Just routine. A man died at the Dean Bridge early Wednesday morning and we've reason to believe he was here immediately before his death.'

'Cammy Lewis, wasn't it? Heard just a few minutes ago.'

'That's him.'

'What can I say? He's one of our regulars. I understand he *was* here Tuesday night into Wednesday morning. Irina, one of our cocktail waitresses, told me he'd lost a lot of money and got very drunk. She was quite worried about him – he tips well, apparently, even when he's losing. He was still at the table when she finished her shift.'

'When would that have been?'

Mortimer checked on his computer. 'Two-thirty.'

The two policemen glanced at each other. They knew the estimated time of death was 3 am, give or take half an hour. While one jotted Mortimer's response in his notebook, the other asked, 'Is Irina here tonight? We should talk to her. And who was dealing at Mr Lewis's table? That's another person we'd like to interview.'

'I don't know what table he was at, so I can't tell you the name of the dealer. But Irina will know. I've just buzzed her. She'll be here in a moment. Can I get you something? Coffee? Soft drink? Something stronger?'

The police officers declined the offer of refreshment. A few seconds later, Irina walked into the office and gave a start as her eyes fell on the uniformed policemen. Her normally pallid complexion turned even whiter.

'Is it my papers again?'

'No, Irina,' Mortimer said. 'Remember we got all that sorted out with the Border Agency at the beginning of the year.' Turning to the officers, he explained, 'Irina's from Bulgaria.'

'Romania,' she corrected him.

'Comes to the same thing. Constantinople, isn't it?'

'Constanţa.'

'Right.'

The policeman with the notebook had stopped writing. 'We're not here about your immigration status, Miss ...'

'Milescu. You can call me Irina.' She smiled nervously.

'You saw Mr Cameron Lewis here on Tuesday night or Wednesday morning, I believe?'

'Yes, he was here. Poor man.' Tears came to her eyes.

'Did you serve him alcohol?'

'That's my job. He was drinking scotch and water, no ice. He got a little drunk, and kept losing money. I was sorry for him, but I'm not allowed to suggest a customer stops playing.'

Mortimer interjected, 'Of course, we encourage a customer to leave the table if he seems to be getting inebriated, but that's not Irina's responsibility. It's up to the dealer.'

'I see,' the policeman without the notebook said. 'So tell me, Irina, when did Mr Lewis leave?'

'I don't know. My shift ended about half past two. I catch a night bus at 2:40. He was still here when I left. By that time he was the only player at Sid's table.'

'Sid?' the note-taker asked. 'What's his full name, Mr Mortimer?'

'John Sidney,' the manager said. 'Let me confirm he was on that night ... yes, he was. In fact he locked up, just after three o'clock on Wednesday morning.'

'Wouldn't that have been Mr Herring's job?'

'Not necessarily. Victor might have gone home and left Sid in charge. Sid's been with us a long time. He's very trustworthy.'

'Mm. One more question for you, Irina. Was Mr Lewis sick? Were you aware of him vomiting? Throwing up?'

'No, sir. I've never seen him do that. He holds his whisky well.'

'Thank you, Irina, that will be all for now. So, Mr Mortimer, can we have a word with Mr Sidney?'

'Not tonight you can't. He went to Brighton with Victor.'

Next morning, Quin woke at four. Careful not to disturb Delia, he tiptoed to the kitchen to make coffee and toast. On the table were printed copies of two handwritten documents, one titled *MY FAMILY: A TRUE MEMOIR*, the other *A NEW STORY OF EDINBURGH'S EARLIEST BEGINNINGS*. By the time Delia surfaced at eight, he had read both from beginning to end.

'I think I know where Charlotte's tower is,' he announced, as Delia poured herself a plate of cereal. 'And could I have some of that, please?'

'Where?'

'In this bowl.'

'No, stupid, the tower. Where is it?'

Quin thumbed through the Memoir, located a page and began reading aloud. '*One of my most vivid childhood memories is of Mama getting me up at midnight, wrapping me in a blanket and hustling me up the steep staircase to the belvedere.* I'd never heard of a *belvedere* before, but it's a glass lookout on the roof of a house. Charlotte's family had one. That was her tower.'

'D'you think?' Delia moved the breakfast dishes to one side and spread a map of Edinburgh on the table. 'Here's where her family lived, 47 York Place. So, if you *cast thine eyes from high atop*, what can you see?' She traced a finger over the map. 'Most of Edinburgh, and quite a lot beyond. Not very helpful.'

'We're looking for *the one thou callest queen*. That should narrow the search a bit.'

'Or a place associated with a queen. Such as the castle. Hermutrude, Eithne and Margaret were all queens mentioned by Charlotte in connection with the castle. Or how about Holyrood Palace? I think it might be visible from the Nasmyth rooftop.'

Quin was puzzled. 'I don't recall Charlotte talking about any queen who lived at Holyrood.'

'No, but lots of queens have had an official residence there. Mary, Queen of Scots, for example. Even Queen Victoria, who gets a mention in the *Memoir*.'

'Why do you think the verse says *the one thou callest queen*? Should we be looking for something *called* "queen"? A building – a church, say? Or a street named for a queen?'

'Queen Street!' Delia exclaimed. 'The westward continuation of York Place!'

'Now we're getting somewhere,' Quin said. 'But what's the message? The message that *hand over heart, will lead thee to her dene*?'

Delia was studying the map again. 'The line of Queen Street running west leads precisely to a *dene*. It's under the Dean Bridge, which features prominently in the *Memoir*. We should take a look, though not today – it's probably still crawling with cops. A man was found dead there the other day.'

'If the verse is supposed to lead us to the Dean Bridge, I'm still wondering what *hand over heart* means.'

'Beats me,' Delia said. 'Let's ponder it for a day or two. My priority is still the five hills where Charlotte painted her series of landscapes.'

'Which of these would be visible from York Place? From her *tower* – the belvedere, I mean?'

'All of them, I guess, except Craiglockhart, which would be hidden behind the Castle Rock. The nearest would be Inverleith.'

'The *Memoir* mentions the view of Inverleith from the belvedere,' Quin said, leafing through the copy on the table. 'Here it is. It's about the botanic garden there. *We enjoyed watching its colours change with the seasons. Behind it lay the firth with its scattering of islands and, still farther beyond, the hills of Fife, the distinctive rounded summit of East Lomond being our marker for due north*. Was it the Inverleith painting, by any chance, that had the verse hidden under the backing?'

'No, it was another one, the view from the Salisbury Crags.' Noticing his bewildered look, she added, 'You're going to be very familiar with all these places in just a few days. Wait a minute – what did you just read?'

'*We enjoyed watching its colours change ...*'

'No, after that, the bit about East Lomond.'

'*... the distinctive rounded summit of East Lomond being our marker for due north.*'

'That hill,' Delia told him, 'has an association with Scotland's most famous queen. Not a particularly strong one, I have to say. When Mary, Queen of Scots was in residence at Falkland Palace, by the foot of East Lomond, she used to delight in hunting and falconry on its slopes.'

'Wow! How do you know that?'

'Three or four weeks ago, when I was doing fieldwork in Fife, I had dinner one night in a small restaurant in Falkland. I picked up a leaflet on the history of the village – I probably still have it somewhere.'

Quin caught her evasive tone. 'Dinner? Just you, or with some of your co-workers?'

She looked him straight in the eye. 'It was a date, right? With a guy who helped me when my stupid company van wouldn't start. It was nothing.'

'You still seeing him?'

'No. He turned out to be a lowlife. It's too embarrassing to talk about.'

'After dinner, did you ...?'

'No!'

'Were you going to tell me?'

'Quin, let's drop it, okay? I haven't quizzed you about who you've been seeing in Chicago.'

'You can if you like. Though there's nothing to tell.'

'Well, same here.' She took hold of his hand and squeezed it, then changed the subject. 'Let's pursue your Inverleith idea. It seems to be the only one of the five hills that Charlotte mentions in connection with her *tower*.'

She picked up her phone. 'Hi, Marcus. Listen, Quin's been reading Charlotte's stuff and ... What's that? He got here yesterday and has been up reading since the middle of the night. Anyway, we think the verse could refer to the hill of Inverleith ... I'll explain later, but the point is this. We need to look again at the *Prospect of Edinburgh* from Inverleith. Can we go back to Kirsty's? ... Yes, again. We should open up the backing like we did with the other one ... Hospital? Right, for a "procedure", she called it. Okay, call me when you've talked to her.'

'So,' Quin said, 'if the verse is meant to point us to the Inverleith painting, who or what is *the one thou callest queen*? And we're still no nearer an answer to *hand over heart*.'

'Maybe it'll become clear if we can take a look at the back of Inverleith. Charlotte didn't want to make this too easy.'

⬠

John Sidney's first reaction to the Kemptown Casino in Brighton was stunned delight. Four times the size of the Learmonth Club, its restoration to regency glory had clearly been a no-expenses-spared labour of love. So *this*, on an even grander scale, was what Rachel Herring was planning for her new casino resort on the outskirts of Edinburgh.

Things were moving fast; could it have been only yesterday that Victor spoke to him about the opportunity? To graduate from croupier to floor manager had certainly been Sid's ambition, but for it to happen so quickly, without any hint this was in Victor's or Rachel's plan – well, it blew him away. Today, Victor and he had taken an afternoon flight to Gatwick, hired a car and driven straight here; a couple of hours on, it was confirmed the job was his, at a salary almost double what he made, even with tips, at Learmonth.

Rachel wanted him to start the very next day; he could arrange later for removal of his furnishings and effects. No problem. There was an attic flat above the casino that he could occupy until he found himself a more permanent place to live.

Everything was going so well that a midnight call on his mobile phone from Police Scotland came as a bit of a shock. 'Was Cameron Lewis playing at your table on Tuesday night into Wednesday morning?'

'Er ... yes.'

'At what time did he leave the club?'

'Just after 3 am; in fact I locked up immediately after Mr Lewis left ... but what is this about?'

'Just routine inquiries, sir; did he leave alone?'

It would cause unnecessary bother if he mentioned Lewis being helped out the back door by Victor. 'I didn't see him leave. I was closing the table, cashing up for the night.'

'Where will you be tomorrow, sir?'

Sid gave the address of the Kemptown Casino.

‘Staying in Brighton, eh? Okay, you can expect a visit from Sussex Police at some point.’

‘Has something happened to Mr Lewis?’

‘I’m afraid so. He went off the Dean Bridge at approximately 3 am on Wednesday. It’s likely you were the last person to see him alive.’

38
DECLARATION OF INTEREST

THE APPROACHING MONTHLY MEETING of the Planning Committee had caused James Swift a few sleepless nights; as the day dawned he felt physically unwell. The arithmetic – a seven-seven split with the convener's casting vote to go against the Herring casino development – was remorseless, even before he learned one of those in favour would miss the meeting. That made it seven-six against, with no need for a casting vote. He had tried to take the matter off this month's agenda, to give him more time to rally support, but the convener refused.

Now he knew exactly how things would play out. There would be no gambling resort; Rachel Herring would make her investment somewhere else. Being the vindictive bitch she was, she would carry out her threat to expose his illegal acceptance of money. Another corruption scandal in Edinburgh local politics – the papers would love it.

These thoughts occupied his mind during consideration of the first five items on the agenda, all of which were passed without a vote. Next up: the casino resort. He gathered his wits; might as well deliver the speech he had prepared, lost cause though it was.

'Councillor Swift, do you wish to speak in favour?' the convener asked.

'I do indeed, Mr Chairman. Edinburgh cannot afford to turn down a project of this scale and quality. It will turn a decaying office campus, one that currently brings little revenue to our coffers, into a world-class resort that will attract high-spending tourists to our city all year round. The trams will bring them in their thousands into Princes Street and St Andrew Square – it will be like Festival time twelve months of the year. The business case, Mr Chairman, is unassailable. Now as to the proposed development itself ...'

Swift droned on for a full twenty minutes, getting into minutiae of the architecture, the landscaping, the interior design. He seemed oblivious to the foot-shuffling and yawning of his colleagues on the committee. Finally, he wrapped up: 'And so, Mr Chairman, I commend this development for the whole-hearted approval of the committee.'

'A strong voice in favour, then,' the convener said. 'Councillor Swift, do you wish to make a declaration of interest in this matter?'

Swift's complexion turned from tomato to beetroot as he replied, 'Indeed I do not, except for my love of this city.'

'Fine. As we are already running over our allotted time, I will not call for any other statements in favour. Does anyone wish to speak against?'

One of the 'antis', a lay preacher, spoke passionately of the damage this 'den of vice' would inflict on Edinburgh, the problems of gambling addiction, and the missed opportunity for a new 'contemplative green space' on the edge of the city.

Another questioned the business case. She reported on a recent visit to Las Vegas where, she said, the overwhelming majority of visitors took a shuttle from the airport to their casino resort, spent their entire time in that resort or the one next door, and took the shuttle back again. There was little or no spin-off benefit to non-gambling venues.

A third was concerned about an influx of low-wage workers driving down local salaries in the service industry.

The SNP man Steven Lawrie said nothing, but Swift knew where he stood. He had tried his damnedest with him, to no avail.

Swift's request to respond to the points made by the 'antis' was turned down. He had taken enough of the committee's time and the matter would now go to a vote. The result was not the foregone conclusion he had expected and feared. The committee voted seven-six *in favour*. Lawrie, who had said, 'My vote *against* is one hundred percent solid,' had switched sides.

A huge wave of relief swept over Councillor Swift, followed by an equally powerful wave of self-congratulation. 'My speech was a stunner,' he told himself. 'I turned him around.'

⬠

The message on Isla's phone was terse. 'Lowell Blackett. You'll be pleased to know I called in a favour from a friend. The Edinburgh Planning Committee has just voted to approve the casino resort development by the airport.'

⬠

Kirsty was happy to see Delia again so soon, and was equally welcoming to the young man she brought along. 'I suppose you want to tear open the backs of more of my paintings,' she said with a wink.

'Actually,' Delia said, 'that's exactly what I want to do, if you can bear it.' She explained why she thought the view from Inverleith might be significant: a view of Inverleith from the rooftop of the Nasmyth family home was specifically mentioned in Charlotte's writings.

'Isn't this exciting!' Kirsty said, in a conspiratorial whisper.

But with the backing removed, there was nothing to see. The stretcher bars looked original, only this time they bore no inscription of any kind. All that was visible was the carapace of a long-dead spider, which had quite possibly been trapped when the painting was originally framed in 1835.

'*Livin' there*,' Delia said, absently.

Kirsty looked in puzzlement at Delia, then at Quin, who shrugged as if to say, 'She does this sometimes.'

'It's a bad habit I have.' Delia explained. 'Pathological, Quin might say. I make anagrams of place-names. Inverleith, *livin' there*.'

Kirsty laughed. 'Funnily enough, I did live in Inverleith for a couple of years. So, d'you want to open up the third painting?'

Though there was no reason to think the Craiglockhart painting was of special significance, the offer was too good to refuse. And again, no writing on the stretcher bars. Not even a dead spider this time.

39
DUMB

BACK AT MARCHMONT ROAD, Delia and Quin returned to the puzzle of the *tower*, the *queen*, the *hand* and the *heart*. The map of Edinburgh was out again.

Thinking aloud, Delia wondered, 'What if the *tower* was just Charlotte's way of referring to the Salisbury Crags where she painted her *Prospect of Edinburgh*, the one with the verse? They certainly tower above Holyrood.' She put her finger on the spot where, according to Marcus, Charlotte must have set up her easel. Suddenly, she gave a whoop. 'Oh my God!' she cried.

'What is it?' Quin asked, peering at the map. 'The Palace of Holyrood? We talked about that as a place of queens, didn't we?'

'Yes we did, but there's something *much* more significant, even closer to her viewpoint on the Crags. Look!'

St Margaret's Well, the map indicated.

'Don't you see, Quin? Margaret, the sainted 11th-century queen, featured in the *New Story*. Wouldn't her well be a place where "limpid water flowed"? In Scotland, a 'well' isn't always a hole in the ground. It can be a spring, the source of a stream. And there might, at one time, have been a hazel grove around it. Come on, if we run across the Meadows we can pick up the 35 bus to take us over there.'

This was the Delia he knew and loved. Always with a plan, always ready to act on it.

Any idea Hendrik Vandenbrouck might have had of absconding with the £770,000 – the balance of the money received for the gold statuette after Rachel Herring's share was deducted – was not acted upon, at least not immediately. Mariane would claim 200K for supplying knowhow and explosive, and there were other bills to pay. That would still leave a cool half-million; after the bridge had blown he might take the opportunity to disappear. A new identity, a new home (Aruba took his fancy) beckoned. He was fed up with this Scottish climate, anyway. Almost as rainy as Belgium.

Time to get the Operation Nightjar team together again, to ensure everything was on track. Though there was no reason to suppose Firth TV & Audio was under surveillance, he announced that Friday's meeting would be held in anonymous premises he had rented for a month – a seedy former nail salon in Pilton.

Mariane reported that the charges would be delivered to an address in Glenrothes on 4th August. Batteries included, only minimal assembly required. Fraser Cadenhead confirmed he would collect the parcel the following day and take it to his boat at North Queensferry for deployment that night. Willie Thomson's responsibility, on which the success of the operation was totally dependent, would be to provide intelligence as to security detail on the Forth Bridge between midnight and 2 am on the 6th, and warn the team of any last-minute changes.

Isla and Hugh, entrusted with planting the bomb, would immediately travel to Belgium for two days of training at VHC *(Vrijheidscentrum)*, a clandestine school for 'freedom fighters' in a converted wartime bunker deep in rural Flanders. Mariane, herself a VHC instructor, would participate in their training.

They would be met at Brussels airport and driven to a large supermarket car-park, where they would transfer to the windowless cargo compartment of a florist's van. The van journey would take two hours in each direction, enough time to reach virtually anywhere in Flanders (or, for that matter, to leave Belgium altogether), though for all they knew they might spend most of that time being driven around in circles.

Once at VHC, Hugh would share a cramped underground sleeping cell with Isla the Goth. He would have been scarcely less enthusiastic had his assigned room-mate been Attila the Hun.

⬠

It was an uncomfortable meeting. In the opinion of Edinburgh's chief superintendent of police it came close to breaching an ethical boundary. Opposite him at his desk sat a grey-haired man in a dark suit, who was urging him to show restraint in pursuing what, according to his detectives and forensic experts, was a suspicious death.

'We're duty bound,' the senior policeman said, 'to follow our lines of inquiry, wherever they may lead.'

'I understand,' his visitor said, 'but on occasion we have to consider the greater good. And the greater good will *not* be served by antagonising the Herring business empire at this critical time, as we've discussed. Mr Lewis's death could have been suicide, could it not?'

'It could, yes, but ...'

'Then let's leave it at that, for the time being.'

⬠

On the way to St Margaret's Well, Delia and Quin came close to convincing themselves that it would turn out to be the site of Neadreth's grove, though they had to admit there remained a puzzle in the third and fourth lines of Charlotte Nasmyth's quatrain. *A message from the one thou callest queen, hand over heart, will lead thee to her dene.* Sure, it made sense that Queen Margaret could be the one sending the *message*, but why was it *her* dene? Wasn't it *Neadreth's* dene they were looking for? And, once again, why '*hand over heart*'?

'It might become clear when we get there,' Delia said, as their bus sat stalled in Friday afternoon traffic.

Eventually getting off at the Scottish Parliament building, they threaded their way through the throngs of tourists outside the royal palace to the open spaces of Holyrood Park. There, at the base of the Salisbury Crags, they soon found themselves face to face with St Margaret's Well.

A plaque on the stone superstructure made it clear they were on a fool's errand. The well had been reconstructed here in 1860, more than 20 years after Charlotte had painted *A Prospect of Edinburgh* on the clifftop above. Its original site was a mile to the east, where it had been in the line of a new railway.

'That was dumb,' Delia said. 'We could have found this out from the internet and saved ourselves the journey.'

'No harm done.'

'Since we're here, let's take a walk and see for ourselves the view Charlotte painted all those years ago.'

They followed the same path Marcus had walked earlier in the summer. As they rounded the spur and began climbing towards the crest of the Crags, the sounds of the city faded. Swallows cleansed the air of tiny insects; somewhere a skylark was singing. They continued their ascent until suddenly the ground beneath them came to an end, and the traffic noise burst upon them again. Another step forward and they would have plunged fifty feet off the sheer cliff.

Before them lay Edinburgh in all its glory. Delia pointed out the landmarks she recognised. Centre-stage stood the castle on its ancient rock, just as it did in 1838 when Charlotte Nasmyth recorded this view in oils on a 34×21-inch canvas – knowingly framing the scene in Pacioli's *divine proportions*. From this spot, the castle just failed to break the skyline formed by the wooded ridge of Corstorphine Hill beyond.

No wonder Charlotte chose this viewpoint. They gazed enraptured at the vista. Quin put his arm around Delia's shoulder and drew her towards him. Their lips locked, until suddenly they realised they were perched on the edge of a precipice. Stepping back from the brink, they simultaneously burst into laughter.

Rachel Herring's attention to detail was part of the secret of her success. True, marrying and shortly afterwards burying a rich old man had been a crucial first step, but since then she had kept an eagle eye on the minutiae of running – and expanding – the late Cyril Herring's casino empire.

So when the crooked little Edinburgh councillor called her at her Isle of Man home to claim his £50,000 for pushing through approval for her new gaming resort, she decided to make sure it had indeed been his intervention that won the day. After all, she had given *Auld Stobby* a chunk of the value of an antique gold statuette to corrupt the planning process; why pay James Swift unless he had truly been instrumental?

A few discreet phone calls gave the information she needed. The crucial member of the planning committee, Councillor Steven Lawrie, had been got at not by Swift but by the well-known *Stobby*-sympathetic MSP Lowell Blackett. So Isla Younie, she of the ashen face, spiky black hair and purple lipstick, had delivered the goods. No need to pay a penny more to Swift. He could remonstrate all he liked; Rachel had him by the balls and there was nothing he could do about it.

Meanwhile, other matters required her close attention.

First and foremost, Sid had to stay in Brighton at least until the heat was off the Learmonth Club in Edinburgh; hence the invention of a 'floor manager' position for him, at a salary which would keep his trap shut about whatever the hell he knew of Cammy Lewis's last few minutes of life.

Plus, she had to control her idiot son. He had no concept that the more he evaded police questioning, the more suspicion would rest on him. If – God forbid – he were to be charged with Lewis's murder, it would be curtains for Learmonth, and for the casino resort. She called him, for the tenth time that day.

'Victor, where are you?'

'On the train, heading into London. Everything's cool in Brighton. No need for me to stay any longer.'

'*London?* For what? A night of clubbing? Whoring? No, don't tell me. There's no bright lights, big city for you tonight, sonny boy. Get back to Edinburgh, *now*, understand?'

'Ma, it's best I stay away for a few days. Let the cops find another death to investigate. Lewis can be written off as a suicide, open and shut. They'll soon lose interest.'

'Jesus, Victor, you've no idea, have you? Look, here's what you'll do. First thing tomorrow morning, you'll walk into police HQ in Edinburgh. You've been away on business, but as soon as you heard the news you wanted to come in and tell them what you know.'

'You want me to cuff myself while I'm at it?'

'I'm serious. Tell them you helped Lewis out the back door. You were going to give him a lift home but didn't want his vomit in your car. You walked him up on to Queensferry Road, pointed him across the Dean Bridge, and left him to make his own way from there. You didn't realise how much booze the damn-fool Romanian girl was giving him, but knew he'd lost a wad of cash at the table. Give them every reason to believe he was suicidal. Tell them he was a good man, you're sad he took his life, you wish you'd walked further with him, blah, blah.'

'I'm nearly at Gatwick. I can try to catch the last flight.'

'Do it. Call me later.'

As she ended the call, Rachel realised she was going to have to coach him further. The cops would say he was seen with Lewis on the bridge, say they found Mogadon residues at Learmonth, anything to unnerve him, get him off his prepared story. He would need another pep talk in the morning. Hell's teeth, if only that son of hers weren't so goddamned dumb.

Had she known the investigators of Cammy Lewis's death were under high-level instructions to play softball with Victor, she would have slept much easier than she did that night.

40
A CHEAP KNOCK-OFF

MARCUS WAS BUSY AT *A Malt O' My Ain* that Saturday, 31st July. Street performers on the Royal Mile drew crowds; though only a tiny fraction of the tourists enjoying the scene ventured into the shop, this was his most profitable time of the year. For him, the search for Neadreth's sacred grove would have to take a back seat for the next month.

Not so for Jody, Delia and Quin, who made their way to Jane Street in Leith for the weekly auction at Ramsay Cornish. Before the sale began at eleven, dealers and collectors previewed the 300 or so lots that were to come under the hammer. On offer this week was an eclectic mix of furniture ranging from faux Chippendale to genuine Ikea, a miscellany of small ornaments, jewellery, coins and watches; oriental rugs; and a gallery of art to suit a variety of tastes, including paintings, engravings and prints from the 19th and 20th centuries.

A Prospect of Edinburgh 'after Nasmyth' hung on the wall between a portrait of a sullen-looking Abyssinian cat and a framed collection of beer bottle tops. When the space around it cleared for a moment, Jody took the opportunity to lift the picture down for a closer look. The signature was indecipherable; the best guess any of them could come up with was 'C. Summer'.

The view was essentially rural: woods and grassy fields stretching towards a distant town, identifiable as Edinburgh by its castle on the rock and a slightly misshapen Arthur's Seat beyond. Two standing and three seated figures in the foreground were dwarfed by trees reaching up to a sky about to deliver a shower of rain. The composition was certainly Nasmythian, but the brushwork showed neither the discipline of Alexander nor the flair of Charlotte. It was Delia who first recognised it for what it was; in less than a minute she brought up an image of Alexander Nasmyth's *Edinburgh from Corstorphine Hill* on her smartphone. The 'C. Summer' painting was a workmanlike copy – or a cheap knock-off, as Jody put it.

A Prospect of Edinburgh from Corstorphine Hill this might be, but it was not the work of Charlotte Nasmyth. Half an hour into the sale it went for £65, purchased by an unkempt man in a raincoat, black trousers and white shoes who, unaccountably, also bought the bottle tops. Time to go.

The Edinburgh Fringe had just opened. Having three tickets for an afternoon drama performance at the Pleasance, Jody invited Delia and Quin to join her. Afterwards they repaired to a nearby pub in St Leonards Street for a drink and a bite. In a quiet corner, their conversation quickly turned to what they'd come to call the 'Neadreth Project'.

Delia brought up Aebbe's monastery at Coldingham. 'A long shot, for sure, but I still keep thinking about the ruined abbey, just like the one in *The Antiquary* with its buried treasure.'

'Does it have a queen connection?'

'Yes, Jody, if you remember, Aebbe gave refuge there to Aethelthryth or St Audrey.'

'Ah yes, the virgin queen. You've done pretty well to recall *both* her names.'

'At least one of them was easy to remember. When I was a kid, I had a cat called Audrey.'

'St Audrey,' Quin remarked, 'is one of the few historical figures whose name gives us a common English word.'

'Huh?' Delia and Jody uttered in unison.

'I checked it out. On her feast day, a great market was held in the town of Ely, outside the cathedral she founded. Among the goods traditionally sold were lace bodices designed to hide a woman's cleavage, in keeping with a cult of chastity inspired by

Audrey's story. Over time, the bodices declined in quality as the townspeople could ill afford fine lace. They even lost their primary function of making their wearer seem demure. The word "tawdry", initially applied to goods bought at St Audrey's fair, came to describe any cheap and crudely made article.'

'Like the tartan tat sold up and down the Royal Mile,' Jody remarked.

'I suppose,' Quin said, though he hadn't yet been exposed to the worst excesses of the Scottish souvenir market.

'So, coming back to Coldingham, you think it's a possibility?'

'Yes,' Delia answered, 'but for the moment we should stay focused on Charlotte's five *Prospect of Edinburgh* landscapes. She hid her little verse in one of them; if that's not a clue, I don't know what is.'

'Pity we're still missing two of the five,' Jody mused. 'I was hopeful that would be one of them at Ramsay Cornish this morning. I'd have willingly paid £65 for it.'

⬠

Not a hundred yards from the pub where that discussion was going on, one of a different kind was in progress at St Leonards police station. Victor had walked in just after 4 pm to 'volunteer' information relating to the last movements of Cammy Lewis.

His mother's admonition that he should do this 'first thing in the day' had been set aside; likewise her advice that he should dress 'professionally'. Victor arrived in his favourite *THIS HOODIE'S NOT FOR HUGGING* leisurewear. The duty officer motioned him to take a seat in the waiting area – 'Someone will be with you shortly, sir' – where he joined a nervous middle-aged woman in a shabby dress and a twenty-something transvestite.

Victor pointedly ignored the tranny's attempt to engage him in conversation. It was of no interest to him that he/she was there to lodge a complaint of sexual harassment by members of a rugby team in a Canongate pub.

A young policewoman walked past. She looked vaguely familiar to Victor, and eventually he placed her. It was PC Shona Kilmartin, one of the two constables who had paid him a call at his mother's building site while investigating the headless body that washed up on Cramond Island. She had said they would like to see the chainsaw he kept in his garage at Merchiston, but there had been no follow-up. Clearly he was not a 'person of interest' in that matter. He hoped that would be the case, too, in the death of Cammy Lewis.

In due course he was summoned through a door and into what he assumed was an interview room. There was no obvious CCTV camera, no one-way mirror like they had on his favourite cop shows. PC Philip Bannerman, a fresh-faced rookie, showed his badge and offered a plastic tumbler of water. Victor declined.

'I have to ask you to lower your hood, sir,' Bannerman said. 'It's a rule.'

Victor's impulse was to tell baby-face, 'Sod off,' or challenge him, 'Would you ask a Muslim woman in a hijab to do the same thing?' But with his mother's coaching still fresh in his mind he quietly complied.

After giving his statement he waited in the interview room while the constable's notes were compiled into a narrative for his signature. All quite painless. He was relieved, and not a little surprised, to be released before 5 pm. He put up his hood again and headed to the nearest pub for a drink. Vodka and Irn Bru.

He paid no attention to the young man and two women engrossed in conversation at a table in the corner. Instead, he quickly finished his drink, ordered another, and called his mother to report that the police seemed happy with his statement and had no further questions. He then sat back to enjoy the football match from Croatia or someplace playing silently on the TV.

41
PHANTOM QUEEN

SUNDAY 1ST AUGUST: D-DAY MINUS FIVE.

The sun was just appearing over the Binn at Burntisland but Fraser Cadenhead had already been out on the firth for an hour and a half. He had timed the crossing from North Queensferry to Inchgarvie and reconnoitred the proposed landing point on the north shore of the tiny island.

He had initially expected to use the jetty on the south side, built to service the fortifications that had occupied Inchgarvie since the reign of James IV. But Willie Thomson had insisted it would be too visible from the platform of the bridge.

The nearest granite plinth supporting the bridge stood on rocks between low and high water marks on the island. As the planned operation would coincide with low tide, access would not be difficult, even with a heavy swell in the firth.

What remained was to estimate the number of minutes it would take to go ashore, reach the plinth and scale it with a lightweight ladder, fix the explosive to the steelwork, and return to the boat. A practice run would be set up when Isla and Hugh got back from Belgium, not on the island – that would be too dangerous – but at an abandoned industrial site in Kirkcaldy that Cadenhead had scoped out a few days ago. This was critical, because the operation had to be timed precisely to fit within a 'blackout window' in the bridge security schedule, when activities on Inchgarvie would briefly escape surveillance.

Watching Cadenhead steer his boat into the harbour at Aberdour, an old man walking his dog on the breakwater called to him, 'Aye, Fraser, ye're on the go early. Catch anything?'

Fraser Cadenhead held up a pair of foot-long mackerel he'd brought from his freezer at home. 'No much daein this mornin, Sandy. Jist enough for a wee fry-up.'

⬠

At that moment, about 6:15 on Sunday morning, Delia and Quin were just coming to. They planned to spend the day going round the remaining four hills where *A Prospect of Edinburgh* had been painted.

The weather was set fair, and after breakfast they made for the nearest viewpoint: Blackford Hill. Craigmillar Park Golf Course skirts the base of the hill, but their goal was the summit to the west. Having passed through the imposing archway and ascended past the Royal Observatory, they arrived at some cliffs of exposed rock known as Corbie's Craig, overlooking a deep wooded defile, the Hermitage of Braid.

A dene for sure; could Neadreth's grove be there? Yet another possibility, but Charlotte's verse made no sense if that was it. Unless there was some queenly association they were unaware of.

Under the Craig they took a breather. On her tablet computer Delia looked up the meaning of *corbie*. Scots for a crow, she found. 'Like the French, *corbeau*,' Quin put in. Certainly there were a few *corbies* patrolling the Craig that morning, the grey-waistcoated species known as the hoodie crow that in the British Isles is largely restricted to Scotland and Ireland.

'Listen to this, Quin,' she said, and proceeded to read aloud. '"In Irish folklore, the hoodie crow is a manifestation of the *Morrigan*, a mythical phantom queen." Could the *corbie* of Corbie's Craig be *the one thou callest queen*? If so, maybe the Hermitage *is* the dene we're looking for.'

'Possible, I suppose, but unlikely. Since we haven't seen Charlotte's *Prospect of Edinburgh* from Blackford Hill, we don't know exactly where she painted it, but wherever it was, she would have had her *back* to the Hermitage.'

'I know. And none of her writing suggests an interest in *Irish* folklore.'

Getting back on their feet, they walked the short distance to the highest point of the hill. Here the map showed remains of a fort, dating probably from pre-Roman times, on what was clearly a strong defensive site, but to the untrained eye no trace of it could be seen. A flat-topped stone plinth on the summit bore a panoramic indicator that showed compass directions and named some of the most conspicuous landmarks. '*Cast thine eyes from high atop thy tower*,' Delia said. 'What do you see?'

'Well, obviously, Edinburgh Castle on its rock, which seems to be pretty much due north from here.'

'The Castle of Maidens, yes. Plenty of queens there.'

'It's so central to everything Charlotte wrote, it seems like it must be the place we're looking for, yet it's hardly what you'd call a *dene*. Quite the opposite, in fact.'

'Yes, but remember the queen gives a *message ... to lead thee to her dene*. The *dene* is somewhere else, if we can figure out what the message is.'

'Something to do with *hand over heart*, presumably.'

'I suppose,' Delia said, 'we'll have to go to the castle. But it's swarming with tourists at this time of year. I can't imagine that we'll pick up the trail there.'

From their perch on Blackford Hill they looked for the remaining three *Prospect of Edinburgh* viewpoints. To their west were the two unmistakable domes of Craiglockhart. They had already decided Easter Craiglockhart had to be the one Charlotte chose, being closer to the city. More distant, to the north-west, was the squat dark mass of Corstorphine Hill. Their final destination would be Inverleith Hill – if hill it could be called – occupied now by the botanic garden and in a direct line behind the castle.

On the panoramic indicator, Delia spread out her map of Edinburgh. 'Okay,' she said, 'here's where we are, Blackford

Hill, there's the castle and there's Inverleith, all in a straight line. Guess what's interesting about the distances from the castle to these other places?'

Quin made a determined but ultimately unsuccessful effort not to roll his eyes. 'Don't tell me, sweetheart. The golden ratio.'

'Exactly.'

'How can you tell that without measuring?'

'My eye is permanently tuned to the golden ratio. But when we get home this afternoon, you can get out a ruler and measure the distances on the map. *Hand over heart,* Quin, you'll find I'm right.'

They laughed, then enjoyed a long kiss, until a sudden breeze picked the map up off the direction finder and they had to run after it.

⬠

A Malt O' My Ain was humming with customers on Sunday morning, many of them ready to spend money. Fortunately Jody had offered to help out, otherwise Marcus couldn't have handled it. He *had* to hire an assistant, at least for weekends – a step in his business development plan he had put off for months.

'Have more faith in yourself, in your idea,' Jody kept telling him.

Easy for *her* to say; she hadn't suffered the jolt to self-esteem that comes with being thrown out of work in the corporate world. But at least today he could see his business model was a good one. Tomorrow he would call an agency to send him some candidates for a part-time sales position.

A man Marcus judged to be in his fifties but coiffed and dressed like someone much younger had been hanging around for half an hour or more, spending some time in the tasting room, purely as a spectator. At a relatively quiet moment, he introduced himself as Dimitri Giannopoulos; though clearly of Greek lineage he had no trace of a foreign accent.

‘I’m in online wines and spirits retail,’ he told Marcus. ‘Based in Swansea but with customers all over the UK and Ireland. You can check us out: www.grape-n-grain.co.uk. If you’ve a minute I’d like to talk to you about a business proposition.’

‘As you can see, Mr ...’

‘Call me Dimitri, or, as I prefer, Jimmy.’

‘... Jimmy, I’m really busy at the moment.’

‘I know, and I’m impressed. Here’s my card. Call me later today when things cool down.’

‘Thanks, I will,’ Marcus said. Seconds later he was engaging a German customer who wanted his whisky in a bottle adorned with a *Schloss*. ‘Send me a photo of your *Schloss* as a jpeg, and I’ll put it on a label for you,’ he promised.

During a lunchtime lull, he told Jody about Jimmy the Greek. ‘Go on, call him,’ she urged. ‘What harm can there be in just talking to him?’

First, he checked out grape-n-grain on the web. He came across a flattering profile of the founder and chief executive, Dimitri (Jimmy) Giannopoulos, together with his picture, in a *Financial Times* from last October. It was him, all right. And he found that grape-n-grain was the fastest-growing online seller of wines and spirits in the country.

The call lasted 20 minutes, during which Jody held the fort. By the time he hung up, Marcus had agreed to a meeting in Swansea on Wednesday, with a view to negotiating a licence for his custom-blending system, for nationwide rollout.

⬠

By noon Delia and Quin stood on Easter Craiglockhart, having made the steep, muddy climb through dense woodland from Morningside. Though much less visited than Blackford, it offered a couple of seats for out-of-breath walkers at the very top.

The Merchants of Edinburgh golf course that had long tamed the south-eastern flank, coming within just a few feet of the summit, enjoyed a view towards the Braid Hills and the Lammermuirs beyond. Except for a clearing to the north-west that afforded a vista over Slateford and Saughton to Corstorphine Hill, most of the city was hidden from sight by tall trees. Charlotte Nasmyth had painted *A Prospect of Edinburgh* here in the 1830s, but little of it was in prospect now.

On the way down, they made a short detour to visit a rocky outcrop from which Edinburgh Castle could be glimpsed through the trees. The island of Inchkeith in the firth lay just to the left of the castle, exactly as it did in Charlotte's painting. Perhaps it was right here, not on the summit, that she had set up her easel.

At the foot they hopped on a 38 bus to Western Corner, where they ate lunch in a small café and planned their next ascent: Corstorphine Hill.

42
LORE MINER

THE SERMON THAT SUNDAY MORNING was a commentary on the famous lines from Psalm 127 that gave Edinburgh its civic motto, *Nisi dominus frustra*. The reading in full was

> *Except the Lord build the house, they labour in vain who build it; except the Lord keep the city, the watchman waketh but in vain.*

James Swift's mind was on another matter entirely. By the time the service ended, he had made a decision.

He would call Rachel Herring again.

Terrified she was going to renege on the deal, he would have to pressure her to pay up. When they spoke two days ago, she had been noncommittal about the money he had earned by pushing through planning approval for her casino resort.

Having complimented the minister on his sermon, he found a seat in a quiet corner outside the church and rang Rachel on his mobile. No time like the present.

'Mrs Herring? James Swift again, following up on our Friday conversation. Hope I'm not disturbing you this Sunday morning.'

'Actually, I'm pretty busy, so make it quick.'

'Just wanted to confirm arrangements for the payment of £50,000 per our agreement.'

'What £50,000 would that be, Councillor Swift?'

Damn the woman to hell, fine she knew. 'As I told you, full planning approval went through for your casino development. Certain members of the committee were hesitant, but through forceful persuasion I turned them around.'

‘Would that include Councillor Lawrie?’

Swift was astonished that she knew who had been key to a favourable decision, that without Steven Lawrie’s last-minute reversal, permission would have been refused. ‘Er ... absolutely. I had a heart-to-heart with him before the meeting, otherwise he would for sure have voted no.’

‘You can fool yourself, Swift, but you can’t fool me. What exactly have you done to earn fifty grand? I happen to know Lawrie turned you down. It was only through intervention from someone else that he supported the development.’

‘Someone else? No, Mrs Herring, that’s incorrect. I don’t know who would have told you such a thing. *I* made this happen.’

‘On the contrary. It was a friend of mine in Holyrood, an MSP, who made it happen. You’ve done well out of me, Swift. There’s not another penny in this for you, am I clear?’

There was silence on the line for a few seconds. ‘Am I clear?’ she repeated.

Recovering his composure, Swift tried a new tack. ‘There was a procedural irregularity in the committee meeting. I have until tomorrow noon to raise it and enter a motion for a revote. If that happens, I can no longer guarantee a vote in favour. But if I say nothing, it’s a done deal. Transfer the money to the usual account by eleven tomorrow and you have your casino development.’

Rachel burst out laughing. ‘Is that the best you can come up with? Go on, raise your “procedural irregularity”. But don’t be surprised if a story appears in the *Scotsman* this week setting out how you’ve been funding your comfortable lifestyle these last few months.’

‘Implicating you as well as me,’ Swift found the words to say. ‘And what will that do to your chances of building your casino in Edinburgh?’

She laughed again. ‘My tracks are covered. There’s no way a single penny of what you’ve taken can be traced back to me.’

Suddenly, her tone changed to one of unmistakable menace. 'Still, if you were to try implicating me, you can expect a visit from some friends of mine. We know where you live.' With that, she ended the call.

⬠

'This Corstorphine Hill covers a big area,' Quin remarked, studying Delia's map spread out on the café table. 'Much bigger than Blackford or Craiglockhart. I think the best place to start is at the supposed site of Thorfinn's encampment.'

'Okay,' Delia agreed, pulling up the *New Story* on her computer. 'Charlotte wrote: ... *in 1035 he sailed into the Firth of Forth, made a landing at Cramond and marched a small army over the hill to a place affording a view of Edinburgh's famous Castle Rock ... Camp was pitched on a south-facing hillside overlooking an expanse of flat marshy land.*'

'Is there a marsh to the south of Corstorphine Hill?'

'Not now there isn't, but there's certainly some floodplain between there and the Water of Leith that probably once was a bit of a swamp.' Delia ran a finger over the map. 'See, the south-facing slope that overlooks the floodplain rises up from what's now Corstorphine Road.'

'Where the zoo is?'

'Yes, but I don't think you can see the castle from there. Thorfinn's camp must have been further east, nearer where we are now.'

They settled their modest bill for lunch and set off walking west along Corstorphine Road, once the main artery leading out of Edinburgh towards Glasgow. At a weathered old milestone reading on one side 'Edinburgh 2 MILES' and on the other 'Glasgow 40 MILES', they turned to face the direction they had come, and were rewarded by a fine view of the castle two miles away to the east. A view the Norse warlord had enjoyed almost a thousand years earlier, in 1035.

A gate gave access to the densely wooded Corstorphine Hill nature reserve; from there a footpath, signposted as part of the John Muir Way, led straight up the hill through the trees.

As they climbed, Quin remarked, 'I can't see Thorfinn setting up camp on ground as steep as this. More likely it would have been on the gentler slope lower down, near the road.'

'Y'know,' Delia said, 'I asked Marcus if the Water Lairds still told the story of Thorfinn's plan to unite Scotland and England under King Knut. He'd never heard it before reading Charlotte's manuscript. And the sagas don't mention it; I haven't seen it on any history, or even pseudohistory, website.'

'So are we on the wrong track here?'

'No, it's quite promising. Charlotte could have invented the whole thing, precisely to provide a clue to the whereabouts of Neadreth's grove.'

'It's not *all* invention,' Quin said, firmly. 'The etymology of Corstorphine, from the cross of Thorfinn, is just too right not to be true. I'm sure the old Norseman was here.'

'Then maybe the Water Lairds *did* at one time tell the story, but it's been lost.'

'Give me the map again,' Quin said. 'I see there's a tower on the top of the hill. *"And cast thine eyes from high atop my tower."* Is *that* the one Charlotte mentions in her verse?'

'It's Clermiston Tower,' Delia told him. '*W. Scott, lore miner.*'

'W. Scott what?'

'*Lore miner*. Sir Walter Scott used to mine Scottish folklore for his poems and novels. The tower was built in 1871 to commemorate the 100th anniversary of his birth.'

'What are we waiting for? Let's get up there.'

'Quin, *eighteen seventy-one*. Charlotte's verse was written sometime in the 1830s. She can't have been referring to Clermiston Tower, can she?'

They nonetheless paid the small entrance fee and climbed the 99 steps, to find themselves at treetop level with the city of

Edinburgh laid out below them. From here, almost all the ancient land of Lothian, once a semi-independent province of Anglian Northumbria and before that the homeland of the Celtic *Gododdin*, could be surveyed.

Together they admired the panoramic view in silence. The flat sheen of the Firth of Forth was interrupted by Cramond Island and, beyond it, Inchmickery. They turned to the east.

Quin was first to talk. 'See, just to the left of the Castle Rock is where we stood on Salisbury Crags. I still think that's the spot Charlotte is drawing our attention to. That's where she painted her *Prospect of Edinburgh*, the one she hid her little four-line poem in. The one whose dimensions are in the golden ratio.'

'What if she wanted us to focus on what she was looking *at*, rather than where the view was *from*?' Delia suggested.

'You mean right here, the top of Corstorphine Hill?'

'Not quite. Remember she placed the castle in the centre of her painting. It's like a gunsight, and directly beyond it is a particular point on the hill.

'If that's so, we're too far to the north. We'd need to head back towards Thorfinn's camp to be on that sight-line.'

'Yes, but not all the way back. There's a spot with a fine view over the city. It's called Rest And Be Thankful. Shortly after I met Jody for the first time, we went there for a run together.'

They descended from their lookout on Clermiston Tower to the woodland floor. Paths, some well-marked, others less travelled, criss-crossed the hill making it difficult to get proper bearings. When they came to the top of a rocky precipice a vista opened up. A golf course stretched down towards the city.

'We're getting near,' Delia announced. 'There's a place over here where we can get to the bottom of these cliffs.'

'What were those words of Scott's about cliffs? In the song of Bonnie Dundee, wasn't it?'

'*On Ravelston's cliffs and in Clermiston's lee*. Clermiston, that the tower's named for, is on the other side of the hill from here. So we're in *Clermiston's lee*. And on this side of the hill are the old lands of Ravelston. These are *Ravelston's cliffs*. Charlotte's ancestors on her mother's side were lairds of Ravelston. This is the very place Scott wrote about.'

As they clambered down a steep slope, Delia's mind was working overtime. There was something about Charlotte's ancestors, the Foulises of Ravelston. The buried treasure that *W. Scott, lore miner* wove into his novel *The Antiquary* was a Foulis family legend. Buried treasure, *store of wealth*: could it be here, at Rest And Be Thankful?

At the foot of the cliff, their way was blocked by a wire-mesh security fence. Inside stood a pale grey 20-foot OOCL shipping container. Though no major excavation had taken place, there were signs of ground disturbance. A heap of brush occupied one corner of the site.

'I don't remember seeing this when I came up with Jody,' Delia said. 'I'm surprised building is being allowed here.'

'Unless the nature reserve stops at the cliff there,' Quin suggested. 'This could be golf course property.'

'I suppose so. Anyway, this can't be the place we're looking for. No limpid water, no dene, no Roman remains – nothing of the kind is mentioned in any of the websites I've consulted.'

'No message, no queen, no hand, no heart,' Quin added. 'Nice idea, though. So I guess it's down to Inverleith. Our last hope.'

'We've done enough for one day. Inverleith can wait. Let's head back down to the main road and grab a bus home. I've a chicken to put in the oven, some vegetables and a bottle of chardonnay in the fridge.'

By 4 pm they were back in Delia's flat. While she was preparing dinner, her phone rang. A colleague at work.

'Delia, I know you were to be taking this week off, but I wondered, would you be able to do a day's fieldwork at Strathconon between now and Thursday? I'm supposed to do it but I've a family funeral to go to in the south of England.'

‘Sorry to hear that.’

‘Yeah, well, these things never happen at the most convenient time, do they? Anyway, the results need to be in by Friday. I’ll be back by then to take care of the report.’

‘That’ll be a big day at NEPA with the Forth Bridge takeover. Isn’t there to be some kind of celebration?’

‘It’ll be a rah-rah session, American style ... oops, Delia, didn’t mean to sound ...’

Delia laughed. ‘I know exactly what you meant. Anyway, I’ve no particular plans for midweek. My boyfriend’s here from Chicago and might welcome a chance to travel up to the Highlands with me. So, no problem. Just email me the protocol and I’ll take care of it.’

43
BONDING

ARRIVING BACK IN EDINBURGH off the short flight from Brussels, Hugh and Isla were surprised to be met at the airport by the enforcer. He would be 'looking after' them between now and Thursday night, he stated, breaking his customary embargo on speech.

Rory drove them not into the city but over the water to Fife, where all three of them would be in 24-hour 'lock-down' for the next three days. 'So we're not to be trusted, is that it?' Hugh asked. He received only a shrug in reply.

Their destination was a rundown-looking cottage on the outskirts of Dunfermline, a single-storey building surrounded by untended hedges and dark spruce trees, scarcely visible from the road. Rory unlocked the front door and ushered them inside.

The interior was unexpectedly clean, tastefully furnished and decorated. In addition to the living-room there were two bedrooms, each with a double bed and an *en suite* bathroom. To the rear was a fully-fitted kitchen with a large well-stocked fridge-freezer, and a utility room with washer and dryer. Hugh couldn't help noticing that every room was equipped with what looked like motion detectors. Or cameras. Someone other than Rory might well be keeping an eye on them while they were here.

'See, ye'll be comfortable enough here,' Rory told his charges. 'Now ye get tae make one call each, then I keep yer phones till efter we're aw din here. Ye dinnae say whaur ye are, hoo long ye'll be here, ony o' that. Just let your husband, wife, lover, next o' kin, whatever, ken ye're fine, awright? We dinnae want ony "missing person reports" filed.' It was the most garrulous their Glaswegian guardian – warder might have been a better description – had been since he collected them at the airport. 'Okay, the lady first.'

'Nobody'll be missing me,' Isla said. 'Here, you can have my phone.' She seemed surprisingly at ease with the situation she found herself in.

Hugh's call was to his great-aunt, recuperating at home after outpatient surgery. 'Hello, Aunt Kirsty. Just calling to see how you're feeling after your op.'

Kirsty gave a long response, quickly getting off the subject of her 'procedure' on to other matters, including the visits by Mr Annandale and his friends to see her Nasmyth paintings. Hugh made appropriate noises – oh? – good – that's good – really? – no way! – until Rory made a 'T' sign with his hands.

'Listen, Aunt Kirsty, things are very hectic here in the office, so I have to go, but I'll call you at the weekend. In fact I'll come over and see you, if that would be okay. Bye now.'

Hugh had prepared for only two days away from home. No one had told him that training in Flanders would be followed by three days' enforced seclusion in Fife. With no means of looking after his professional responsibilities, he mentioned to Rory that the Crown Office might be trying to get in touch with him.

'The Croon Oafis? Whit's that?'

'The office of the Procurators Fiscal, the public prosecution service in Scotland. I do investigations for them. I need to let them know I'll be unavailable for the rest of this week.'

The Glaswegian clearly smelled a rat. He looked at Isla.

'It's right enough, Rory.' Then in a mocking tone, 'He's a *forensic accountant*, believe it or not.'

'Ye kin dae whit ye like for a livin,' Rory declared, 'but ye're phonin nae Croon Oafis. I'll let ye send an email fae my computer. *If* I see whit ye write an tell ye it's okay.'

Hugh's draft to iksmith@copfs.gsi.gov.uk was brief and to the point:

Ian:

On an unexpected trip to deal with a family emergency, plan to be back Friday, will call you then.

Hugh.

Rory insisted on deleting 'an unexpected' and 'plan to be', thinking they looked like some kind of coded message to I.K. Smith – whoever *that* was. Uncomfortable with 'emergency', he eventually settled for 'matter'. The email went out at 4:37 pm.

While Rory rustled up a meal, Isla settled down to watch TV and Hugh put some clothes in the washer before joining her in the living-room. He was pleased that Rory had bought some reading material and he picked up the *Scotsman*. A story on an inside page caught his attention. 'See this, Isla. Our friend Victor Herring gets a mention in today's paper.'

'What's he been up to? Nothing to do with the wee gold chariot, I hope?'

'No, it's something else altogether.' He read the story aloud.

The death of a man who fell from the Dean Bridge in the early hours of Wednesday 28th July was 'not suspicious', police said last night. Identified as Cameron Lewis, 40, a building contractor of Dalry Road, Edinburgh, he is believed to have committed suicide following a marital breakdown and heavy gambling losses. A report has been sent to the procurator fiscal.

Having taken a voluntary statement from Mr Victor Herring, 27, director of a small casino near the Dean Bridge, police have ruled out foul play. Mr Lewis had spent several hours in the casino, drinking and playing the tables, just prior to his death. During that time his losses amounted to several thousand pounds.

When it became clear Mr Lewis had too much to drink, Mr Herring ordered closure of his table, escorted him out to the street, and set him towards the Dean Bridge, which was on his way home.

Police commended Mr Herring for his responsible actions and his help in completing their inquiries. Mr Herring told the Scotsman *he was 'devastated' to learn of Mr Lewis's death. 'He was a good man who loved his family, and was going through a difficult patch,' he said.*

'Quite the hero, our Mr Herring,' Isla commented.

Hugh put down the paper and moved over to the sofa beside her to watch TV. During their two days together in Belgium he had begun to see through the uncompromisingly hostile exterior to a more likeable Isla hidden inside; she, in turn, had started to trust him better. They were in the early stages of a bonding process that was no doubt part of the plan; a process set to continue until D-day.

'I know you're nervous,' she said, 'and you hate being cooped up like this. I don't like it either, but I can understand why it's necessary. And really, it's an honour to have been selected to plant the explosive. We just have to go along with it.' Something in her tone suggested she was less comfortable with her role in Operation Nightjar than her words implied, but he said nothing.

Rory's cooking was amazingly good – it turned out he had been a sous-chef in one of Glasgow's most prestigious hotels, before landing in jail for assault on a co-worker with a meat cleaver. The meal was accompanied by a fine Bordeaux and followed by a selection of single malts. By mid-evening Hugh felt quite mellow. *No point in fighting it,* he thought, *just go with the flow. I'll be out of here on Thursday.*

As dictated by their captor, Hugh and Isla would share the larger bedroom while he would have the smaller one. 'Shouldnae be a problem tae yiz,' he said. Indeed, they had shared a bed during their two nights in Flanders, both of them keeping chastely and resolutely to their own half. Three more nights of the same would be bearable.

Some time after eleven, Hugh was in bed, eyes closed in a pretence of sleep. He heard Isla emerge from the bathroom and was aware of the mattress adjusting to her weight as she slipped under the duvet behind him. A moment later, he felt a naked body against his back. An arm flopped over him and a cold hand came to rest on his belly, before travelling south.

'For God's sake, Isla,' he said, opening his eyes and turning over on his back, 'what are you doing?' Her hair was wet and she smelled of vanilla shower gel.

'Shh,' she whispered. 'I'm cold and was hoping you could fix that for me. And by the feel of it, I'm pretty sure you can.'

'This isn't a good idea,' he protested, though at that moment his whole body was telling him otherwise.

'Hugh, I know I'm not your first choice – hell, you're not mine, but we're all we've got for the next three nights. After that, who knows? Chances are we'll be spending years in separate jails. Won't we regret not taking this opportunity?'

'Jail? You're thinking we'll be caught?'

'Aren't you?'

'The possibility has crossed my mind, yes. *And* the possibility that our mission will fail. But didn't they din it into us during training that we mustn't contemplate failure?'

'Right,' Isla said, throwing off the duvet and pulling his boxer shorts down to his knees. 'No failure. Let's go for it, Forensic.'

44
THE VAIN QUEEN OF JOPPA

THE VALLEY OF STRATHCONON was one of the catchments that would feed NEPA's aqueduct. Stretching 30 miles inland from the Cromarty Firth, its lower reaches were blessed with a patchwork of farmland and forest, and a scattering of tiny villages. A series of hydro-electric power stations showed NEPA was not alone in seeking to exploit the enormous water-collection potential of the valley.

Farther west the strath was wild and uninhabited, seldom visited even by dedicated hill-walkers or Munro-baggers. Delia's task was to retrieve a number of insect traps her colleague had placed along the River Meig and its tributaries, identify each species caught and count the number of individuals. The results would be a baseline for future environmental impact studies.

It was Tuesday 3rd August. On the drive up the A9 to Inverness and on to Beauly, where a comfortable B&B awaited them, Delia and Quin talked intermittently about the riddle of the verse. He recited it aloud once again:

Come yesterday, at ten upon the hour,
And cast thine eyes from high atop my tower.
A message from the one thou callest queen,
Hand over heart, will lead thee to her dene.

'I'm still convinced *"my tower"* refers to the York Place belvedere,' he said. 'What would the Nasmyth family most likely cast their eyes on, when they went up there?'

Delia wondered why she hadn't realised it before. The main interest of watchers in the belvedere wasn't in the city around them, or the hills and waters beyond. It was the sky *above* them. 'Charlotte and her brothers used to observe the heavens – particularly towards the north where the air was clearer.'

'Right. She talks specifically about the northern lights.'

'Yes, but also the stars in the northern sky. What were her words again?'

Quin found the passage. '*The circumpolar constellations – those that wheeled around the North Star without ever dipping below the horizon – became as familiar to us as the streets of our city.*'

'Let me see that,' Delia said, pulling off into a lay-by. 'The circumpolar constellations – of course!'

Quin had no idea what she was talking about. Seeing his blank expression, she explained. 'Only a few constellations are truly circumpolar. One gets a mention, not in the *Memoir* but in the *New Story*. Cassiopeia. A group of five bright stars that straddle the Milky Way. Five, note.'

Now he was getting it. 'To the Angles, Cassiopeia was the heavenly manifestation of Neadreth. In classical mythology, Cassiopeia was a queen!'

'*The one thou callest queen*!'

'Exactly! Now what's the *message* that *will lead thee to her dene*?'

Excited though they were at what seemed a breakthrough, they were still stumped. How would a set of five stars send a *message*? Some online research was needed.

At that moment, Marcus was heading south on a train to Swansea, changing at Crewe. His meeting the following day would reveal what Jimmy the Greek had in mind. It was hard to see how *A Malt O' My Ain* could fit an online business model, given the need for a tasting session to design a custom blend. Yet, he supposed, if people bought shoes online – which increasingly they were doing – it shouldn't be beyond the bounds of ingenuity.

Jody, meanwhile, sat at her desk in a tiny office in the bowels of the National Museum of Scotland in Chambers Street, Edinburgh. No travel for her this week. She was quietly relishing a couple of evenings home alone.

⬠

'Will you be wanting dinner in?' Mrs MacNeil asked her newly-arrived guests. 'Or have you plans to go out? Just so you know, I have broccoli and stilton soup, rosemary-infused game hen with vegetables from my garden, and a variety of desserts. I'm not licensed to serve wine, but if you've a bottle I can provide glasses.'

Delia and Quin needed little further encouragement to select the dine-in option. It was five o'clock, giving them two hours of internet time before they ate. Already a suitable division of labour was agreed: Quin would find out everything he could about Cassiopeia, *the one thou callest queen*, in classical myth, while Delia would investigate the celestial Cassiopeia. By dinner-time, they knew more about the queen and her five-star manifestation than they could possibly have dreamed of.

Quin had downloaded the myth:

> *Cassiopeia's realm was centred on the coastal city of Joppa, now known as Jaffa in present-day Israel. She was possessed of great beauty and had an equally beautiful daughter, Andromeda. Mother and daughter were praised so often, by true admirers and sycophants, that Cassiopeia came to believe they were the most beautiful women in all the world. As in the Snow White legend of northern Europe, the vanity of a queen was to prove her downfall.*
>
> *A group of 50 water-nymphs was said to roam the seas, giving protection to sailors. The queen's boast that her daughter was fairer than any of them angered*

the ruling sea-god Poseidon, who vowed to teach her a lesson. How dared she, a mere mortal, question the beauty of his water-nymphs? After all, Joppa's ships were kept safe from sea-monsters and sirens by these lovely maidens, the Nereids as they were called. Their father Nereus was a primeval god, a Titan, and their mother Doris was the goddess of the bounty of the seas.

(*Nereid? Neadreth? Could there be a connection?* There was more to this story than Quin and Delia were expecting. *And what about this Joppa? Edinburgh has a Joppa too.*)

Poseidon warned the queen that he would send the sea-monster Cetus to destroy the coast of Joppa, on which the wealth of her realm depended. An oracle advised her that, to ward off the threat, she must offer her daughter in sacrifice to the sea-monster.

Was this the best suggestion he had?

Yes, the oracle insisted.

With sorrow in her heart, she chained Andromeda to a rock at the foot of a sea-cliff and waited for Cetus to claim his prize.

By fortunate coincidence, just as the sea-monster approached, who should happen by, flying on winged sandals, but the great hero Perseus, bearing in a sack the head of the Gorgon Medusa he had just slain. The Gorgon would literally petrify any creature that gazed upon her; evidently even her severed head was powerful enough to have this effect.

Perseus quickly sized up the situation. Averting his own eyes, he opened the sack and brandished Medusa's head before Cetus, instantly turning him to stone.

Upon freeing the beautiful young woman from her chains, the hero with wings on his heels instantly fell in love with her, and in due course took her in marriage.

Furious that Cassiopeia's boast had thus gone unpunished, Poseidon had the queen bound to a chair and placed in the heavens, her head towards the North Star. For all eternity she was doomed to circle the sky, spending half of each year upside-down on her torturous throne.

Now it was Delia's turn. 'My story is less colourful than yours, and maybe no more helpful.' She showed Quin a simple star-map of the constellation named for the vain queen of Joppa.

Caph
Segin
Shedir
Ruchbah

'What's the starburst thing at the top?' Quin asked.

'It's the closest I've been able to find to *a message from the one thou callest queen*. In 1572 a brilliant new star appeared in the Milky Way at that position. Many sky-watchers reported it, but the Danish astronomer Tycho Brahe gave the most accurate and detailed account, and it's become known as Tycho's Star.'

'Maybe the verse should end, *"lead thee to her Dane"*, not *"dene"*.'

'Yeah, yeah. Anyway, for a few days it was the brightest star in the heavens, visible even in daylight. But it gradually faded, until by 1574 it had disappeared from view.'

'A supernova, I suppose?'

'Yes. Apparently its remnants can still be seen with a radio telescope. Like other supernovae – the Christmas star is the best-known example – Tycho's Star was seen as a message from on high. A portent.'

'Of what?'

'In Scotland, some said it spelled doom for the Earl of Morton. Appointed regent for James VI as the star appeared, he threw a banquet at Dalkeith Palace for a number of dignitaries, including his predecessor the Earl of Mar. Mar fell violently sick and died immediately after the banquet. Though fingers were pointed at Morton, already a suspect in the murder of the king's father Lord Darnley, he was confirmed as regent, becoming the most powerful noble in the country.'

'His star was in the ascendant, obviously.'

'For a while. In 1579 Darnley's cousin the Earl of Lennox engaged James, at the age of 13, in a homosexual relationship.'

'Another vain queen, by the sound of it.'

Delia laughed. 'Yes, in a manner of speaking. Soon after, at Lennox's instigation, Morton was deposed, tried and beheaded.'

'So the new star in Cassiopeia wasn't good news for Morton.'

'No, but what kind of message are *we* supposed to get from the vain queen of Joppa?'

Quin was silent for a moment. He was looking at the star-map again. Then his fingers began racing over the keyboard of his laptop.

'What are you looking at there?' Delia asked.

'An online Arabic dictionary.'

'Arabic?'

'I know a few words, and a couple of the names of those stars seemed familiar. *Segin* doesn't look Arabic. But *ruchbah* means "knee". I suppose it refers to the knee of the seated queen. *Shedir* – that's easy, another part of the queen's anatomy, her breast.'

'And *caph*?'

'It means "palm".'

'That makes sense,' Delia said. 'In medieval pictures of the constellations, Cassiopeia is shown bearing a palm frond.'

'Yes, but *caph* can also mean the palm of the hand. I think we've solved *hand over heart*, Delia. Caph is the hand, Shedir the breast – for which read heart.'

'A message from the one thou callest queen, hand over heart, will lead thee to her dene. You're right! Caph and Shedir are the two brightest stars in Cassiopeia. I bet they act as pointers! If we take the line from Caph to Shedir and continue it downwards, we'll find ... uh, oh.'

'What's the problem?'

'Cassiopeia revolves around the pole daily. Our pointers are constantly shifting in relation to the ground.'

'Yes, but the first line of the verse says *at ten upon the hour*. Presumably it means ten at night. Doesn't that fix the line for us?'

'If only. The stars have an annual as well as a diurnal cycle. So unless we know the time of year, *ten upon the hour* leaves us none the wiser.'

45
A GOOD CITIZEN

TUESDAY EVENING AT THE Learmonth Club. Seven o'clock, nothing much doing yet. Chances were it would start to get busy around eleven.

Victor was feeling good. So good, in fact, he decided to take off for a couple of hours. The staff would manage just fine until he came back.

Celebration was in order. The *Scotsman* had told everyone what a good citizen he was. His mother disapproved of his talking to the press, but, though he said it himself, his line about Lewis being a devoted family man who loved his wife and kids was genius. And on Thursday work was to start on the foundations for Ma's new house on Corstorphine Hill. He'd go there tomorrow afternoon and make sure all was in order for delivery of some heavy machinery the following morning.

But, right now, pleasure beckoned. He fired up the Harley and made for Leith.

He saw what he was looking for in the doorway of a 'sauna'. He negotiated a price for two hours, to include a bit of rough, and paid up front. The girl looked about twenty-two but was probably younger, and seemed to be a novice; she didn't pass the money to a minder before fulfilling the contract. He liked that. Giving her a spare helmet carried specifically for this kind of situation, he set her on the pillion behind him then headed west, careful to stay within the speed limit until he was out of the city.

Soon he arrived at the very spot on the shore of the firth near Carriden where he had disposed of most of Bob Bowman. Only tonight it was warm and dry, unlike the last time he was here.

The girl protested as he led her into tall grass. 'What's your problem, bitch?' he said. 'You're happy enough to screw in a back doorway in Leith, with rats running around your feet. This is luxury compared to your usual place of business.'

He had to smack her about a bit before she would give him the precise services he wanted, but eventually he had satisfaction. In a burst of generosity he lit her a cigarette as he took one for himself. An almost irresistible thought came into his head. He could kill this dirty young whore, right here and now, and dump her in the firth like he did with Bowman. Well, not *exactly* like that – he didn't have the means to sever her head – but it would make a nice end to a fun outing. Naturally, he'd take back his money before she went in the water.

Reluctantly, however, he let her get back on the bike behind him for the ride back to Leith. From the movement of the water he could see the body would not be carried away. Next time he'd check the tide tables.

46
SOLVED

DINNER WAS EXCELLENT. Delia asked Mrs MacNeil how she found time to grow her own vegetables while running a busy B&B.

'Neil does the garden,' she said. 'He has a good way with vegetables. Fruit too.'

'Your husband's name is Neil MacNeil?'

'Yes,' the landlady affirmed with a laugh. 'His parents weren't the most imaginative.'

Delia and Quin had shared a table with a couple from Sheffield, and decided to take a little walk in the fresh Highland air before settling down for the night. It was after nine o'clock. Twilight was descending from a clear and moonless sky.

'Within the next half hour or so,' Delia said, 'we'll be able to see the brightest stars. I wonder where Cassiopeia is right now.'

By 10 pm, the W-shaped constellation had become visible in the darkening north-eastern sky. The two stars forming the right-hand side of the W, *hand over heart*, pointed almost vertically down.

'*Come yesterday at ten upon the hour,*' Delia recited. 'If that meant right now, Cassiopeia would be pointing to a spot north-east of Charlotte's tower. But if *yesterday* was any other date, she'd point somewhere else. It all hinges on that date. I guess I should have realised *yesterday* was important. Charlotte gave it a capital *Y*.'

'Say that again,' Quin said.

'She wrote *Yesterday* with a capital *Y*. She also began *Queen* and *Dene* with capitals, and if I remember right, *Hand* and

Heart as well. When I copied the verse, I didn't bother with the capitals – I thought it was just some 19th-century way of writing.'

'The upper-case *Y* could be significant. In her *New Story*, Charlotte talked about the gods the early Angles worshipped – other than Neadreth, I mean.'

'I remember a thunder-god, for sure, and a war-god, and didn't she mention a dawn-goddess?'

'Sure she did,' Quin said, a note of triumph in his voice. 'The Anglo-Saxon goddess of the dawn was Eostre. Her name is from the same root as "east". She brought the dawn of each day, also the dawn of each new year – the spring equinox, hence her feast day, 21st March. This pagan goddess gave her name to the Christian festival of spring, Easter.'

'So you think *Yesterday* means Easter Day?'

'Not exactly. I think it means 21st March. Can we find out where Cassiopeia is on that date, and where her *hand* and *heart* are pointing?'

'No problem.'

Back at Mrs MacNeil's, the WiFi connection was slow, but soon Delia was calling up a planetarium app from the 'cloud'. She entered the place – Edinburgh; date – 21st March; then the time – 22:00. A simulation of the night sky filled the screen. Moving around the 'sky' she centred the view on Cassiopeia.

The 'pointer' stars were now directed to a spot on the horizon a few degrees south of due west.

'As seen from Charlotte's belvedere,' Delia pronounced, '*hand over heart* points to Corstorphine Hill, more precisely to Rest And Be Thankful, where we were the other day.'

'I remember. The beauty spot that's now a building site with an ugly shipping container. Why don't you give Jody a call?'

⬠

In his hotel room in Swansea, Marcus answered his phone. Jody was scarcely able to contain her excitement on the other end of the line. 'Delia's solved the riddle, I'm sure of it. Neadreth's grove has to be at Rest And Be Thankful. It all fits.'

Marcus was sceptical, even when she filled in the details. 'There's no water there, Jody, no deep little valley that could be called a *dene*. I still like Faucheldean, under the shale bing, or the valley under the Dean Bridge. Both are west of Charlotte's belvedere, so Cassiopeia's pointers work just as well for them. They're both genuine *denes*. Faucheldean's our best shot – the water bears Neadreth's name, remember? The Niddry Burn.'

'You could be right,' Jody admitted reluctantly. 'Once you're back, we can take another look at those places. Are you all set for your meeting tomorrow?'

'Think so. Wish me luck!'

⬠

That Tuesday evening, Hugh and Isla were taken for a dry run with their boatman Fraser Cadenhead. Rory kept careful watch the whole time, and brought them back to the cottage around eleven o'clock. 'Enjoy the rest o' yer evenin,' he said with a leer before retiring.

If either one of Rory's charges contemplated making a run for it, that was as far as it went. The forensic accountant and the Goth were in this together; neither could admit to cold feet.

The second night of their 'captivity' culminated much like the first. Hugh sensed a vulnerability in his co-conspirator, and in their post-coital embrace he ventured to ask, 'Did you realise what you were getting into, Isla? Did you ever expect to be playing a leading role in anything as big, anything as *bad*?'

'To be honest, no. I knew the money I was raising was for a major operation. But I never suspected *this*. How about you?'

'Me neither. Somehow we passed a point of no return without ever noticing.'

'I know. Between me and you and these bed-sheets I wish we weren't going to do such damage to that lovely old bridge.'

'We can't back out now.'

'No, of course not. Don't get me wrong, Hugh. I'm committed to the cause. I just wonder if this will do more harm than good.'

He pulled her closer. 'I have the same concern,' he said.

⬠

The weather next day was perfect for going up into Strathconon. Though a map showed the location of all the insect traps, Delia was glad of Quin's help in uncovering them. They took the car as far as the road permitted, then proceeded on foot. For hours on end they saw not another soul. Miles out of range for mobile phone communication, they rejoiced in the solitude of this beautiful wilderness.

By early afternoon it was becoming clear there was more than a regular day's work involved. Rather than come back tomorrow to finish the job, delaying their return to Edinburgh until Friday, they would complete the work that day. It would be dark by the time they were headed back to their digs in Beauly.

⬠

Jody had gone early to the office so that she could finish by 3 pm. She tidied her desk and went home to change into her running gear: olive-green top, black three-quarter length leggings, red Nike shoes. It was a beautiful day for a run – dry and bright, no direct sunshine.

Her destination was not a conscious decision, but at 4:15 she found herself by the Water of Leith at Stockbridge. Heading upriver as she had done many times before, she was soon directly under one of the imposing arches of Telford's Dean Bridge.

All evidence of police activity following last week's tragic suicide was gone, and the area was busy with walkers and joggers. Pausing for a breather, she glanced up at the massive stonework of one of the bridge's pillars, right beside the walkway.

There was a sign on the stonework, one she'd never noticed before. She snapped a photo of it with her smartphone:

and immediately forwarded it to her email address, with copies for Marcus and Delia.

For an instant Jody was convinced she had arrived, not just at 'The Dene', but at the *dene* promised by Charlotte Nasmyth's four-line verse. Yet almost at once she began to have doubts.

Beyond the wall, the river tumbled over rocks on its way to the firth. A *limpid flow*? Not somehow an apt description for such a torrent of water. Perhaps those words referred to the mineral spring known as St Bernard's Well, where Charlotte's father had fashioned the classical caprice Jody passed a few minutes earlier. Either way, so much 18th- and 19th-century development had taken place here as mills were built to harness the river and as the New Town expanded westward, it was unlikely any 6th-century Anglian or 2nd-century Roman remains would have survived.

Marcus was right: this *dene* was in exactly the right direction – a few degrees south of due west – from the Nasmyth belvedere. But why, Jody wondered, would Charlotte have chosen the view from Salisbury Crags as a hiding place for her cryptic little verse? This *dene* wasn't even visible from there, hidden as it was behind the Castle Rock. No, whatever Marcus said, Delia's idea that Neadreth's *dene* was farther west, at Rest And Be Thankful, made more sense.

47
OBLIVIOUS

SHE CLIMBED THE STEEP PATH to the Gallery of Modern Art, then crossed to Ravelston Dykes to continue her run west. Soon she reached the start of the track that ascends through the Murrayfield golf course towards Rest And Be Thankful, an elevated spot known to many but visited by few. The ancient estates of Ravelston to the east and Clermiston to the west met here, as immortalised by Scott in *Bonnie Dundee*.

Despite ill-health, Robert Louis Stevenson had come here and found it a perfect setting for the parting of his protagonist David Balfour from Alan Breck Stewart in the final passage of his 1886 classic *Kidnapped*. (A monument on Corstorphine Road near Western Corner celebrates the fictional moment.)

And in 1920, Alexander Graham Bell, returning in old age from Nova Scotia for a last visit to his native city, fondly recalled his walks here as a boy, but was no longer able to make the ascent.

Now Jody Stair was looking for evidence of a much older role for Rest And Be Thankful – as a shrine to an Anglian goddess and perhaps, even earlier, a Roman bathing place.

Delia had mentioned that much of the beauty spot was now fenced off, apparently in preparation for some kind of construction work. Jody was nonetheless unprepared for the visual assault of a 2-metre-high wire mesh fence backed with nylon screening, surrounding an area of perhaps half a hectare between the golf course and the woods that clothe the summit of Corstorphine Hill. All she could make out inside the fence was a grey shipping container and a tall heap of brush.

Who allowed this? It had to be some misguided council project. Edinburgh's planners had a patchy record in the capital's western sector. Citizens could protest all they wished; the planners always 'knew best'.

But Jody was on a mission. Regardless of what was to be created on this beautiful site, she had to see what was in the process of being destroyed. Then she could alert her city councillors, her MP, her MSPs and MEPs, the press, the BBC, the Friends of Corstorphine Hill, whoever might be an ally in getting Rest And Be Thankful restored to its proper tranquil state.

The gate into the enclosure was firmly chained and padlocked. She scrambled around the perimeter among rocks and gorse bushes, looking for a way in. The site abutted a vertical cliff and for a moment she considered jumping down from its crest to land inside. The image of being hauled down from here on a stretcher with an injured foot or broken limb was enough to force abandonment of *that* idea.

However, with a museum curator's attention to small detail, she observed that each join between sections of the fence was secured by three steel clips, top, middle and bottom. If even one of those clips was missing or loose, she reckoned, she might be able to force the panels apart sufficiently to accommodate her slim frame. Finding just such a spot, she used all her strength to prise open a gap. First an arm was through, then a leg, then her head. She snaked her body through the gap, snagging her running top. Thank providence for small pelvis and breasts; thank Decathlon for a tight-fitting and protective sports bra!

Making first for the OOCL box, she found it even more securely locked than the gate. Then as she combed over the uneven ground, she almost turned her ankle where a hole had been dug and only loosely refilled under a layer of turf.

When she came to the heap of brush, she worked around it, but gradually became curious as to what might be underneath.

It was all horribly prickly – mostly gorse, wild rose and bramble – and she started gingerly dragging branches off the heap. The job was going to take a while, but she had plenty of time. No golfers or passers-by would ask awkward questions, since she was hidden by the nylon privacy screening on the fence.

⬠

Though he sometimes objected to her nagging, Victor seldom ignored his mother's demands. At her insistence, his Land Rover had been professionally cleaned and detailed, outside and in.

He wasn't about to get it all dirty again driving up the rutted track to Rest And Be Thankful. Instead he left the vehicle on Murrayfield Road and set off on foot. Approaching the gate in the fence, he was relieved as always to see it was secure.

At the far end of the enclosure, Jody was as oblivious to Victor as he initially was to her. Hauling a particularly large piece of brush off the heap, she exposed a neatly stacked pile of sandstone slabs of varying size and shape. Reaching in for one of the smaller pieces, she recognised it as a paving stone. One face had traces of topsoil but was otherwise clean; it showed signs of wear, whether by feet, hooves or wheels she couldn't immediately tell. The other face was coated with a layer of hardened clay. With some effort she pulled out another slab, and another. They all looked similar, clean and worn on one side, clay-encrusted on the other.

Recalling the hole where she had almost injured her ankle, she realised the stones had been dug up on this very site. Stones exactly like those excavated from Dere Street in the 1920s and now at her place of work.

Wow. Right here could be the Roman bathing place appropriated by the 6th-century Angles as a place of worship for their water-goddess.

Jody's excitement at this discovery was tempered with anger that the ground had been seriously disturbed – vandalised was the word that came to mind. *Didn't the planning people insist on an archaeological survey before any excavation took place here?*

Still, at least the sandstone pavers had been preserved. Some of them, at any rate. Perhaps they could be relaid in some approximation of the original Roman terrace. She got out her smartphone to take photographs. Intent on the task, she was unaware of a heavily-built, bearded young man in a hoodie creeping up behind her, carrying the steel chain that had been fastening the gate.

48

SMASHED

EXERCISING ALL THE SKILLS HONED in his previous life as a marketing executive, Marcus negotiated a business arrangement with Jimmy Giannopoulos that would serve his interests well. The handshake came just after 4 pm, at which point Jimmy complimented him on having driven a hard bargain.

'I suppose you're familiar with ouzo,' he said.

'Yes,' Marcus replied, 'though I've only ever drunk it on holiday in Greece.'

'Have you tasted *Pitsilad*e? It's one of the highest-quality traditionally distilled products from the island of Lesbos. It's in my online catalogue at three times the price of my more generic ouzos. Follow me.'

From Jimmy's warehouse where they'd been in discussion since 9 am, they walked along a succession of narrow lanes to an inconspicuous *taverna* with a sign above the door in Greek letters. Marcus was surprised to find such an establishment in Swansea, but was assured the town's expatriate Hellenic population was large enough to keep such a place in business.

At the bar, Jimmy joked in Greek with Stavros the owner, then joined Marcus at a marble-topped table by the window. They were served a small carafe of ouzo, two glasses filled with ice and a jug of water. Then a young woman brought a platter of *mezedes* – grilled sardines, calamari, feta cheese, kalamata olives, sliced tomato sprinkled with herbs, and a few other delicacies.

Following his host's lead, Marcus poured a small amount of the crystal-clear, viscous ouzo over the ice in his glass, added a similar amount of water and watched as it turned cloudy, almost milky white.

'There,' Jimmy said, 'just like a malt whisky tasting.'

'Yes, except for the ice.'

'Of course. Now taste your *Pitsilade*, and tell me if it's not the finest ouzo you've ever had. *Yiamas!*'

With no further business to discuss, the two men settled into a friendly chat. At Marcus's mention of his girlfriend Jody, Jimmy said, 'Yes, the pretty young lady who was helping you in the shop on Sunday. I figured she was more than just an assistant.'

'I should give her a call, if you don't mind. She'll be interested to know we've reached an agreement. It's almost five; she should be finishing up at work.'

'Please go ahead. While you do that, I'll have another word with Stavros at the bar. Then I'll introduce you to a very different ouzo.'

'Sounds good, Jimmy. But that'll be my last. Don't want to get smashed tonight – I've an early train to catch in the morning.'

⬠

Day three at the cottage seemed to drag. Isla and Hugh could do nothing but watch television; Rory forbade them even to step outside the back door to appreciate the fine early August weather. Isla checked her watch: not five o'clock yet, though it felt like seven or later.

They sat on the sofa, he in a polo shirt and jeans and she in a sleeveless mini-dress that zipped up the front, while Rory busied himself in the kitchen, humming tunelessly. Hugh put his arm around the diminutive young woman who would be his partner in crime the following night, drawing her to him and tenderly stroking her bare shoulder. Keeping the TV on, they spoke in whispers, knowing the room was bugged.

'After tomorrow,' Hugh said, 'why don't we both quit this whole business? We'll have made our mark for *Auld Stobby* and for Scotland. We deserve a quieter life.'

'We? As in ... you and me? Together?'

'That's what I meant.'

'I can think of two reasons why that's not going to happen.' Hugh made to withdraw his caressing hand, but she protested and it remained in place. 'One, you're not going to want someone like me. You're a professional man, you'll want a prim boring wife who won't embarrass you in polite company.'

'Boring? If I wanted boring, I would hardly have signed up to destroy the Forth Bridge, now would I?'

She smiled briefly and gave him a peck on the cheek, before turning serious. 'Two, after tomorrow we'll be locked up, maybe for the rest of our lives.'

'What makes you think we'll be caught?'

'I dunno. It just seems, well, impossible that we'd get away with such a bold attack. Better to get our knees smashed by Rory's baseball bat than grow old in jail.' To Hugh's surprise, Isla's eyes welled up and a tear ran down her pale cheek, carrying a blob of mascara with it.

'You want to make a run for it, now, before it's too late?' he asked.

'What do you think?'

'I'm interested in what *you* think, Isla.' Was she testing his resolve, again looking for a sign that he wasn't to be trusted? Yet that mascara-laden tear looked very genuine.

'This whole operation is fucking stupid. We've been manoeuvred into it by those Belgians who don't give a damn about Scotland or *Auld Stobby*. *They've* got the money, *they'll* get clean away, *we're* left holding the baby.'

'Hendrik and Mariane? You believe they're going to scarper with what's left of the funds?'

'The more I think about it, the more sure I get.'

At that moment, Rory emerged from the kitchen. 'Ye look real cosy there, the pair o' yiz,' he said, a glint of suspicion in his eyes. 'Whit wur ye whisperin? Sweet nuthins, eh?' He turned down the volume on the TV.

While Isla buried her mascara-streaked face in a tissue, Hugh said, 'We were just wondering, where's Hendrik going to be when the blast goes off? And Mariane?'

'They'll be watchin yiz wi' a guid pair o' binoculars. Ye didnae think they were gaun tae leave us tae get on wi' it oorsels?'

'No, no. It's just that Hendrik never mentioned what his plans, or Mariane's, were for D-day. We were curious, that's all. Anyway, if you came through to ask what we're drinking, mine's a scotch, with water. What about you, Isla?'

'Me too. But go easy on the water, Rory.'

Generous drams having been poured, Rory returned to his kitchen fastness and Hugh turned the TV volume back up.

'So you're thinking our glorious leader won't be seen for dust?' Hugh said, resuming the whispered conversation with Isla. 'You're not buying Rory's theory that he'll be watching us?'

'If I was Hendrik, and had the shit-load of used twenties that he still has, even after paying Mariane for the explosives and our training, I wouldn't hang around. Would you?'

'No, I suppose not.'

'D'you realise what this means, Hugh?'

'What, that we're on our own?'

'Yes, and if we choose not to go through with the operation, who's going to come after us?'

'Rory, with his Louisville slugger, that's who.'

'But won't he see he's been left in the shit just as much as we are?'

'He's not the sharpest knife in the kitchen, our Rory. That's one reason he's so reliable at what he does.'

Isla was silent for a moment, apparently digesting Hugh's words. She gulped down a mouthful of whisky before speaking again. 'You're right. We're committed, stuck with it and we'll have to see it through. I just hope nobody's squealed.'

'I'll drink to that,' Hugh said, draining his tumbler.

⬠

By some sixth sense, Jody caught a movement behind her and turned round sharply to come face to face with Victor Herring. In a fraction of a second she took in his angry expression and the menacing swing of a chain from his right hand.

Whoever this is, she thought, *he's bad news. I can outrun him if I can get to the gate. But how the hell do I do that?*

'Well, Missy,' Victor said, 'what do we have here?'

Play for time, Jody. 'What does it look like?'

'You're trespassing on private property. You've no business here.' He moved a step closer.

Think, girl, think. 'Actually, I have. I'm with the National Museum. We believe this is the site of a Roman bathing place.'

'Nothing like that here,' Victor said. 'If there was, the city archaeologists would have found it by now and halted our development. Looks like you're mistaken, Missy.'

'These paving stones, where did they come from?'

'Some demolition site somewhere. Bought 'em a few weeks ago. They'll make a nice patio once the house is up.'

House? Somebody's got planning permission for a house at Rest And Be Thankful?

'Did I see you taking photos?'

'Yes, to show my colleagues at the museum.' In a weak attempt at levity, Jody continued, 'They'll be a bit sceptical otherwise, you know, just because *they* didn't find them. These stones are definitely from a Roman plaza of some kind.'

'Let me see.' Victor held out his left hand for Jody's smartphone, which she held in her right. When she demurred, he made a lunge for it, prompting her to put her right hand behind her back. That gave him the opportunity he needed to whip the chain sharply around her knees, bringing her to the ground. She uttered a scream of pain and terror, which he quickly silenced by grasping her throat. Though she struggled against the powerful hand choking her, she now felt his full weight on top of her and lacked the strength to fight him off.

Soon she was still. Gingerly, Victor relaxed his grip on her neck. She made no movement, no sound. Putting an ear to her mouth, he felt no breath. *Pity. Could've had some fun with this chick out by the firth before dumping her in the water.* The appetite whetted by the Leith whore just a few days ago could have been sated.

He opened up the OOCL box, then dragged the carcass towards it. The girl was remarkably light. So much easier than dealing with Bob Bowman.

The next step: wrap her in builder's polythene. That way there would be no DNA or other contamination of his 'office'. It would be a nuisance to have to arrange *another* container switch.

After dark, he would return with the Land Rover to take the body out to the firth. He'd better check those tide tables again.

As he was preparing the polythene shroud, he heard a low groan. The girl's eyelids flickered. *All right! Brilliant, she's alive! Change of plan. Forget the polythene. And it's best if she recovers a little before her outing to the Carriden shore.*

With a roll of duct tape to hand, Victor wasted no time in covering Jody's mouth and eyes, and binding her hands and feet. Before she fully regained consciousness, he'd have to get her into the OOCL box and tie her securely to the anchoring straps on the interior walls. Couldn't risk her making a din, though chances were nobody would pay any attention. Soon he'd move her to a better place, until she was ready to be taken to the firth. He had just such a 'better place' in mind.

The job was soon complete. By 7 pm he had enjoyed an Irn Bru and a cigarette and was stepping jauntily down the hill to his waiting vehicle. There was time to eat before coming back.

Jody slipped in and out of consciousness a few times before becoming fully awake. She was unable to move, see or shout for help, but she was alive. The pain in her legs was almost unbearable – the chain he felled her with had probably smashed her knees – and her neck hurt from the attempted strangulation.

Listening intently, she heard the sound of wind in trees and, faintly but distinctly, the occasional thwack of a golf club hitting a ball, sometimes followed by a shouted expletive. She was still at Rest And Be Thankful, obviously now inside that shipping container with four letters painted on the outside. *What were they? OO something? What the hell does it matter?*

It was difficult to guess the time, but the golf sounds told her it was still daytime. Or was it the *next* day? Somehow it didn't feel as if she'd been out that long.

She supposed that animal had taken her smartphone. Pity she hadn't managed to email any of the photos she'd taken of those paving stones. She *had* sent a photo from under the Dean Bridge; at least Marcus and Delia would know she'd been there. Maybe they'd surmise she'd gone on to Rest And Be Thankful. Just maybe. But they were nowhere near – Marcus in Swansea and Delia in the Highlands.

Time dragged. Sounds from the golf course became few and far between. An owl hooted. Jody figured it must be after nine o'clock. This was *not* how she'd planned to spend her evening.

The hum of a motor vehicle. The click of a car door opening and the thump of it closing. A metallic sound – the gate being opened. Click and thump again, then revving and drumming as the vehicle was brought inside the compound. One more click and thump, closer this time. Jody braced herself for what she knew was coming next – a key in the lock of her prison.

As the door opened, any hope that rescue was at hand was dashed when a now-familiar voice said, 'Well, Missy, I see you're awake. I have some new accommodation for you. Don't struggle, and you won't get hurt.' She wished she could believe it.

49
THE WASTE-PIPE

MARCUS'S 5 PM CALL TO JODY from the Swansea *taverna* went unanswered. Minutes before, a message from her mobile had come in with no text, just a photo of a stone wall bearing a sign for 'The Dene'. It was snapped at 4:23 pm that day, Wednesday 4th August.

Ah well, he thought, *all will become clear very soon.* He left a brief voicemail that there was good news on the deal with Jimmy the Greek, he would be catching the first train in the morning, and he loved her.

With no response by seven, he called again. This time he was informed that the number was 'not available on this network'. What did that mean? He kept trying every ten minutes or so, always getting the same message. Strange ... if Jody was having technical problems with her mobile, she could always use her landline.

At 9 pm he called Delia, who was enjoying a late supper with Quin in a Beauly pub. She too had tried to contact Jody, without success. There was probably a simple explanation – she'd gone to a festival event and had turned off her phone, she'd forgotten to charge her battery, she'd ...

Still, Marcus was worried something bad had happened. He checked online for a night train that would get him into Edinburgh by early morning. No such luck; if he left at 10:30, one hour from now, with a change in Cardiff he could be in Crewe by 2:30 am, but the next train to Edinburgh from there was scheduled to leave at 10:20, arriving sometime mid-afternoon!

Could he get a flight from Cardiff? Not tonight – the last one had left at 8:30. For a fare of over £200, he could fly next morning, to get home by eleven. Still not fast enough, at any price.

In desperation, he arranged for delivery of a rental car at ten o'clock. If he left at midnight – to allow time for his metabolism to work off the ouzo he'd drunk with Jimmy – he could be at Jody's door by 7 am. He set his alarm, slept fitfully for two hours, and was on the road a couple of minutes before twelve.

⬠

The journey from Rest And Be Thankful had been painful but mercifully short. Like a sack of potatoes she had been transported in what felt like a wheelbarrow along what sounded like a gravel path through what smelled like a lavender-scented garden. Finally dragged down a flight of stone steps to a musty cellar.

Her captor had propped her on a heavy chair with a tubular steel frame then removed the duct tape from her eyes, peeling off much of her eyebrows as he did so. Her eyes quickly adjusted to the light of a single dim bulb.

'I'm going to take the tape off your mouth, Missy, but don't even think about making a noise, or I'll punch you in the face. Nobody's going to hear you anyway.'

She nodded.

He whipped off the tape. For a moment her cheeks and jaw felt as if they were on fire. The sensation passed, though the gluey taste on her lips would linger.

'I need the bathroom,' she said.

Victor looked surprised, as if he hadn't thought of such a thing. 'I'll bring a bucket, okay?'

As he bound her ankles and wrists to the chair, she looked around in disgust, saying, 'But how do you expect me to ...'

'I'm not some kind of monster, you know. I'll free you so you can use the bucket – under my supervision.'

Afterwards, she was once again immobilised in the chair. He gave her a drink of water before putting some fresh duct tape over her mouth, then left. She heard him lock the cellar door behind him. To her relief he left the light on, her eyes uncovered.

Jody's universe for the next few hours was a clammy windowless cellar with stone walls, a cracked concrete foundation and a ceiling formed of beams supporting the floor above. From the breadth of the floorboards and the spacing of the beams she was pretty sure she was somewhere in the New Town, in a building dating from the late 18th or early 19th century. A waste-pipe came down from the ceiling in a corner about 5 metres away; the occasional rush of water as a toilet was flushed upstairs proved the building above was occupied. From time to time she heard other sounds overhead – footfall, muffled voices and the slamming of a door. Straining to catch even a single word being spoken, she gradually became aware of a faint but constant background noise that seemed to come from further away.

What was that noise? A jangling of discordant bells? It took her a few minutes to identify it, but once she did she was absolutely sure. There had to be a slot-machine arcade or a casino nearby.

Two storeys above, on the gaming floor of the Learmonth Club, Ciaran the manager happened to ask Victor why he'd come in that evening. He didn't usually show up on a Wednesday.

Tetchily, Victor reminded him who *owned* this club; as the owner's son he was free to come and go as he pleased.

Around midnight, he sought out Irina to demand some sandwiches on a covered tray, and a bottle of still mineral water with a straw. The order was unusual: Victor hardly ever ate in the club, and absolutely never drank water. And what was with the straw? But Irina knew better than to ask questions.

Having exited by the back door into the dark garden, Victor felt rather pleased with himself as he groped his way down the steps to the cellar door. The very existence of this space below the Learmonth Club was known to few, and only he had a key. His mother had a long-term plan to convert the basement into a luxuriously furnished room for private upmarket poker games, but those damned fire regulations had so far proved an insurmountable obstacle. (Well, not *totally* insurmountable: money in the right hands would eventually resolve the issue.)

He recognised fear in his hostage's eyes as he approached her. 'No need to be afraid, Missy,' he said. 'I thought you might be peckish so brought you a sandwich.'

He peeled the tape off her face and thrust the food towards her mouth, but she turned her head this way and that to avoid his offering. 'There's nothing wrong with it. See?' he insisted, taking a bite of the sandwich himself.

Still she refused, though she accepted the bottle of water with its apparently unbroken seal.

Her throat moistened with the welcome drink, she screamed 'Help me!' at the top of her voice. Hardly had the words left her mouth than she was gagged again with duct tape; to complete the punishment her tormentor viciously slapped the side of her face with his open hand.

Two minutes later he had abandoned her to her prison, this time turning off the light to leave her in total darkness. *That's it,* he said to himself as he turned the key in the lock once more, *no more Mister Nice Guy.*

⬠

Shortly after 2 am on Thursday, Gibby Wishart was dropped off at his council house in Kirkliston, after his late shift on the Forth Bridge security team. As he fumbled for his keys, a voice behind him said, 'Aye, Gibby, anither day in, eh?'

'Is that you, Willie? God, man, ye could mak a body shite himsel, scarin him like that. Whit are ye daein here at this oor?'

Willie Thomson, *Auld Stobby* operative and former Forth Bridge maintenance engineer, approached and gave Wishart a friendly pat on the shoulder. 'I've a few cans o' yer favourite lager here, Gibby. Thocht we could hae a blether. Ye cannae find a pub open at this time in the mornin, but I ken ye like a wee drink when ye come aff yer shift, eh?'

'That I dae, Willie, that I dae. Come on in, but keep yer voice doon. I dinnae want the wife roused.'

In Wishart's tiny front room, the two men settled down to drink their way through the eight cans of lager Thomson had brought. The conversation began with football and became quite lively, Wishart being a Hibernian supporter and his former colleague a dyed-in-the-wool Hearts fan. When the debate about which team would fare better in the new season foundered in a messy stalemate, Thomson took the opportunity to begin gently probing as to the current state of security on the bridge.

'Nuthin much his chynged,' Wishart said. 'Still three shifts, ten tae six, six tae two in the mornin, two tae ten. I've been on the six-tae-two for a coupla months. The wife nants, but I like it fine.'

'I suppose it gets real quate?'

'Aye, Willie, it does. Atween you and me, I usually hae a fly wee nap efter I dae the midnight inspection. I set the alarm on my phone, then dae a quick round afore the graveyard shift comes on at two.'

Thomson knew this was common practice but was delighted to hear it still went on. Now it only remained to broach the most sensitive subject: disabling the security camera that scanned the area of the firth around Inchgarvie.

Wishart controlled the conversation for a bit – he wondered what Thomson was up to these days; reminisced fondly about the night they both got plastered in Linlithgow and woke up together in a police cell; complained that the lager wasn't as strong as it used to be, and went to the kitchen for the whisky bottle. When he returned, and poured a good two inches into each tumbler, Thomson judged the moment was right.

'We go back a lang wye thigither, Gibby,' he began. 'So I'm no gaun tae lee tae ye. Ye asked whit I wis up tae, and I didnae tell ye the full story.'

'Oh aye?'

Thomson spun him a tale about a boat that would come up the firth the following night, laden with contraband Scotch whisky labelled for export to Russia. He was in on the deal, he said, and would cut Wishart in if he was interested. 'Could be five hundred in it for ye,' was the pitch. All Wishart had to do was turn off the Inchgarvie camera for a few hours. 'Is that something ye can dae?'

Wishart took a swig of whisky, washed it down with lager, and laughed heartily.

'It's no a joke, Gibby.'

'That's no whit's amusin me,' Wishart said, trying to contain his mirth. 'That camera's been oot for the last month. Like a lot o' things that need daein on the bridge, it willnae be fixed until efter the takeover. NEPA's gaun tae hiv tae pey for it. So yer boat'll be safe enough, eh? Aye, I'd still like the five hundred, mind, for tellin ye this.'

'It's a deal, man. Soon as I get my cut, I'll be roond wi yours.'

⬠

Not even a chink of light relieved the blackness. Jody had memorised the layout of the cellar, and knew where she wanted to get to, if she were able to move. Painful though it was, she found that, by shifting her weight from one hip to the other, she could rock the steel-framed chair slightly on the uneven floor. By twisting her body at the same time, she could turn the chair a few degrees as it rocked. After twenty such twists, she knew it was working; the sound of water in the waste-pipe was now coming from a different direction.

On and on she laboured. Listening for the periodic flow of water, she judged it was now marginally closer. Encouraged, she completed another slow rotation on her chair, then another. The pipe now seemed close to her ear. By a stroke of good luck – boy, could she use one – there was a depression in the concrete by the pipe, allowing her greater movement.

Eventually, Jody manoeuvred the chair to knock its frame against the waste-pipe with a satisfying clunk. Now, she set up a rhythmic rocking: *clunk-clunk-clunk; clunk-clunk-clunk; clunk-clunk-clunk*. Somebody upstairs was bound to hear it.

Upstairs, somebody *did* hear it. Irina was using the ladies' room before heading out for her night bus. *Clunk-clunk-clunk*, it went. Sitting on the toilet, she thought she could even feel the vibration.

Taking out her house key, she tapped as hard as she could on the porcelain. *Chink-chink-chink*. Back it came: *clunk-clunk-clunk*.

She tried *chink-chink*. A moment later: *clunk-clunk*.

Chink-chink-chink-chink; clunk-clunk-clunk-clunk.

At the risk of missing her bus, she sought out Ciaran.

'Time you went home,' he told her. 'You're imagining things.'

Okay, she thought, *not my worry*. She left, and had to run to catch the bus.

50
PATIENCE

VICTOR AWOKE TO THE RING of his mobile. Struggling to focus his eyes on the alarm clock he established the time: coming up to 6 am. He'd only got to bed at one. After his midnight act of mercy had been so underappreciated, he had locked the cellar door and driven straight home without going back inside the club. He picked up the phone, looked at the display, then answered.

'Hello, Ma.'

'Sounds like you're not up yet, Victor. Don't forget the guys will be at the site by 7:30. Did you check the place yesterday?'

You bet he did. And got a surprise, which was a damn nuisance to have to deal with, though he planned to turn business into pleasure – maybe as soon as tomorrow, down by the firth. But he mentioned none of this to his mother. She'd just worry.

'Yes, Ma, everything's in order. I'll be there by seven or so.'

'Thanks, son. I'm off to Nottingham today. Got a filly in the 3:25, think she's in with a chance. Then I thought I'd take the train up to Edinburgh, should get in around midnight.'

'Jeez, Ma, wish I'd known. The flat's a bit of a mess. Been so busy ...'

'Don't worry, I'll stay at the Balmoral. You can take me up to see the ground-breaking for my house tomorrow.'

'Won't they break ground today?'

'Shouldn't think so. It'll just be a pole-dance with surveying instruments.'

'Okay, Ma, no problem. I'll pick you up at the Balmoral at – what – nine?'

'Make it ten. I'll have had a late night.'

Me too, Victor thought but didn't say. *If Ma's to be in Edinburgh tomorrow, I'd better dispose of the girl tonight. First task: check the tide tables.*

Marcus made good time driving up from Swansea through the night. The road was dry, traffic was light and he managed the whole trip with only one ten-minute stop at Tebay on the M6. It was just 6:40 when he pulled up outside the Morningside flat. Ignoring the 'permit holders only' sign, he parked in a space right behind Jody's car. Hoping against hope she'd be in bed, possibly just getting up, the first sign that something was wrong came as he let himself in with his key. The chain was off. It was a little early, even for Jody, to have gone for a run.

'Jody! Sweetheart?' He made his way to her bedroom.

No reply came. The bed was made up, obviously unslept-in. He checked every room; nothing seemed amiss except that there was no trace of Jody. He called the police, wishing he'd done so twelve hours earlier.

Against all her expectations, she had slept on and off. Now, though, Jody was wide awake, taking stock of her predicament.

Her body clock told her it was several hours since she had heard the faint response to her knocking on the waste-pipe. Her hopes had been raised, then everything had gone quiet. No toilet flushed; even the constant jingling background of slot machines had stilled. And so it remained, a silence as black as the darkness that pervaded her lonely dungeon.

One more time, her mind ran through the chain of events that would, she prayed, release her from this hell. Her last communication to Marcus – and to Delia – was the photo she emailed of the sign at The Dene. At least one of them would surely guess she'd gone off alone in search of Neadreth's grove.

Then they'd realise she was bound to go to Rest And Be Thankful. Something must have happened to her there, or on the way, otherwise she'd have sent another photo, wouldn't she? Or a text message, perhaps? The police would get involved, and soon be on the trail of the hooded thug.

Meanwhile, she'd just have to be patient, at least until she heard signs of life upstairs. Then she'd begin knocking on the pipe again.

⬠

At the police station Marcus handed his phone to the young officer assigned to the case. He immediately recognised the location of the sign in the photo.

'The Dene,' he said. 'Part of the Water of Leith walkway. That sign is actually on a pillar of the Dean Bridge, where there was a suicide just last week. You probably heard about it.'

'I never knew it was called The Dene,' Marcus said, 'but it makes perfect sense she was there.' He explained that he and Jody were investigating medieval and Roman sites in and around Edinburgh, and that was one of the places that had caught their interest.

'We'll have a look,' the officer said. 'But first things first. We need a description, including what she might have been wearing yesterday. Have you a photograph of Ms Stair?'

Marcus produced one from his wallet. 'She was probably in her running gear. Black leggings and a coloured top – don't know which one she had on yesterday – but definitely red shoes. Nikes.'

'Okay, that's a start. Now where else might she have gone?'

'Another place we've looked at is Faucheldean, between Broxburn and Winchburgh. But she'd have needed her car for that, and it's parked at her flat. Then there's Corstorphine Hill. You know Rest And Be Thankful?'

'Sure. There's a building site up there for a new house.'

'So I've heard. Jody might have headed there after The Dene.'

'But there were no more photos? Any texts or missed calls?'

'Nothing like that, I'm afraid.'

'We'll check out Rest And Be Thankful. Any other ideas?'

'Since she'd gone for a run, she might have decided to follow the walkway, either up or downriver from where she took the photo of the sign. She typically runs eight to ten miles.'

The policeman's mobile beeped; there had been no hospital admission of anyone answering Jody's description.

The interrogation that followed about Marcus's own movements left him upset. The rental car, delivered in Swansea at ten the previous night and now parked outside Jody's flat, should be proof enough that he could have no involvement, he thought.

'Now, Mr Annandale, this email was sent by Ms Stair at 4:25 pm yesterday, attaching a photo taken at The Dene at 4:23.'

'Yes, what about it?'

'I see there was one other recipient.'

'That would be Delia Cobb, a friend of ours, who's in the Highlands on a work trip. She's a NEPA employee. You'll want to check with her.'

'We will, thank you. All right, we have enough to be going on with for the moment. If anything else occurs to you, call us right away.'

⬠

By the time two constables arrived at Rest And Be Thankful, the surveying crew were on site, measuring and levelling. The heavy excavating machinery was expected by noon. The same officer who had interviewed Marcus that morning talked to the foreman. Neither he nor any of his crew had seen the missing woman.

After rooting around inside and outside the fence, the police began their trek back down towards Ravelston Dykes. On the way, a call came in.

'Hi, this is PC Shona Kilmartin. I'm at home – start nightshift tonight – but heard from HQ you were on a missing person case.'

'Correct. So what?'

'There's a house-building site at Rest And Be Thankful.'

'Just coming away from there.'

'I paid a visit there in June, with PC Crawford.'

'And?'

There was a pause while PC Kilmartin checked her notes. 'It was about the headless body on Cramond Island. The victim's car was found abandoned off Ravelston Dykes, near Murrayfield golf course. A groundskeeper remembered directing a man with a metal detector up to Rest And Be Thankful, just off the fairway. There we talked to Victor Herring, who said it was the site of a house for his mother, Mrs Rachel Herring.'

'Did Herring become a suspect in the case?'

'Not officially.'

'It's still unsolved, that headless murder. What was the guy's name again? Bowland?'

'Bowman. There are still no good leads. But here's a strange thing. I happened to see Herring again, just last Saturday, in St Leonards, giving a statement on the Dean Bridge suicide. A bit of a coincidence that you're looking for him on yet another case.'

'Coincidence, you think? But we've no reason to link this missing person with the Cramond Island body, far less Mogadon Man. She'll turn up in a day or two, like they mostly do. It's not even 24 hours since she was last heard of.'

Kilmartin gave them Victor's address and mobile number, then ended the call. Immediately they rang him – no reply. They drove to the Learmonth Club – closed, no one there at that time on a Thursday morning. Finally, they went to Victor's flat – again, nobody about. A neighbour told them Mr Herring's movements were very erratic and he didn't talk much.

No problem; they'd catch up with him later. Only thing left to do meantime was talk to Jody Stair's colleagues at the museum. She might have confided in somebody that she was going away somewhere. Other than that, they'd keep an eye on the boyfriend. His alibi was tight, but, well, nine times out of ten ...

⬠

At the precise moment the two police officers were ringing the bell at the locked front door of the Learmonth Club, Victor was in the cellar of that very building attending to the basic bodily needs of his hostage. By now she knew better than to make a noise when he let her use the bucket or removed her gag to give her a drink.

Oddly, he failed to notice that she had moved her chair a few metres and was now close by the descending waste-pipe. She begged him to leave the light on this time.

Liking her submissive tone, he magnanimously agreed. *This is a step in the right direction,* he thought. Before he left, he told her she only had a few more hours to spend in the cellar. He had something in mind that would be a different kind of experience for her.

51
SOFTLY, SOFTLY

DETECTIVE SERGEANT KENNY FYFE was in charge of the Jody Stair missing person inquiry. A veteran who had joined Lothian and Borders Police not long after the 1975 reorganisation that swept away local constabularies, he had survived the creation in 2013 of Police Scotland. One of those who felt an opportunity had been missed to name the new national force 'The Polis', Fyfe was also among the Edinburgh ranks who resented what they saw as a takeover by Glasgow.

Eligible for retirement for the last 6 years, he had stayed on through sheer inertia. But the writing was now on the wall; he had been given progressively more insignificant desk jobs and it looked like he would be gone by Christmas.

When told he was getting the Stair case, he deadpanned, 'Staircase? Why dae ye no just show me the door?' Clearly his new assignment was a routine matter that had fallen through the deep litter system to land on his desk.

Fyfe looked at the thin file on his computer screen. Female, 34, unmarried, works at the museum. Goes for a run. *A woman her age should have a more demanding job, better still keep a man fed, rear two or three bairns and be pregnant again, instead of wasting her energy running.*

He was sure the case would take care of itself. She'd have gone to a Fringe show, got drunk and crashed out at a friend's house. That was doubtless the type of her.

It was now 2 pm the following day; her hangover would have worn off. *She'll turn up at home in the next couple of hours or so.*

Fyfe made no protest when told the uniforms who'd been on the case were being reassigned to a more important operation.

At 3:30, a young constable arrived at his desk. *Nice looking, but could do to lose a few pounds off those hips.*

She introduced herself as PC Shona Kilmartin. 'I was wondering if your men have caught up with Victor Herring yet.'

Fyfe almost said, 'Who?' Instead he bit his lip. 'What's it to you?'

'He was briefly a person of interest in that death at the Dean Bridge last weekend ...'

'Mogadon Man, aye. Turned out to be a suicide, didn't it?'

'Well, yes, but I also ran into him on the Cramond Island murder.'

'The man who lost his head, eh? And did Herring assist you with your inquiries?'

'Only as a witness. But this is the third case he's cropped up in this year. I think we need to question him.'

'You do, do you? Based on what?'

'I understand the missing woman might have gone to Rest And Be Thankful yesterday. Herring's having a house built up there, for his mother.'

'Aye, Rachel Herring, the casino queen. She's bringing a big new development to the city. Wouldn't want to get too heavy-handed there.'

'I'm not saying get heavy-handed. Just talk to the guy. If Jody Stair went up there yesterday, he might have seen her, that's all.'

'I've no manpower at this minute. But once I have, I'll get right on to it.'

Shona Kilmartin saw she was getting nowhere. She turned on her heel and Fyfe watched her backside for a moment as she walked away.

'Constable?' he called out.

She paused and looked back at him. 'Sergeant?'

'What's the first rule in any missing person case, eh?'

'Er ... the sooner you search, the better the chance of a good outcome.'

'No. Husbands, wives and lovers. They *always* know more than they're willing to tell you. Stair has a boyfriend, Marcus Annandale. Reported her missing at seven this morning. Conveniently, he has an alibi for the whole period from her last communication until that time. *Too* conveniently, in my book. *He*'s the one we're keeping an eye on, not your Victor Herring.'

She shrugged and left, frustrated at the older man's complacency but more so by her own inability to sell him on her idea. Herring *must* somehow be involved.

Why was she bothered? She wasn't supposed to come on duty until six, yet here she was, two and a half hours early, trying – and failing – to breathe life into an investigation that had nothing to do with her. For a moment she considered going after Herring herself, but decided against. It was possible Fyfe did have some softly, softly operation in progress that he wouldn't talk about to the likes of her.

If she went blundering in, she could ruin everything.

⬠

By the time Victor arrived back at the building site, the surveyors had begun to pack up. The lines of the foundation walls were now clearly marked out with posts and string for the excavation to begin tomorrow. The digger and earth-mover were here, and a hut had been set up to double as site office and store for tools and instruments.

He was looking forward to bringing his mother up in the morning to witness ground-breaking. Already he had picked the starting point: the precise spot where Bob Bowman's metal detector had located the gold statuette, later dug up by Cammy Lewis. Whatever else might remain there would be destroyed – the sooner the better.

Once the workmen had left for the day, Victor opened the door of his OOCL box. This was his first chance to clean up inside, to get rid of anything the girl might have touched. Fortunately there had been no bleeding from the injury he inflicted with the chain, but there might be traces of hair or saliva on the floor or walls.

He stopped to think for a moment – something Ma told him he should do more often.

There was *no way* he could remove every last atom of forensic evidence that the girl had been in the shipping container. So why try? He just needed to make sure there were no scraps of duct tape lying around. And he'd come up with some kind of plausible story, if the police should ever come asking.

Okay, she could have been at the site before I got there yesterday afternoon.

And ... oh yes! I'd forgotten to lock the container. I checked, nothing was missing. But I suppose she might have gone in there and rooted around – for what, I can't imagine.

Around 4:30 he headed with a light heart to the Learmonth Club. *Between now and picking Ma up at ten tomorrow, it's me time.*

⬠

Delia and Quin were delayed for an hour and a half by a multi-vehicle pile-up on the A9. Their arrival in Morningside was clocked by a police officer in an unmarked car. Now they were in Jody's kitchen with Marcus, endlessly rehashing explanations for her disappearance.

'She agreed with me that Neadreth's grove has to be at Rest And Be Thankful,' Delia said. 'I'm sure that's where she went.'

Marcus remained sceptical. 'There's no *limpid flow* there. Nothing you could call a *dene*. No remains of a Roman bathing place.'

'Only as far as we know.'

'It doesn't bear Neadreth's name, as Charlotte said it did.'

'Still,' Delia insisted, 'I think Jody was sufficiently taken with the idea to have gone there yesterday.'

'Well, I think something happened to her at The Dene. I'd like a good look around the spot where she took the photograph. But I'm reluctant to leave the flat, in case she arrives home.'

Quin volunteered to hold the fort; together Marcus and Delia drove off, tailed by the policeman in the unmarked vehicle. Marcus got out at Stockbridge and began following the Water of Leith walkway towards the site of Jody's last photograph.

Alone now, Delia continued to Ravelston Dykes and was soon striding briskly up the hill to Rest And Be Thankful. She encountered walkers and a kid on a mountain bike, then had to step aside for a green Land Rover bumping down the track. As it passed, she glimpsed the driver, who wore a dark-coloured hoodie. His rear windows were blacked out, or heavily tinted. She thought little of it, as her mind was suddenly taken up by a stinging sensation all over her bare arms and the backs of her hands. She had stepped into a bed of tall nettles.

Ignoring the discomfort, she continued to the fence she had seen last Sunday with Quin. Only now there was a digger and a machine like a small bulldozer in the enclosure. Development of the site was under way. But the gate was securely locked and there was no one around.

If I were in Jody's shoes and I thought Neadreth's grove could be in there, I'd be determined to get in somehow for a look.

Clambering over the barricade didn't seem like an option Jody would have considered – she'd have been too conspicuous to walkers or players on the adjacent golf course. No, she'd have looked for another way in.

Before long Delia found the tiny gap between fencing panels that had been the point of entry. She herself couldn't contemplate wriggling through that space, but Jody's slender frame could gain access where others couldn't. Trying unsuccessfully to prise the panels further apart, Delia noticed a scrap of olive-green fabric hanging from a loose wire that projected into the gap.

Jody had a running top just that colour. Instantly she knew Jody had been there.

My God! She could still be here!

Delia called Marcus to tell him. 'I'm gonna call the police.'

'Don't bother,' he said. 'A cop's been tailing me ever since you dropped me off – thinks I haven't noticed him. I'm waving him over.'

On the open phone line Delia heard the call going out for police and ambulance backup.

The officer then spoke to Delia. 'Stay right where you are. Don't touch anything. We'll be there as soon as we can.'

⬠

Irina arrived in good time for her shift, due to start at five. Still puzzled by the knocking sounds she'd heard in the ladies' room, she went there before clocking in. Listened, but heard nothing. Began tapping on the plumbing with her key. No response. Repeated a few times, always pausing to listen. Still nothing. 'I must have imagined it,' she said to herself.

She flushed the toilet and was washing her hands when she thought she heard it again. The sound of the cistern filling? Waiting until all was silent once more, she tapped three times. *Chink-chink-chink.*

It was unmistakable. *Clunk-clunk-clunk* came back.

Running out into the corridor, she almost bumped into Victor Herring, who had just entered through the back door.

'Mr Herring, there's a funny knocking sound in the plumbing. Like somebody's trying to attract attention. I heard it last night too. Come and listen.'

'No, no, Irina, I believe you,' Victor said in as soothing a voice as he could muster. 'I'll have all the toilets checked right away. Now, shouldn't you be at work?'

52
THE LAST SUPPER

'WHY DOES THIS FEEL LIKE the Last Supper?' Isla wondered aloud as she separated the bones from Rory's *truite aux amandes*.

It was 7:30. In just three hours she and Hugh would leave their five-star prison and set in motion their assault on the Forth Bridge, still the property of Network Rail. By the time a call was made to a particular mobile phone number, at exactly 1:30 am, the bridge would legally belong to NEPA.

Scotland would awake on Friday morning to a blizzard of news about the audacious attack. But after the initial shock, Isla told herself, public anger would gradually be directed away from the patriots of *Auld Stobby* and on to NEPA, those English chancers in spiv suits. *They* were the real villains. Not content with stealing Scotland's precious water, *they* had put that magnificent structure in harm's way. Nobody was going to blow up a bridge owned and operated by stuffy old Network Rail. But the moment it became NEPA's, all bets were off. Their crowing about acquiring it for one pound would be silenced at a stroke.

So why the sense of impending doom? Was it fear of being caught in the act? That was always a risk, though it had been confirmed that bridge security would have a one-hour blackout from 12:30 am; plenty of time to land on Inchgarvie, plant the explosive and get away again.

Was it a different outcome that worried her? One where the explosive went off prematurely, making them suicide bombers? Those damned Belgians had nothing to lose by having them die in the explosion.

Hugh had tried to banish Isla's fears on that score by proposing she withdraw to a safe distance, after the explosive was in place but before the phone connection was activated. He would make the final connection alone before making a swift retreat. The worst that could happen was that he would die and she would escape.

'You said yourself, Isla, after this is all over, we have no future as a couple. We're going to go our separate ways. So surely it's better that *one* of us survives, and it might as well be you, don't you think?'

She had ultimately accepted that logic. Yet somehow it *still* felt like the Last Supper.

Any option Kenny Fyfe might have had to stall the search for Victor Herring into the evening hours evaporated when a shred of the missing woman's clothing was found at the building site. He despatched four constables in a 4×4, reluctantly agreeing that Shona Kilmartin should be one of them. With that vehicle they could have negotiated the deeply potholed track from Ravelston Dykes up to Rest And Be Thankful, but to the horror of club officials they opted for a faster approach, along the fairways of Murrayfield golf course.

At the Learmonth Club Ciaran Mortimer said Victor had been there an hour or so earlier but had left without saying where he was going. The premises were searched and staff and customers interviewed.

Though nervous of talking to the police, Irina made a point of telling a uniformed officer she had spoken to Victor just before coming on duty at five o'clock. She even told him what they had discussed. A strange knocking sound coming through the plumbing. The policeman showed no interest in such details.

Another employee mentioned Victor's use of the back door, which led through a small garden to a private lane and a garage where he often parked his car or his motorbike. Out there, the police found neither vehicle, but did notice a wheelbarrow with indications of recent use: a wheel-track led from its present position through a side-door and along a gravel footpath to a flight of steps down to a cellar.

Only Victor had a key to the cellar, the officers were told. But they had sufficient reason to break in. In a corner, where a waste-pipe descended from the building above, was a steel-framed chair with strips of duct tape stuck to it. Scuff-marks on the concrete floor showed the chair had been dragged to its present position from about three metres away.

But there was no Jody Stair, alive or dead.

Back at police HQ, the registration number of Victor Herring's green Land Rover had been traced and all police patrols within fifty miles of Edinburgh notified.

At 7:30, Kenny Fyfe received a call he'd been dreading. The voice said, 'You gave your word, sergeant. Victor Herring would not be harassed. So why do I hear that you've put an alert out on his car?'

'It's out of my hands,' Fyfe replied, shifting uneasily in his chair. 'We believe he's abducted a young woman and her life may be in danger. This was definitely not in the plan.'

'Everything we've been working towards, these last few months, could be blown. You realise that?'

'Even if I wanted to I can't turn a blind eye to a crime as serious as this. Look, it could turn out we're wrong, that he's got nothing to do with the missing girl. He'll get kid-glove treatment, I promise you.'

'You've already made too many promises,' the voice said. The call ended.

⬠

Marcus, Delia and Quin were together again, in Jody's flat. Quin had prepared some food for them all.

Time dragged as they waited impotently for any news. If only to suppress the unbearable thought that Jody might be seriously harmed, or worse, they talked of inconsequentialities.

'I'd intended to go to the Water Lairds tonight,' Marcus said. 'Remember Kirsty Morton's grandnephew, whom I'd nominated for membership until I discovered he was part of an extremist group? I was going to formally withdraw the nomination at tonight's meeting. But it can wait until next time.'

'He joined *Auld Stobby*, a militant ultra-nationalist organisation,' Delia explained to Quin.

'*Auld Stobby?*'

'It's a reference to the Scotch thistle – old prickly.'

'From the language of the Angles,' Quin said. '*Stybb*: a sharp-pointed thing, a thorn or prickle.'

'Hey, Quin, you should come to *Inglisleid* one night with Jody and me.' Marcus's eyes filled at the voicing of her name. Then, recovering, he turned to Delia. 'I owe you an apology. You were probably right about Rest And Be Thankful. I was too wedded to the idea that the place we were looking for bore Neadreth's name in some form or another. If I'd sent the police up there the minute I got back from Swansea ...'

'They wouldn't necessarily have found the scrap from Jody's top. Even if they had, they mightn't have thought it was significant.'

At that moment, Marcus's phone rang.

'Just to keep you in the loop, Mr Annandale, we've a camera shot of Herring's Land Rover travelling west on Queensferry Road near Cramond Brig at 6:22 pm. There's no sign of it having crossed the firth. So we're now focusing the search on West Lothian, Falkirk, Stirling and North Lanarkshire.'

To Marcus, it didn't sound like much of a focus.

53
METICULOUS PLANNING

ELEVEN PM. HOWEVER THEY WERE feeling on the inside, the two patriots about to blow a hole in the Forth Bridge projected an aura of calm. Identically dressed in black from boots to hoodies and with blackened faces, Hugh Leggat and Isla Younie had crossed the line. They were terrorists.

Having helped Fraser Cadenhead load his little boat on the dark shore just outside North Queensferry, they launched without delay into the silent darkness of the bay. There they would wait until they received the signal to head for Inchgarvie.

Less than a mile away, at St David's Harbour, Hendrik Vandenbrouck kept watch through night-vision binoculars. From there he would monitor the entire operation, and at the same time get early warning of police approach.

Not that he expected such a thing. First, he had received no intelligence suggesting any kind of security alert. Second, radio chatter indicated the police had their hands full with an entirely different matter. Some woman had been abducted in Edinburgh and a major search was in progress. How lucky was that?

The Nightjar team were under strict orders: no mobile phone use. The whole operation was a masterpiece of meticulous planning with no need for further communication. Only two calls would be made, both by Vandenbrouck himself. The first would be the 'go' signal to Cadenhead, at 12:15 am unless some unforeseen event such as a ship passing under the bridge necessitated a short delay. The second would be to the mobile that Younie and Leggat would wire to the explosive charge. He had told his team to expect that at 1:30 am precisely.

⬠

At police HQ, the mood had turned pessimistic. No further sighting of Herring's Land Rover had been reported. The quarry had gone to ground, almost certainly in the countryside somewhere to the west of Edinburgh. He had stayed off major roads, avoided towns and villages and was probably now in some hidey-hole in a farm building or forestry plantation. If his hostage was still alive, the chances were slim that she would survive the night.

Almost five hours since the last sighting, Herring and the girl might be anywhere. There were uncomfortable reminders of the 2010 abduction of Suzanne Pilley in Edinburgh, which culminated in an ultimately fruitless search for her remains in a remote part of Argyll.

It was a lowly uniformed officer, PC Shona Kilmartin, who came up with a credible theory. If Herring had been the killer in the Cramond Island case, he might have taken Jody Stair to the very same spot where he had dumped the headless body of Robert Bowman in the firth. She argued that place had to be on the south shore – Herring would have been caught on camera if he had crossed any of the bridges. He would favour an unfrequented place, perhaps accessible only by Land Rover.

Some of her colleagues dismissed her simplistic thinking, in the absence of any hard evidence linking Herring to the Bowman murder. But none had a better idea.

Thus it was that, at 11:45 pm, the green Land Rover was spotted on the shoreline just east of Carriden.

Three minutes later, Jody was found in long grass a few metres from the vehicle, bound and gagged, injured but alive. Still wearing only the light running gear she had set out in 30 hours before, she was cold and dehydrated. Quickly her duct-tape binding was removed, and an ambulance was soon on the scene.

Victor Herring was discovered at 11:59, cowering in some bushes less than 200 metres from his intended victim.

⬠

On the stroke of midnight, a train rolled to a stop in Edinburgh Waverley station. Among the passengers alighting sleepily from the first-class coach was Rachel Herring, to be met by a surprise welcoming party in police uniforms and high-vis jackets.

Meanwhile, the Caledonian sleeper from Aberdeen to London was hurtling south an hour behind schedule, after a signal failure near Montrose. Its 75 passengers and crew would, at this rate, find themselves on the Forth Bridge shortly after one in the morning.

⬠

As soon as Marcus got word that Jody was safe and on her way to Western General Hospital, he headed over there. Having stayed all evening with him during the long wait for news, Delia and Quin went home to bed.

She checked the time before turning out the light. It was just after one o'clock. Until now she hadn't given it a moment's thought, but for some reason it came into her mind. NEPA, her employer, had been the proud owner of the Forth Bridge for precisely one hour.

⬠

At that very moment, two black-clad, black-faced operatives were perched on a granite plinth under one of the mighty steel towers of NEPA's new acquisition.

A rumbling sound signalled the arrival of the Caledonian, slowing to under 50 mph as it approached. *Good thing,* Isla thought, *that this train will be miles away by half-past one when the bridge blows.*

It was a two-person job to lift the charges into position around the tower. That done, all that remained was to connect the detonator to the mobile phone and activate the connection – a simple flick of a switch.

Hugh motioned to her to get back down the ladder. She lingered for a moment, then threw her arms around him. 'Wish we hadn't had to do this,' she said, leaving him alone on the plinth.

Vandenbrouck seethed as he watched from his lookout. He saw clearly that only one figure remained with the explosive charge, while the smaller one retreated to a safe distance. This was a serious breach. Hugh Leggat could not be trusted to connect and activate the detonator unsupervised by the other.

He saw Leggat move towards the ladder, just as the front coach of the sleeper train passed directly above. Instantly, the Belgian took out his mobile and made the call.

No blinding flash, no thunderous bang. With calm insouciance, the Caledonian continued its southward crossing of the firth.

'Klootzak!' With that Flemish utterance he made another call, to Cadenhead.

Over the clatter of the train above him, Hugh heard the mobile ring, and knew he was supposed to be a dead man. It came as no surprise that the Belgian would try to kill him, but even Hugh was astounded that the passage of a train at the critical moment hadn't given Vandenbrouck pause. Quickly shinning down the ladder, he rejoined Isla. Without a word, they made for the boat that was waiting for them. Before they got there, Cadenhead started up the engine and took off at speed into the firth, leaving them stranded on Inchgarvie.

Isla was aghast at this turn of events, then astonished to see that Hugh seemed unperturbed. 'What the hell's going on?' she asked.

'Okay,' Hugh said calmly, 'I didn't activate the charge. The phone rang while I was still on the plinth, and I'm still alive. So are all the people on that train. Here's what's going to happen now.'

⬠

Cadenhead returned to shore and found Vandenbrouck waiting for him. To the surprise of both, police 4×4s closed in on them from two opposite directions, sirens blaring, lights flashing. There was no escape; they were cuffed and bundled into separate vehicles.

A police launch sped out from North Queensferry. As they watched from their castaway island, Hugh said, 'You were right not to trust me, Isla.'

'I *knew* it! You're a fucking infiltrator! What are you? MI5?'

'Let's just say I'm a Scottish, and British, patriot. Like you, I want what's best for my country, though we differ in what we think is best and certainly on how to achieve it.'

'And the last three days? Does all that mean nothing to you?' She raised her fists in impotent rage.

Grabbing both her wrists, he said, 'I'll tell them you didn't want to go through with this. That you even tried to persuade me we could make a run for it. All of which is true, Isla. I might even embellish the story a little. Say we agreed together not to activate the explosive.'

She broke down in tears. Eventually, in a small voice, she said, 'I'm glad.'

'You're glad that what? That the police are on their way?'

She shook her head.

'That the bridge didn't blow?'

'I couldn't see how I was going to live with myself after this. Just do what you can, Hugh. Do what you can to lighten my sentence.'

'Trust me,' he said.

The sobbing ceased and she managed a grin. '*Trust* you?' she echoed. 'Are you crazy?'

The launch arrived with three police officers. 'Mr Leggat, I presume?' one of them said.

'Yes,' Hugh affirmed, 'and my partner in saving the Forth Bridge, Ms Isla Younie.'

⬠

It was close to 3 am before Marcus was allowed to see Jody. Despite painful-looking bruises on her face and neck, she was in remarkably good spirits. Even after a seriously traumatic experience and 45 hours without proper sleep, she managed a smile and held her arms out for a hug.

'How are you feeling, sweetheart?' he said, gently clasping her hand.

Her eyes welled. 'Okay, I guess. My knees are going to need some surgery, so I won't be running for a little while. But other than that, I got off light.'

He kissed her, then watched tenderly as her eyes closed and sleep overcame her.

54
THE GREY-HAIRED MAN

THE EDINBURGH FESTIVAL and its famous Fringe were over once again; on the Castle Esplanade the stands for the Tattoo were being dismantled. The next big city-centre party, Hogmanay, was still months away, and now the city was settling down to its core businesses: beer, finance, the pursuit of knowledge and, above all, government and bureaucracy.

For the last four weeks, the papers and blogs had been filled with breathless and often speculative reporting around what had come to be called the Inchgarvie Plot, its unmasking and aftermath. Until 6th August, most citizens would have been hard-pressed to name the tiny island on which the middle section of the Forth Bridge rested; since that date its name had been on everyone's lips. One paper had even seen fit to regurgitate the old playground riddle:

> Q. *What is the narrowest firth in Scotland?*
> A. *The Firth of Forth – there are only four 'inches' between its shores (Inchkeith, Inchmickery, Inchcolm and Inchgarvie).*

Also on the agenda of every after-dinner conversation in Edinburgh: the almost certain demise of *Auld Stobby*, whose fingerprints were all over the affair. New arrests were being made on a daily basis, it seemed. Thomson, Wishart, that Rory guy ...

... and one Paul Bissett, a minor *Stobby* operative who had 'borrowed' the identity of a cycle-shop manager, Lex Durno. Thanks to a detailed description from an American girl, the police had tracked him down in Dundee. She was an employee of NEPA and, having fallen briefly for his charms, had inadvertently 'leaked' to *Stobby* her company's plan for the Forth Bridge.

Competing with the Inchgarvie Plot for column inches and website traffic was another story with endless ramifications, one that, bizarrely, unfolded on the very same night. The abduction of Jody Stair, an NMS curator, had ended in her safe recovery and the arrest of Victor Herring, son of Rachel the casino lady. Charged not only with 'assault to serious injury' (what in English law would be referred to as grievous bodily harm) in the forcible kidnap, he now faced two murder raps and remained in custody.

Rachel herself was accused of conspiracy in the two earlier murders though not in the seizure, assault and imprisonment of Jody Stair. Having secured the services of one of Scotland's leading defence lawyers, she was currently free on bail.

She was also under investigation for corrupt business practices relating to planning applications. Details were still sketchy but James Swift had resigned from the council to 'spend more time with his family' and shortly afterwards had been charged by the police with accepting bribes.

Though some commentators had attempted to draw links between the Inchgarvie Plot and the Herring affair, the intricate nexus of the two stories had yet to emerge. Rachel's bankrolling of the foiled attack on the bridge, in particular the part played by a certain precious gold artefact, had not been revealed.

Furthermore, it had not yet been reported that Victor Herring's two alleged murders and the Stair abduction were apparent attempts to conceal important archaeological remains on his mother's house-building site at Rest And Be Thankful.

Though Jody had found ancient Roman paving stones on that site and surmised that a paved terrace, associated perhaps with a ritual bathing place, had existed there, neither she nor Marcus yet knew of the existence of the gold statuette that had lain undisturbed for centuries under that terrace. Having been released from hospital on 12th August, she was making a good recovery. Marcus was spending a lot of time with her, helping out with housework and shopping and joining her in visits to her physiotherapist. He'd finally hired an assistant manager for his business, something he had the confidence to do following the deal with Jimmy the Greek.

Now, on 3rd September, an invitation arrived by the curiously old-fashioned medium of the Royal Mail. It was addressed formally to Ms Jody Stair, Mr Marcus Annandale, Ms Delia Cobb and Dr Quinton Johnson. The card read:

Mrs Kirsty Morton respectfully requests
the company of the addressees in a *conversazione*
at her home on Friday 10th September at 4:30 pm.
Refreshments and a light meal will be provided.
RSVP.

The stiff tone of the invitation was tempered by a handwritten note at the bottom of the card.

I promise: you won't want to miss this. KM.

'What the hell's a *conversazione*?' Marcus asked.

'It's Italian for a *blether*,' Jody said. 'Should be fun ... let's go. Pity Quin's gone home to Chicago, but I'm sure Delia will be up for it.'

'I think I know what this is about,' Marcus said. 'At the Water Lairds last night, everyone wanted to know if I was still supporting the induction of Kirsty's grandnephew. I had to tell them that until Hugh's involvement with *Auld Stobby* was fully explained, I couldn't commit one way or the other. Most wanted to fast-track the membership of one of the two 'heroes of Inchgarvie', but Craig Wetherby of NEPA was understandably cool on the idea.'

'So you think this is about the Water Lairds?' Jody asked, a puzzled expression on her face.

Marcus laughed. 'No, I didn't mean that. Hugh and I have spoken a couple of times since 6th August. I've asked him if there's a connection between the Inchgarvie Plot and the Herrings. He's told me he can't say much – which I take to mean there *is* a connection – but that he should be able to tell us more by the middle of September. *That's* what we're going to hear about at Kirsty's *conversazione*.'

'So you think Hugh will be there?'

'I'd lay money on it.'

The grey-haired man in a dark suit facing Hugh in his office was the same person who had persuaded the chief superintendent to hold back on investigation of Victor Herring in the Dean Bridge death; and his had been the voice on Sergeant Kenny Fyfe's phone making a last-ditch effort to stop the 'harassment' of Herring during the search for Jody Stair. Hugh knew perfectly well who he was, and what organisation he belonged to.

'Mr Smith,' he said. 'I've been waiting weeks for this meeting.'

'As you probably guessed, Ian Smith is not my real name. No matter. The email you sent me from Dunfermline was perfect, thank you.' He pushed a print-out across the desk.

> Ian:
>
> On a trip, plan to be back Friday, will call you then.
>
> Hugh.

'The first word of the message told us all we wanted to know. The attack on the bridge was *on*. It was the agreed signal.'

'What about the money?' Hugh asked. 'All those used twenties? Have you been able to recover any of it?'

'Marked notes make a perfect paper trail. Of the £80,000 you gave Rachel Herring, we've already recovered about 64K, mostly in casino payouts in Blackpool. She also bet a wad of your twenties at the Nottingham racecourse on the day before her arrest.'

'But what about Vandenbrouck's haul?'

'Well of course while he's in custody he isn't spending any. And as for Colonel Mariane Rombouts of the Free Flanders Army, we tracked her to London by what she spent along the way. She took the Eurostar to Brussels and is now being held by the Belgian authorities. They have a list of terrorism-related charges to throw at her. At some point she'll probably be extradited to face a Scottish court. You might even get involved in her prosecution in your professional capacity. We believe she has the bulk of the money hidden somewhere in Flanders.'

'Maybe at the terrorist school Isla and I attended. Have the Belgian police located it?'

'Not yet. I gather they're interested in talking to you both about your experiences there, with a view to finding it and shutting it down.'

'I'll help them in any way I can. So will Isla.'

'Smith' paced across Hugh's small office to look out of the window. 'This brings me to my next subject.'

'I'm listening.'

'Some uncharitable colleagues of mine object to your defence of Ms Younie. She was, after all, a member of Vandenbrouck's inner circle, up to her scrawny neck in the plot.'

Hugh bristled slightly at the unwarranted dig.

'While we appreciate,' his visitor went on, 'her willingness to testify against her co-conspirators, she *was* involved in illegal activity and should have her day in court. As an accused, not just as a witness.'

'She was no more involved in the Forth Bridge operation than I was. In fact, she several times tried to persuade me that we should get out, make a run for it. That, of course, would have blown the sting, so I had to get her back on side. I was *agent provocateur*; I persuaded her to see the attack through.'

'That's for the court to decide. In any case, there are many other offences she could be charged with: blackmail, receiving the proceeds of theft, conspiring to deliver a false report, ...'

'The *badger* thing?'

'A relatively minor one, I grant you. But there's more. Conspiring to conceal treasure trove, ...'

'Now you're getting ridiculous. She had no idea where the gold statuette came from, had no concept of its archaeological significance.'

'You've become involved with her, haven't you? I mean in a personal way – a sexual way, no doubt.'

Hugh uttered no denial.

'You may be compelled to give evidence against her. Even if you marry her.'

The question of marriage had never entered Hugh's mind. Isla *had* moved in with him, but as far as they both were concerned it was an arrangement that could change at any time. He got to his feet. 'I think we're done here,' he told 'Smith' as he opened the door to usher him out.

55
CONVERSAZIONE

'THANK YOU, BUT REALLY there was no need to bring a gift,' Kirsty said as she was handed the flat package at the door. 'So glad you could come to my *conversazione*. We'll be in *this* room.'

She showed Marcus, Jody and Delia into an elegantly furnished drawing-room, a formal space reserved for receiving guests. A huge Persian carpet covered most of the floor; the ceiling was elaborately corniced; a large bay window, framed with heavy curtains, overlooked the garden and a koi pond. They immediately noticed Kirsty's three Charlotte Nasmyths, now taking pride of place on a wall uncluttered by any other items from her substantial art collection.

Opening the package, she squealed with delight to see it contained bound copies of two manuscripts in the artist's delicate hand.

'You already have the third sample of Charlotte's writings,' Jody said. 'It's under the backing of that painting.' She pointed to the largest of the three landscapes, *A Prospect of Edinburgh* from the Salisbury Crags.

In her American accent, Delia recited the verse from memory.

Come yesterday, at ten upon the hour,
And cast thine eyes from high atop my tower.
A message from the one thou callest queen,
Hand over heart, will lead thee to her dene.

'And so it did,' Marcus said, 'though for Jody not in the way any of us wanted.'

'No, my dear,' Kirsty said, turning to Jody. 'You had such a dreadful experience. I'm sure I don't know the half of it. But look at you now.'

Jody's embarrassment increased with Marcus's next remark. 'Isn't she beautiful? Well, I certainly think so, and today, three hours ago to be precise, she agreed to marry me.'

She held up her left hand to display a sparkling diamond. Kirsty tinkled a little bell from a side table. 'We have more to celebrate than I thought!'

The door opened and a young man walked in carrying a tray with six foaming glasses of champagne. Behind him, bearing a salver of canapés, walked a petite woman with a pale complexion, studiously unkempt raven-black hair, and deep purple lipstick with eye-shadow and fingernails to match.

'Marcus,' Kirsty said by way of introduction, 'you know my grandnephew Hugh, but I don't think any of you have met his partner Isla.'

⬠

There was much to talk about. Hugh told of his recruitment by a 'national security organisation' – he would not confirm it was MI5 – to infiltrate *Auld Stobby*. Upon his report that Rachel Herring was funding Operation Nightjar, his paymasters believed she was party to the plot. Even when they suspected foul play in the death of Cameron Lewis at the Dean Bridge, the police had to bide their time, lest the whole sting were blown.

'Pity the cops couldn't do their job,' Marcus said bitterly. 'Then Jody wouldn't have been put through such an ordeal.'

'Marcus is right,' Hugh said. 'Our security services have a lot to answer for. They hung Jody out to dry, now they want to put Isla through the wringer.'

'What made you decide to help foil the plot?' Delia asked Isla.

'Well ... I followed orders up to the end, but I always hated the thought of damaging that bridge.'

‘So how did the two of you get together?’

‘Hugh and I were sent to negotiate with Rachel Herring for the gold statuette that would fund the whole operation.’

‘Gold statuette?’ Delia, Jody and Marcus repeated in unison.

Hugh went over to an antique chest that sat in the bay window, and brought out a heavy object wrapped in a green cloth. He laid it on a low table in front of them and slowly removed the cloth. The pure gold gleamed as it had done when the object was first cast, 1500 years before.

Again almost in unison, Delia, Jody and Marcus cried out, ‘Neadreth!’ The symbolism was obvious: the Anglian goddess with two water barrels in her chariot, pulled by a pair of heifers. The pattern engraved on both sides of the chariot: five stars, in the unmistakable W-shape of Cassiopeia.

‘So let me guess,’ Jody said. ‘Victor Herring found this when he was digging up the Roman paving stones at his mother’s house-building site.’

‘We believe so, yes,’ Hugh confirmed.

‘My God, she’s beautiful. Did you know who she was?’

‘I had her examined by Trimble the goldsmith. He said she was Nerthus.’

‘Her name as latinised by Tacitus.’

‘She must be solid gold, is she?’ Marcus asked.

‘Yes, and of the highest purity. Trimble reckons she was made from melted-down Roman coins – *aurei* – from the time of Septimius Severus.’

Jody looked puzzled. ‘You can’t mean this is a Roman artefact?’

‘No. The original coins were Roman, but the statuette was cast later.’

‘Much later, I think. Severus was 2nd or 3rd century; the Angles arrived in the 6th century. They must have found a hoard of Roman gold and used it to glorify their water-goddess. Then, with the spread of Christianity, they hid the statuette under paving the Romans had laid centuries before, where it remained until the site was vandalised by Victor Herring.'

Kirsty interrupted to announce that a buffet had been laid out in the dining room and invite the party to move through and continue the *conversazione* over some food. The 'light meal' she had promised turned out to be quite a splendid affair. To compliments from her guests, she protested that she had not gone to a lot of trouble, that Isla had done most of the preparation. *Isla? Who would have guessed?* Marcus thought. *Appearances are really deceiving.*

The talk then turned to the execution of the Inchgarvie Plot.

'Inchgarvie,' Delia said without thinking. '*Having rice.*'

Jody and Marcus looked at each other in amusement. Delia's face reddened. 'I must try this rice salad.'

⬠

After the meal, they retired to the drawing-room for after-dinner drinks. Hugh had brought a bottle of his *Poacher's Poison*; he, Isla and Marcus sampled it while Kirsty, Jody and Delia enjoyed something less demanding. 'We have still to hear what led you to Rest And Be Thankful as the place where the Anglian water-goddess had her sacred grove.'

'It's all in those Charlotte Nasmyth manuscripts we've given to Kirsty,' Jody replied, 'and in the verse behind that painting.'

'I can't understand how a 19th-century landscape artist knew about the gold statuette.'

'She may not have known about it – hell, neither did we until tonight. But based on tales her brother had heard at meetings of the Water Lairds, she believed there was a sacred grove dedicated to Neadreth and somehow guessed it was at Rest And Be Thankful. You could call it intuition, or a sixth sense. Fact is, Charlotte was a very clever lady as well as a fine artist.'

Marcus picked up the story, admitting he had been too stuck on the idea of a place bearing Neadreth's name in some form or another. 'Let me read you a passage by Charlotte,' he said, picking up one of the bound manuscripts.

> *... the Romans used certain locations as bathing places, dedicated to their gods. One such location was the shady hazel grove later rediscovered by the Angles and consecrated in the name of their goddess Neadreth ...*

Marcus repeated the words *'consecrated in the name of their goddess Neadreth'* before continuing:

> *... believing the remains of Roman construction at the site to be the work of her mystical priesthood. Though there were other deities in their pantheon, they revered Neadreth as the fountainhead, the wellspring of all their fortune ...*

Kirsty waited while he concluded the reading, then abruptly left the room.

'The *store of wealth* legend has turned out to be true,' Jody said. 'A priceless gold statuette, hidden for centuries under Roman stonework. And the curse on anyone attempting to steal it. Herring's first murder victim, Robert Bowman, was a metal detector hobbyist. First to detect the presence of gold at Rest And Be Thankful, killed and beheaded for his discovery.'

Isla gave a shiver. 'I read that a wristwatch with his initials was found in Victor Herring's flat. Bet he's having difficulty explaining how that came to be in his possession.'

'For sure,' Marcus said. 'And the curse also landed on his second victim, Cameron Lewis. Lewis's DNA was found at Rest And Be Thankful, in traces of blood on rose thorns. He was the one who excavated all those paving stones.'

'In which case,' Hugh put in, 'he may have been the first person in modern times to lay his hands on the statuette.'

'And for his pains, Victor threw him off the Dean Bridge. Sat him on the parapet spikes, grabbed his heels and tipped him back. I gather Victor's fingerprints are on Lewis's shoes.'

Anxious to change the subject away from Victor, Jody announced she had good news. The City of Edinburgh had revoked all planning permissions and were now proceeding to repossess, without compensation, the land they had sold to Rachel Herring for the building of her house. An archaeological dig was already under way on the site, and it had been found that impressions remained in the clay of each of the paving stones that had been lifted. It would be possible to replace them exactly as they had originally been laid.

'And,' she went on, 'some colleagues of mine are now working on a theory that Ravelston Dykes, and its continuation as a track up to Rest And Be Thankful, follow the line of a Roman road. A road that once ran from a fording point on the Water of Leith near Stockbridge to a sacred bathing place on the Corstorphine Hill.'

'A place that became the site of Neadreth's grove but never received her name,' Marcus said.

'I wouldn't be so sure,' Kirsty said, having just returned to the room with a large framed map, which she set on an easel.

'Marcus,' she said, 'I want you to look at this Ordnance Survey map from 1852. Find the site of the sacred grove, and tell me the name of the closest habitation at the time this map was made.'

He peered at some tiny print, then turned to face the others with a triumphant smile. 'There was a cottage, or a farmstead, right there. It's called Fountainhead.' He picked up Charlotte Nasmyth's manuscript and read aloud once again:

> *They revered Neadreth as the fountainhead, the wellspring of all their fortune.*

AUTHOR'S NOTE

Groups and organisations featured in *Scotch and Water* are real, except that NEPA, the Ancient Edinburgh Society of Water Lairds, *Inglisleid* and *Auld Stobby* are drawn entirely from my imagination.

Contemporary characters and events are fictional except for a few well-known public-domain figures. Characters from the 18th and 19th centuries are real but fictionalised in a way that I believe to be consistent with recorded fact. In particular, details of the Nasmyth family (except again for membership of the Water Lairds) are broadly factual. Charlotte Nasmyth's manuscripts (her *True Memoir* and *New Story of Edinburgh's Earliest Beginnings*) are, of course, fictional but most of the characters and events they depict are known from history or legend. Her suite of five paintings under the title *A Prospect of Edinburgh* is also a fictional device. For the life of George Nasmyth, I have drawn heavily from the research of J.A. Cantrell (see Acknowledgements).

I have taken liberties in applying the name 'Neadreth' to the Anglian goddess called 'Nerthus' by Tacitus, and in deriving from her the place-name Niddrie. The arrival of the Norseman Thorfinn Sigurdsson in the vicinity of Edinburgh in 1035, and his sending of an emissary to Jorvik at that time, are matters of my invention. Otherwise, characters and events up to the 11th century are broadly consistent with accepted history.

Places mentioned in *Scotch and Water* are real except for premises such as the Learmonth Club, Firth TV & Audio, *A Malt O' My Ain* and Two-Wheeler Dealer. For precise locations of places featured, readers are invited to consult Ordnance Survey Explorer (1:25,000) Sheet 350 and adjacent sheets.

Jim Forbes.

ACKNOWLEDGEMENTS

I am deeply indebted to my dear wife Elinor (the novelist Elinor Hunter) for her very thorough editing of my manuscript and for her indispensable critique of *Scotch and Water* as it took shape. Thanks also to Naida Forbes for her excellent suggestions on plot points. Any errors and shortcomings that remain are, however, mine.

Sources relied on for the lives of the Nasmyth family and their ancestors include:

Cantrell, J.A. (2003) Two Maudslay protégés: Francis Lewis and George Nasmyth. *Transactions of the Newcomen Society* Vol. 73, pp. 257–274.

Fothergill, G.A. (1909) George Foulis (1569–1633) and the carved stones of Ravelston. *Proceedings of the Society of Antiquaries of Scotland,* Vol. 44, pp. 76–89.

Johnson, P. & Money, E. (1977) *The Nasmyth family of Painters*. Leigh-on-Sea: F. Lewis.

London Gazette, The (1884) Charlotte Nasmyth, executry notice (12th September, p. 4096).

Smiles, S. (ed., 1883) *James Nasmyth, Engineer: Autobiography*. London: John Murray.

Sources of myth and history up to the 11th century include:

Carr, A.A. (1836) *A History of Coldingham Priory*. Edinburgh: A. & C. Black.

Fry, M. (2009) *Edinburgh, a History of the City*. London: Pan Books.

Grant, J. (ca. 1883) *Cassell's Old and New Edinburgh* (6 vols.) London: Cassell.

Higham, N.J. (1993) *The Kingdom of Northumbria, AD 300–1100*. Stroud: Sutton Publishing.

Meehan, B. (1976) The siege of Durham, the battle of Carham and the cession of Lothian. *Scottish Historical Review,* Vol. 55, pp. 1–19.

Rollason, D. (2003) *Northumbria 500–1000: Creation and Destruction of a Kingdom*. Cambridge: University Press.

Saxo Grammaticus (ca. 1185) *Gesta Danorum*.

Smyth, A.P. (1989) *Warlords and Holy Men: Scotland AD 80–1000*. Edinburgh University Press.

Also from Kinord Books:

Taran's Wheel by Jim Forbes
(*Incomers*: Book 1)

A riddle from beyond the grave sets Delia on a search for an ancient talisman, taking her from Chicago to the 'Pleasant Vale' of Cromar in Scotland, where the dramatic story of the Vale and its people is revealed. But can this story lead her to Taran's Wheel, or will sinister forces deny her the prize, even threaten her life?

A Bad Woman by Elinor Hunter

Though Queen Victoria's affair with John Brown raises barely an eyebrow, it's a different story for her working-class subjects. Bella and Isa each discover the harsh realities of loss and single parenthood. Like Victoria, the supposed moral compass of the nation, they risk their reputations to survive tragedy and retain their sanity, only their efforts are met with public censure and humiliation.

The fates of all three share uncanny parallels, yet posterity will brand one of them ***a bad woman***. But then nothing is ever as it seems ...

Sharpster by Elinor Hunter

A psychological drama which opens in the late 1960s. After a year in Aberdeen, American student Kelton MacLeod returns to the States with a Scottish wife in tow. Too late, she discovers he is a serial womaniser and a psychopath. Though wealth and career success follow, Kelton is the husband – and the boss – from hell. He seems untouchable ... but will his past catch up with him?

www.kinordbooks.com

Printed in Germany
by Amazon Distribution
GmbH, Leipzig